THE SECOND COMING
OF CURLY RED

a novel by

JODY SEAY

Firebrand
Books
Ithaca, New York

This book may not be reproduced in whole or in part, except in the case of
reviews, without permission from Firebrand Books, 141 The Commons, Ithaca,
New York 14850.

Book and cover design by Sunset Design

Printed in Canada

10 9 8 7 6 5 4 3 2 1

Library of Congress Cataloging-in-Publication Data

Seay, Jody
     The second coming of Curly Red : a novel / by Jody Seay.
     p. cm.
     ISBN 1–56341–115–6 (alk. paper)—ISBN 1–56341–114–8 (pbk.:
     alk.paper)
     I. Title
     PS 3569.E243 S43 1999
     813'.54 21—dc21
                                                                99–045456

ACKNOWLEDGMENTS

The birthing of this book could not have happened without the encouragement and support of many people. Time and space limit my ability to list each person by name—those of you who have been cheering this story's launch for so long. Let me say I know who you are and I won't ever forget you. I offer you my love and my deepest gratitude.

There are others, however, to whom I am particularly grateful and want to acknowledge personally here. To my wonderful and tenacious agent, Sheree Bykofsky, and her crew, Janet Rosen in particular—thanks, pals, for not giving up.

Thank you to my publisher, Nancy Bereano of Firebrand Books, for taking a chance and for wrestling with me through rewrites and duke-outs and still remaining friends.

Many thanks to my friend and fellow author, Susan McElroy, for the critique, and for seeing me as a good writer, then challenging me to be that.

Thanks to Phyllis for the editing, and to my friend Sheila "on-line" for the computer help, pulling my technologically impaired ass out of cyberspace more than once.

Eternal thanks to Beth Sawyer, Judy Wood, Sheryl Reese, Lynda Jacobs, Carol Ann Kerman, Betsy Pless, Sharla Taylor, Mickey Garrison, and Marjorie Porter for holding my head above water when the river ran through me. I owe you my life.

A very special thank you goes to Patricia for loving me when I needed it most and for the gift of entering me in the Mendocino Coast Writer's Contest. Thanks to the sweet folks at MCWC as well.

A thousand thank-you's to my very spectacular and supportive Rolfing clients and colleagues in Oregon, Texas, and Oklahoma. Your friendship and trust is both my honor and my joy. And thank you to my friend, Stephen Saunders, who has carried my Rolfing bag for years and years and never complained. Not once.

Thank you to Stef, who dusted off and recycled my heart just when I thought I'd used up the last of my tokens.

And finally, thanks to all of you who choose love over hate, truth over lies, courage over fear, and who use each encounter as a chance to do the dance once more. It is for you that this book was written, and it is you who will give it life. Thanks for the dance.

*This book is dedicated to my friends Shirley (1939–1999),
Judith, and Tina, who clubbed together a while ago and bought me
a typewriter for my birthday; and to my friend Lou (1945–1998)
who always laughed the loudest; and to my mother (1922–1986)
who said, "Written anything on your new typewriter yet?"
I will always wish I'd had the courage to tell her what.*

*For everyone who has ever loved the soul of another person,
and for Julian C. "Chape" Harris (1911–1995),
a good-hearted hero if there ever was one.*

·1·

Of all the things Jimmy Heron ever imagined he'd do in his most predictable life, driving his dead wife's body home in the back of their truck was not one of them. But there she lay in the camper, Lou Heron, just deader'n hell, as Miz Bridwell would say, packed down tight in a particle-board box with a bullet hole the size of a cigar butt beside her left eye.

Jimmy sucked in his breath at the thought of it as tears streamed down his cheeks in great rivers, snaking their way through the gray stubble on his jaw and hanging there like raindrops on a roof's edge before dripping onto his neck and chest. He was a man still in shock: if a growling chainsaw suddenly got tossed into the cab of the truck and ground his nose off, he might not even have noticed.

Shivering, assuming he must be cold, Jimmy rolled the window up against the chill of a Texas October night. He'd been driving for six hours, his back sweating and his shirt getting stiff on him from the salt and the blood and the *meringue*, for God's sake. But now they were almost home, and Jimmy Heron shuddered. Home, he knew, would never be the same again.

Jimmy felt something in his mind move, almost a sound, like a file drawer clicking open and sliding out, as he remembered this woman he'd loved for almost fifty years. She was the force in the blood that flowed through him, the light that warmed his heart with a steady glow, and he'd known it from the first time he saw her.

It was at a USO dance in Fort Worth in 1943. Valentine's Day. He and Curly Red, his best friend, were fresh out of basic training, creased and spit-shined as much as new soldiers could be, waiting to hear back from OCS about their acceptance. Lou had double-clutched her daddy's Ford down from the chalk-rocked hills by Mineral Wells, *ka-powing* and grinding the old car all the way in on Highway 80 with her cousin Irene, both girls curled and powdered and smelling like spring, the seams on their stockings straight as plumb lines.

Leaning against a post holding a fresh pack of Luckies, Jimmy was laughing to himself each time Curly Red scuttled past with some blonde. Fox trot, waltz, or jitterbug, it didn't seem to matter—Curly Red danced like he had a crab in the seat of his pants.

Jimmy had felt Lou, felt her presence, really, before he ever saw her, like someone had juiced the electricity in the room up higher, as if his bones had started to buzz. Turning to his right he locked eyes with the girl he knew, instantly, would be his wife. It took his breath away.

"In town long, soldier?" Lou had asked.

It would not be the last time her remarks would tickle, thrill, embarrass, and delight him all at once. And Jimmy had said to Lou the very thing he would say to her for the next forty-eight years whenever his heart left his body and jumped right out on the table to dance around at the sight of her.

"Marry me," he had said.

And Lou, the brunette with all the joy in the world radiating from behind those hazel eyes, had taken hold of his big hand and said, "I thought you'd never ask."

Jimmy Heron jerked his head, trying to shake the memories out, and ran his fingers over his face and chin. He wanted to feel his own skin, to see if he was still real, still here, hoping somewhere down deep that he was not, that none of this was real. They'd been on their vacation—things like this didn't happen on vacation. It all seemed so long ago, a million miles away from the reality of only this morning when they climbed in the truck to head back home.

Jimmy and Lou Heron drove across Texas once each year, from the top to the bottom, in order to spend a week vacationing on the Texas coast. They alternated seasons; this year was fall. Jimmy said he didn't know why they did this since the Texas coast looks exactly the same year 'round, but Lou insisted she liked the one tiny pinpoint of variety in their marriage. Other than this, she often told him, their lives were as steady as metronomes.

They walked hand in hand on the beach, making a contest of finding shells that most closely resembled the thick, gray toenails of their elderly neighbor, Miz Bridwell. They made love and took naps in the afternoon. Their love life, although no longer exactly spewing volcanic flame, was still sparked with plenty of heat and was thrilling to them both. In their tender times together, they vowed to never let the flame die out and were certain their passion for each other would be there when their old bones were banging together like bags of dominoes.

These two were the breath of each other, their flesh and fur commingled for so many years that no one could imagine one without the other. Their relationship was one of balance, with each bringing to the table special gifts. Their common thread, though, was goodness; it ran through both of them as brilliantly as a turquoise stripe on a burlap sack. And also their rituals, including this annual vacation.

During the early years of their marriage, when they were still youngbloods, as Lou liked to say—in love, but so broke they couldn't sit up to pay attention—Jimmy and his wife began making pies as Christmas gifts for family and friends. They got good at it, too. Excellent, as a matter of fact. Jimmy would mix up the dough—genuine shortening, not lard, blanket of flour, a sprinkle or two of water, pinch of salt, and a whisper of cinnamon blown off an open palm the way his mama had shown him—and roll out crust after crust, starting a new batch in a clean bowl for each pie. "Takes a delicate touch to make it flake just right," he'd say, knowing full well it really burned Lou's ass that his crust was lighter than hers.

Lou's job was the filling, and she liked using as many local ingredients as she could find: pecans and peaches from their own trees; milk and cream from their ancient, reliable Jersey cows, Curds and Whey; sweet blueberries and lockjaw-tangy wild plums from Miz Bridwell up the road.

Sour cream-raisin pie had been their personal favorite for years until Lou lost a tooth filling on a raisin and they switched over to coconut meringue. They'd been feuding about the *favorite* designation ever since, because right about the same time they discovered that no matter how good theirs was, no matter how creamy and cool and slippery they created it, they could never quite make as perfect a coconut meringue pie as the one at Judd's Cafeteria. Neither of them thought so, anyway, although not a single soul who'd eaten one of the Herons' coconut meringue pies ever found anything lacking.

Something about it eluded Jimmy and Lou, however. Lou said it was a dash more salt in the filling; Jimmy was sure it was cream of tartar in the meringue. Deciphering this mystery became the tastiest of challenges, one they might never really want to conquer since it afforded them the opportunity to stop once on the way down to the coast and once on the way back, plus taking a couple of extra pieces along in the truck for "research." It was their diligence and dedication to solving this puzzle that inspired them to turn off Interstate 35 and onto Highway 190 toward Killeen. Besides, the coconut meringue pie at the Judd's Cafeteria there was just so damned delicious.

"Honey," Lou shouted above the blast of the air conditioner as they roared down the highway, "if we're going to open our own pie shop, then let's just do it. We can find a place for it in Bowie—that's not too far—and we can call it A Slice Of Life, or Pie In The Sky. Or even, Cholesterol R Us. We can be open from noon 'til three, then back home in plenty of time to feed the critters and have our supper."

"Oh, I don't know," Jimmy said, his voice hesitant. "I'd kind of like to wait until we retire."

Lou rolled her eyes, weary of this conversation. "Jimmy," she said, "if we get anymore retired than we are now, we'll be horizontal. They'll be shoveling dirt on us before we know what hit us. We lease out the land now. We haven't run cattle or horses in years." Lou waited, just a little half-beat of syncopation, to let the stew bubble. "Years, Jimmy," she added for emphasis. "We piddle in the garden all morning, eat lunch, snooze in our recliners, then watch Oprah. Haven't you noticed, Jimmy? Here, watch my mouth move. *We Are So Very Much Retiiiirrrrrred.*" Lou slowly leaned over in the seat and pretended to snore. Her volley complete, she peeked out of one eye, watching her husband's face for his return shot, and here it came.

"Don't you think people are worried about their cholesterol?" Jimmy asked, ever the pragmatist. He'd just read in a *Newsweek* magazine at the barbershop that he should be watching his triglycerides, his HDLs, his LDLs—and his Ps and Qs, for that matter.

"I say if the pie's good enough," Lou replied, straightening herself up, "people will kiss their arteries good-bye. 'Member what Uncle Bob said the time we made that pecan pie for him? Remember what he said? He said it pained him to think he was going to have to share it. Said if he could drive far out into the pasture and eat the whole thing all by himself, he'd die a happy man right then and there." Lou cocked her chin in the air, like that had settled the issue.

"If you recall," Jimmy responded, "he for sure almost did die right then and there."

"Not from the pie, Jimmy," Lou admonished righteously. "That snotty, mean bull ran over him almost as soon as he climbed out of the truck. Uncle Bob had only eaten a bite or two of the pie when he got there."

"Well," said Jimmy, "I still say if it hadn't been for us making him that pie, he would never have gotten hurt."

Rounding a long curve in the highway, something caught Jimmy's eye on a pasture hillside up ahead of them another half mile and off to the right. "What the heck is that?" he asked. Lou, with her reading glasses poised on her nose and an ancient Texas road map accordioned out across her legs like a fan, never glanced up.

"It's a fifteen-year-old map," she said. "I'm trying to figure out which little towns have disappeared while we weren't looking. They're getting gobbled up faster than savings and loans."

"No, I mean up *there*." Jimmy pointed, and Lou followed the line of his finger upward from the highway where two large white signs were braced against the hillside. A third was being sledge-hammered into place by a middle-aged man who, except for a slight beer gut, seemed to be all muscle slapped tight against his bones. His shirt was open, flapping as he swung the hammer high up over his head, and sweat glistened on his chest and neck like lacquer. His mouth was pulled taut across the bottom of his face, looking more like a thick, pink scar than a set of lips. Jimmy slowed the truck down so they could read the signs, the first of which was the U.S. flag with the words GOD BLESS AMERICA painted across the front. The second sign read, DON'T LET THE GOVERNMENT USE YOUR TAXES TO SUPPORT WICKEDNESS! REPENT NOW, AMERICA! The third sign, which shook with each hammered blow of the grim-faced man, said in large red letters: GOD HATES HOMOSEXUALS! READ LEVITI-CUS 18:22.

"He looks like a happy guy," Lou said, as Jimmy gassed the truck and they picked up speed. "Didn't I read about him somewhere? Isn't he the one who keeps getting in trouble with the county or the state or somebody for those signs?"

"Are you joking? Why would he get in trouble for that?"

"Because they are so hateful, Jimmy, and no, I'm not joking. It's nothing to joke about. People have been protesting, and I don't blame them."

"If it's his land, though," Jimmy said, "seems like he ought to be able to do what he wants on it."

"Not if it puts the lives of other people at risk, Jimmy. Think about it, honey. Use your head. Suppose some maniac read a sign like that up in Massachusetts and decided to murder Della and Bonnie. What would you say to that?"

"I'd say he was a fool with too much free time on his hands. Bonnie and Della are both almost ninety for goodness sake. You'd think he'd have something better to do than pick on two old lesbians. Besides, I'm not so sure anyone would want to tangle with Della, old lady or not. She might be creaky, but she's smart and she's tough. Tougher than I am, I'll tell you that."

Lou sat back and smiled at her first memory of her sister-in-law, so long ago now. Della was almost forty then, steady and strong, struggling to wrestle a stocky young steer to the ground on an April day when Jimmy brought Lou home to meet his family. They had climbed up to sit on the top rail of the fence with Bonnie and were watching Della and her bovine opponent locked in a gritty, passionate dance.

The dirt in the corral was deep and loose that day, the steer a stubborn one. Della's boots were dug in up past the ankles and her arm was wrapped around the steer's head. She gripped his horns to pull his head up, then pushed back against his hard-packed shoulders with all her might. Her neck muscles stuck out like steel cables beneath her skin. Trying to gain enough leverage to take him down, Della grimaced as an occasional pain shot through her from an old hip injury.

"Hold on," she had shouted to them over the pants and farts and frantic, shuddering bellows of the steer. "I'll be right there."

"Take your time," Lou had shouted back.

"I'm not takin' my time," yelled Della. "This damned steer is takin' my time. *All* my time." Exasperated, she hauled off and punched the steer in the nose with her gloved fist, watched his eyes cross, then leaned back and sat on him as he sank to his knees, rolled over onto his side, and heaved a belch and bawl of surrender. "Bring me that brand, Jim," she said, pitching her leather gloves to her brother. Jimmy hopped off the fence, loped over to the fire, and picked up a red-hot JH branding iron with a rawhide strap wrapped around the handle. "Go ahead," Della said, nodding to Jimmy, who put his foot on the steer's leg, bent over, and seared the family brand onto its rump.

As Della let the steer up and it bolted off, she had turned toward Lou, grinned her crinkly grin, and swooped her thick mane of hair back from her face with one hand. Still going against the grain, she was a cowgirl who never wore a hat except for pictures. And she hadn't even broken much of a sweat. "You must be the young woman who's makin' my baby brother walk on air and smile like a Cheshire cat," she said. "We've been hearing about you."

"I've already met Bonnie," Lou responded. "You must be Della."

"I must be—or I'm scorching the wrong cattle."

"Are you going to brand the whole herd all by yourself?" Lou asked.

"Nope, just the newest ones," Della replied, "and the meanest ones. I saved the sissy ones for Dad."

Lou had let out a sigh as the whole memory of that day flooded back to her, as rich and satisfying as a favorite meal, then she reached over and patted Jimmy's hand. "My point, sweetheart, is that hateful words inspire hateful actions. That guy back there wants everyone to hate the people he hates, and the group he hates just happens to include two of the people we love most in the world, plus a whole lot of good people we won't ever know. So, do I want him to get away with blasting everyone who drives on this highway with that kind of message? Not on your life, Jimmy Heron, not me, not in a million years. Our taxes pay for these highways, and we shouldn't have to look at hate messages as we drive on them. It's worse than graffiti—it's poison. You can bet I'll be calling the highway department and the attorney general's office and anyone else I can think to complain to just as soon as we get home." Then she gathered her thoughts and her actions back toward the tattered road map still on her lap.

Jimmy Heron glanced at his wife and smiled. Oh, how he loved the fire in her. Her passion for fairness and justice in the world surprised him still, after all these years. He watched the dimple in her left cheek form as she concentrated on the red and blue and gray squiggly lines on the map. The tip of her tongue stuck out from beneath her upper lip, pink and glistening. He had loved Lou Heron now for almost half a century, more than any man alive could ever have loved anyone, and today it just got deeper. Jimmy turned his eyes toward the road ahead of them and gripped the steering wheel. "You're right," was all he said.

·2·

A little later and further on up the road toward home, toward the end of lunchtime, Jimmy eased the blue truck to a stop in the parking lot at Judd's in Killeen, Texas. The date was October 16th, a brilliantly golden fall day, temperature in the low eighties already, warm, but not unusual for Texas. Lou lifted her sunglasses and squinted into the sun. "Looks hot out there," she said. "You know how I hate the thought of sweating on my vacation." Jimmy patted her hand.

"Nah," he said, "it's just bright. I could carry you piggyback, if you want." She snorted at him.

"You and John Deere," she said, and began removing her sweater. Their new truck had an air conditioner powerful enough to blow a coat off a rack, and since Jimmy kept it cranked up to hypothermia, Lou insisted an extra sweater stay in the cab at all times.

They climbed out of the big Chevy, and Jimmy carefully checked locks on doors and on the camper in his methodical way. He reached for Lou's hand as she slipped her smaller palm up against his, an act as unconscious and natural to them as breathing. Then they sauntered, in the easy rhythm of the lovers they still were, into Judd's Cafeteria to do research by having yet another luscious piece of coconut meringue pie.

National Boss's Day had swelled the lunchtime crowd at Judd's to around 150—people staying longer than usual, tables crowded with co-workers, bosses in shirt sleeves and ties, funny cards being passed around. The air buzzed with excitement and good feelings.

Jimmy and Lou had just sat down with their pie and coffee, had a few bites and sips, and were sparring about whether men should be forced to wear hairnets to work, when BOOM! the explosion of shattering glass hit the room with the force of a bomb. Murder had arrived

15

in a 1987 Ford Ranger as it plowed through the front glass window and into the dining room, its engine growling, the tires grinding on broken glass and crunching bits of shattered plastic.

What followed was a stunned, hazy silence. A muscular, dark-headed man in a green shirt calmly got out of the truck and began firing two 9-mm semi-automatic weapons. The air was suddenly sucked out of the room and the aroma of food disappeared, replaced by the metallic odor of gunpowder and the sickly sweet smell of blood. Movement came in slow motion.

"This is what Bell County did to me!" the man screamed, as he walked through the dining room. Except for the gunfire, the silence was thick as fog. "All women are vipers," the killer hissed. "Tell me, is it worth it? Is it worth it?" Then the *pop pop pop* of gunfire rang out.

The sound of bullets entering someone's body made a bumping noise, like a bag being punched or a mattress being kicked. *Bump bump bump.* There was not a cry, not even a whimper, from whoever had just been murdered, only the horrifying stillness of death.

Jimmy saw some people run out through the hole left by the truck, bursting into the sunlight like newborns, screeching through the parking lot like maniacs. He heard traffic whiz by like it must every day, like nothing was wrong. A siren wailed in the distance, too far away to stop the carnage happening right now, too far away to help.

Lou jumped when a spoon clattered against the tile floor in the kitchen, exposing the secretive sound of life hiding out from death.

Someone was gasping for air not far from Jimmy and Lou. Lungs rattled against a chest wall for the final time, bloody bubbles foamed up and burst like soap. Jimmy remembered that sound from the war: the memory never goes away. Nor does the putrid stench.

Pop pop pop. The shots rang out from somewhere close. A woman crumpled to the floor, her chair shooting out from under her with its brass casters spinning and crashing against a serving cart. "No, don't," a man pleaded, before another *pop pop* ended his life.

Jimmy slid across the table, pushing Lou to the floor as the horror boiled throughout the room. They lay there together, their hearts pounding, their breath ragged and stale. Her hand grabbed hold of his belt buckle, pulling him closer. They and the others were what was left.

Targets for the hatred of some crazed man they didn't even know. A woman wept softly on the other side of the room. A man groaned. "Oh, God," sobbed a woman's voice, just before a burst of automatic gunfire.

"He must have had the liver and onions," Lou whispered, and Jimmy stared at her, appalled, but not altogether surprised, that she could even think of such a thing—a joke, for God's sake—right now. He pulled her hand away from his belt and kissed her fingers.

"Hush," he said, and positioned himself to turn the table over as gently and quietly as he could to hide her. It was heavy, much heavier than he had imagined, slipping from Jimmy's sweaty, desperate grip just inches from the carpet.

Jimmy saw the man in the green shirt turn at the clunking sound of the table hitting the floor. *Oh God, dear God, help us now.*

Knowing he had just made the mistake of his life, Jimmy Heron rose to his knees as the man approached and they stared at each other. This was a showdown.

Oh, please, dear God, don't let him see her, don't let him see her was all that ran through Jimmy's mind. The acrid residue of gunpowder filled his nose and made his eyes water. He thought his heart would explode it was beating so fast. His mouth tasted like ash.

"What's the problem, gramps?" the killer said, taunting him. "You gettin' a little nervous, huh? Afraid?" he jeered, as he slowly placed the blistering barrel of the Ruger P-89 against the old man's chest. James Jefferson Heron, certain this was the last day of his life, stared back into the flat eyes of a man who had died long before. Jimmy spoke up.

"I'm not afraid of you, you chickenshit bastard," he said.

"No?" the killer said. "Well, maybe you oughta be—"

"JIMMY!" Lou screamed, wild-eyed and lunging over the top of the table as the killer calmly shifted and pulled the trigger. Then he quickly walked away, gliding past Jimmy and Lou Heron as deftly as a pickpocket at a carnival.

Jimmy scrambled around the table, gathering his wife to his chest, scooping up her rag doll form, watching in horror as her head lolled to one side. Her mouth hung open and a hissing sound escaped from deep in her lungs, like an air mattress with a slow leak.

"NO NO NO NO NO," was all Jimmy could say, cupping his arm around her sleeping face, rocking her, holding her close, squeezing his fingers over the bullet hole beside her left eye, wiping coconut meringue pie off her cheek.

Jimmy watched Lou's face as the last electrical storm buzzed through her brain, causing her eyelids to flutter before closing forever. It seemed to him that if he pressed his fingers hard enough over the hole, her blood would not leak out, her life could not slip away. *Yes, yes. That's what he would do. He would just hold her until she woke up. She would have a chance to wake up if he just held her long enough.*

Jimmy Heron looked down at the woman he loved, her face, her body already smaller, transforming into a shell which had held the treasure that was Lou. "NO," he said, "no, no, no," as the light in his heart faded away. "No. Please. No."

The man who killed Lou Heron had taken his own life after murdering twenty-four people and wounding twenty-seven others, Jimmy learned later that day. There had been many slaughtered after Lou, then a shootout of some sort, of which Jimmy had been oblivious. He found out that this murderer, George somebody, hated Blacks, Jews, Latinos, gays, and women. Hated his own mother. None of this mattered to Jimmy Heron, however, even though he felt that it should. What mattered was the fact that the woman he had adored for more than half his life was dead. He had not been able to protect her, he had not been able to save his own wife. His heart ached even more knowing that she had given up her life for him, taking the very bullet into her brain that was destined for his heart.

Jimmy felt numb, sick, like he would puke. He wished that he could die, take it back, do it all over, forget this day, go back to yesterday. Something. Anything! But he could not. What he could do was sit quietly and answer the questions of policemen as paramedics loaded his wife's body into the zippered bag for transport to the funeral home. There was no hurry, no bustling about with IVs and monitors like earlier. The woman was dead, it was easy to see. Someone handed him Lou's purse, from which a road map of the state of Texas hung limply out the side pocket. The leather smelled of White Shoulders cologne.

Toward dusk, on the six-hour drive back home, Jimmy remembered the kindness of paramedics who knelt to talk to him in their soothing way as they carefully pried his wife's body away from him.

"Mr. Heron, please," the young man said, "we've got to take her now. I promise you we'll treat her gently."

Jimmy recalled the concerned manner of police officers as they sat knee to knee with him, softly asking him questions, apologizing over and over for having to do so.

"Your wife was from Fort Worth?" the detective asked.

"Mineral Wells," Jimmy replied, in a daze.

He remembered the feel of a warm, soapy dishtowel as a young woman, one of Judd's employees, knelt beside his chair with a bowl of sudsy water. She quietly washed meringue and blood off his hand, methodically soaping between his fingers and around his wedding band. Thin and waiflike, she appeared as if from a vapor coming off the steam tables in the serving line, an angel or vision as she made her way through the veil of gunsmoke and horror still in the room. She had been so distraught, so desperate to do something to help heal this awful wound for all of them.

"Oh, I am so sorry, sir," the young woman kept saying, as she swiped at the cream gravy on his pants leg and the blood and meringue on his shirt. Tears coursed down her face and dripped off her chin. "I am so sorry this happened to you," the young woman said. She wept openly, suddenly whipping off her hairnet and leaning her head on his chest. Her pain was real, and Jimmy instinctively put his arm around her shoulders and softly stroked her head. He noticed the name tag on her uniform said RUTH, and it startled him. That had been his mother's middle name. In Hebrew it meant compassion.

"Shhhh, Ruth, shhhh," he said, in a voice and words he wasn't sure were his. "Don't you worry. We will all be okay."

·3·

Time steps aside, takes a nap, goes out for coffee whenever tragedy strikes, making yesterday seem like weeks ago and today a century long. Driving up Interstate 35 north of Dallas toward home, Jimmy could smell how the cool night air of a Texas October would send whiffs of Lou—her cologne, her sweater, a sudden chocolate blast of Ultra Slimfast—swirling around inside the cab of the truck. He would have to pull over to the side of the road and cry. Great, heaving sobs would wrack his body, and then he would moan the low, mournful sound of lost love, the cracking sound from one of God's creatures who had mated for life.

Turning off the interstate just outside Krum, heading west toward Bolivar on FM 453, Jimmy eased the truck off the two-lane highway and onto the grass. He got out to relieve himself. It was almost midnight. He'd been driving for hours in the dark and only now realized he was still wearing his sunglasses.

Lou would never have let him get away with this, he thought, peeing into a road ditch by the back wheel of the truck. She said one of the truly unfair things in this life was that men could stand up to urinate and women could not. Truth was, Lou could never figure out how to squat and pee without splashing on her shoes.

"This marriage is a partnership, Jimmy Heron," she said to him. "You and me, fifty-fifty, even-steven, and I'll not have you emptying your bladder when mine's about to blow. Besides, wasn't neither of us raised in a barn. From now on, we'll just stop at a gas station like civilized folks have been doing since the beginning of time."

"Since the beginning of time, huh?"

"Well, since Christ was born, anyway."

"And how do you know this, Miss Smarty?"

"The star. Remember the star the wise men followed to find the Baby Jesus?"

"Yeah, I'm listening."

"It was a new Texaco station opening up in Bethlehem."

Jimmy found himself chuckling as he zipped up, reliving this funny memory of his life with Lou. Then it hit—the pain, a knifepoint in his gut, quick as a snakebite—the reality that she was gone. He steadied himself on the back of the truck. "Just checking for a low tire, darlin'," he said, patting the camper door behind which his wife's body rested in a particle-board box. "Don't you worry now," he said, "we're almost home."

By the time he had passed through Forestburg, turning left out onto Boggy Road toward their ranch, Jimmy knew he could not go through a funeral service regardless of how many people got their noses out of joint. "Some people around here just live for death." That's what he remembered Lou saying about Winnie Bridwell's excitement over getting to attend three funerals in one week, funerals and church being Miz Bridwell's primary social outlet.

The Herons were childless, with no close living relatives other than his elderly sister in Cambridge, and Lou's cousin Irene, who had been homebound with emphysema in Mineral Wells for years and couldn't walk eighty feet without having to lie down for several days. He would call them.

A funeral for Lou would be too much, too painful, Jimmy decided, like watching her die, having to give her up all over again. His mind was made up and his conscience clear by the time he arrived at their ranch on this cool October night. Lou Heron's burial would be his own private matter.

Headlights and truck tires on the gravel drive at one in the morning brought Web Hardy's dogs, in a tangle of dog hair and excitement, scurrying down the road and into Jimmy's yard. Both of them Australian shepherds—Canyon and Cliff were their names—they fancied themselves guardians of every creature on Boggy Road, especially after Buck, the Herons' black Lab, died, and had run down now to make sure none of their herd was loose.

"Hi, woofers," Jimmy said, making his way to the barn. "Got some sadness here today." His breath grabbed on him as he exhaled. He took shovels and a Coleman lantern, and looped a couple of pieces of sturdy rope around his left shoulder. After filling the lantern, he pumped it a few times and lit the mantle. Then, wearing grief across his shoulders like a yoke, Jimmy walked with the dogs on either side of him, a priest and his acolytes, out to the edge of the pasture toward Buck's grave, where the knotted, gnarled live oak, as huge and old as life, waited with her arms outstretched to gather them in.

It was still dark around four-thirty in the morning when Jimmy gingerly lowered the heavy wooden coffin into the grave he had spent all night digging.

Jimmy brought the tractor around with the grate blade hooked on and pushed most of the dirt back into the grave. The last few shovels full he tossed on the mound himself, then sat down cross-legged in the dirt next to the grave. Wind hit his back where sweat had soaked through his shirt, causing him to shiver.

The dogs were still with him—Canyon, on her belly, ears perked and watching, and Cliff, on his back, asleep and gently snortling away, a clod of dirt stuck to the end of his nose. Slowly, through hacking sobs, Jimmy said good-bye to Lou.

"You were always the very best part of my life," he told her, "more than enough in every way for me, braver than I would ever be. You *were* my life. Oh, please forgive me. I am so sorry." His big shoulders shook with each sob. Then, looking up at the sky, he held up his arms to his wife. "I promise I'll find you again and love you forever just as much as I do now," he said. "I promise. Oh, Lou, I promise."

Tears ran in rivulets down the old man's cheeks. Canyon moved in closer to Jimmy's ribs, whimpering her support as he combed his hand through the blonde and reddish-brown hair on her back. Cliff, awake now and feeling confused, walked over to Jimmy and quickly licked him on the ear, then threw back his head and howled at the remnants of the moon.

·4·

ometimes when a story gets so big, it's just gotta get itself told and that's what I aim to help this one do. Elsewise, nobody would ever know the whole thing except maybe folks on this side. If it got told on the other side, it might get told wrong, and I'd sure as hell hate to go through the rest of eternity kickin' myself because I let that happen.

Now, I gotta let you know I'm breakin' some rules here by doing this—takin' time out from my duties to tell this story. I mean, what with me bein' dead and all. Did I mention that? No? Well, I am. Dead. A corpse, a stiff, our dearly departed has bought the farm, croaked, snuffed, been nailed, is doing the dirt dance, pushin' up daisies. R.I.P., that spells me. At least, the part of me that was visible on the other side. And, seein' as how I'm dead and all, I think it gives me a unique perspective from which to tell this story.

James Jefferson Heron is one hell of a great guy. You might not know it even if you had the chance to meet him. Jimmy still doesn't know it himself, although I suspect he's gettin' closer to realizin' it by now. But then, jeez, maybe that's part of my job, too. I'll have to check with the Big Guy to find out what my marchin' orders are on that one.

See, really, this is a cush job, one most folks could do just layin' on their side, which makes you wonder why everybody's so afraid of dyin'. When you come across to this side, they give you a chance to get settled in and then they give you assignments. Mostly good stuff, ways to learn what you didn't know before, different ways of lookin' at things. Sure shakes up a lot of your opinions, I can tell you that for damned sure. But the most highly prized job is angel duty. Fun, too, and a challenge.

First time on the job liked to have scared the bejeezus outta me. See, this five-year-old kid was fallin' off a second-story balcony, headin' right down toward a patio. Straight down, head first, mind you. I got the word *just before it happened. "Save That Boy, Curly Red!" is all He says to me in that voice of his that makes him sound like John Huston. What with me bein' brand new at this and all, well, I wasn't exactly sure what to do, so I just flipped the kid in mid-air and whammy! he lands with his little front teeth stuck in a redwood planter on the patio. Kid even left his body for a bit, just long enough to see me and say thanks.*

Now, I ain't sayin' it was the perfect save, and the kid did have to wear braces once his big teeth came in. But shit, it spared his life, and he's grown up to be a fine young man. Got a cute smile, too. I hear he's had a life-long aversion to geraniums nobody can figure out. That's been twenty years now in earth time, and I guess everybody's forgotten what kind of flowers his mama had growin' in the redwood planter that day. But I haven't.

·5·

immy? Lou? You seen my dogs?" Web Hardy's voice boomed through
the back screen door, causing Canyon and Cliff to jump and begin
barking. They scrambled to the door, all wiggles and whines when
they saw who it was. "There you are," he said, easing the door open.
"Get a better breakfast down here, do you?" Web rubbed Canyon's head
as she jumped up, whimpering, wrapping her paws around his middle. Cliff hung his head like he always did when he thought he was in
trouble, looking up at Web through soulful eyes. His nub of a tail pointed
down and barely wiggled. "And you," Web said, grabbing Cliff's muz-
zle, "I know you, you've got a crush on the lady of the house. Lou?
There's no coffee going in here. You two aren't getting healthy on me
now, are you?"

Web looked around the kitchen. Too tidy, he thought, for people
just back from the coast. No Igloo cooler on the counter, no road map
or suntan lotion on the table, no sandy sneakers by the back door. Something was wrong. "Lou!" he yelled, bounding through the kitchen and
dining room, rounding left into the den with the dogs on his heels.
What Web Hardy saw made his heart stop. He felt skid marks clawing their way across his chest wall.

Jimmy, mercifully, had been taken to the underworld of the unconscious, where the pain of tragic loss is temporarily set aside so the gap-
ing wound can slowly start to close. He was asleep tilting back in his
recliner, his mouth open, his hands and trousers filthy with dirt. His
Beltones rested in a dish on the TV tray. Some of Lou's spattered blood
was dried on his shirt, squirted across the front of him like paint. Web
Hardy thought his friend Jimmy Heron was dead.

"Oh, God," he said under his breath, leaping across the den in two
giant steps. "Jimmy!" he screamed, and grabbed the old man by the

ankle. Jimmy tried to stand, panting, his eyes blasted open and terrified. Web knelt beside the recliner, easing Jimmy back into it and holding him gently. "It's okay," he said, trying to sound as soothing as he could. "It's just me. I'm here."

"Oh, Lord," Jimmy said, "I had the most awful dream. Lou and I were swimming in the gulf and the waves kept pulling her away from me. I swam out to her, calling her name. I could even touch her hand, then the waves would pull her further out." He looked Web full in the face. "I couldn't save her," he said. Web let go of his friend and handed him his hearing aids. He knew better than to try to have a conversation without them stuck in Jimmy's ears. The left one squealed, and Jimmy grimaced as he adjusted it.

Turning back to face Web and say the truth, Jimmy's eyes were red-rimmed and raw looking. His chin wrinkled up and began to quiver. "She's dead, Web," he cried, burying his face in his hands. "Oh dear God, she's dead, and I got her killed. The bastard shot her right in the head, just took the gun out of my chest and shot her when she reached for me. Oh, Jesus-God," he sobbed, "this is too hard." Jimmy wept like someone being slapped, his head jerking back and forth, writhing, as if snared in a trap.

Web sank down beside Jimmy's chair. He feld kicked in the chest, like all the air had just been pushed from his lungs. He glanced over at Lou's empty chair. Next to some scissors and clipped coupons, a women's magazine rested on the TV tray opened to a recipe section declaring, "Squash Those Winter Blues!" A pair of newly crocheted house slippers rested on top of Lou's plastic bag of yarn. Everything smelled of her—White Shoulders cologne and Clorets gum—and Web Hardy did the only thing a sweet man could do: he pulled his friend close and rocked him like a baby.

Over the next half hour, stepping out of the embarrassment that comes from men caring for each other, Web Hardy got Jimmy Heron in the shower and cleaned up. He laid out clean khakis with a fresh handkerchief as Jimmy recounted the previous day's tragedy and Lou's burial next to Buck under the big oak. Web glanced out the window to see the mound of dirt at the edge of the pasture, pushing away the thought of his friend's body beneath it. Trying to help, he flicked on

Jimmy's ancient Remington, but the thing was vibrating so badly he dropped it in the sink. "Goddamn, Jimmy," he said, "that thing's as loud as a chainsaw."

"Swarm of hornets," Jimmy replied. "That's what Lou said. Always said it sounded like a swarm of hornets coming down the hall. Made her want to run out the back door and head for the creek. They both laughed, then suddenly stopped short with the realization that the funniest woman they ever knew was dead. Jimmy's eyes began to water and Web quickly looked away. Jimmy pulled out his handkerchief and gave his nose a good honk. "Well," he said, "I'll finish up in here. Why don't you go make us some coffee."

Folger's perking away filled the house with comfort. They entered that land of make-believe so easy to visit when someone dies, pretending the loved one just stepped out for a bit. Web hung up the phone and headed down the hall when he heard cupboard doors banging and the cast-iron skillet clanging onto the stove. Jimmy was already in the kitchen. A box of Alpha-Bits sat on the table beside the carton of milk, set out just like always for Buster Dan.

"Where's the bitty-boy?" Jimmy asked.

"Over at Miz Bridwell's," Web said, "helping her wash out jars. I just talked to her. He's only washed out one so far, but he's done it about a hundred times. She says she likes a man that's thorough. She'll send him along—the horse knows the way."

Daniel Webster Hardy, Jr. was six years old, very small, and very slow. He had been cursed with colic his first six months, a father who didn't have a clue about being a dad, and a mother who thought this job was going to be a whole lot easier. The baby wouldn't smile, couldn't turn himself over, and didn't come anywhere close to sitting up or walking when other babies his age were practically riding the rodeo circuit. Hell, Linda Dee, his mother had thought when the kid was first born, he wouldn't even take a breast unless she forced it on him. Actually, this had been fine with her since the last thing she needed in this life was a pair of saggy titties, especially if she didn't even have a GED. It had all gurgled and churned inside her until her autistic son's third birthday, when Linda Dee Hardy roared away in the Torino, a Marlboro in her mouth, and never looked back.

After that, word leaked out on Boggy Road that Web Hardy had taken to drinking, something he couldn't do very well even in the best of times. Folks around Web then sort of took over for him, in that silent way people do when times are painful and words get stuck.

Jimmy looked after the small herd of cattle Web grazed on the land he leased from them, and Lou set out bowls of scraps and bones for his dogs. Miz Bridwell, as ancient and hunkered over as she was, lugged a huge pot of soup over to Web's and left it on the porch with the lid taped on tight to keep out the critters. "The man can drink hisself to death if he wants, but I'm sure worried about that little boy," she told Lou on the phone late one afternoon. Lou and Jimmy, on a mission, stormed over to Web's, snatched up the kettle of soup from the porch, and barged right in without knocking.

Web Hardy sat in the darkened room, skinny and chain-smoking, wearing only his underwear. George Strait crooned "…Amarillo by mornin'…" from the cassette player. Lou punched the music off and bustled through the house opening shades and curtains. She muttered something under her breath about the conditions being right for growing penicillin. Jimmy, meanwhile, went off in search of some pants, offended that Web hadn't even attempted to cover himself when a lady walked in. Emerging from the bedroom with Levi's and a shirt, Jimmy tossed them onto Web's lap. "Put your clothes on, man," he said sternly. "Don't be a jackass." He motioned with his head toward the kitchen where Lou was. "She'll make you sorry about it."

On the kitchen floor sat little Danny, right in the middle of a Spaghetti-O's mess, laying out the noodles in long chains of OOOOOs on the linoleum and carefully eating every fifth one. Lou scooped him up before he had a chance to squawk or pull away, sat him on the counter, and wiped his hands and face with a mildewy sponge. Wrinkling her nose at the smell of him, the sponge, or both, Lou carried the boy to the bathroom. Her hazel eyes blazing, she paused for a second in the living room to stare at Web, who sat all caved in on the couch like a fifth grader in the principal's office. "Don't you move a muscle, mister," she told him, pointing her finger like a fiery scepter. "I want to talk to you." Then she stomped off down the hall, slamming the door behind her.

When he heard water going in the tub, Web thought briefly about running away but, hell, Linda Dee had taken the only vehicle that would start. He supposed he could set out on foot, although Lou was so pissed at him he was sure she'd stomp him in the middle of Boggy Road and throw his body in a ditch. Jimmy had noticed the flicker of escape in Web's eyes from across the room. He stood up and headed toward the kitchen. "Don't even think about boltin' outta here, bud," he said. "You'd best just stay put and take your licks like a man."

By the time Jimmy had the kitchen cleaned and Miz Bridwell's soup simmering on the stove, Lou had gotten Danny scrubbed and pajamaed and in his bed with his favorite stuffed toy. Although she had calmed down some, she was restless, moving about the kitchen like a woman with something on her mind, some scorching truth that needed saying before her hair caught fire.

Jimmy sipped his coffee. He had learned not to run off at the mouth when his wife was collecting her thoughts and was absent-mindedly humming "Mexicali Rose" until she glared at him.

Finally, when Web had finished his soup, Lou sat down at the table. "Web," she said, "you got your heart broken and we're both real sorry about that, sorry you have to bear that pain. But Linda Dee's not cut out for this life and never was. Her idea of ranch life is rodeos and chili cookoffs and dressing up like Reba McIntire to get her picture snapped at Olan Mills. Well, it's not like that at all and, now that she knows it, you couldn't drag her back here with a tractor. We're not saying a heartache's the easiest thing in the world to get over, but life's for living and you sure as the world can't do that when you're sittin' around a dark house in your underpants playing sad songs and drinking. Besides, there's another heart in this house that gets broken every time you ignore it and that's your boy's in there." She pointed toward Danny's bedroom. Web hung his head, feeling chastised and blue.

"It's true," Lou continued, "he's not the brightest apple to fall from the tree but he's your apple, and it's your job to be a good daddy to him." Web began to cry, and Lou, feeling only a twinge of an urge to back off, decided not to let it slow her down. "Babies are a gift from God, Web Hardy," she continued, "and nobody realizes that more than the ones who never made the gift list."

Jimmy nodded in agreement, knowing she meant the two of them. An outbreak of meningitis in an army hospital during the war had nearly killed him, rendering him sterile as a gelding.

Lou patted her hand on the formica table and continued. "What you need to understand is that babies come from God with a lease agreement, Web. If you don't take care of them, you don't get to keep them. It's that simple. Either God takes 'em back, or the county takes 'em away. Now, what's it going to be?"

Thoroughly ashamed of himself, Web wept into his hands. "I want to keep my boy," he sobbed, accepting the handkerchief Jimmy handed him. Web gave his snout a solid blow.

"That's clear enough, then," Lou said. "Remember, I don't want to hear any more about this drinking, or sitting around playing sad songs and poor me."

"Okay," came Web's weak reply.

"You're a strong, capable man with a ranch to run and a son to raise."

"Yes, ma'am."

"And I expect you'll do a good job."

Jimmy glanced at his wife, in awe again at her ability to take a man to his knees, then lift him to the stars, all in the same breath, without even breaking stride.

"Because if you don't...," Lou paused for effect.

"Yes, ma'am?"

"I'll be forced to send my man, here," she said, pointing to Jimmy with her thumb, "down the road in the middle of a dark night to kick your butt all over this pasture."

Jimmy felt a little shocked at her statement, seeing as how he hadn't kicked anybody's butt in a serious way since the ninth grade, and here he was practically seventy years old. Finally, he took his cue from Lou's stare and leaned right down in Web Hardy's face to say, "And I'd really hate to have to do that, son."

"Well, then," said Lou, standing up from the table and straightening her dress, "this issue is settled. Jimmy and I have business in Bowie tomorrow, so we'll be leaving early, but the next day we want you and Danny joining us for breakfast. We eat at seven o'clock."

Then the two of them walked out into the hot August night as Jimmy asked, "When did we plan a trip to Bowie?"

"About two seconds before I said it."

"And what's the purpose of this trip?"

"Jimmy Heron, you and I are going to see a man about a horse."

Breakfast two days later at the House of Heron was served on four placemats instead of the usual two. Cornflakes with peaches, toast, jam, juice, and coffee for the grown-ups, Alpha-Bits and a banana for the boy. As Web was taking his second cup, Jimmy said he needed to check on something and in a few minutes yelled for everybody to come outside and take a look.

Standing under the pecan tree, next to Jimmy, was a boy-size horse, his mane combed, his shiny black coat curried, his tack and hooves all polished and gleaming. He seemed reserved in his new surroundings.

Jimmy picked up Danny, whose eyes were as big as silver dollars, and said in a low, soothing voice, "Come here, little man, you're about to meet your very best friend. Now, hold your hand out like this by his nose so he can smell you and know who you are." And Danny did just that. "Now, blow real easy right at his nose, like this," Jimmy said, "so he'll know you're his family now." Danny did exactly that, too. Lou walked over and slapped a cowboy hat on the boy's head. It slipped down over his bright blue eyes and pushed his ears straight out. "Ladies and gentlemen," Jimmy said, "I am proud to present Buster Dan and his faithful horse."

So, Daniel Webster Hardy, Jr., thus became Buster Dan, riding the range up and down Boggy Road astride his trusty steed. Even though he rarely spoke, Buster Dan became a much happier little guy. The patient, tiny horse seemed to draw the boy out, as gentle animals often do, communicating through the silent, sweetest part of the heart, where love is true and forever.

On this crisp October morning, the day after Lou Heron's death, Jimmy lifted Buster Dan off his horse as Web got breakfast on the table. "Just us gents today, little man," he said, carrying the boy inside, trying to push away the full meaning of what he'd said.

They ate mostly in silence, piddling with their food and muttering a sentence or two about football and horses. The loudest thing in the room, the absence of Lou Heron, screamed at the three of them from her empty chair. It was what Buster Dan did, though, that flicked the scab off and opened the wound in the hearts of the two grown men. On the placemat beside his cereal bowl, the little boy had spelled out with soggy Alpha-Bits the name L O U. Having seen it, both men began to cry. The drenching sadness poured down on all of them, as relentless as an autumn rain, as steady as the beat of a little boy's heart.

·6·

nyway, I don't know if you've ever had the privilege of savin' a life, but it's a thrill, I mean to say so. I've done it now on both sides, but savin' the kid that day just fired me up so, I wanted to zoom around and save everybody. That's when He took me aside and told me about the blueprints. See, this is such a simple idea, it's no wonder we humans never thought of it.

Every life lived has a blueprint, a way of livin' and dyin' that each person's spirit has already agreed to before they came back to old schoolhouse earth. Seems it's all just a honin' process—learnin' this, lettin' go of that, lovin' yourself enough to love each other. The purpose of guardian angels is to make sure humans don't screw up the plan. Simple, huh?

The nice part is that you don't have to be dead to be a guardian angel. The difference is, once you're dead, you know when you're pullin' angel duty. Before that, you just think you got lucky. Joke's on you. Know what He told me about the Ten Commandments and the Bible? If He had to do it all over, He'd rethink the whole thing, probably do away with it altogether. And, if you wanna know the truth, He wasn't just pickin' on the Bible, either. He'd do the same with the Torah, the Koran, the book of Mormon, and every other book mankind has come up with to try to explain the purpose of life, especially since there's been jillions of 'em written, seems like, and all of 'em with a different take on things. Too many rules, too many interpretations. Too many people so quick to twist His words, that's what really gets on His nerves.

Anyway, the Big Guy says if He was redoing the whole Christianity thing, He'd whittle the entire Bible/Commandments idea down to a short bio on His son Jesus. He'd slap a picture of Jesus on one page, and below it He'd write just these three things:

1. Be like him.

2. Love each other.

3. Cheer for the Cubs (and He wouldn't say if He meant the ball team or baby bears or both).

If humans could incorporate those three things into their lives, why, He just bet that'd take care of all the other commandments and rules in every spiritual book ever written. But, hey, who knew rule books would turn out to be such a problem? You know, for somebody who's all powerful, this God person is really a down-to-earth kind of guy.

·7·

Jimmy Heron stared out the window at the gnarled oak near the edge of the pasture and watched a sudden autumn wind kick dirt off the top of Lou's grave, sending it spiraling away like so many dreams. This was his third day without her. Their picture box rested in his lap. His Colt .44 sat on the lamp table beside his recliner, shiny and oiled, even though the smell of such a weapon now made his gut twist. Reaching over toward the table, he slid his fingers along the smooth dark metal from the cylinder to the sight bead, then lifted his hand toward his nose and gave it a sniff. The taste of bile and too-warm saliva crept up his throat and into his mouth. No doubt about it, if Jimmy Heron was going to blow a hole in his own heart, he'd have to hold his breath while he pulled the trigger.

But he couldn't pull the trigger, couldn't even come close, without hearing the voices of his parents. "Life is a gift, boys," his dad said to him and Curly Red one day up on the bluff. "Don't ever forget it, and don't ever turn it down. It'll be the unluckiest thing you'll ever do." That was right after one of their county's not-so-well-balanced elderly ladies shot herself dead right on the porch at her family reunion and, except for a rousing game of horseshoes in the late afternoon, pretty much messed up the event for her entire clan.

"Taking your own life is like thumbing your nose at the Lord," was what Jimmy's mother had said, but that was enough, and her simple statement had stuck with him all these years. It was why, even with pain so piercing and hollow he could almost feel a blasting winter wind scraping through him, James Jefferson Heron could do no more with this gun of his but shake and cry at the sight of it, grow nauseous and weak at the smell of it.

Glancing at the box where he and Lou kept their pictures, Jimmy spotted a packet of plastic in the corner and gently pulled it out. He opened it and shook the contents loose. They were the love letters the two of them had written during World War II, bundled and tied delicately with a bright red ribbon.

He had been stationed first in France and then in Germany as the Allied troops moved in. In some nondescript German village, in 1944, he'd been wounded and Curly Red had gotten his ear sliced off. Trapped in the bottom of a bombed-out building, they were almost killed when the retreating Nazis up above dropped a grenade down the ventilator shaft he and his men had stuffed with rags and straw. God, they were scared, he remembered that. Jimmy, a young, green lieutenant, was in charge of this bunch, all of them just kids, it seemed, most just barely out of school.

The first grenade blew the stuffing out. The second one came clanging down and rolled onto the floor right in the middle of them. Jimmy grabbed it and threw it back up the shaft only an instant before it exploded, sending shrapnel and sheet metal flying. He caught some shrapnel right between the eyes and—*shoomp!*—felt part of his head fly away like a chunk of melon hit with a knife. Diving in front of Jimmy's chest to protect him from the blast, Curly Red's ear was sawed off by a piece of metal, clean as a whistle, like he'd been shaved.

Nobody else had been hurt that day, something they'd both always been thankful for, but life and death had been a close call for Jimmy Heron. Curly Red, bleeding like a stuck pig himself, had held his friend's head together with his hands until the medics got there. "Don't you be scootin' out on me now, Jimmy," he said. "It ain't your time. Lou would shoot me for sure and shove my body down the well if I fooled around and let you get yourself killed. You hang on now, you hear me? You hear me?" That was the last Jimmy did hear before he slipped into unconsciousness.

He was taken to a hospital in Holland where surgeons worked valiantly and managed to save his eye. Later on, he was sent to a hospital in Belgium, to one in Paris, and finally to an army hospital in England, where meningitis nearly killed him. But Jimmy hardly remembered any of that. What he remembered most was his C.O. delivering a medal to him, a commendation of some sort for valor, and a letter from Lou, the very one he now held in his hand almost fifty years later. He opened it carefully so the delicate paper wouldn't tear, and read:

Sept. 20, 1944

My darling Jimmy,

Curly Red called the second he got back to tell me you are okay, but losing part of your skull doesn't sound much like an okay thing to me. I finally got six of your letters all at once, which explains why I thought you had left me in the spring.

Della and Bonnie have been here all week helping your dad ship some cattle to the army, so your lunch may be someone you recognize pretty soon, if Della doesn't wear us all out before the end of this week. I swear, she can get more done on a ranch than any six cowboys put together, and she works from dark 'til dark, way too long for the rest of us. She has almost taught me to rope. I snared Bonnie twice, but yanked too hard the second time, pulled her over, and she got a bloody nose, so we went back to shelling peas. They are moving to Massachusetts to teach and practice law. Your mother says she hopes they don't become full-fledged Yankees, a fate worse than death in her mind. They promised to write, but I'm sure we'll have to count on Bonnie for that. You know Della— won't even pick up a pen to write a check except at gunpoint.

There's a party tonight to welcome Curly Red back home. I hope he's not so shy he won't go, since he is the guest of honor and all. He looks good, but still way too skinny, no matter how hard we've all tried to fatten him up. Keeps a bandage over his ear hole so his brains won't fall out, he says. Della told him some must have already leaked through the gauze and he laughed, then looked in the mirror. Ha! Surgery is planned soon at the VA hospital in Dallas. He follows me around like a puppy, but I think he's mostly missing you. I think he thinks if he stares at me long enough, you will appear. Oh, how I wish that were true!

I have to go make a pie now for Uncle Bob, as I promised to make one special, just for him. Come home to me soon, Jimmy, the bed is too wide without you. If you really did have to get a plate in your head, I hope it matches your mother's china.

I love you, Jimbo,
Your Lulu

Jimmy Heron held Lou's letter against his cheek and cried, then kissed it lightly and slipped it back inside the plastic sheath. Fishing around in the picture box, he found a photograph of Lou taken on the ranch the weekend he'd brought her home to meet his family. She sat on their big horse, Ramsey, who tended to paw at his stomach with a back hoof like a dog scratching for fleas—which is just what he was doing in this picture. This struck Lou as the oddest thing and tickled her no end. Her head was thrown back and she was laughing so hard it appeared she might topple off the horse backwards. Jimmy smiled as he remembered the day and the joy of it before the sadness settled over him again. Then, kicking back in his recliner, Jimmy Heron clutched the photo to his chest as he drifted off to sleep, hoping, somehow, to be able to see her just once more.

<h1 style="text-align:center">·8·</h1>

immy did not remember coming to this resolution but awoke several mornings later knowing what must be done. He drove to the county courthouse in Montague and filed a quitclaim deed to his property, making sure to fill out everything correctly so there would be no confusion. That afternoon and into the evening as he went about his chores, cleaning up after himself and putting things away, he noticed a feeling of peace, almost of lightness, had come over him. It was slight, just a whisper of tranquility, but it boosted his spirits and made him think that maybe, just maybe, he wouldn't be going crazy as he'd expected. He picked up the phone and dialed Web's number.

"I'm lonesome for you guys," was all he said to Web. "Can you and Buster Dan be here in the morning?"

"Sure," said Web.

"Early?" Jimmy asked.

"Yeah, Jimmy, sure," Web replied, and they hung up the phone.

At 6:45 the next morning, Web Hardy was surprised to see Jimmy's house still dark as he walked up with Buster Dan. Jimmy had seemed so insistent they get there early. Tacked to the back door was a note that read: *This place belongs to the first person who shows up.* It had James Jefferson Heron's signature on it. Along with the note there was an envelope containing keys and pertinent papers, as well as a second envelope addressed to Ted Lanier, a friend and stone cutter over in Bowie. Inside it were ten crisp one hundred dollar bills and instructions for a headstone for Lou.

Web carried Buster Dan inside the sandstone house, easing open the back door which had never been locked, not once, since the house was built in 1937. He turned on the lights and noticed cereal bowls and silverware already set out for them. Coffee was in the plaid thermos on the counter. A simple note rested by the napkin holder in the middle of the kitchen table. All it said was: *Welcome to your new home. Be sure to look at the step.*

Feeling a little thunderstruck, Web flicked on the light and walked back out on the porch. Scratched into the concrete on the bottom step was writing he'd never noticed before. It stated the simple truth: PEOPLE LIVE HERE WHO LOVE EACH OTHER.

By seven o'clock that same morning, Jimmy Heron was two hours out on the highway, heading toward Amarillo. He had no idea where he was going to wind up. He only knew that he could not stay where he and Lou had lived together and remain a sane man. It was with resolve that he had packed his gear—just a few changes of clothes, his shaving kit, their pictures and letters—and set out on the road, staying one step ahead of insanity and one step behind his heartache. He had pinned the papers to the door with faith, pretty much certain, but hoping with all his heart nonetheless, that the first people to see them would be Web Hardy and Buster Dan.

·9·

By dawn the next day, Jimmy Heron was standing on the summit at Flagstaff mountain just outside Boulder, Colorado. He had driven all night and had no trouble with the weather, even though the waitress at the diner in Raton, New Mexico had said there might be ice on the pass. There was not.

Standing there in the early morning, Jimmy looked out onto the canyon below and wondered if Lou could see him from wherever she was. Did she know how much he missed her? Could she let him know in some way that she was all right? Would he ever be with her again?

Snow had dusted the tops of the mountains off in the distance and the clouds hung low, pregnant and gray. The mist which had coated his glasses earlier was now turning to white powder. The wind blew up from the bottom of the canyon, sending swirling poofs of dirt and snow spiraling up from the rocks below.

Jimmy zipped his jacket against the cold and sat on a big rock, letting his feet dangle off the edge and over the empty space. He picked up a pebble and sailed it off into the abyss. While nobody would ever have deemed them religious, Jimmy Heron and his wife were very spiritual people, grateful all their life together for everything they had been given and quick to ask for guidance when they needed it.

They considered themselves to be Christians, which meant to them that they chose to live their lives in a loving way. This is how they had been taught. "I'd rather live a Christian life than yap about it all the time," Lou had said. "People who can't be quiet about it are either trying to convince themselves or trying to convince me to write a check." Besides, televangelists and preachers of hate made her mad as hell.

Jimmy Heron sat on the cliff at Flagstaff mountain, so deep in his thoughts that even the cold of an approaching early storm didn't bother him. He clasped his hands together to pray, just as his mother had shown him when he was a boy.

"Dear God," he said, "I am sorry to keep having to ask for help with this...I feel I should be stronger on my own. But I don't know how to bring peace to my heart without some assistance. I'm not sure where to go, or where I'm supposed to be. That's the bottom line of it. I don't know what the plan is for me and I miss my wife too much to think clearly anymore. I need a sign, if you don't mind, and I'll try to pay more attention. Also, if it's not too much trouble, please tell Lou I love her. I am trying not to be angry with you for taking her away from me, but I am struggling with it and need some help with this. I miss her. I miss..."

The biting wind from the canyon had crusted the tears on Jimmy Heron's cheeks. He was staring absently out across the mountains when he noticed there was a warm spot right in the middle of his back, very warm, like a heat gun or hair dryer was pointed directly at him. A tiny space up in the clouds had opened just enough to let a laser of sunshine zap him right between the shoulder blades. It made him smile. He jammed his hands further into the pockets of his jacket and was surprised to feel something. Slowly he pulled it out.

It was a letter—how could he have missed it? The postmark was from Cambridge, Massachusetts, four days ago. Must be from Della, Jimmy thought, turning the envelope over. Sure enough, just as she'd done all her life, Della Heron had sealed the letter with shiny Scotch tape and affixed a wax seal with a replica of the JH brand they'd used on the cattle. Della always said the thought of some stranger reading her personal missives was a worrisome thing and had thus sealed each of her letters, scarce though they were, in this fashion.

Shaking the letter out of the envelope and opening it, Jimmy was shocked at just how long it had been since Della had retired from her law practice. The letterhead address was marked with a postal zone rather than a zip code. He realized that this yellowed stationery, which might even have been white at one time, had probably been printed some thirty years ago. It was tasteful and simple, the way Jimmy expected his big sister's life had always been.

There were three pages, quite a long letter for Della Heron to write.

The pages fluttered in the wind as Jimmy held them close to his eyes so he could decipher the palsied script.

Della Heron
Attorney and Counselor at Law
973 Newell Ave.
Cambridge, 08, Massachusetts

October 20th

Dearest Jim,

Winnie Bridwell phoned me about Lou's death and my heart aches for you. I recall how we all felt truly blessed when you found and brought into our family such a sparkling and wonderful girl. I know you will miss her, especially since the end came so tragically, but remember you are from strong stock with the JH brand on your heart.

We are still creeping along up here, living in the north but never becoming Yankees, just to keep Mother happy. We did not expect to get this old. Bonnie is much damaged by two strokes and I must care for her, so we do no traveling. It is hard to see someone so vibrant diminished in such a way, but the goodness of her still shines through. She cried and touched her heart when I told her of Lou's passing, and I know she sends her love and warmest thoughts to you.

As for me, I am taking medication for my heart and finally found some blackstrap molasses like Dad fed to the cattle to take for my blood. The smarty-pants child doctor I see was appalled but she has given up arguing with me, at least for the moment. My bad hip bothers me some and the workings of my inner ear have turned to powder. Other than that, I am in fine shape.

Do not worry about us as we have many friends to help us out, including two young women who own a food co-op close by. They bring us granola and alfalfa sprouts to graze on (even though we would both rather have fried chicken), but they are lively and fun to know.

I have a feeling you won't stay at the ranch and I understand. Write to me from wherever you wind up. God knows, Bonnie and I aren't going anywhere, and I'm sure we'll both ride the horse on into the barn from here.

Remember Mother's words, from the hymn, just before she died: "In the sweet, bye and bye, we will meet at that beautiful shore." Living on this earth is just a phase, Jim. I honestly think that's true. After death is when the real living starts.

I love you,

Sis

P.S. If you talk to Winnie, please apologize to her for me. We mostly shouted at each other on the phone since I cannot hear thunder anymore and her grammar is atrocious.

Jimmy Heron hung his head in awe for just a moment as he refolded the letter and slid it back in his pocket. Della's wisdom, humor, and clarity had always amazed and humbled him. It honored him, somehow, that she was his big sister and loved him so much. He knew it with a feeling as solid and sturdy as granite.

Crawling from the ledge, Jimmy dusted off his pants and made his way back up the hill to his truck. The heater in the big Chevy felt good. Even though he still didn't know where the path was taking him, he felt sure he would be given a sign if he would just pay attention. Was he supposed to be in Colorado? He wasn't sure. Return to Texas? No, he could not. That much he knew.

Heading back down Flagstaff, back down Canyon Boulevard toward the city of Boulder, Jimmy noticed a young man trudging up the hill. The skinny kid wore a University of Colorado sweatshirt, baseball cap, hiking boots, and baggy shorts, of all things, and was braced against the wind. The boy had a scraggly almost-beard and a grim, determined look on his face, his shoulders hunched up toward his ears. He looked almost brittle, as if the strong wind would snap him in two.

Jimmy slowed the truck and rolled down his window. He wanted to tell the kid he'd just been up to the summit and it was windy and cold. There was a storm coming, he was going to say, and he'd be happy to give the boy a ride back into town. The young man glanced across the road toward Jimmy's truck and seeing his Texas license tags, instantly shot Jimmy the finger, scowling at him.

"Take your fucking pickup back to Texas!" the kid shouted. "We don't want you here!"

Jimmy Heron was startled. After all, he had only intended to help and couldn't remember anyone flipping him the bird before. He had read how people from Colorado didn't much like people from Texas. Seems Aspen or Vail or one of those big, fancy ski resorts had been built with Texas money. That brought a lot of rich, loud-mouthed Texans to Colorado, the kind of people who got drunk and rowdy and banged their beer bottles on the table and threatened to buy the place if the service didn't get better. Obnoxious jerks, Jimmy thought, but he couldn't believe the kid could think that he, Jimmy Heron, in his blue Chevrolet truck with a camper, was one of them. Shoot, he thought, he didn't even have whitewalls. Why would he want to live someplace where he was hated already and didn't even have whitewalls?

He took this as his first sign and laughed to himself, a laugh tinged with sadness and irony, about how the Lord sure works in mysterious ways. Then he headed back out Highway 36 toward Denver so he could hit Interstate 25 going north.

Winter storms threatened but never really happened. Having spent most of his life in Texas, Jimmy Heron was not sure what he would do if he were caught in a blizzard. He had some chains in the back, still shiny in their original box. Whenever ice or snow hit north Texas, the personal policy Jimmy and Lou Heron always adhered to was to feed all the animals and then crawl back in bed and snuggle all day. Lou actually thought that that was what snow and icestorms were for. Rainstorms, too, if she had her way.

Further north, in the purple darkness of early morning before daybreak, Jimmy Heron stopped at Sharon's Cafe in Chugwater, Wyoming.

It was so early he was surprised to see the restaurant already open. The caramel smell of strong coffee brewing and maple bacon frying gave the place a homey feel. Country music played on the kitchen radio. Jimmy had always savored the sound and smell of a day shaking off its blanket and sizzling itself awake.

Besides a couple of road workers, he was the only customer. The restaurant was just one big room with deer and elk antlers here and there on the knotty pine walls. Most of the booths didn't match, and there was a fair share of duct tape strapped on to hide rips and keep the foam rubber from burping out. But the floor was clean and a sign hung in front of the cash register which read: SKINNY COOKS CAN'T BE TRUSTED.

Sharon, the owner-waitress-cook, was in her forties, Jimmy figured, a strong-looking woman, all muscle and bone, with curly, ash blonde hair pulled back at her neck, and clear gray eyes. They were kind eyes, belonging to someone who had touched the face of the dragon and lived to tell about it. She brought him coffee and a glass of water, then handed him a menu as he took his first sip of the strong brew.

"You up from Texas, mister?" she said. "I saw your tags."

Jimmy nodded.

"Where're you headed?" she asked.

"Not sure," he said.

"You lose somebody special?"

Jimmy nodded again, somewhat surprised that his loss was written all over him. "Lost my wife," he said. "She was killed, actually. It's been very hard for me. How could you tell?"

Sharon slid into the booth across from Jimmy, facing him with those clear eyes. "I know that look, mister. Had it myself more than once," she said. "People don't drive through this kind of country at this time of year without being sure of where they're going. Unless they're running away from something painful. Or the law. And you don't look much like an outlaw to me."

She reached across the table and brushed his hand, patting his knuckles with her fingers. Jimmy was touched by the instant connection and didn't pull away or clam up like men often do when their tender core is exposed.

"I lived in Texas for a while, at Fort Hood, close to Killeen," she said. "My husband was stationed there in the army."

Jimmy felt a knife in his stomach at the sound of the word *Killeen* and he winced.

"My wife was killed in Killeen," he said, "a couple of weeks ago."

Sharon looked at Jimmy, leaning back in the booth and let out a long, low whistle through her bottom teeth. A smoky sadness seeped into her eyes, which turned down at the edges as she stared at him.

"At that cafeteria?" she asked. Jimmy nodded.

"You heard about it?" he asked. "All the way up here?"

"Read it in the paper. I am really sorry for you, mister. What a terrible and tragic and stupid thing," she said, putting particular emphasis on the word *stupid*.

"What about your husband?" Jimmy asked. "He still in the military?"

"Oh Lord, I hope not," Sharon said. "The last thing we need is the military in heaven. He was killed in Vietnam. Got shot in the neck and bled to death before anybody found him, so I guess it wasn't too painful. At least that's what they said."

"I am sorry, too, for your loss," Jimmy said.

"Thank you," Sharon replied. "It was a long time ago. We were newlyweds, married just four months when he shipped out. Hearing he'd been killed pretty much knocked my props out. That's how I got to Wyoming. Just drove and drove until I ran out of gas and money. I wasn't even sure what state I was in when I took a job waitressing here. Finally saved up enough to buy the place when the owner retired. It keeps me busy and out of trouble."

"Well," Jimmy said, "it's a nice place. And the coffee's good, too." He waggled his cup toward her, like a half-salute.

"Say," Sharon said, sliding out of the booth, "I've got some elk sausage in the back a fella gave me the other day. How about I fry up a couple of patties for you, no charge. If it makes you sick, I'll give you your money back on whatever else you order."

"You're on," Jimmy said. "I'll have a pancake, just one, and the sausage."

Jimmy Heron ate his breakfast in silence as Sharon greeted more customers coming in. He noticed how she had that same energy good

47

waitresses have had since the beginning of restaurants, the ability to keep everything coming or going and never really getting flustered or mad enough to throw food or punch some fool in the nose. He admired that quality, and so had Lou, who often left a tip equal to the price of the meal if she'd been especially pleased with the service.

Jimmy smiled at the memory, then hung his head for a second as another small wave of pain rose inside him. When he looked up, he saw Sharon sashaying toward his table, pulling his ticket out of her shirt pocket with her left hand and holding the coffee pot with her right.

"One for the road?" she asked, and he shook his head no. "How 'bout that sausage? You sick yet?"

"No," he said, "it was fine. Very good, actually. Thank you."

Jimmy placed some money for his meal and tip on the table, adding an extra couple of bucks to the pile when Sharon wasn't looking. She set the coffee pot down on the table and put both her hands on his left one. Squatting down so they could be face to face, she rubbed her thumb back and forth on his wedding band and looked directly into his eyes. "Mister," she said, "I know it doesn't feel like it just now, but it will get better. You will heal from this. It's one of the magical things about being human." She patted his hand. "Safe travels," she said.

Jimmy Heron pulled out onto the highway in his truck just as dawn cracked like an egg in the eastern sky. The gold and pinkish light beckoned the chilling gusts of fall, which whistled down through the mountains of Wyoming, forming a vacuum that sucked him along the road toward a new life. He could not say where he was going, only letting the wind pull him there.

·10·

Like I said, Jimmy Heron is one hell of a guy, and I ought to know because I knew him all my life. My folks had a place out by where the town of Uz used to be, before it burned down, close to Forestburg. Nothin' left there now but an old shack leanin' hard to the right where old Marvin used to beat the daylights outta me for nothin' more than bein' the red-headed stepchild I was.

Flu and pneumonia took my folks and my sister in 1928. I was only five years old and got shuffled off to live with this relative and then that one. Most of 'em had too many kids and not enough money, so I wound up with a drunk named Marvin LeCroix. He wasn't my grandpa but he'd been married to my grandmother for a short time before she passed away. Rumor had it that he'd beat her up bad enough that she'd never recovered, but since folks clammed up about that kind of thing back then, I never knew for sure. And I wasn't sure why he took me in, either, except to have a punchin' bag, or an opponent too small to fight back. Maybe it saved him a trip into town on Saturday night. I do know I came close to starvin' to death while I lived there. He'd fix himself somethin' to eat, then I could have whatever was left over before he threw it out. Never any more than that, though, and I couldn't dare let him see me get it. Just lookin' at me chewin' somethin' really pissed him off.

Oh, Marvin had a mean streak! Lucky for me he was a drunk and spent a fair amount of time passed out, 'cause when he was awake and I was within reach, his arm would snake out lightnin' fast and I'd get slapped or punched or thrown up against a wall. Made me quick, though, and kept me on my toes. Made me stay alert, I'll say that for the sonofabitch.

I tried hard to make myself invisible back then. Seems like he was maddest at me for just takin' up space. My mother's people were part

Cherokee, and she'd shown me how to walk and breathe like an Indian, puttin' my toes down first and exhalin' to the rhythm of the wind. I crept around like that, tryin' to disguise myself as a piece of air. Hard to do with my hair so red and curly it looked like a bowl of cherry tomatoes balanced on my head.

My name was Curtis Robert Parsons in that life, but most everybody called me Curly Red, except my mother. She called me Robbie. There was always the oddest, most wonderful smell around my mother. Lemons and roses was what it smelled like, so I could tell when she was close by. I'd just follow my nose until I found her. She said if she didn't know better, she'd swear I was part hound dog. After she died, and the whole time I had to live with Marvin, I'd smell lemons and roses in my room late at night, and I'd sneak through the house looking for her, then cry myself to sleep.

The smell stopped showing up at night the day I left Marvin's house and went to live with Jimmy Heron. I guess my mother felt I was finally safe and she didn't have to keep lookin' in on me. She was right. Jimmy Heron saved my life.

I'd heard folks say how old Marvin must've had a rough boyhood, what with him bein' so ornery and all, but I figured he couldn't have had a rougher one than the one I was havin'. So one morning after I was sure he was gone from the house, I stuffed all my worldly goods, which consisted of six marbles, a pair of socks, a wrinkled photograph of my parents, and a three-legged lizard named Twig, into a pillowcase, then headed barefoot down the road as far as I could run from the meanest man I ever knew.

By early afternoon I was sittin' on a big branch of a scrub oak across the road from Jimmy Heron's, tryin' to remember the smell of lemons and roses, tryin' to remember what clean sheets felt like, tryin' to keep from cryin'.

Me and Jimmy didn't really know each other then. We'd only seen one another a couple of times down by the creek. Muddy Boggy Creek ran through at the end of the Herons' property line. That's where I'd go hunt for lizards and frogs and whatever else I could find.

What I wasn't huntin' for the first time Jimmy saved me was a big old cottonmouth water moccasin. He was just layin' out there sunnin'

*himself as I hopped from one rock right over to the one Mr. Snake was
using as his own personal piece of beach property. The snake raised up
his head and opened his mouth real wide just to let me know who I was
dealin' with. He was hissing at me when BLAMMY! he got blind-sided
by a rock almost as big as my head tossed by none other than Dead-Eye
Dick, Jimmy Heron.*

*Well, I'm pretty sure it didn't kill the snake, but it sure as hell rang
his bell. I saw his eyes roll and he just sort of laid back down on the rock
in slow motion and slithered over sideways until he was almost belly-
side up. I was still frozen where I'd been standin', with my skinny little
knees shakin' so hard they were bangin' together. Next thing I know, Jimmy's
got my scrawny arm in his hand and gives me a good shake. "Pay attention to where you're going!" is all he says to me, then takes on off up the
hill toward home.*

*I've always had a fondness for the sound of the word home. Marvin
had a house, sort of; Jimmy's folks had a home. As I sat on the big branch
of the scrub oak, just starin' at Jimmy Heron's home all afternoon, I realized why I was there. I was takin' Jimmy's advice. I was paying attention to where I was goin'.*

*Toward suppertime, Jimmy came out and ambled down the gentle
hill in their front yard. I remember watchin' his russet-colored hair bounce
on his head with each step, like a fella's hair will do when it's freshly cut.
He walked across the road and right up to the tree where I was sittin'
just quiet as snow and yelled up at me, "My mama says that guests in
our home are expected to wash up and join us at the table for supper."
I didn't say nothin' at all, just handed Jimmy my sack to hold while I
climbed down. We walked back up the hill in silence, new friends for life
with a hell of a big story ahead.*

·11·

J immy Heron had driven all the way to the Pacific Ocean like a man possessed, stopping only to eat and catch a few hours sleep. When he reached the vast expanse of water, he parked his truck up from the beach and trudged, almost in a trance, across the sand and into the sea until he was standing knee-deep in the fifty-five-degree water. The roiling, bone-chilling waves of the Oregon coast spewed and foamed against the rocks beside him. He found himself wishing one would grab him and drag him out to sea, pulling him under until his lungs and nose and mouth filled with brine and kelp, until otters and seals and sharks could gnaw his flesh to shreds and the ceaseless ache in his heart would stop.

Jimmy dropped to his knees just as an angry wave crashed, slamming into his chest and rolling him over backwards. The icy chill and the power of the sea took his wind away. Even though his natural instinct was to struggle against it, he felt oddly at peace, hoping this was it, praying it would be quick. As he opened his mouth to let the sea rush into his lungs, Jimmy Heron felt two powerful arms, arms with the strength of many men, scoop him up and stand him straight up in the water, leaving him there to sputter and cough and spit. Salt water poured off of him. A sea lion on one of the rocks further out began barking wildly at him, chastising him, it felt like, and the voice belonging to the arms of whoever or whatever had saved him thundered right behind his head.

Curly Red's voice shouted at him: *"Not your time, Jimmy! Stay alive, will ya?"*

Jimmy's neck snapped as he quickly looked behind him, searching the shoreline with his eyes. He saw no one, nothing but the stone-colored beach and a few gulls dipping in the wind. Someone flew a lonesome kite off in the distance, a spiraling windsock with rainbow-colored streamers attached.

He had no idea how long he'd been standing there when he noticed the tips of his fingers beginning to turn blue. It had frightened him, getting this close to suicide, because the thought of it had come so easily. Death didn't seem that far off. It was right over…there.

He dragged himself out of the surf and back up the beach, shivering in the gray and wind of the Oregon coast. It was not the place for him, he decided. Not the sand, not the salt water. Jimmy Heron changed his clothes and warmed himself by the truck's heater. Then he took himself southeast to the high desert of central Oregon, to horse country.

Within two days he had purchased five acres of land outside a wisp of a town called Reliance, Oregon. The drive there had been a long one, but the land reminded him a little bit of Texas, only not so much as to make him homesick every time he glanced out the window. Mostly, it reminded him of New Mexico, a place he and Lou had enjoyed in the early years of their marriage. Or maybe it was the rock formations and their resemblance to the Palo Duro Canyon, up on the cap rock in the panhandle back home. It didn't matter. The place felt good to him, and he liked being near the mountains. Let's see, he thought, there's Faith, Hope, and Charity, the Three Sisters. Then there's Black Butte, Three-Fingered Jack, and Mt. Jefferson. He was glad the service station attendant in Reliance had been patient enough to point out all the mountains, and he made a mental note to learn the names of the ones he couldn't remember by the end of the week.

Jimmy Heron bought the first place he saw for sale. A garrulous woman named Millie Jensen sold it to him before moving to her daughter's in North Dakota. They agreed on a price and shook hands on the deal. Before Jimmy knew it, Millie was pulling pictures off the refrigerator and stuffing them into her bag.

She had skinny arms and spindly legs and a gut that tugged at the seams of her polyester stretch pants. Her faded flannel shirt might have been stolen off the back of a sixth-grade boy. Or it just as easily could have been hers forever. Life and the weather had settled hard on her face, and the soiled John Deere cap she wore pretty much told her story.

But Millie was a woman who liked to chat and figured she owed Jimmy an explanation of the cheap price for the land and everything on it. All she planned to take with her were her pictures and her small ugly dog, Troll.

"First my daughter thinks I'm going to burn the place down with my cigarettes," she said, "even though I tell her I gave up my smokes in '82. Next she's sure I'll forget and leave the iron on or something dumb like that. I haven't even owned an iron since her last year in high school—I threw the goddamned thing out the window and don't have any plans to buy one. Then she starts crying and says to me, 'Oh, Mama, please come live with us. I don't want the kids to grow up without knowing their grandma.' I thought, well, shitfire, I don't want that either, and so I'm going. Those kids might not like what they see for their grandma, but this is what they're gonna get."

She stuffed Troll's food dish into her bag and slipped some space-age looking sunglasses on. She noticed how Jimmy was taken aback at her choice in eyewear. "I know, I know," she said, doing a last-minute check for any essential items, "these are really not my style. Found 'em on the road out front. But they do the trick. And I think they make me look like Catwoman. Troll hates 'em, growls at me every time I put them on. Don'tcha?" She bared her teeth, sticking her face right down next to the homely dog, who, as if on cue, growled so hard it made his eyes bug out. "God, you're a dreadful-looking little bastard," Millie said to the dog. He instantly stopped growling and began trying to wag his corkscrew tail without falling over. She gave him a few long strokes all the way down his bony back.

"Let's go," Millie said to Troll, "time to saddle up." And she banged her way out the front door of the trailer.

Jimmy followed her out to the truck, an ancient Dodge the color of a chalky Army cot. "Load up, dogface," she told her pet, letting him jump up into the cab, "and stay on your blanket. If you don't, I'll throw you out the window."

Millie handed Jimmy a piece of paper with her daughter's address and phone number on it. "Here's where you send the checks," she said. "Call if there's anything you can't figure out. Fixed just about everything myself, except for that big dent. But don't worry, it's just ugly—

won't leak on you or anything. Sort of like my third husband.

"Reliance is a good place as long as you don't let people meddle in your business. Most folks will help you out if you need it, though. The girls who live up on the hill are the sweetest. You can count on 'em. But watch out for that fat preacher—fella named Dimmer—he's a snake."

With that, Millie Jensen swung her worn frame up into the cab, braced her saggy belly with her free hand, and fired the truck's engine. It went off as loud as a rifle shot, and Jimmy instinctively ducked his head. Millie cackled and whapped her hand on the steering wheel. "By God," she yelled, "I like a truck that shoots back!" She wheeled the big banger around in the driveway with an amazing grace and stuck her head out the window. "My son-in-law's a real estate attorney—God, what a snoozer of a job that must be, can you imagine? He'll do the paperwork and send you the documents. Anyway, I gotta scoot. If I'm lucky, I'll beat the snow!" With that, she gunned the engine and spun the tires, spewing gravel and dirt everywhere as she roared away, leaving Jimmy Heron in her dust.

Jimmy watched Millie's rattletrap truck pull out onto the highway, straw and dirt swirling up and flying out the back. He heard it backfire once more before disappearing over the ridge. Then he looked down at the dust settling on the toes of his shoes and realized he had hardly said anything more to her than, "How much for your place?" She had done just about all the talking.

He turned back and surveyed the trailer, his new home. Aside from the fact that it was faded turquoise with rusty screens and had a big dent in the top where a dead tree had fallen on it, he decided the place didn't look too bad. Ugly, sure. Smelly, yeah. But not uninhabitable.

Jimmy zipped his jacket higher and took a stroll around his five acres: mostly ponderosa pines, some creosote bushes, some juniper, and lots and lots of rocks. Good, he thought, nothing to mow. Rocks are the easiest things in the world to ranch—no feeding, no milking, no shoeing, or worming.

He would have to drive into Bend the next day to handle his business affairs. He would set up a bank account, transfer money, get the phone line switched over to his name, apply for an Oregon driver's license, and get new tags for his truck. But for right now, he wanted to stand on the land and get the feel of the earth, let the wind blow gently into his nose until he and this place could start to feel like family.

The ponderosa pines swayed. Jimmy Heron climbed on some boulders just down from his trailer, the dry, cold air of the Oregon high desert spiraling around his head. He chuckled to himself at how completely daredevilish this would seem to Lou and Curly Red. Jimmy was a cautious and pragmatic man, weighing most decisions far too long for either one of them. They were always in the front of the roller coaster with their arms straight up, screaming and laughing, while he was still standing at the ticket counter, wondering if the ride would make him throw up on his new shirt.

Leaving the ranch and driving clear across the country was certainly out of character for him. He half expected to see roots and clods of dirt dangling from his shoes, so uprooted did he feel, so ripped away and raw, torn from the life and land he had loved all his days.

He glanced up toward the hill. The afternoon sun hitting the west side of it caused the lupine and sage and red volcanic rock to combine in the most wonderful color. Lavender, he thought. He stood there, awestruck by the beauty of it. Then he spotted a log house in the clearing, a home for someone. Wood smoke curled from the chimney, doing a lover's dance with the wind. Jimmy Heron walked back up to the turquoise trailer, his new home, wondering what the rest of his life would be like. He added picking up a box of oatmeal and other staples to his list of things to do in town.

.12.

nna Leigh O'Brien was horrified. And pissed. She had just found the body of a dead kitten in their mailbox, its head severed and missing. The sign she and her partner Cory had made and carefully tacked to their mailbox post was torn in two. HATE-FREE ZONE. NO ORS MATERIAL, PLEASE, the sign said." One-half of it was stuffed into the mailbox with the body of the dead animal Someone had written on it in black felt pen, DYKES DIE EARLY. YOU'RE NEXT.

Leigh gagged, and then she began to cry. She picked up the newspaper, which had been pulled from the slot and tossed on the ground, and wrapped the kitten's body in the classified section. On the front page the headline screamed, SHERIFF SAYS HATE CRIMES ON THE RISE. No kidding, Leigh thought, and felt the baby move.

Forty years old and into her sixth month of her first pregnancy, Leigh felt herself continually in awe of the entire process of motherhood. She marveled at the changes she saw happening to her body on the outside, as well as the ones she felt going on within. Instinctively, she rubbed her belly with her left hand, soothing the small package of life budding inside her. She began making her way back up the drive toward their log house. The autumn sun glistened on her dark auburn hair. In her right hand, she held a small package of death, a reminder of hate.

The initials ORS stood for the Oregon Reformation Society, an organization developed solely for the purpose of eliminating gay and lesbian rights in Oregon, part of a larger plan boiling up across the nation. Before the group led by local accountant Wendell Metcalf took hold in central Oregon, nobody in Reliance paid much attention to the sexual habits of their neighbors. Now it seemed to be what people talked about the most. An atmosphere of fear and mistrust had seeped into the town, a dark fog of secrecy and wariness that brought window shades down and made lifelong friends shy away from each other.

Joining forces with Rev. Darryl Dimmer of the Mt. Goshen Church of the Righteous and various statewide churches, and with support from powerful and wealthy national organizations, the ORS had managed to get enough signatures across the state to propose an initiative which they planned to put on the ballot in the next election. If passed, it would change the Oregon constitution to declare homosexuality "…abnormal, wrong, unnatural and perverse." It would allow the firing of any state employee even suspected of being homosexual. It would encourage discrimination and violence. No wonder people were feeling beleaguered.

With the election a little over a year away, things were looking good for the ORS. They had their own newspaper, *The Moral Code*, in which they repeatedly published what they called the "militant homosexual agenda," a "plan" known only to them and other organizations of the Christian Right. Neither Leigh nor her partner, Cory Miller, nor any other gay person they knew had any idea that they'd ever had an agenda at all.

It was certainly true that most of Leigh and Cory's gay friends were too busy making a living and saving for retirement to have an agenda. They were helping put their kids or nieces and nephews through college, going to work every day, mowing their yards, ordering pizza and watching a ball game—just living their lives.

The Moral Code was distributed at night, slipped into mailboxes and under doormats when nobody was looking. This seemed, from Leigh O'Brien's point of view, an extremely odd way for the truly righteous to behave.

At times it felt like a monster, something sinister and calculating loose on the land. Painting its face, traveling at night, the ORS laid its eggs in the murky swampland of fear. It left no tracks, circling back again and again, trailing a residue of literature and the miasma of hate. Talking love and engendering hate was creepy, Leigh thought, just plain creepy.

There were many people, she believed, good people, who harbored no hatred for the homosexual community. These folks, the ORS and

Darryl Dimmer in particular, held in check with a kind of spiritual blackmail. There was no room for tolerance in this debate, no place for compromise.

Feeling winded, Leigh pulled her sweater closer around her as she got to the top of the drive, and stopped for a moment to admire the lavender color on the side of the hill. Wind blew up from the valley and the pines swayed like geriatric hula dancers. It was getting colder, she thought, might even snow by the weekend. Hard to tell in this part of the country.

She glanced back at their log house, glad it was so snug and warm, even more glad they'd given up on the idea of building it themselves. What a nightmare that had been. If it had gone on much longer, someone was bound to have been badly pounded with a claw hammer.

Leigh snooped around the porch for a shovel or some sort of gardening tool to dig a grave for the kitten. Finding none, she left the body in its newspaper wrapping on the porch swing and walked into the house looking for Cory to help her, and for a tissue with which to wipe her nose.

Cory Miller was sitting on the floor with one shoe and sock off, examining the top of her foot by lamplight. Her reading glasses were perched on the end of her nose. The sore place she was inspecting, the by-product of an unfortunate encounter with a nail gun some months earlier, was almost healed. Only a purple bruise on top of a small bump remained. She glanced up, recognizing a particular look on Leigh's face which had become all too familiar in the past few months.

"Is the beast on the loose again?" Cory asked, as Leigh slumped heavily into the rocker, nodding her head, almost on the verge of tears. "What happened? They knock over the mailbox again? Leave dog shit in it? Or is it just the usual warm and wonderful reading material which, come to think of it, is not much different—only dog shit will wash off. What happened?"

"They cut off the head of a kitten and put its body in the mailbox," Leigh said. "It's horrible. I tore up the sign they left…it was just too awful." She began to cry softly.

"Oh God, no," Cory said. "Where's the kitten?"

"I left the body wrapped in newspaper on the swing. We need to bury it. Oh, Cory, I am so tired of this." Cory leaned across and took Leigh's hand, holding her fingers lightly.

"I know," she said, "I know. We don't have to stay here, Leigh-O. We can go anywhere in the world we want to."

Leigh sniffed, then suddenly straightened herself up in the chair. A look of resolve settled across her face. Her freckles actually became more vivid. "No," she said, "this is our home and this is where we'll stay. My ancestors came here on the Oregon Trail. I'm not going to be run off the land by a bunch of bigots who think they need to tell everybody how to live." She stood up, heading toward the back of the house as Cory scrambled to get her sock and shoe back on. "I'll get a spade," Leigh said. "You get your jacket and the kitten and meet me by the barn."

This was not the first time the two of them had buried a dead animal left for them as a message of hate. There had been a dog draped across their mailbox, three squirrels skinned and placed in a row on their driveway, and a stringer of trout hung to rot on the gate. The hardest thing to take, however, had been the murder of their steer, Sir Loin, and the wounding of their Guernsey cow, Mimi, which had occurred about three months before.

Cory had rescued the cattle from doom by purchasing them at an auction. Neither she nor Leigh had any intention of letting their bovine pals do anything other than live out their days grazing and looking sweet out in the meadow at the bottom of the hill. To lose Sir Loin from a rifle shot to the head and see Mimi forever maimed and limping from bullet fragments still buried deep in the muscle and bone of her shoulder was to remind the women of the nature of violence and hatred targeted at them for nothing more than telling the truth about their lives.

It seemed out of place, somehow lopsided and misshapen, that love could beget this much anger and violence. Yet, each Sunday across America, preachers raged against homosexuals as if the future of the planet depended upon the annihilation of every lesbian and gay man on earth. Indeed, the coffers of those same preachers had grown fat as they actively sought and successfully persuaded their congregations and supporters to send more money to help them fight their war against the evil, depraved homosexuals of America. The money taken in was, of course, tax free.

Nobody in the world appreciated a tax-exempt status more than the Reverend Darryl Dimmer, fiery minister and self-appointed prophet of the Mt. Goshen Church of the Righteous on the edge of town. With the American flag waving right outside his office window at the church, Darryl Dimmer loved counting the money received in the Sunday offering; loved it when shiny coins slid out of envelopes and bounced across his desk; loved it when even he was shocked at the dollar amount on a check from some family struggling to pay the rent. It was then he felt certain he was doing the job he was called to do.

TAKE AMERICA BACK! Those were the words this week on the church's marquis. It would be Rev. Dimmer's sermon for this Sunday. Last Sunday it was "Don't Cheat God!" and the money had poured in, just poured in.

Darryl Dimmer rubbed his chubby hands together, thinking of the delightful possibilities, remembering the fire in his belly, the wrath in his voice. Recalling the looks on their faces.

"Are you going to hell over fifty dollars?" he had railed at them from the pulpit. "If you make five hundred dollars a week, God wants 10 percent of it right now—in this basket! You can cheat the stinking Internal Revenue Service, but YOU CAN'T CHEAT GOD!" he had shouted at them, his face purple with rage, spit flying out of the corners of his mouth.

He flourished his Bible in the air as he marched back and forth across the blue carpeted stage. He mopped his sweaty face and neck, wiping up under his double chin and the folds of skin around his shirt collar until his handkerchief was soaked through. He worked his congregation into a frenzy until they were waving their arms in the air and begging Jesus to forgive them for not making even more money from which to donate their 10 percent.

Darryl Dimmer said there was a way out of sin. He said he was the only one who knew the way. If they followed him, let him lead them out of their wicked paths, well, there just might be a chance for them. Maybe, just a slight chance, that he could help them get their foot in heaven's door. But they had to make a reservation for this trip and this trip had a cost. He knew they had it to give for the work of the Lord.

He rolled their emotions around the stage like a ball, taking them up, pulling them back down, going in for the kill. The slam-dunk for Jesus, he called it. When Darryl Dimmer was done, they applauded. They stood on the pews of the church, their Bibles raised, and swayed back and forth. They reached out to the Reverend Darryl Dimmer, hoping he would reach back, hoping a drop of his sweat would get slung their way, perhaps even splatter on them, anointing them. And they would be blessed.

He had been a handsome man not so long ago. He kept a picture of himself and his wife on the bookshelf in his office. Both of them appeared clear-eyed and purposeful, their hands joined together on top of his red leather Bible, just starting out in their ministry, eager to serve the Lord. But something had soured in them in the past few years. They plumped up, got jowly, and in their eyes came the desperate look of people who need to make their point of view the only one. They couldn't see it when they looked at each other, but it was there, just as surely as the stain on a paisley tie always shows up. Soon it's the only thing there is to see.

Darryl Dimmer used to stare lovingly at that photograph. Now, he stared lovingly at the carton of videotapes and cassettes of his previous sermons, his babies, the very ones he had begun selling by mail order and would sell to the members of his congregation every chance he got. He saw no reason why they wouldn't want to recapture the feeling of power and ecstasy, the presence of the Holy Spirit, by experiencing his brilliance again on their VCRs.

Why, it was only a matter of time before his sermons would be picked up by one of the religious television stations across the country, only a matter of time. Within the next two years he knew he would successfully rid the state of Oregon of homosexuals—like St. Patrick driving the snakes from Ireland, like the Puritans ridding Salem of its witches. Darryl Dimmer bet he'd be close personal friends by then with Pat Robertson and Jerry Falwell and the big shots in Christian broadcasting. Yes, he just bet he would.

Reverend Dimmer looked out his office window and savored the sight of Old Glory waving there in the autumn breeze. He liked hearing the snap of the flag and the clang of the metal clip on the rope against the pole. By God, he did love America, especially the free market economy part, which was making him a man of importance and wealth, particularly since all of his wealth came, praise God, tax free.

From their vantage point in back of their creaky old barn, Cory and Leigh could see all the way down through the meadow and into the valley. Although the ponderosa pines blocked their view of Millie Jensen's trailer, smoke from the wood stove generally let them know if anybody was home. Millie was not one to burn up her fuel supply just for the heck of it.

The two women finished burying the tiny cat by placing its body in the grave with some stones, dried sage, and catnip. They added a coupon for fifty cents off a large bag of Meow Mix, the personal favorite of their own fat gray cat with the busted left front toe, Jerry Garcia. Leigh looked off down the valley. "I thought Millie Jensen moved away," she said.

"She did," Cory said. "Willis filled up her truck at the BP station. She told him she was headed to Fargo. Apparently Darryl Dimmer pulled his Cadillac up to the next pump and Millie shot him the bird. Then she peeled off and threw gravel all over the good reverend's new car. Said Millie yelled *viper* out the window of her truck before she sped away."

"So, who bought Millie's place?" Leigh asked. "There's smoke coming from the chimney."

"Don't know for sure. An older man, up from Texas, Willis said. My kind of guy."

Leigh turned to look at Cory, who had her fingers in the famous Hook 'em Horns position of the University of Texas, her hand over her heart.

"You Texans, I swear," Leigh said. "You stick together, no matter what. He could be a serial killer, for all you know. A Rush Limbaugh maniac."

"Who's Russ Linbong?" Cory asked.

"You don't want to hear about him. Believe me. And he's not a Texan."

"Good," Cory said, "because we have a simple philosophy in the Lone Star state. We figure it's either hang together now or hang separately later on. I'm going to go introduce us tomorrow. Want to come along?"

"Maybe. Can't say for sure. Sally will be here for my check-up, then I've got lots of papers to grade and a lesson plan to write before Monday. The fifth grade never stops, you know."

"Until it gets to its first tube of Clearasil. Or to middle school, right?"

"Let's hope. I would dread the thought of having to teach a few of these children again. This has not been an easy year."

Cory bent over and patted the kitten's small grave, smoothing the dirt out with her fingers. She placed a pretty stone right in the center of the little mound. There was a lump in her throat. "I am sorry your life was so short," she whispered.

Then, with their arms around each other, the two women walked back to the log house. The warmth from the woodstove called them in and held them close in the late afternoon of a chilly autumn day in central Oregon.

·13·

endell Metcalf was a man obsessed. Since he had taken the position as head of the ORS in central Oregon, his life had become a whirlwind of activity—he was in constant demand as a speaker at various events and antigay rallies across the state. He had never been as popular or well-known before. He was, after all, not a bad man, just one who needed to be noticed, and this need gnawed at his gut, burning inside him like a coal afire.

Wendell's business as a certified public accountant had suffered some, both due to time constraints and from people taking their business elsewhere because of his politics. The salary he was paying himself and his wife Suzette from ORS donations, however, more than made up for the lost income. As a matter of fact, it was the most money he'd had in his life. Although he could not have foreseen it, Wendell Metcalf quickly found out that this was a heck of a way to make a very comfortable living.

In spite of his basic good looks, Wendell Metcalf was awkward in social settings, generally content to stay in his office until late at night, balancing the books of some idiot who couldn't even reconcile his own checkbook.

He was continually amazed at how stupid people were. And gullible. As the membership in the Oregon Reformation Society grew, he realized he could tell people almost anything. He could pull statistics right out of his ass if he wanted to, it seemed, and these people would never know, never think a thing about his being anything other than exactly right. They trusted him, poor slobs, and that was proof to him of just how stupid they were.

But Wendell Metcalf knew there was a faggot in him. He knew it from the first time he and David Mack had masturbated each other when they were eleven years old. It had been only a little puddle, just a drop or two of white goo into David's hand, but it had taken Wendell's breath away. He clung to David's shoulder and cried in a mixture of ecstasy and shame.

"Do you think we're queer?" he asked his friend, and David laughed out loud at him.

"No, dummy, not a chance," he had said. "Do we look like guys who would wear a dress?"

"No," Wendell said.

"Well, then we're not queer. Now, you do me." And David placed Wendell's shaky hand on his penis.

Over the next two years in the clubhouse they built into the side of a hill behind David's house, they camped out, played army, swapped baseball cards, talked about girls and school, and hid out from the rest of the world. The two boys explored their budding sexuality by looking at magazines David had swiped from his dad's collection under the mattress and then masturbating each other. When David took Wendell into his mouth one night, Wendell was horrified but could not pull away, could not bring himself to push David's head from him, and his orgasm felt like an explosion from the depths of someplace he could not even name. When David asked him to do the same, Wendell could not. He could only shake his head no and whimper, rubbing David's erupting penis against the soft adolescent hair on his belly.

For Wendell Metcalf, there had been no more homosexual encounters after that. But a peculiar longing would overtake him from time to time. Before the end of high school, David Mack had moved away, joined the Marines, and later married some mousy-looking girl named Patsy. Their wedding picture appeared one day in the *Reliance Record-Chronicle.* David was in his dress blues and Patsy, appropriately, was wearing something gray or beige. Mouse colors, Wendell thought.

When word got back to Reliance that David had been killed in a car wreck on his way to the naval air station just outside Memphis, Wendell Metcalf felt only gratitude. He was relieved David was gone since he dreaded the temptation David represented to him. More than that, though, David was the only other person in the world who could've told what actually happened between the two of them, and now that threat was gone.

Wendell thought of it as a virus inside him, something to be battled and destroyed. Each time he did not act on the impulse, he felt stronger and even more resolved to rid the world of homosexuality. Stinking faggots.

He went to college, became a CPA, then married Suzette. He'd met her in a tax class he took at night over at the community college in Bend. Wendell thought of her as dumb, which is how he thought of most people. Her talent for rooting out tax deductions and loopholes, however, had surprised him, and even attracted him to her, although it was not why he married her. Suzette was nice to him, unlike other girlfriends he'd had before who had left him. Because of her propensity for doe-like devotion, he knew Suzette would stay. Even though she sometimes called him Daddy-Bear because of his hairy chest, that nickname was as close to parenthood as either of them cared to get.

Wendell Metcalf even ran for City Council once. He was soundly defeated, mainly because nobody in Reliance could remember who in the world he was. It had enraged him, actually. Well, they wouldn't be wondering who he was any more, damn them. By now he had as much name recognition in the state as the governor. Nobody could laugh about that, certainly not all those howling fags who yelled at him whenever he showed up in Salem to get the ORS initiative on the ballot and hold another press conference.

Just last week after one of those press conferences—he remembered this vividly—a young man with the clearest blue eyes and a sweet smile had taken his arm and led him gently to the side, out of range of cameras and microphones. "I need to speak with you," he had said. The young man looked so clean-cut, so average, so normal, Wendell was sure the guy was going to ask him about the ORS and how to join. Maybe he would congratulate Wendell for doing such a great job, perhaps even ask him to do a radio interview or a TV talk show. But the young man with the clear blue eyes had looked right at him, smiling as he said, "You know, Wendell, it has occurred to me that if you were more secure in your own sexuality, you wouldn't be getting so concerned about everybody else's. I believe maybe you should think about that." Then the guy had simply walked off, vanishing into the crowd.

This evening, Wendell Metcalf did think about all of these things. He squirmed in his chair and looked at his watch. It was almost nine o'clock. If he left right now, he could get home to Suzette before she removed her makeup with some kind of greasy goop, before she rubbed lime juice and vitamin E cream all over her body. He could take her up the stairs and into their big bed before she had time to make herself smell like a giant key lime pie. Although he did not think of her as especially bright, he knew his Suzette was a good lay. He could part those big white thighs with his muscular, tan body and she would squeal with delight and claw at his back, just like he wanted her to, and help burst the blister of shame seared on his soul.

And later, just this time, Suzette would take him into her mouth, something he could never bring himself to do for her. He could buck and groan and thrust his hips and watch in the mirror on the closet door. He could look past Suzette's jiggling mound of buttocks, and ignore her pendulum-like breasts swinging back and forth. He could imagine her bouncing blonde curls in a crew cut, and see David Mack's head right there, on him, once again. *Semper Fidelis.*

·14·

don't rightly remember when it came upon me, but sometime after I started livin' with Marvin I began to stutter and stammer, really bad. Oh, it was awful. It was so bad, in fact, that I got to where I couldn't say hardly any of my letters or sounds right at all and, well, it wasn't too long before it just seemed easiest not to talk. Called Jimmy Heron "Bimmy" for the longest time and would still do it every so often after we got all grown up. Especially if I was scared, it would just slip out.

Well, Jimmy told his folks I had a mild case of the shut-ups brought on by havin' to live with somebody so mean. If I lived with them, why, he just bet I'd get over it. Besides, he told them, he'd heard that havin' a red-headed person livin' in your house was almost as lucky as havin' a cardinal in your backyard.

I was standin' in the next room peekin' through a keyhole when Jimmy said that, and I saw his daddy roll his eyes. But his mama just laughed. "James Jefferson Heron, I swear," she said to him, "someday we're going to enter you in the Texas State Fair. Now you run along and tell Curtis that all members of this household are expected to have clean feet and clean teeth before they go to bed."

Jimmy let out a yelp like a pup, then sombered himself real quick to say, "Yes, ma'am," and came to get me. What Jimmy didn't know was that his folks would have been dragged across barbed wire by a team of mules before they let me go back to live with old Marvin. My grandmother had helped deliver their daughter Della.

Jimmy's folks were older, so Della was already about seventeen when Jimmy was born, and she was a woman to be admired, yes indeedy. She was a tomboy, no doubt about it, smarter and faster than all the girls and most of the boys her age. She was the first woman in Montague County to ride astride, on a big bay gelding she called Dandy. He was seventeen hands high if he was an inch, that's what everybody said, all muscle and good horse sense. Almost as smart as Della.

She and that big horse loved each other, that was for sure. One story I heard about was when Della was fourteen and runnin' her horse along the fence line in the north pasture. Dandy stepped right in a red ant sinkhole and flipped 'em both just ass over tea kettle. That big horse landed on Della and dislocated her hip, nearly broke it. Cracked three of her ribs, too. She must have been in terrible pain, but I tell you what—Dandy stood there right beside Della all day, makin' shade for her with his body, yes he did, movin' as the sun moved, and wouldn't leave her for a minute.

When Mr. Heron found 'em, he got just mad as a hornet, thinkin' Dandy had raked his daughter off on the fence. He was just pullin' his 30.06 out of the scabbard when Della dragged herself up, hangin' onto the saddle horn. "Your bullet's gonna have to go through me, Dad," she said, just as steady and fierce as a buzz saw. "This horse didn't do a bit of wrong."

They created quite a stir, as you might imagine, Della ridin' just like a man, in pants, her hair all wild and flyin' in the wind. But everybody seemed to forgive her for it when they figured out she could bulldog a steer at age fifteen almost as good as any ranchhand around.

By the time I came to live with Jimmy and his folks, Della had already graduated from college, a pretty unusual feat for a woman from those parts then, and headed for law school down at the University of Texas in Austin.

Yep, she was quite a gal, that Della. Jimmy always said, when we were teenagers, if he could grow up to be half the man his sister was he'd be a happy guy. He said it in a jokin' way, but I knew he meant it down deep 'cause he admired his big sister so much. Everybody did.

Now, going from a place I hated to a place I loved callin' home was a big adjustment for me, but Jimmy's folks were just as patient and sweet as any two people you'd ever find.

Mrs. Heron called me Curtis and she taught me about manners and neatness. She'd say, "Curtis, every gentleman has an easier time in this world if he speaks his mind and keeps himself clean." When she said that I knew it was my cue to get in the tub and get myself scrubbed.

Mr. Heron called me Red and sometimes he'd say, "Red, let's us gents go thank the Lord for this land he lets us borrow." And we'd saddle up and ride to the top of the bluff where we could see several hundred acres and all the way down to the creek. Sometimes I'd swear we could see Oklahoma if we squinted and held our heads just right.

Growin' up at the Herons' was a blessing for me, and I know it now that I'm dead even more than I did when I was alive. Jimmy and me, well, we were just average fellas doing average things, but every night when we sat down to supper, Mr. Heron would include us in his prayers. He was a grateful man, so his prayers were generally long. Every single time, without fail, he'd add, "And thank you, Dear Lord, for these two fine sons who bring us joy and contentment each day."

Well, after that, there wasn't much me and Jimmy could do but clean our plates, wash up the dishes, and get ourselves to sleep on time. Neither of us ever had the heart to let 'em down, especially after all that gratitude.

·15·

immy Heron awoke from a deep sleep and a strange dream about buffalo and a wagon train. Someone was knocking on the door of the trailer. In the few days he had been there, he had managed to make the place feel a little more like his own by cleaning out a lot of the junk Millie left behind and hauling some of the stacks and stacks of magazines she had strewn everywhere over to the recycling center in Bend. It was no wonder the place had seemed dingy and crowded. He welcomed the extra room in which to move around.

Still, it was a battered old trailer with a shower so puny it made his bones ache to get in and out of it. The bed was cramped, really too small for him. Most of all, he missed his wife. Lou Heron's absence was like a knife in his back.

The knocking on the door was so persistent, Jimmy finally decided to answer it. Popping in his Beltones, finding his slippers and his watch, he was surprised to see it was already nine-thirty in the morning. It was unlike him to sleep late and he felt embarrassed, even though what people thought about him was of no concern to him. Besides, he did-n't know a soul up here in this faraway state.

Jimmy opened the door and peeked out. A gust of wind blew his wispy gray hair straight up. At the bottom of the steps stood Cory Miller holding a jar of homemade salsa, a bag of chips, and some flowers wrapped in cellophane. A big yellow dog sat beside her. The dog's droopy ear and an equally droopy eye made him look suspicious. Cory smiled an infectious smile at Jimmy. He couldn't help grinning back at her.

"I'm not usually so bold," she said, "but I heard there was another Texan on the loose up here and I brought a peace offering." She held out the chips and salsa. "I'm Cory Miller," she said. "I live up on the hill with my beloved. Her name is Leigh. We call it Lavender Hill because of the color when the sun hits it. You've seen it?"

Jimmy nodded. "Yes," he said. "It's beautiful, very pretty."

"Oh, and these are for you, too." She held out the flowers and he took them. "They were his idea," she said, pointing with her thumb to the dog. "His name is Ned. Grateful Ned some of the time. He doesn't always remember just what a lucky dog he is."

The dog's eyes brightened at the sound of his name, and he stood and began wagging his big, swooping tail. His droopy parts perked right up, making him look more like a regular dog.

"Heron's my name, Jimmy Heron, and I thank you for the gifts," Jimmy said. "It's always nice to be welcomed, I suppose. I appreciate it. Would you and Ned like to join me for coffee?"

Ever the gentleman, he said it, but didn't really mean it. He didn't want company of any sort right this moment. Cory could see it in his eyes.

"Oh, no, thanks, Jimmy," she said. "We just wanted to stop by and say hidy. Ned always likes to know who he's looking out for in this valley. Gotta do his dog-job. Say, if you get lonesome for some company, give us a call or just come on by. Leigh teaches fifth grade, but I'm almost always home. Ned won't bite you or even bark too much now that he knows who you are."

Cory handed Jimmy a business card out of her shirt pocket. Then she snared Ned by the collar, since the dog had decided Jimmy was okay and was making his way up the steps of the trailer. "Come on, buddy," she said, yanking at Ned, whose legs had stiffened up like branding irons and were sticking straight out as she pivoted him around, making him look flash-frozen. Cory placed the jar of salsa and the bag of chips on the steps of the trailer. "Call us if you need anything," she said to Jimmy, as she waved and backed away. "We sold the business on that card, but the number's still good, so call us, okay? Anytime, day or night. We both wake up quick and easy and don't hold a grudge about it, either. Really, day or night."

Cory kept looking at Jimmy, waiting for him to say something, something that would give her a clue about his life, but all he could do was nod his head. "Well," she said, finally, "glad you're here. We needed another Texan up in these parts. I've got eighty jars of Pecos Fire Salsa in my basement and nobody brave enough to share it with me. Cowards is what they are, basically. I tell 'em they should just be glad I no longer make margaritas."

Jimmy noticed how the sunlight filtering through the trees made the gray in her hair glisten like silver. Then she smiled at him again with her twinkly brown eyes. Something about her reminded him of his sister Della, just a particular look Della would get on her face sometimes when she smiled. There was something strong and capable and steady and true about women who smiled like that, something that would hold the world together.

Jimmy closed the door to the trailer, swiped at his windblown hair, and found his glasses on the table. He looked at the business card Cory had given him. It read:

CORY MILLER

Pecos Fire

Meatless Chili & Thunderbolt Salsa

"This ain't no sissy food!"

(503)555-4343

He stuck the card under the edge of the phone and thought for a moment. How much energy would it take to get himself cleaned up and take on the task of making new friends in this strange place? He decided it would be too hard. Mostly, it would just be too sad, and he didn't want to have to tell the story of Lou's death over and over like some morose wind-up toy. He didn't want to talk about his broken heart. He didn't even think he could look anybody in the eye.

Jimmy squinted out through the curtains and could see Cory and Ned making their way up the road toward the log house on the hill. The dog had picked up what appeared to be a tree branch. He was prancing around with this huge thing in his mouth, ears pinned back, like he'd just found the Holy Grail. Jimmy saw Cory stop for a minute by the fence along the road as a large old crippled-looking Guernsey limped over to get petted. The cow placed her big head across the fence and brushed cheeks with Cory. She got her ears scratched and neck rubbed as well. He watched as Cory put both arms around the cow's neck and hugged her. Then she gave the Guernsey a big, smacking kiss right in the middle of her forehead before continuing on. It was a sweet sight that made Jimmy Heron smile. He wished Lou had been here to share it with him.

He lay back down on his cramped bed and thought about what might be in store for the rest of his life. He drew a blank. Then he tried to think about what his life would have been like if he'd never met Lou—if he'd never let Curly Red talk him into getting all scrubbed up to go to that USO dance. He could not. Probably would have gotten his silly head blown right off in Germany just like a lot of other poor guys did. Probably what kept him alive at all was his and Lou's love for each other. After he met her, he felt like the most special guy in the world, as if, somehow, God had him by the hair, just guiding him along.

Jimmy Heron knew right from the start he could never have found anyone more perfect for him than the wife he picked, and for almost fifty years, day after day, she had proved him right. Oh, they could get crossways with each other, there was no denying that. She'd become ring-tailed and obstinate, and he'd be sullen and brooding. But they never let it drag on long enough to create a real problem, and they could josh each other out of just about any disagreement. And at night, when they held each other, the stars came out to twinkle over the rolling pastureland of north Texas, and the moonlight beamed only for them. And they were grateful.

Cory Miller stopped on the road for a moment to admire their snug little log house before going up the drive. She liked it that the whole place was almost picture perfect. Not posh or foreboding, but sweet and inviting, like a postcard or a painting on the wall by somebody's grandmother. Mostly, though, she was certain that what made the place so inviting was Leigh and the love they shared.

Sometimes it was hard for Cory to remember what her life was like before they met. She drank too much, she could remember parts of that. And she'd had the wild woman in her, with a penchant for standing on the hood of her Jeep truck and singing "Born Free" at the top of her lungs. She could remember parts of that, too. Probably meeting Leigh saved her life. Certainly, it saved her liver: Leigh O'Brien would put up with a lot, but being drunk wasn't on the list and she let that be known right off. Cory Miller had quit cold turkey and was thoroughly surprised at how much better she felt. Too good to go visit the Jose Cuervo party hacienda ever again.

Oh, Cory thought, they'd had their disagreements, there was no doubt about that. When they attempted, at first, to build their log house themselves, and both of them discovered they were Typhoid Mary when it came to power tools, well, that turned into one huge, two-month marathon of teeth-gnashing which really put their relationship to the test. Leigh had that Irish temper and could throw a champion fit if pressed. She, Cory, was slower to anger, but could get silent and pouty, holding onto a hurt or slight until it grew mold. It was not a trait she was proud of, and she knew it needed work.

They finally decided to end the torture and have Glenn Taylor build the house for them. It was one of the wisest choices they'd ever made, and they both knew it. Deciding to have a baby was one of the scariest.

Their life together in Reliance was no secret, and yet, it was also something rarely talked about. When they announced Leigh's pregnancy, the attitudes of some of the people in the town changed toward them. They expected this, but that didn't make it any less difficult to take.

Still, raising a child together was something they were both committed to. They saw it as a natural extension of the love they felt for each other. No matter what it took, no matter how hard things got, both women were in this one for the long haul. In love. Spoken for. Dug in. Married. Family. That's how both women felt. And at night, when they held each other, when stardust sprinkled itself like powdered sugar along the branches of the ponderosa pines, the moon would peak over the edge of the mountains to shine its light only on them. And they were grateful.

.16.

ally Peterson Taylor, Leigh's midwife, emerged from the bathroom drying her hands, her stethoscope draped around her neck. She was a big Swedish woman with straight blonde hair, bright, cornflower blue eyes, and pink, shiny cheeks. She walked with a slight limp from what looked to be a clubfoot and had a thick leather lift built into the heel of her left Birkenstock. Sally Taylor was as dedicated to her sandals as she was to her patients and wore them year 'round. With wool socks and galoshes to slog through the winter snow, with no socks the rest of the time. Her toes were callused and fat.

"Well, Leigh-O," she said, "looks like we've got a healthy baby on the way. Right around New Year's would be my guess. How's your appetite? You getting plenty to eat? Sleeping okay? Taking your vitamins? You look skinny to me." Leigh nodded her head and chuckled at the remark. Everybody looked too skinny to Sally.

"Yes, Sally," Leigh said, "don't worry about it. I feel like I'm already waterlogged on protein drink and vitamins. I eat tons, Sally. I eat plenty." She gave Sally a shove toward the living room where Sally's bear of a husband, Glenn, was slumped down on the couch and snoring next to Jerry Garcia. He was asleep on his back and doing the same, with Glenn's right hand buried in the thick gray fur on the cat's belly.

Glenn was a lumberjack and a carpenter, a huge man with curly black hair and an unruly beard flecked with gray. On his lap, in a wool sock, was the Taylors' neurotic Chihuahua, Felipe. The dog shivered even when he was sound asleep and shook all the time he was awake, as if he had some kind of built-in Richter scale Doppler radar and a volcano was about to blow somewhere in the Cascade mountain range. Or maybe Guatemala. Ever mindful of impending doom, Felipe stayed on RED ALERT all the time, even while napping with Glenn, to whom he was devoted.

Sally stopped in the doorway for a second to admire them. "Aww," she said, "is that not just the dearest thing you've ever seen?" She sat down next to Glenn, easing her large frame up gently next to him. "Sweetie?" she said, and Glenn instinctively brought Felipe up close to his chest with his free hand.

Glenn Taylor was a silent man, preferring to let his actions speak for him. This particular protective maneuver with the dog meant: *Don't worry, honey, I won't let him slide off my lap and onto the floorboard, or let him get bonked in the head with an empty tequila bottle like I did that time in Matamoros. I promise.* Sally smiled at him since she knew exactly what he was not talking about. She touched Glenn's leg.

"Sweetie," she said, "it's time to go." Glenn and Felipe both jerked completely awake simultaneously, with that same bug-eyed, terrified look on their faces. Jerry Garcia merely flipped himself over until he rolled completely off the couch and landed on the floor with a *whump*, like a big sack of Meow Mix, of which he was probably dreaming. He awoke only for a second and, not smelling food, went back to sleep in his new location.

Glenn pulled on his jacket and slipped the dog, in his own special sock, into the side pocket. Leigh jammed a fifty-dollar bill into the hip pocket of Sally's jeans. She knew Glenn, recently laid off from his job at the timber mill, and Sally, a school nurse and part-time midwife, were always strapped for cash.

"Thanks, Doc," Leigh said.

"Nurse."

"Okay. Nurse. I appreciate it. Will I see you at school this week?"

"Only on Thursday. The county has me on a scaled-back rotation—budget cuts—so, let's keep our fingers crossed that Tuna Surprise isn't on the school lunch menu until then."

"We can only hope. I'll tell the kids they can't heave until they see you."

"Thanks, pal," Sally said, squeezing Leigh's shoulder.

Glenn bent down to hug Leigh which, for him, meant almost bending over double. Straightening up, he smiled his gentle smile at her through his big beard and tenderly touched her cheek. She placed her hand on top of his.

"He thinks you look especially beautiful as a mother-to-be," Sally said. "He thinks you and Cory have never looked happier."

"You're right, Glenn," Leigh said. "Thanks for saying so."

Leigh reached into Glenn's pocket to feel the smooth silkiness of Felipe's cold, silvery little ear. "Take it easy, Don Knotts," she said to him, rubbing his flappy ear. The dog stared at her and shook, half-expecting her to pinch it off, flick it real hard, grab him by it and swing him around, or something worse. Relieved that she did none of those things, he shook.

Leigh walked Glenn and Sally out to their faded powder blue and rusty VW bus and looked off down the valley toward Jimmy's to see if she could spot her partner. "Cory must have found a friend," she said. "There's a new guy up from Texas who bought Millie's place. She went down to meet him and hasn't made it back yet. I'll tell her you both say hi and that Felipe will be starting on Thorazine soon."

Glenn cranked the bus up and the throttle stuck, making the engine roar until it sounded like the space shuttle about to lift off. Or blow an O-ring. He stomped the accelerator, the engine calmed down, and they could hear each other talk again.

"Watch out for any dead animals you might see in our driveway," Leigh said, shaking her head.

"The ORS again?" Sally asked, "or is it Dimmer's crowd?"

"Not sure," Leigh replied. "There has been some really vicious stuff—maybe too gruesome even for them. But you never know about hate and what it can do to people."

Sally reached across Glenn and out the window, taking her friend by the hand. "You two be careful, Leigh-O," she said. "I mean it. No sense in trying to fight off these hatemongers all alone. Call us anytime if you need us. Promise me?"

"Promise," Leigh replied, then she waved to them until they pulled out of sight and down the driveway to the road.

As Leigh walked in the front door, Cory came in the back door. Leigh was shocked to see her.

"Where were you?" she asked.

"Out in the bunkhouse talking to Jonah," Cory said.

"He's back already? I thought you were still visiting with our new neighbor."

"No, that was a short visit. He looks like a man with a pretty sad story to tell—only he's not ready to tell it yet. His name's Jimmy Heron. Glenn and Sally didn't stay long; I thought they'd still be here."

"Nope, they had to scoot. And our little bambino bundle is doing just beautifully, so sayeth Nurse Taylor."

"That's music to the ears of our family tree," Cory said.

"So," Leigh said, "how was Jonah's elk hunting adventure? Did he see any elk?"

"Lots."

"He didn't shoot any, did he?"

"Not a chance. He says hunting is the sport, killing's not. He just takes the gun along for show. I haven't had any bullets for it since the seventh grade, when I shot a grasshopper off the butane tank and my dad threatened to shoot me with my own gun. Can you imagine? With my own gun!"

"Yes," said Leigh, "I absolutely can. I might even have shot you over that one. But not with your own gun, I don't think. No, I would have borrowed a larger caliber gun and shot you with that."

"You are so good to me," Cory said.

"It's true."

"You know," Cory said in a conspiratorial voice, "it's really the oddest thing Jonah does when he hunts. And I can tell you if he was in my home state, those bubbas would have locked him up in the loony bin by now. All he does is hunt the elk or the deer or whatever it is down and then squat there and watch it. He doesn't shoot it with a gun; doesn't try to nail it with a crossbow; doesn't even take its picture. All he does is watch it for a while, and then he walks home. Where I come from, that's not hunting—that's being a Peeping Tom. Besides, he says he's allergic to red meat. And bullets."

"So, how does he know when to give it up and come home?" Leigh asked. "When his knees give out? When the elk runs off? When another hunter takes a shot at him?"

"Oh," Cory said, "you know Jonah. He does everything according to Indian time, which is when the time is right. I guess that works out okay for him if he never has to catch a plane."

·17·

onah Sullivan was meditating. He sat alone in the bunkhouse back beyond Cory and Leigh's barn, listening to Native American flute music and chanting a Lakota Sioux prayer song until his mind became still. His heartbeat slowed, and the chatter of the world shut itself off. This he did every day, sometimes more than once—surrounding himself with white candles, pink candles, and purple candles, becoming still and listening for the voice of God.

On the table he had perfectly adorned with special stones, feathers, and herbs, Jonah kept a picture of Jesus, a small painting of Buddha, and a photograph of Gurumayi Chidvilasananda. There was also one of a trusted family friend, Jerome Three Bears, a Lakota shaman and intertribal medicine man he had known as a boy.

Jonah viewed his spiritual journey as one mountain with many roads. The eclectic mix of avenues by which he sought to achieve his reunion with Tunkashila, the Great Spirit, was not of concern to him. Nor was it his intent to worship the people in the pictures occupying the place of honor at his altar. He only sought to emulate them, since he saw them as people who lived their lives and made life choices from a state of grace. This was true of Jonah Sullivan as well.

He was a young man, twenty-five, with dark, straight hair and the regal, chiseled features of his mother's Sioux heritage. His olive skin was flawless and, in a particular light, sometimes seemed to almost glow. Only a stubble or two of whiskers ever appeared on his chin, and a cowlick at his part on the right kept a shock of black hair draped across his forehead. He was a physically beautiful man, muscular and lithe, with a look of compassion about him, as if he knew an exquisite secret almost too good to tell.

There was some kind of peace that others perceived in him, though he did not see it himself and struggled with questions of his spirit and purpose. Still, he was a gentle man with a loving heart and a lively sense of humor. It seemed that the only things Jonah had inherited from Thomas Sullivan, the hard-drinking father he barely remembered, were his green eyes and his last name.

Enlightenment came early for Jonah Sullivan. He realized he was living a special life and that feeling had never left him. When he found himself falling from a second-story balcony head first toward the patio, only the briefest of thoughts told him that he would die. In the next instant, in a flurry of wind and light, something—*someone*—had grabbed him by the ankles and flipped him, turning him completely over in mid-air. Instead of landing on the back of his skull on the concrete, Jonah landed with his baby teeth stuck into a redwood planter full of geraniums.

He remembered leaving his body, could remember seeing himself limp and unconscious as his mother screamed and ran back inside the house to call an ambulance. His spirit followed her around, trying to comfort her. Back outside, as his mother clutched her son's lifeless body, rocking him and singing a Lakota prayer song, Jonah's spirit saw another being with red hair hovering close by, like a protector or guardian.

"Are you my guardian angel?" he had asked the being. The being looked back at him rather puzzled, as if trying to decide.

"Well, I ain't sure," the being said. "I'm new at this. If you don't die, I suppose I am. If you do, well, then maybe I need some more trainin'."

"I won't die," Jonah had said, "not yet. Thank you."

And as Jonah's spirit reentered his body, the red-headed being disappeared just as quickly as it had come.

Jonah's parents separated while he was recovering, and he and his mother went to live with his mother's people, mostly in Montana. When she became gravely ill, Jerome Three Bears took Jonah in to teach him the Lakota way. Among those things was peaceful living, a way of being— dwelling lightly on the land and keeping an open heart. Jerome even paid for the braces and retainers needed to fix Jonah's teeth.

On her deathbed, Jonah's mother had told him the truth. His own father, in a drunken rage, had thrown him off the balcony that day.

And Jonah could feel only gratitude.

His life choices had brought him from Oklahoma and Texas oil fields, to the loading dock at a warehouse in Billings, Montana, and finally, to this place in Reliance, Oregon. These two women, Leigh and Cory, had become his friends and taken him in. Their lives were intertwined but not entangled. Each of them felt blessed with the simple goodness of knowing the other two.

After Jonah had lived at their place for a year, Leigh and Cory began discussing having a baby together. Often the three of them sat up until dawn weighing the decision. Leigh was almost forty, Cory forty-two, and they had been together for five years. When they asked Jonah how he felt about being the biological father of their child, he was shocked. He left for the river for three days to think. When he returned home, he meditated in the private space of the bunkhouse where he lived. Only Ned had let them know Jonah was back by howling at his door until he came out.

Leigh and Cory and Jonah walked together to Cerebrum Rock, a dark red volcanic boulder in the shape of a brain—spewed up and tossed there from Mount Mazama's blast seven hundred years before— where they liked to sit and think. It was on the edge of the hill by the barn. The wind blowing up the hill from the valley made the ponderosa pines sway back and forth and the support timbers in the old barn creak and groan. Mimi and Sir Loin, and their horses, grazed lazily in the meadow below them. Cory and Leigh waited in silence until Jonah spoke.

"Jonah of the Bible was a Hebrew prophet," he said, "who was tossed overboard in a storm for disobeying God. He was swallowed by a big fish, but three days later he was burped up and washed on the shore unharmed."

Cory and Leigh glanced at each other, somewhat in awe, seeing as how this was the longest string of words they'd ever heard Jonah utter in a row. They kept silent, though, wondering what point their friend was about to make. Jonah picked up a small stone and sailed it off down the hill.

"So Jonah, according to the dictionary," he continued, "is often thought of as someone or something who brings bad luck just by being present." He stopped and was still, gathering himself, and then said, "There have been times in my life when I felt I was in the belly of the beast. Other times I thought I was the beast itself. But since I've been with the two of you, I often feel myself to be the luckiest man alive. I have witnessed so much love—not just between you, but in how you treat other people, as well as your animals and your land. I think you've made Jonah a lucky name. I have prayed about this, and God has told me it would be an honor for me to help you create a child to be born into this much love. My honor."

Sally Taylor had been in charge of the artificial insemination process, even to the point of sending Glenn to the convenience store for a *Penthouse* magazine, which she offered to Jonah along with a sterile specimen cup. He politely refused it, taking into the bathroom only the cup.

"I am a twenty-five-year-old American male, Sally," he had said to her, "and I'm half Irish. I think I can manage this."

And so the conception of Cory and Leigh's baby had taken place on a cool, moonlit night at the end of March. To send Jonah's sperm swimming toward their rendezvous with Leigh's egg, Sally had used a Sharpvet reusable nylon syringe, almost the size of a large caliber handgun. She was relieved a few weeks later when they found out Leigh was pregnant. Sally could not stand the thought of having to try this again with a turkey baster.

Now, as Jonah sat deep in meditation on this October day, God eased his heart by answering his questions about a recurring dream. In this dream, Jonah saw himself sweeping—the bunkhouse, the forest, along the edges of the river, Leigh and Cory's cabin. Cobwebs and dustballs and mounds of animal hair and dead leaves were swept and swept until what he was pushing around with his broom looked like an enormous tumbleweed bigger than the barn. Always in this dream he was barefoot, sometimes with smoke shooting in spurts from the top of his head like a steam engine. A road appeared before him, a sapphire road, that wound upward through the mountains until it disappeared up into the clouds. He knew his job was to push this tumbleweed all the way up, along the blue road to heaven. In each of the previous dreams, Jonah had awakened before he had figured out his job. In the dream last night, he knew.

As he came up from the depths of the stillness, his consciousness reentered the room. His hands stopped vibrating, and Jonah Sullivan opened his eyes and smiled into the kind faces of the people on his altar. The message in his heart was clear: he would be leaving soon. His house was almost in order, his job almost complete. Soon it would be time to go.

.18.

You wanna know what it's like to die? Well, I'll tell you, it's like the most spectacular, thrill-you-to-the guts fun ride you ever took. Like goin' off the top at Turner Falls up in Oklahoma and splashin' into the coolest, clearest water on the hottest day of summer. For me, it was joyous and beautiful, but it sure was a surprise.

I'd been in Forestburg all morning, just goofin' around, visitin' with folks I'd see here and there, pickin' up a few groceries. I was standin' in the post office, leanin' in the window jawin' with Meb and Roxie Dunn. They ran the place back then—sweetest folks you'd ever want to meet. Anyway, they'd just oiled the floor to help keep the dust down. The smell was so strong I began to feel sick to my stomach and had to sit right down there on the floor for a spell.

Lou and I had been havin' one of our salsa wars the night before—our own little contest to see who could make the fieriest salsa this side of Mexico. "Hellfire in a brimstone bowl" is what Jimmy called the stuff, 'cause he just couldn't eat it like me and Lou. Anyway, I thought maybe the extra cracked pepper I'd thrown in my batch was double-crossin' me, fightin' back.

Roxie poured some water out of Meb's thermos onto a rag and put it on the back of my neck until my head cleared and I began to feel better.

I remember what Meb said to me just before I walked out of there. He said, "Curly Red, what you've got is an equilibrium problem. If you'd get that other ear put on, I bet it'd clear up." Well, I told him I was as balanced as any other sidewinder in Montague County and besides, since I knew I could only believe half of what I heard I figured having one ear would keep me ahead of the game.

Truth was, I had three operations at the VA hospital with them tryin' to fashion an ear out of extra skin and then drag it in stages up my neck.

Never did work right, and looked like hell. Ugly old flappy thing, so I gave it up. Had 'em slice that nasty-lookin' wad of skin off and just kept a bandage over the hole on the side of my head.

Anyway, I managed to drive my pickup home, back to my trailer behind Jimmy and Lou's house. I was feelin' pretty punk by the time I got there, like my chest was on fire and somebody in a big pair of boots was tryin' to put it out. It was a lovely spring day though, kinda cool, so I opened the windows up and lay down to take a nap.

Had a dream about my mother driving a motorcycle down the highway, of all things, and I was ridin' in the sidecar. Had my arms straight up in the air, Mother and I both just laughin' our heads off. When I woke up a couple of hours later, I fixed a cup of coffee and sat down at the table. I was pourin' in my Carnation milk when all of a sudden, whoof!, right in through the window comes that smell of her, lemons and roses. I looked around, almost in a panic because it was so real. I felt a pain in my chest like I'd been kicked by a colt. The next thing I knew I was zoomin' through the most beautiful tunnel, colors of the rainbow sweepin' past my head. It was scary, but I didn't want to leave, didn't want to be anyplace else. Then I heard this music, glorious music, and then, well, I saw the light. I gotta tell you, it's somethin' you don't ever want to miss.

That's when it first occurred to me what had happened. I had hopped the fence, bounced right over, slick as a whistle. And it had happened so quick that I didn't have a chance to pack a razor or even say good-bye to Jimmy and Lou. But you know what? I wouldn't have changed a thing. Not a thing.

I made sure I tracked down Meb Dunn, though, when he got here a few years later. I just had to tell that old know-it-all, "Equilibrium problem, my ass."

Yep, those two were sad, Jimmy and Lou, they sure were, after I left. We'd all been such good friends for so long. I did my best to comfort them whenever I could slip away. They had the nicest funeral for me, too. Laid my skinny old body to rest at the Perryman Cemetery, outside of Forestburg. I did get to see that—almost like a bird perched in a tree. Folks came from all over Montague County, some folks I didn't even like very much, but I appreciated being remembered by them and I enjoyed the beautiful flowers everybody brought.

Jimmy and Lou had just gotten this new pup, a black Lab they named Buck. He was a tiny guy, and they brought him along with them to the funeral ridin' in Jimmy's jacket pocket. They pulled him out to let him stretch his legs and run around for a bit right after the service. The very first thing he did was squat and take a leak on the edge of my grave. Well, Jimmy and Lou got so tickled that they busted out laughin' and I was laughin' at them laughin'. I swear, I could have stayed there forever, just hoverin' right above them, lookin' out for them. But that's against the rules, you see. Elsewise, everybody would be hangin' around tryin' to take care of people they left behind and then nobody would ever learn any lessons and nothin' would ever get done on this side. Heaven isn't all of us just floatin' around on clouds playin' harps, I can tell you that. There's lots and lots to do, lots to learn.

Each person dies eventually, so everybody gets let in on the big secret in the long run. But it's hard to see people you love bein' sad and missin' you so much. What we think of as the other side is really not that far away, you know. Just right over here, almost like looking through a glass wall, sometimes more like a screen door. It's not so far away at all.

.19.

Jimmy Heron was awake by dawn the next day, brought up from the depths of sleep by the shape-shifting caw of a crow echoing through the pines. He showered, shaved, and dug out fresh clothes, even splashed on Old Spice before he walked outside. It felt good to be clean, although he noticed that he'd lost weight. His pants had begun to bag on him, dragging in the seat like some extra somebody had just moved out of them.

Staring at himself in the mirror when he first awoke, Jimmy Heron struggled to remember what he'd looked like on October 15th, the day before his life had shattered so completely. He could not. All he knew was that right now, and maybe for the rest of his life, he had that same blank, dazed, and confused look of someone who'd just been bucked off.

Walking up the hill and across the back section of his property, Jimmy stopped for just a moment to admire the lavender color on the hillside. He felt something almost comforting in the beauty of it, something that seemed to want to pull him in, hold him close. He couldn't define it, could not have described it accurately to someone else, but it was an intense feeling, and it was real.

Jimmy Heron allowed that feeling to fill up his heart, allowed himself to savor the arms of Mother Earth enfolding, holding, and rocking him for the moment. It was just enough. He climbed the fence and headed toward the Deschutes River, where it trickles along through lava tubes and then suddenly bubbles up, forming large, deep, luscious pools.

The morning was dazzlingly bright and snap-apple crisp, with the smell of fall and wood smoke in the air.

Jimmy jumped from rock to rock, surprising himself at the strength he still had in his legs. He recalled the time down at Muddy Boggy Creek when he'd saved Curly Red from the cottonmouth snake, and how they'd become best friends for life after that. The memory made his eyes well up, and he pushed it away. Just as he had to keep pushing away thoughts of his wife, so terrified was he of losing control, losing his mind, losing his way.

Spotting what he thought was the perfect ledge upon which to land, he sprang with all his strength from the boulder where he stood. The thin stone ledge shattered when he hit, sending rocks and dirt and Jimmy sliding and sprawling the half-dozen yards down to the river, clutching at sagebrush along the way. A gray lizard slid right beside the old man, scrambling for a foothold.

When the world stopped spinning and the dust had cleared, Jimmy Heron lifted his head and saw the bird.

At the water's edge by a large rock lay a great blue heron tangled in fishing line. There was no way to tell how long the bird had been stranded this way, although it appeared to be half dead. Its eyes had that hooded look of resignation, its head lolling to one side.

Jimmy watched for a minute and could see shallow breaths coming every so often. The heron's bluish-gray feathers were separated and ragged, oily-looking. With each breath the will to live surged through the bird, and it yanked its head up, crashing its great wings against the water and clawing the air with its long black legs.

Jimmy could see the fishing line wrapped around one of the legs. It extended up across the torso, a wing, and the bird's neck, before coming back down into a wad now tangled and snagged under the rock. By its own struggling, the heron was actually pulling its head under the water, killing itself in its effort to stay alive.

Jimmy took a few steps toward the heron, easing his rusty old pocketknife out of his pants. He wished he'd bought a new one back in the summer when he was thinking about it. Seeing Jimmy, the bird began flailing its massive wings. Its eyes became wild and terrified. Jimmy could think of nothing else to do to calm the creature except talk to it as he would a scared calf or a skittish colt. "Hey bub, hey bub," Jimmy said over and over. "Hey bub, you're okay now."

Easing himself into the water, he fought off the urge to shriek from the cold. Jimmy began stroking the heron's matted feathers, talking to it in a voice as low and calming as he could. The bird had its head turned to the right, leaning toward its shoulder. And then they saw each other. Really saw each other. Heron to heron, deep into the left eye, straight into the heart of the other, they saw. Colors swirled inside Jimmy's head with the magic of the moment. Looking at his own hands, Jimmy realized he couldn't exactly tell where he stopped and the heron began. Their essences had blurred together.

Terrified only seconds before, the bird now became still as snow. It seemed trusting and resigned, as if in the moment before death, and let Jimmy Heron begin to set it free. The huge bird waited patiently, not struggling or trying to move until Jimmy had cut and completely unwrapped the line from its body.

Jimmy smoothed the bird's feathers and then helped it stand, scooping the big creature up in his arms as he would a child. Both Herons looked dazed, fuzzy and befuddled by what had just occurred between the two of them. They behaved like two old men, the dearest of friends, who had hugged each other for the first time in their lives.

It was a connection as pure as a baby's laughter. With a quick dip of its sleek head toward Jimmy, the bird flapped its huge wings, bent its spindly legs, and was off. It brushed Jimmy Heron's shoulder with an ebony wingtip before first circling and then soaring away with the low, humming sound of a heron in flight.

Jimmy was standing almost waist-deep in the river, shading his eyes against the sun with one hand as he turned and turned, watching the majestic creature circle before it flew away. As he glanced toward the hill he'd just tumbled down, Jimmy noticed a young man watching him, crouched on a boulder and staring, like a cat about to spring.

The young man did just that, bounding down the rocks toward the river, his black hair, green eyes, and movements all panther-like and exact. He stopped on the big rock right by the water's edge and looked down at Jimmy.

"That was a wonderful thing you did, saving the heron," he said.

"Well, he was in a heap of trouble," Jimmy replied.

"Not everyone would have known what to do."

"Neither did I."

"But you did it anyway."

"Yes. I suppose I did." Jimmy stepped out of the water and stared up at Jonah. He put his hands on his hips, and Jonah jumped down off the rock and extended his hand to Jimmy. It was then that Jimmy noticed his own hands were raw and bloody from his fall. They were beginning to swell, to ache and stiffen up.

"Jonah Sullivan is my name," Jonah said. "I am a friend of Leigh and Cory who live up on the hill. You've met them?"

"Only Cory," Jimmy said.

"Looks like you got yourself pretty scratched up," Jonah said. "This volcanic rock will scrape you to the bone. Come on, I'll help you take care of it."

Jonah led the old man by the arm, back up the rocks and the hill, all the way across the property to Jimmy's dilapidated trailer. He scrubbed out Jimmy's hands with soap and water, and found some hydrogen peroxide under the bathroom sink to finish the job. After helping Jimmy into dry clothes, the two of them sat down together at the table and got to know each other.

The younger man filled a couple of plastic glasses with ice and Coca-Cola. By the time the fizz had died down, Jonah and Jimmy had decided they liked each other quite a bit. It was male bonding in its most streamlined fashion, and they were both happy for the company. Even Jonah, who mostly preferred his solitude.

Jimmy Heron told his story over the next hour. He shared his sorrow and made a new friend. When it was time for Jonah to leave, he reached across the table and caught Jimmy by the wrist.

"It was no accident that the life you saved today was that bird's, Jimmy," he said, "no accident at all. And certainly quite a remarkable thing that a heron was saved by a Heron, don't you think?" Jonah smiled at Jimmy and released his grip.

"It was odd," Jimmy said, "but when we looked at each other, when he calmed down and became so still, it was like we knew each other, like he saw inside me, like he *was* me. Or maybe I had become him. Oh, I know this must sound nuts. And here I was, so sure I could keep from losing my mind."

Jimmy rubbed his eyes with the backs of both hands. Jonah smiled at him.

"You aren't losing your mind," he said. "It sounds like God wants you to stick around."

Jonah took a deep breath and locked his green eyes onto Jimmy Heron's blue ones. "There is so much to think about in this world, Jimmy," he said, "to wonder why things happen the way they do. Now that, my friend, can make you nuts."

Jimmy cleared his throat and shifted in his seat. Jonah reached over and put his hand on Jimmy's shoulder.

"In Lakota culture," he said, "surrender is not giving up; it is starting anew. In Eastern cultures, surrender is not giving up; it is being still and allowing the process to happen, just like that bird did this morning. I'd say the heron you saved could turn out to be one of your most important teachers."

Jonah stood up. "I have to go now," he said.

Jimmy stood, too, looking at his hands, now crusty and swollen. Not knowing what else to do, he held out both his arms to his new friend. They wrapped each other in a bear hug, then each gave the other a manly bang with their arms, like men do when it's time to let go.

"Raw honey makes a good antiseptic for scrapes like that," Jonah said, as he made his way out of the trailer and onto the gravel drive. "That's what my Uncle Jerome always told me. He was a medicine man."

"Yeah?" asked Jimmy, surprised at all the things this young man seemed to know.

"But I like Neosporin better," said Jonah. "It's not so sticky."

With that, Jonah Sullivan was off like a cat through the woods, leaping from log to ledge to boulder, over the fence and then disappearing into the bright autumn day, almost like a whirlwind.

Jimmy Heron set the empty glasses in the sink and peered through the blinds at the sun glancing off the tops of the mountains. He wondered how far away the great blue heron was by now, wondered about the slow turn he could feel his life beginning to take. Maybe this was as good a day as any to wave a pair of his white boxer shorts out the window and surrender.

·20·

onnie Zoeller liked to hate. It filled him up. It was also what he did best, aside from stealing cars, that is. But stealing a car—which he could do in less than a minute—required effort. Driving it all the way down to Medford to get it torched and chopped without getting caught required skill. Those things he only did for money. Hate and fear and hurt were the things Donnie Zoeller did for fun.

By the time he was fifteen, Donnie Zoeller had been a guest of the California Youth Authority for almost half his life. When he got out the last time, he had headed to Oregon, the new Mecca for skinheads, or so he had heard. Second only to Idaho. That's where Aryan Nation and other hard-core survivalists and white supremacists were, Donnie knew, and that's where he planned to go someday. First, though, he had to gain some respect, make a name for himself, and that seemed easy enough to do in this podunk state, especially now.

He had been busted twice in Portland, once for assault and once for disorderly conduct. He had managed to find others scavenging the city like rodents, and several of them moved to central Oregon when things had gotten too hot for them. Although they were more easily recognizable here, they could coast in on the wake of fear and mistrust already being cultivated by the ORS. All Donnie Zoeller and his friends had to do was lay low and do their work at night. His skinhead pals had scurried away one by one, bored by the quiet of rural life. There were only two of them left, but it really just took one person with some brains to do what he did, and Donnie Zoeller had learned not to trust anyone else early in his life.

Their money came from stolen cars and burglaries, and one arson job they did for pay. Their fun came at night from harassment, vandalism, and the feeling of power they got from instilling fear.

Intimidation was the most thrilling, like the stuff they'd been doing recently to spook the dykes up on the hill. And nothing was spookier, Donnie knew, than finding dead animals around and knowing their killing could just as easily have been you. That would make anybody sweat a little harder, maybe even sleep with a gun under the pillow. Donnie Zoeller laughed out loud just thinking about it.

Killing animals came easy for him, as easy as hitting some stupid animal on the road. *Splatt-bump!* Just like that. The excitement of it roared up his spine, like when he'd cut off the head of the kitten. Now you see it, now you don't—just like that. He felt no more remorse for the deed than for having squashed a mosquito on the back of his neck.

Donnie Zoeller was big, almost 6' 2" and 190 pounds, and he liked lifting weights to keep himself strong. Although not really as ugly as he first appeared, the rage inside him, a black hole of anger, made him quite unappealing.

His nose was flat, busted one too many times by his old man. That, and a chipped front tooth from a fall on a Dr. Pepper bottle as a kid, forced a whistling sound from his mouth when he talked. He kept his blond hair very short but not shaved in order to avoid suspicion. Besides, Donnie didn't much care for the scrotum-head look. Home-done tattoos, in varying levels of artistic skill, sat on his skin like mashed blue spiders: a Z on his forearm, made to resemble a swastika, was his favorite.

Donnie Zoeller often spoke of himself in the third person, as if the Z he referred to was his hero, someone to be admired. "Nobody's gonna be fuckin' with Z anymore," he would say as he watched himself lift weights in front of the cracked mirror. He and his friend Mo, short for Moron, had taken over the basement of an abandoned building on the edge of town.

Nobody seemed to know who owned the building where Donnie and Mo lived, and people appeared unconcerned with their presence, if they even knew they were there. Donnie and Mo tended to sleep most of the day and keep their activities under wraps by blacking out the windows.

They enjoyed the ritual of living by candlelight. Soda bottles and empty potato chip sacks littered the area by their sleeping bags. A sneaker was permanently stuck in the hardened cheese on a pizza box.

Across the room, beneath a Nazi flag, there was a table covered by a velvet cloth. It was as neat, well-kept, and out of place amidst their grunge as freshly folded laundry. On the table were stacks of leaflets from Aryan Nation, a framed newspaper photo of a Ku Klux Klan rally, and the latest information from the Oregon Reformation Society.

The table had the eerie sense of being an altar, although Donnie did have the presence of mind to suspend a rolled-up American flag directly above the Nazi one. That way he could drop it down quickly over the swastika and scrape all the leaflets off the table and into a box if anyone ever showed up to hassle them. Nobody ever did.

Donnie Zoeller did not especially hate gay people. That is, he didn't hate them more than he hated everybody else. He didn't hate them any less, either. The simple fact was that the atmosphere was ripe for this kind of homophobic hatred. He could get away with acting on it like never before. And that was good. He was twenty now and less likely to be given second chances.

He'd pretty much gotten the system down as a kid. He would hang his head and look contrite and talk to his juvenile probation officer about his rough childhood and his strong desire to get himself back in school and educated. Especially if the officer was a woman, he would look in her eyes and make her feel sad for him. So sad that, by the time he left her office and was back out on the streets, he was surprised she hadn't written him a personal check just to help him out. One female officer had actually pressed a couple of twenty dollar bills into his hand before he left. Stupid bitch.

Yeah, things were tougher now, and nobody was more aware than Donnie Zoeller that he had only so many tokens left before he'd be sent away for good. He guarded his moves and his activities closely. Besides, faggots and dykes were more scattered and disorganized than some other groups, like Blacks and Jews, and the easiest target Donnie Zoeller had ever encountered. If they got beat up or bombed out, most of them would just leave. They were far too afraid, especially now, to say what had happened to them and why.

This was Donnie's favorite part, the easy part. All he had to do was stay behind the dust of hatred being stirred up by the Reverend Darryl Dimmer, Wendell Metcalf, and the Oregon Reformation Society.

Donnie knew he had them to thank for this golden opportunity. But, hell, he hated them too—the rich bastards.

.21.

By mid-November, Jimmy Heron had handled all of his business affairs. He had even sent off for a home-study locksmith course, which arrived promptly and occupied a good portion of his days. He had talked himself into thinking he needed to have a profession when, in fact, he just needed something to occupy his time. He had notified everyone who needed to know of his new address—Box 2, 408 Wild Horse Road, Reliance, Oregon 97046—and had begun to hear from various people he loved who thought he had left them behind and out of his heart forever.

Winnie Bridwell, who wasn't much of a letter writer since the telephone had been invented, even phoned one morning at 4:00 A.M. to chat. It was 6:00 A.M. in the state of Texas, so according to Winnie's reality, it was the same time everywhere else in the world. Keeping up with time zones, she said, gave her a headache, a "migrant," she called it.

Ted Lanier sent a nice card along with a Polaroid picture of the headstone he had carved for Lou's grave. Jimmy wiped his hand across the photo and held it close to his eyes. It was a grainy black-and-white shot and hard to see. The granite slab was light gray and low to the ground, but raised up at a thirty-degree angle. It read:

ETTA LOU HERON

DEVOTED WIFE, GENTLE SOUL

68 YEARS ON EARTH, FOREVER IN HEAVEN

WE WILL MEET AGAIN

Jimmy stared at the photograph and saw another headstone, a smaller one, to the left of Lou's. All it said was: BUCK—FAITHFUL FRIEND.

The headstone had a drawing of a bone carved into its end, something Jimmy knew had to have been done by hand. Ted Lanier, without having been told or asked, had carved a stone for the final resting place of the Herons' black Lab. Jimmy was so touched by the sweet gesture, he got choked up and began to cry. He found himself, just sometimes, but more and more recently, amazed at the genuine goodness of people. Considering what had happened to Lou, it was not always easy to remember this. And harder still to stay in touch with. It felt good to him, though, to know he didn't see the world as all bad.

He sat down at the table, cried a little more, and was wiping his eyes when he heard the knock at his door. It was late in the day, almost dark. Checking to make sure his hearing aids were in, he opened the door to see a lovely, pregnant woman carrying a big pot and grinning up at him. Her hair was dark auburn and curly, pulled back at her neck. She had a mass of shiny freckles on her nose and cheeks, and straight, very white teeth. Steam curled up from the pot she was holding with a pair of hot mitts that looked like sharks.

"I made too much stew," she said. "Could you help me out and take some off my hands?"

"Sure," Jimmy said, "I'd be more than happy to help out. Here, let me take that." He came down the steps and took the mitts and pot from her, motioning with his elbow and his head for her to go on up the steps and inside.

"I'm Leigh O'Brien," she said, as Jimmy set the stew on the stove. "You've met Cory and Jonah. I'm sorry it's taken me so long to get down here to say hello."

"No need to apologize," Jimmy said. "I've been kind of a hermit myself. I lost my wife just before I came here, I guess Jonah told you. It's been a very hard time for me."

"Yes, he did tell us and we are very sorry for your loss, Jimmy. That's your name, right? Jimmy Heron? Please let us know if we can help you in any way. I've lost both my parents, Cory's mother died when she was very small from breast cancer, and Jonah's mom died when he was a teenager. His father left when he was little. So, we have all experienced some major losses in our lives, maybe not exactly like the one you've just gone through, but enough to empathize." She touched his elbow, and he placed his hand on top of hers.

"It's always easier to get through things when you have some support, Jimmy," she said. "Please allow us that honor."

He took a step back and stared at her. He had never heard it expressed that way before—as if helping someone through a painful time or a difficult loss were a privilege. He smiled at her. "You're right," he said, "I should reach out more. I've just never been through anything this hard." He drew a deep breath. "So, what kind of stew did you make too much of?"

"Chicken and vegetables," Leigh said. "Some we grew, some we bought. There's barley in there, too, and herbs. It's pretty good, even if it was a collaboration—those don't always turn out to be our best efforts. Oh, and here are some biscuits Cory made." She pulled a plastic bag from her jacket. "They're good, but you wouldn't want to get hit with one."

"Kinda heavy, huh?" Jimmy asked.

"Like a sack of doubloons," she said, handing the bag to Jimmy. He dropped his arm down to the floor and looked at her wide-eyed.

"Oh my," he said. "I guess if I get an urge to lift some weights I'll know where to go."

"Right," Leigh replied. "I'll tell her to make extra, just in case you want to buff up. Get strong enough, and you can shovel the road between our house and here. That is, if the weather gets fierce. We've been lucky so far; it's only snowed up on the mountains. Seems to be getting colder almost every day, though."

Jimmy looked at Leigh's barn jacket and noticed how it didn't even cover her belly, pregnant as she was. He grabbed his wool coat hanging on the rack.

"Here, put this on over your jacket. It's plenty big enough to go around both you and the baby and it'll keep you nice and warm." He draped the coat over her shoulders with a flourish. "There," he said, "you look warmer already."

"Jimmy," Leigh protested, "I have another coat—a bigger one—at home."

"Please," he said, "let me help you. Just for now. It would be an honor for me to do so." They locked eyes and smiled at each other.

"Okay, I'll get it back to you. And I promise I won't put any of Cory's biscuits in the pockets and run the risk of dragging it on the ground."

Leigh headed out the door, turning to face Jimmy as she reached the bottom of the steps. When she looked up and smiled at him, he was stunned at how beautiful she was.

"Keep the coat as long as you like," he said. "I have another one."

"Thank you, Jimmy," she said, stuffing the shark mitts into the pocket. "Take care. And call us anytime you need someone to talk to, okay? I mean it. Anytime." Jimmy nodded his head that he would.

Leigh waved and turned to walk away, then spun around so quickly the momentum of her pregnant belly almost threw her over. "Oh," she said, "I nearly forgot. We're having our annual Thanksgiving feast. If you'd like to join us, we'd love to have you. Cory's Dad will even be here for the day and he's always a hoot. Please, Jimmy, we'd love you to be with us."

"Thank you," he said, "but I can't say for sure. I never know from one day to the next how I'm going to feel. Most of the time I don't feel very sociable."

"You think it over," Leigh replied. "If the mood hits you, then just show up. You don't even have to call. We eat at two o'clock on Thanksgiving Day and we always have plenty. And no biscuits." She gave Jimmy the thumbs-up sign, and he just as quickly gave it right back to her. The joyous spontaneity of his own action surprised him.

Jimmy Heron watched his new friend through the window as she headed out the gravel drive and onto the road until the darkness swallowed her up. Glancing up the hill, he could see lights on in the log home she shared with Cory. He felt comforted to know that love, real love, lived so close by. It felt safe and sweet, and seemed as natural to him as had his own.

.22.

The Reverend Darryl Dimmer's "Take America Back!" sermon had been such a tremendous success, he decided to extend it all the way through to the next year. Heaven only knew how many demons, devils, and ogres America needed to wrestle down. Darryl Dimmer knew he was the one to inspire his congregation to do just that.

He stood at the pulpit in front of them, watching closely, waiting for just the right moment when their tender underbelly was exposed and ready to take his message in.

"We are soldiers for God in the fight for the soul of this nation," he said, "and we have every right to use every might—say it with me—*we have every right to use every might*—at our disposal to wrench America out of the grasp of those who would seek to destroy the Judeo-Christian principles upon which this great country was founded.

"We have the right, say it with me—*we have the RIGHT!*—as Christians and the moral leaders of America, to stand up and say NO! to the bleeding-heart liberals who want to tax you to death and tax your churches and give all your money away to welfare mothers and lazy homeless bums who won't work."

Darryl Dimmer was beginning to sweat and he knew that when he began to sweat, things were starting to roll. There was a time in the past when preachers preached to get a message across. Applause and cheering would have been as out of place in such a sacred setting as cheerleaders and pompoms. In Darryl Dimmer's church, though, the reverend liked to hear applause. He paused in his sermon and wiped sweat on his handkerchief whenever he wanted the praise of his followers. They never let him down. He lowered his voice to continue.

"Jesus spoke to me last night, brothers and sisters," he whispered to them. "Jesus said, 'Brother Dimmer, NOW is the time,' and I knew in my heart just what he meant. NOW is the time for action, say it with me—*NOW is the time for action!*—NOW is the time that the battle lines are being drawn, NOW is the time for the church of God to stand up and say NO!—to the environmental wackos who value trees and owls over families and jobs. NO!—to the radical feminists who want to take away a man's natural role. And, by God, I mean NO! NO! NO!—to the militant homosexuals who want to take over our schools and teach their depraved behavior to our children, to ram their agenda down the throats of the American people."

Darryl Dimmer paused to wipe his face and waited for the applause to die down. He lowered his voice. "Let me tell you something, brothers and sisters. Jesus himself said this, and if he didn't, he should have. The only excuse for poverty is sin. I'll say it again: the only excuse for poverty is sin. The only reason to hug a tree is to measure for what size saw you'll need to lay it out in board feet. The only reason to listen to radical feminists is to castrate men and disobey God. And the only reason to live a homosexual lifestyle is to turn this great nation of ours into Sodom. Sex in the streets, sex with children, sex with animals. That's it, pure and simple. I don't care what statistics you read in *Newsweek* magazine written by that bunch of New York liberals. Do you think they are going to tell you the truth? If you want this country to go straight to hell, then don't do anything and it will! The only place you are going to hear the truth is within these four walls. And the truth within these four walls of God's house is the truth that will set you free!" He paused for a moment to let that sink in.

"Jesus said it himself, 'Onward Christian soldiers, fighting as to war,' say it with me—*fighting as to war!*—and if you don't think this is an all-out war, then don't be running beside me as we charge up the hill. Don't stand beside me if I can't count on you to take up the sword of righteousness and slay the demons in this nation. Will you charge with me? Will you fight beside me? Will you take up the sword, the banner of the church of God, and fight with me for Jesus?"

The people of the Mt. Goshen Church of the Righteous cheered for their minister. Reverend Darryl Dimmer closed his crimson Bible and pulled his handkerchief from his pocket to wipe the sweat from his face. He unbuttoned his baby blue blazer and discreetly checked to make sure his eight hundred dollar head of synthetic hair from Topper's in San Francisco was still adhesived and lacquered in place.

With what appeared to be the last of his strength, Reverend Dimmer charged across the deep blue carpet to take his seat in a massive red velvet chair, allowing himself to slump down for the moment. He looked spent, like a prizefighter between rounds. He removed his steel-rimmed glasses and began cleaning them with his soggy handkerchief.

The congregation was on its feet by now, applauding, waving Bibles in the air. The organist boomed out "Onward Christian Soldiers" as the baskets for donations were passed.

In the balcony of the church, in the last row, sat a young man with short blond hair. He wore black jeans and a white shirt. His skinny black tie had something smeared on it, Cheez-Whiz or something. The sleeves of his shirt had been carefully buttoned to hide the swastika tattoo on his arm. The look on his face was of someone about to puke. It was Donnie Zoeller.

As the organist launched into the final phrases of "Onward Christian Soldiers," just before people began filing out into the bright midday sun where Wendell Metcalf and members of the ORS waited to pass out leaflets and solicit applications for membership, the donation basket finally made its way to Donnie Zoeller. He stuck his gum in it.

·23·

om Mason, sheriff of Reliance, made his way to the family car, a
dark blue Isuzu Trooper, with one arm around the shoulders of
his wife, Kate, and one around the shoulders of their twelve-year-
old daughter, Jenny. Their dress clothes had that wrinkled, fresh-
out-of-church look. In the bright sun, with all three of them just as
blond as they could be, it was hard to look at them in a group. It was
hard for them to look at each other, too, and they squinted like moles
until they got inside the shade of the car. All of them seemed troubled, weary and beaten down by something they could not even
name. Except Jenny. She knew exactly what it was.

Tom started the car while Kate stared silently out the window at
the Mt. Goshen Church of the Righteous. Jenny sat in the back with
her arms folded across her chest and looked as if she were pouting as
they pulled out onto the road heading for home. Tom glanced in the
rearview mirror at his beautiful daughter scowling in the back seat.

"Why the long face, Jen?" he asked.

"It's that preacher." She sounded disgusted.

"Who? Reverend Dimmer?"

"Duh...who else. I can't stand him. He gives me the creeps."

"Oh, now honey, Reverend Dimmer just gets a little carried away
in his sermons. And you don't like fire and brimstone preachers. Never
have. I remember when you were around two and we went to a
revival. Some loud preacher kept ranting on and on, and you stood
up in my lap, glared at him, and started saying, 'Shuddup...Shuddup...'
The louder he got, the louder you got. I couldn't stop laughing, but
your mom made me take you and go sit in the car, she was so embarrassed. Do you remember that, honey?"

Jenny's face softened, and she grinned at her dad's eyes in the mirror. He seemed to remember every cute thing she ever did.

"No, Dad, I don't, but you've told the story so many times I feel like I could. Or should. I do remember the first time we went to this church, though. I was seven and I said, 'Daddy, I don't like that man.' Well, I'm twelve now and I still don't like him. And I don't like that stupid son of his, either."

Tom glanced at Kate, who was the principal of the school Jenny and the preacher's son, Rodney, attended.

"Rodney Dimmer is one of our more challenging students," Kate said.

Jenny snorted. "Challenging? Moth-er! I don't understand why everybody always has to be so…so…what's that word?"

"Diplomatic," Kate offered.

"Yeah, diplomatic," Jenny said. "Rodney Dimmer is a jerk."

"What does he do that's so bad?" Tom asked.

"For starters, he calls everybody who has a different opinion from him a Commie liberal and says they don't love America. He talks about everyone else behind their backs. He tells kids who don't go to his father's church that Jesus hates them and that they're going to hell. And he sticks his ugly face with his garbage-breath right in your face and says, 'Kiss me. You know you want to.' If you tell him to get away, or even just politely say no, he calls you a lesbian. Like that's the worst thing in the world. Like being Rodney Dimmer's girlfriend isn't what you'd really hate. *Yech.*"

Tom looked at Kate. "Is this true?" he asked, and Kate nodded her head. Her eyes gave a slow, weary blink.

"Have you talked to Darryl and Juanita about this behavior?"

"Only Juanita. Darryl was too busy to come to our meeting, so he sent her." Kate touched her husband's arm and flashed him an I'll-talk-to-you-about-this-later look.

"Wow," Tom said. He sounded flabbergasted.

"But it's not just Rodney, Dad," Jenny piped up from the back. "I never feel good when I leave church, not ever, and I thought we were supposed to feel good about loving God. You know, like Jesus loves everybody. Reverend Dimmer just wants us to hate people. I don't think he reads his Bible—I think he just waves it around and uses it like a weapon." Jenny folded her arms and stared out the window.

"Well, now honey—"

But Kate cut him short. "Jen's right, Tom. I think Darryl makes up scripture just to suit his own means. "Onward Christian Soldiers" is a hymn, for goodness sake, not a command from Jesus Christ. We're supposed to love one another, not shoot each other dead in the street over religious beliefs. Or political beliefs, for that matter."

"And if Rodney Dimmer says one more bad thing about Miss O'Brien, I'm gonna slug him in the nose," Jenny added. "Will I get in trouble for that, Mom?"

"Yes, you will."

"Then I don't care, I'll do it anyway. I love Miss O'Brien. She's the absolute best teacher I ever had. She and Cory taught me to ride a horse, and Cory showed me how to shoot a gun."

"She what?" said Tom. This conversation was making him sweat.

"Relax, Dad," Jenny said, "it was only a pellet gun and we shot at cans on the hillside. Cory said it would keep me from having to wear bifocals as an old lady—that's her theory. She said if she'd kept her target eye strong, she wouldn't have to wear glasses to read. Also, if I get to be a good shot, I can help her keep the crows out of the corn. What are bifocals?"

"Glasses lots of older people have to wear," Kate said.

"Do you have to wear them, Dad?"

"Not yet, but I may by the time we get home."

"Well," Jenny said, "I don't care if Miss O'Brien and Cory are gay."

"They are?" Tom jerked the steering wheel and the front tire ka-whammed off the pavement and buzzed along in the gravel for several seconds before he composed himself and righted the vehicle.

"Oh, Tom," Kate said. "Honestly, everybody knows that. They're even having a baby together. It surprises me sometimes how much you don't know about the people who live in our town. And you're the sheriff."

The Mason family arrived at their neat white house with the green shutters just as the chicken concoction Kate had thought up that morning announced itself as done in the crockpot. The most wonderful blend of aromas wafted through the house. Some Minute Rice with peas and mushrooms, a quick salad of canned pears and cottage cheese on bib lettuce, and they were in business.

The three of them ate their Sunday dinner in a good mood, with no talk of the Dimmer family or church. Their conversation focused mainly on Jenny's science project, which consisted of sprouting various kinds of beans in paper cups and keeping a photographic journal of their progress. Trapper, their miniature schnauzer, had chewed up a good portion of the first effort until Tom had set up a new "laboratory" for Jenny by the window in the garage. A forced-air space heater and fluorescent lights kept the place warm enough for the plants to germinate.

When Jenny announced she was going up to her room to finish her homework, Tom helped Kate gather the dishes and the two of them set about cleaning the kitchen.

"So, back to our conversation in the car," Tom said. "What *did* Juanita have to say about Rodney's behavior?"

"She said she was sure the girls were just fantasizing, getting all worked up over nothing. 'You know how young girls are,' she said to me. And as far as Rodney's political and religious views are concerned, well, in her opinion, he is just exercising his right to free speech. She's certain we wouldn't want to 'run the risk of a lawsuit by stifling the boy in any way.' This was her not-so-veiled threat to me. I tell you, Tom, the woman is hopeless, a teacher's worst nightmare."

"And what about the younger boy, Jason? He's what—seven years old? A first-grader? How's his behavior?"

"Well, according to his teacher, Elaine Farmer, Jason's most annoying habit is his propensity for trying to baptize all the other children in the bathroom after lunch. He won't stop when she tells him to; he won't stop even if the children are crying and trying to get away from him. He won't quit until he is sure all of them have been 'saved,' and this is apparently something he thinks has to be done every day."

"And you told this to Juanita as well?"

"I did."

"And she said?"

"She held up her hand at me like this and said, 'First Amendment, Mrs. Mason. First Amendment.' My feeling is that Jason's antics actually thrilled her—she thinks it's the most wonderful thing the pushy little snot has ever done. Can you see the problem this is developing into?"

"I can. Wow. So, then tell me this, how can my daughter know about people being gay when she doesn't even know about bifocals?" He finished scrubbing out the crockpot and began drying it. Kate wiped off the counter.

"Honestly, Tom, you amaze me sometimes. Kids these days know everything about everything. Maybe not much about bifocals, but certainly about everything else. Trust me on this one. Most of the kids are much more aware of what's going on than our generation ever was. That's why all this antigay rhetoric, the hateful stuff we hear in church, the piles and piles of literature Wendell Metcalf and the ORS keep pumping out, really scares me."

"Do you think there'll be trouble? Violence?"

"There already has been. What do you think is behind the recent vandalism you've told me about? And there's a lot that hasn't been reported. Leigh and Cory have had animals killed and left to rot by their mailbox. And there've been others, too, other gay people they know who've had similar experiences. People are being harassed and threatened. I'm telling you, honey, this is scary stuff that's going on."

"Well, if it's so upsetting, why don't they report it? After all, I'm the sheriff. It's my job to protect them against things like this."

"You can't stop what you don't see. All of this stuff happens at night or when they are gone, that's what Leigh says. And even you can't be on patrol twenty-four hours a day. Besides, most of the gay people in this community are frightened to let people know who they are. Think about it—why are you so shocked when you find out someone is gay? It's because you're sure you don't know any gay people, and I say you know more than you think you do. This is not a safe time or place to come out of the closet, Tom. It just isn't."

"So, how do you know so much about this subject?"

"Leigh O'Brien is one of the best teachers I have. And she's been my good friend since college. Our great-grandparents helped settle this part of Oregon. It seems like our families have known each other forever, maybe since God was a brunette, and I just can't bring judgment on how she lives her life, Tom. I can't, regardless of what Darryl Dimmer says. I think Jenny's right about him."

"You do?" Tom asked.

"I do, Tom. I don't think Darryl Dimmer's church is a healthy place for us to be. It hasn't been for a long time."

"Well, I'm not sure that Darryl Dimmer is such an ogre. After all, he helped with the soup kitchen when the mill in Redmond closed, and he and Juanita do other good things in our community. Besides, did Leigh or Cory ever stop to think that if they changed their behavior, their 'lifestyle choice,' maybe they wouldn't be the target of so much antagonism?"

"Tom Mason, I can't believe you just said that. I think what Leigh and Cory and many others have decided to do by telling the truth about their lives is extraordinarily courageous. Wouldn't you get tired of having to live your life in secret? Suppose the tables were turned and you had to slink around and pretend to be something you're not. How would that make you feel? I don't care how many bowls of soup Darryl and Juanita dish up—if their message engenders hate, how can that possibly be good for our community?"

Kate was getting pretty steamed and slammed a couple of cabinet doors before she calmed down. She turned to look at her husband, her hands on her hips and the dishtowel draped over her shoulder. "What I'm saying," Kate continued, "is that Cory and Leigh and the others are good people who have done nothing to deserve this kind of treatment."

"And all I'm saying," Tom replied, "is that if sexuality is a choice, then my religion tells me that they made the wrong one."

"Your religion tells you that, your church tells you that, your preacher tells you that, but Jesus Christ never told you that. Besides, how do we know sexuality is a choice? Because Darryl Dimmer and the ORS keep saying so?"

There was no stopping Kate now.

"Even if sexuality really is a choice for some people, what business is it of ours?" she continued. "What right do any of us have to tell anybody else who they can love? What goes on between consenting adults is nobody's business but their own, Tom. Come on, do you ever sit around and wonder about what goes on sexually between Darryl and Juanita in bed?" Tom almost grimaced at the thought and then shook his head no. "Would you want them or anyone else focused on what we do in our bedroom?" Kate asked. Again, Tom shook his head no. "I wouldn't, either," Kate said, "and I am not ready to sacrifice my privacy, my personal liberty or my beliefs to people who have set themselves up as the sex police, the thought police, the spiritual police, or whatever it is they think they are for the rest of us. If Cory and Leigh both changed their minds tomorrow and decided to be heterosexual, I'd still feel the same way. Two adults who love each other should not have to fight the rest of society because they do. How can we not want for other people the same happiness we want for ourselves?"

Kate saw Tom, slumped in one of the kitchen chairs, a tormented look on his face. She felt herself soften toward him because she loved him and knew how difficult it was for him to challenge what he believed. She squatted down and placed her hand on his knee.

"Honey," Kate said, "remember when Jenny was eight and we got Trapper for her because she saw him at the neighbor's and thought she would die if she didn't have a schnauzer puppy?" Tom nodded, sniffing, and Kate continued. "Then remember how, after we'd had him for about two months, she decided what she really wanted Trapper to be was a cat? And every day she'd say, 'Here kitty, here kitty,' and get mad at me if I didn't buy cat food and litter for him. I almost had to hide the Puppy Chow so she wouldn't see it.

"Then one day she had this revelation. She said, 'Mom, you know, I've been thinking. I've been trying and trying to make Trapper into something he never was. He's a *dog*, Mom. He's not a cat. And he could never be happy as a cat—it goes against his nature.' Honest to God, Tom, that's exactly what she said. *It goes against his nature.* I almost drove the car into a ditch, I was so shocked to hear such big ideas coming out of the mouth of our baby girl. I guess that's when I first realized she wasn't a baby anymore."

Kate Mason patted her husband's shoulder and kissed his cheek before rising and going to the den to do paperwork. Tom kept his head down, watching his reflection in the spit-shine of his shoes, wondering if he liked the image he saw.

·24·

By 1:30 on Thanksgiving Day Jimmy Heron's peach cobbler was cooling on the trivet by the stove, puffing little bubbles of sticky goo over the edges of the toasty crust. The cinnamon-baked smell filling the trailer reminded him of home. At the last minute he had decided to go join in the festivities up on Lavender Hill at Leigh and Cory's. With what he considered to be a tremendous amount of good luck, he had managed to dig deep enough into the frosty cavern of Millie Jensen's freezer compartment to find three plastic bags marked PEACHES. God only knew how long they had been in there. Even though they didn't look or smell freezer-burned, Jimmy still felt he would like to have known in which decade they'd been picked.

Leigh had told him he didn't need to bring anything, but Mary Heron and her legacy of good manners won out.

Jimmy could not get himself to mix up the dough and roll out a pie crust without Lou, so he thawed the bags of peaches in a bowl of warm water and came up with a box of Bisquik, sugar, and milk. In just a few minutes, with the help of some cinnamon, vanilla, and a squeeze of lemon juice, he had a cobbler ready to slide into the oven. Not a bad effort, he thought.

While the cobbler bubbled and baked, Jimmy Heron polished his boots, his Dan Post dress pair. They now stood tall and alert on newspaper spread out on the table, as shiny and proud as sentries. Then he showered and shaved, splashing on Old Spice and slapping a few extra swipes of deodorant under each arm. He was sure he hadn't smelled quite this nice in well over a month.

His dress slacks, the western-cut light tan ones, now bagged on him a bit, but they still looked pretty spiffy. His white shirt with the snap pockets was not as wrinkled as he'd feared when he finally found it in the tiny closet. His belt, made of the same whiskey color leather as his boots, had a silver buckle Lou'd had made for him for his birthday one year. It was the JH symbol, the same as their cattle brand. He polished it with his handkerchief.

Jimmy stared at himself in the dresser mirror, making a couple of quick rakes across his thinning hair with a pocket comb. He had decided against wearing a tie. That's what he almost always decided, and it was a good thing, too, seeing as how the three he owned were hanging in the closet he left behind in Texas.

All in all, Jimmy Heron thought, at this time, at this place, considering everything that had happened, he looked pretty sharp. Sharp enough to go calling, anyway.

He walked back through the kitchen, slipped into his jacket, flopped his hat on his head, and jammed his hands into his brown leather gloves. Then he picked up the warm cobbler and headed out the door of his trailer, crunching across the frosty gravel drive.

Up the road toward Lavender Hill, his new friends waited and wondered if Jimmy Heron would show up hungry.

The number of cars at Leigh and Cory's surprised him since he hadn't expected much of a crowd. In truth, he might have backed out and just stayed home, eaten some soup and watched a football game, if he'd known before. Jimmy took a deep breath and banged the door knocker, the black face of a cow with its tongue hanging way out. It was the tongue that whammed against the door when he let it go. In a few seconds, Cory opened the door and the warmth from inside whooshed out, fogging Jimmy's glasses up. It made them both laugh.

"Hi, Jimmy," Cory said. "Glad you're here. Come on in. Here, let me take that while you wipe your glasses. You look like Rod Steiger."

"Who?"

"Rod Steiger, *In the Heat of the Night*. Remember the movie where he wore those sunglasses?"

"Oh, yes," Jimmy said, "with Sidney Poitier, right? We saw that movie in Fort Worth one time. It was years ago. My wife and I enjoyed going to the movies, even though we didn't get to go much. Lou was beside herself when we got HBO." Jimmy smiled at her, a weak, awkward smile, as he realized he was rambling, searching for any topic of conversation.

Cory felt antsy, not knowing exactly how to comment at Jimmy's mention of his dead wife, so she just grinned at him. "I'll put your cobbler in here on the buffet," she said. "You really didn't have to bring anything, you know. We always have way too much food. If you have dinner with us every day through March, maybe we can get it all eaten up."

"Oh, it was no trouble," Jimmy said. "I enjoy cooking now and then, and it's always nice to bring something to share."

"Well, the cobbler looks wonderful. Come with me and I'll introduce you."

Cory took Jimmy by the hand into the large living room. The log house had a delicate pine smell and a wood stove kept it toasty warm. The floor was tile, a dusty teal color. There were Berber rugs and Native American blankets in various tribal patterns all around, on the wall and across the furniture. Candles burned in a soft glow here and there, and Ned, their dog, was asleep on his side by the stove.

To Jimmy's great relief, there were not as many people as he had thought. A guy he recognized from the gas station in town, plus a young, thin woman snuggled close to him, sat on a couch. He saw a couple of women in sensible shoes, a very skinny, nervous, middle-aged man, a lumberjack-looking guy with a large, blonde woman, and a great big, ruddy-faced man who wore lots of big diamond rings and a gold Rolex. Except for his western belt and suspenders with oil derricks painted on them, he was dressed an awful lot like Jimmy Heron. The man was chewing on a fat, stubbed-out cigar. They all became instantly quiet and looked up.

"Everybody," Cory said, "this is our new neighbor, Jimmy Heron. He's the nice man I told you about. I also told him you would be on your best behavior and not throw food or cheer for the wrong football team like last year. Now, Jimmy, we don't expect you to remember everyone's name right off, but if you don't, you have to make breakfast for us all tomorrow.

"This is Willis, who owns the BP station in town. I think you two may have already met, right? Anyway, he's a good mechanic and won't cheat you. This is his sweetheart, Michelle. Michelle works at the Wigwam Restaurant in town and will give you extra bacon on your BLT if you show up early and ask nice. A big tip helps, too. Right here is our carpenter, Glenn, and his faithful companion, Felipe, otherwise known as the Amazing Vibrating Sock. Glenn's other faithful companion is Sally, our midwife and nurse and true friend for life." Glenn waved to Jimmy and brought shaky little Felipe up to his chest. Sally blushed, her pink cheeks flushing into a bright red.

"Pleased to meet you, Jimmy," she said.

"Now, these two scalawags," Cory continued, "are Betty and Ted—excuse me, Theodora. They live over in Sisters, and would ride fifty miles on a motorcycle in a blizzard to help you out if you needed it."

"If we had a motorcycle," said Betty.

"Which we don't," said Ted, then quickly added, "but call us anyway if you need help. We do have a tractor. And we have Betty's son, Mitchell, who's almost as strong as a tractor, only he eats more. If we can get him started on a cold day."

"But the tractor won't talk back," said Betty, "remember that part."

"Well, yeah, there's that," added Ted.

"You two are a mess," Cory said. "Now, this nice man is Ray. Ray owns the florist shop in town and is the only person we know who can name a Peruvian lily on sight. We pay him extra for that talent."

"Leigh pays me extra for that because Cory thinks every flower is a dandelion," said Ray. "Nice to meet you, Jimmy."

"And this big sidewinder," Cory said, waving her arm with a flourish, "is my daddy, A. L. Miller. You can call him Al."

"Just don't call me Daddy," said Al, standing to offer Jimmy his big bear's paw of a hand, "and don't call me collect, either, as my daughter has often been known to do." He nodded his head toward Cory as he and Jimmy shook hands.

"It's a pleasure meeting all of you," Jimmy said, "and if I forget some names, well, I hope everyone likes pancakes. Where's Leigh? And Jonah?"

"Right here, Jimmy," Leigh said, as she walked up behind him and slipped her arm through his. "We're all very glad you decided to join us. And the cobbler you made looks wonderful."

"Hi, Jimmy," Jonah called from the dining room, where he was lighting the last of the candles, "I hope you're hungry."

"My friends," Cory announced, "shall we all go sit down and be thankful together?"

Cory and Leigh ushered everyone into the dining room where the oval oak table was so heaped with food it almost sagged in the middle. A twenty-pound turkey dominated the scene, a roasted golden brown bird with the skin pulled tight across the breast and juice dribbling down. There was a tangle of tossed salad in a wooden bowl, a hill-like mound of green beans, mashed potatoes, creamed onions, yam casserole, fruit salad, plus turkey gravy and two kinds of stuffing.

"You'll be happy to know, Jimmy," Cory said, "that in this household, we always have cornbread dressing, although I have learned to call it stuffing. If I don't, everybody thinks I'm talking about salad dressing, which I most certainly am not. And we also make a token batch of that icky, mushy, Yankee whitebread stuffing, too, just for variety."

"Cory thinks she'll go to hell if she doesn't have cornbread dressing with her turkey," Leigh said.

"She will!" cried Al, making his way into the dining room. "It's against every law in the state of Texas!"

"My daddy taught me to feel sorry for people who didn't have cornbread dressing with their turkey dinner," Cory said. "He and I would put our heads together and sing, 'Pooooooooor Yankeeeeeees.' I always make about six pans too much of the stuff, so we want you to be sure and take some home with you. The neat part is that it's so heavy, if you don't eat it all, you can stick it in the back of your truck for winter and it will keep you from sliding around in the snow. It's my own homemade load leveler."

"You don't really do that," said Jimmy.

"Well, no," said Cory, "but I bet it would work better than a bale of hay."

Ray caught Jimmy's arm and whispered in his ear, "What they really do with all the extra food is haul it over to the homeless shelter in Bend. They cook a couple of extra turkeys and take them along, too. They think I don't know this, but I have connections." Ray wiggled his eyebrows conspiratorially at Jimmy for emphasis.

After everyone was seated and Cory and Leigh had wedged Jimmy in between them and right across from Jonah, Leigh offered her hands to Jimmy and Cory and led the group in a prayer.

"As we gather for this meal with our family and friends," she said, "we offer our thanks and ask that our hearts be opened. We are grateful to have found our new friend, Jimmy, and we ask for special guidance in helping him. And we are especially grateful for the new life about to join our family. Thank you so much for this bounty. May all be loved, and may all be fed."

Leigh squeezed the hands of Jimmy and Cory. They, in turn, squeezed hands with the others until the circle had been completed around the table. Jimmy Heron felt a lump in his throat, knowing that each of the guests knew of his pain and were focusing their energy on helping him heal.

This was not how he grew up, not what he was taught when he was raised. In his family, death and loss were burdens you shouldered on your own. You just struggled along under the weight of them until they eased up, or else they got the best of you, as they had his own father. Jimmy felt a warm spot on the back side of his heart, a budding trust that he would not be alone, that the handling of pain and sadness was a team effort. He felt his throat close up and he thought he might cry, hoping he would not embarrass himself.

Cory rose and leaned across the table, handing what was almost a saber to her father. "Here, you old knife fighter," she said, "you do the honors."

An hour or so later, dinner was finished. Some people went off to a bedroom to watch football on TV. Others were cleaning up in the kitchen. Jimmy took advantage of this chance to spend some time alone with Cory's dad.

"These women make me wear my teeth in the house and smoke outside," Al said. "Care to come along?" He handed Jimmy a jacket as they both stepped out the front door, where the cold wind hit them full force.

"Cory told me you lost your wife recently and I wanted to say how sorry I am to hear that. I know it's a tremendous pain. I lost my wife when Cory was only eight and it was a bad lick. *I mean,* it was a bad lick."

Al and Jimmy both looked down at their shiny cowboy boots and shook their heads at the memory of each loss.

"I feel really lucky to have made friends with the three of them," Jimmy said, picturing Cory, Leigh, and Jonah together.

"Oh yes," said Al, "they're fine young people. Just as good as gold, yessirreebob, good as gold." Al popped one of his suspenders with a thumb, then paused for a moment to let cigar smoke stream out of his mouth. He watched it float up and away toward the mountains.

"I know this must look like an odd setup to a lot of folks," Al said, "but I quit worryin' about what folks think a long time ago. All I want is for my daughter to be happy, and right now she's the happiest I've ever seen her. It's not exactly how I imagined I'd become a grandpa, but it'll do. I'm glad to see the whole thing doesn't bother you any, Jimmy. That's a comfort, actually."

"No, to tell you the truth, it really doesn't. I have an older sister in Massachusetts who has lived with her kindred spirit for over sixty years now. Of course, it wasn't anything people ever talked about back then; we just accepted Bonnie as part of our family the same way everybody did when I married Lou. My mother called it 'nature's variation on a theme,' and that's all I ever remember anybody ever saying about it. People are more open now, although I can't imagine it's a conversation I'd ever have with Della—that's my sister."

"Well," said Al, "the world can be a scary place. And life is short. I say grab hold of love when you find it, no matter what it looks like, and don't let go. I sure didn't intend to."

"Neither did I," said Jimmy.

Al finished his cigar, stubbed it out with his boot and stuck the butt back in the box. He and Jimmy Heron looked at each other and clapped one another on the shoulder, a hallmark of Texas men who've just shared a big fat wad of intimacy. Then Jimmy held the door and they joined the others back inside.

Al Miller, overloaded on turkey and good feelings, rambled off somewhere to take a nap. Jimmy decided to gather his things and say goodbye. Amidst the activity in the kitchen, he could see Ned wolfing leftovers out of his big dish. Jerry Garcia skittered back and forth on his stubby feet, meowing desperately for something—anything—in the way of scraps to be set aside for him. Giblets, his particular delight, would be especially fine. In his holiday sweater with the pumpkins on it, Felipe stood quivering on the kitchen counter. He delicately nibbled some chopped boiled turkey liver and waited for the world to end. His very last meal, the tiny, nervous dog was sure of it.

Cory and Leigh spotted Jimmy from the kitchen. "You're not leaving, are you, Jimmy?" Leigh asked.

"I thought I'd best be heading on back. I'm very full and kind of sleepy and I thought I'd lie down for a bit."

"If you come back later, we'll make turkey sandwiches. My specialty," Cory said. "Oh, but here, we packed up some leftovers for you. I split the good stuff between you and Ned. Sorry, but there wasn't much of your cobbler left—it was just too tasty, I guess."

Jimmy gathered all of the containers together with Jonah's help, who put them into a box for him. One by one, the guests wandered through the kitchen saying their good-byes.

"Bring your rig in and let's get some fresh antifreeze in her before winter sets in too hard," said Willis.

"And be sure to stop by the Wigwam for a bite to eat, Jimmy," Michelle told him. "The first batch of onion rings is on the house."

"Call us anytime, Jimmy," said Betty. "We don't do much more than sit around and wait for the telephone to ring, anyway. Ted is afraid Ed McMahon will phone to tell us we've won the sweepstakes and won't deliver the goods unless we're there."

"Actually," whispered Ted, "if you need help doing any heavy stuff, talk to Betty or Mitch. If you need a canasta partner or if you want to pitch some horseshoes, call me."

Leigh got Jimmy's coat collar turned up and wiggled his hat onto his head, then kissed him on the cheek. She slipped a piece of paper in his jacket pocket with the name, address, and phone number of everyone at the party.

"Thanks for coming, Jimmy," she said. "That took a heap of courage."

"Glad you were here, Jimmy, really glad," Cory said as she hugged his neck. "Come and see us again. Deal?"

"Deal. I enjoyed myself and all of you very much," Jimmy said. "Thank you. Thanks a lot."

Jimmy Heron slowly shuffled and crunched his way down the drive toward the road with his box of leftovers, a little uncertain of his footing on the frosty ground. One thing kept popping into his mind as he made his way back home: there were people in this world who were good, who cared for him, and who would help him through the most awful pain of his life. All he had to remember to do—and this was the hard part—was ask.

·25·

Suzette Metcalf loaded the dishwasher, making sure the plates were facing the same direction. She lined up the cups and glasses and saucers and bowls as perfectly symmetrical as a marching band. It made her feel good to see them all clean and sparkling and in perfect rows whenever she opened the door to unload the dishwasher. Order. Suzette Metcalf liked order. And neatness. Nothing out of place, nothing to wonder about, nothing to get lost or messy.

Her Christmas card list and her client list and her business associates list were in the same condition: perfectly alphabetical, completely up-to-date. Her attention to detail was one of the things her husband liked about her, she could tell. Donating her lists to the cause of fighting those nasty old homosexuals was something she was more than willing to do.

Why couldn't the rest of the world just be like the two of them, she wondered. Why did this gay rights and human rights and special rights stuff have to get so...so icky? Everybody had rights, for goodness sakes, this was America. Some people, the better ones, the normal ones, just deserved more rights, that was all. Why was that so hard for everybody to understand? No wonder America was in such bad shape these days.

Well, Suzette decided, she and Wendell would just have to clean it up, that's all there was to it. Just sweep the mess away like crumbs off the counter. How could the world not be grateful for that?

The Metcalfs' Thanksgiving Day dinner had been shared by the two of them which, as luck would have it, was exactly how they wanted it. They could have their usual Thanksgiving rib roast, baked potato, and lima bean dinner. They would not have to bear the scorn of everyone they knew for not eating turkey and some kind of gloppy stuffing. She would not have to eat the mushy casseroles the relatives always brought, which she and Wendell hated. Suzette also knew that if they dined alone, she would not have to clean up after a bunch of distasteful relatives, or put up with noisy rug rats.

The best part, though, was that neither she nor her husband would have to explain again to some pain-in-the-neck relation why it was that she and Wendell ate the food on their plates separately—meat, then potato, then lima beans—and why neither of them could stand the thought of any of their food touching. Wendell liked the taste of everything, each individual food, S-E-P-A-R-A-T-E-L-Y. Not all mixed together. Suzette simply knew that foods running together, whether it was on her plate or in her mouth, felt messy.

When they began dating, Suzette realized they ate their food the same way the first time they went out to dinner. She knew then, in her heart, they were meant for each other. And later that evening, as Wendell was driving her home, they began humming the same tune in the same key at the same time. Well, Suzette just took that as a sign from God. So exuberant was she at the thought of snaring such a suitable fellow that she set her sights on winning this man by becoming whatever he wanted her to be. Mostly, Wendell Metcalf wanted Suzette to find him always right, always brilliant, and always someone to be adored.

It was not too much to ask of a wife, Wendell thought, although he was certain he could never feel the same toward her. The best component of this setup, of course, was the part Wendell Metcalf knew for sure: Suzette Metcalf, his wife, was too stupid to ever notice.

In his office near Reliance's town square, Wendell sat in front of his computer screen arranging and rearranging words and letters for the most potent impact. He had been at his desk since early afternoon and now it was almost 8:00 P.M. on Thanksgiving Day. He could not go home, however, not now, not until he had completed the first circular to be sent out since the petition drive started.

The ORS needed 89,028 valid signatures by July 6th, ninety days before the November election, to get their constitutional amendment on the ballot. This number represented 8 percent of the total votes cast for all gubernatorial candidates in the previous election. Everything had to be approved by the secretary of state's office in Salem. Every little piss-ant thing they tried to do, it seemed to him, had to be gone over and poked through and written and rewritten until they were blue in the face. It just proved to Wendell Metcalf that the stupid liberals in state government were even more determined to let the queers run everybody else's lives.

He stared at the computer screen until the words came to him, like molten drops of lava spewing from the ends of his fingers, and he keyed them in. His hands felt electric:

UNLESS THEY ARE STOPPED, THE HOMOSEX-
UALS IN THE STATE OF OREGON WILL FORCE
YOU TO:
1. Hire them to work for you even if you don't want to.
2. Rent a room to them in your home even if you don't want to.
3. Teach your children that homosexuality is an acceptable "alternative lifestyle."
4. Use your tax dollars to promote homosexuality, bestiality, sadomasochism, and perversity.
5. Give up your right to decide what is best for your children.
6. Substitute anti-American liberal values for traditional family values.
7. Make a mockery of church-sanctioned heterosexual marriage by claiming their own "marriages" to be of equal status.
8. Give up your right to protect your family from the onslaught of the militant homosexuals, the radical feminists, and the liberal left.

FOR THESE REASONS AND MANY MORE, THE
OREGON REFORMATION SOCIETY URGES
YOUR SUPPORT IN STOPPING THE MILITANT
HOMOSEXUAL AGENDA IN THE STATE OF

OREGON. SIGN THE PETITION TO HAVE THE
ORS CONSTITUTIONAL AMENDMENT ON
THE BALLOT IN NOVEMBER. SAY NO TO THE
HOMOSEXUALS—NO SPECIAL RIGHTS!

Wendell leaned back in his chair and stared at the screen. He liked what he had written, even though he was getting pretty tired of toning down his rhetoric, being so goddamned nice about it. He knew better than to go blasting away with his computer, however, knew better than to make it look like the poor homosexuals were the ones being attacked.

By now, in fact, Wendell Metcalf knew just how to play this song to the independent-minded Oregonians. All he had to do was explain that the homosexuals were the ones taking away the rights of the others—the hard-working overtaxed God-fearing church-going flag-waving Americans—and there'd be a war, all right.

Wendell made a quick decision to stop by the hardware store tomorrow to pick up some buckets. He'd have Suzette spraypaint them red, white, and blue so they could be set up beside the tables wherever people signed the petitions. Why, he just bet people would be so fired up, they'd be happy to write out a check to the ORS then and there and drop it right in the bucket. As long as they were signing their name once, they might as well sign it twice, right? Yes, this was just one more brilliant idea and one he wouldn't even have to ask the ORS bigshots in Portland about, or run it past those piss-ants in Salem.

Even if they found out, even if they said no and made him take the buckets away, he knew of at least ten businesses in the area who would be happy to set a donation bucket right out on the counter. All they needed was something to catch the eye. Wendell pulled up the screen on the computer and typed:

WHAT IF YOUR SON CAME HOME FROM
SCHOOL AND TOLD YOU HE WAS GAY? THE
ORS NEEDS YOUR FINANCIAL SUPPORT TO
STOP THE MILITANT HOMOSEXUAL AGENDA.
PLEASE DONATE TO SAVE OUR CHILDREN.

He ran twenty-five copies, making the print extra big, cutting the signs to the appropriate size. Tomorrow he would pick up buckets, paint, and tape, and by next week they'd be ready to roll. *Save our children*—yes, that was a nice touch. After all, everybody wants to save the children. As long as the money kept pouring in, Wendell Metcalf knew he was the one to help them do just that.

·26·

Jimmy Heron was squinting into a broken lock, spritzing it every so often with some liquid graphite he'd picked up at the hardware store. When he heard the knock at his door he yelled, "Come on in! It's open," and began searching for a rag to get his filthy hands cleaned up. With more energy than he was used to seeing in one mass, Cory, Leigh, and Al burst up the steps to the trailer and into Jimmy's tiny home. Ned was right behind them. The dog began sniffing the place as soon as he was inside, making him look just as suspicious as always. He sniffed around and around until he finally stuck his big yellow head up onto Jimmy Heron's table. A snoot full of liquid graphite made him sneeze, and he called off his own search and flopped down by the woodstove. Within two seconds of a big sigh, he was asleep.

"Hi, Jimmy," Cory said. "You studying to be a safe cracker?"

"A jailer," Jimmy replied.

"Better make a run for it, Al," said Leigh.

"Darn," Al said, "and I packed up my tenny-shoes."

"We decided to stop by for Daddy to say good-bye. We're taking him over to Bend—he's flying out today. He thinks Texas will fall back into the hands of Mexico if he's not there to protect it. It was their land, you know, Daddy."

"I know, I know. You have reminded me of that for almost all of your adult life, my darlin' girl. Makes me feel guilty every time I eat a plate of enchiladas."

"It was sure a pleasure meeting you, Al," Jimmy said. "I hope you make your way back here soon. You be around for Christmas?"

"Thanks, Jimmy, but no. If all goes well, I'll be in Bermuda gettin' a tan on this old lily white carcass of mine. I'm countin' on you to help

Jonah look out for the womenfolk," Al said, "and the new baby."

"Big Al," Leigh said, cocking her head at him, "the last of the old time chauvinists, but we love the poor doofus anyway."

"I am a gentleman from Texas," Al said, indignantly, "and it's my duty to ask for help in seeing to the well-being of those I love when I'm not there to do it myself. Ain't that right, Jimmy?"

"Yes," said Jimmy, "it is, actually. It's really a man-to-man kind of thing." He looked a little sheepish. "We just don't know how else to do it."

"Well, then," said Leigh, "we forgive you. And we love you even more."

"We'd better go," said Cory. "Sky King or Jimmy Doolittle or whoever it is you're ridin' with isn't going to wait for you forever. How'd you find this guy, anyway?"

"I knew his dad. We flew the hump together in Burma. Best damn pilot I ever saw. Walked into a prop one day and chopped himself clean in two. Maybe three."

"I thought you just said he was a great pilot."

"He was! In the air, wasn't anybody better. On the ground, though, well, maybe he wasn't as smart as we'd all thought."

"You don't have to wear goggles and a leather helmet to fly in this rig, do you?" Cory asked.

"Only a parachute and rosary beads," said Al, "and my boots, of course."

Jimmy and Al shook hands, and with a quick scramble of energy and motion, the whole group was out the door and gone. Taking stock of the mess on his table, Jimmy chucked the busted lock into the garbage can and gathered up the newspapers and stuffed them into the wood stove.

This was tedious busywork, he decided, but it kept him occupied. He'd grown almost proficient at picking a lock by now and thought someday soon he might set himself up in business, you just never know.

He and Lou had planned to open up their pie shop, their dream, but that was out of the question now. God, how he missed her!

Washing up in the kitchen sink, Jimmy gazed out at the snow-covered mountains and thought about the power of love. It bound us together like an invisible spider web, he almost said aloud, linking people no matter how far away. Love was a string of light from heart to heart, as tiny as the twinkle in an eye, and as powerful as all the stars lighting the universe.

It suddenly made sense to him that if Al knew he was loved by Cory and Leigh all the way down in Texas, knew it even when he was off gallivanting around the world and didn't speak to them for months at a time, then Lou must know how much he still loved her, wherever she was. Love just went on forever and ever, no matter what, no matter where. And heaven, Jimmy Heron was sure, couldn't be much further away than Texas.

·27·

The Thanksgiving holiday ended, and the country picked up speed as it headed into the Christmas season. Amidst the talk of love and good will, it became increasingly apparent that hatred in America was becoming big business. Christian fundamentalists in the state of Colorado put forth their own amendment to the state constitution to limit gay rights. Even though the language of the amendment was softer than its counterpart in Oregon, the intent was the same.

Word spread from city to city as more and more preachers heeded the call to jump on the antihomosexual bandwagon. A sharp rise in hate crimes bore witness to increasing levels of anger, intolerance, and violence directed at gays and lesbians.

Love the sinner and hate the sin was what most ministers urged their congregations to do. The unspoken phrase, the most dangerous one, however, was...*unless they refuse to change.* This hypocrisy undergirded the fundamentalist movement. Contempt filtered down through the ranks, from preachers, through congregations, out the doors of churches and into the streets across America. When it reached people like Donnie Zoeller, in whom hatred and anger knew no moderation, who had no personal pressure release valve, the atmosphere became particularly turbulent. It was charged with possibilities about to explode. From it sprang the rage and hatred that could kill.

Darryl Dimmer did not care if his inflammatory rhetoric inspired some half-crazy person to kill homosexuals. The world would be better off without them, anyway. He just hoped it would take a long time, one victory after another, a slow, slow march with the Lamb of God, milking the public for all the tax-free dollars it could give in the fight to take America back.

If some idiot blew off a next-door neighbor's head because he was queer, well, there was no way in the world anybody could pin that on Darryl Dimmer, not in a million years. He was a man of the cloth, after all, a shepherd leading his flock, doing God's work. He couldn't help it if, on the way to Glory, one of his sheep bolted from his guidance and went berserk.

Reverend Dimmer rubbed his hands over the surface of his mahogany desk in his church office. He could still feel traces of lemon oil from its most recent polishing. Even though he hated having grease on his hands, he loved the lemony smell of the oil. It gave him a sense of grandness, of being wealthy and important.

He took a deep breath, inhaling the scent deep into his body, then glanced in the mirror he kept on his desk. Daryl Dimmer checked his acrylic hair, punched on the tape recorder, and watched as the cassette began to turn on the sprockets. He moved the polished brass mirror to the center of his desk so he could look directly at himself when he spoke. He had to be able to see what the rest of America would imagine when they listened to him. It was important to look and sound honest and sincere and genuinely concerned about the welfare of each soul he would touch with his message.

He smiled at his reflection and began to speak. This would be the tape that would set things on fire, the speech that put the Mt. Goshen Church of the Righteous on the map. It would be the flagship program of the series he planned to distribute across the country by Christmas. Soon the Reverend Darryl Dimmer would become a household name, a name to be recognized among the spiritually chosen.

"My friends," he said, "there is a cancer loose in America today and it is eating away at the very flesh and soul of this nation. This cancer is homosexuality. It is dangerous, it is depraved, and it is after your family…."

·28·

K ate Mason was developing a throbbing headache.

"We do not send our son to school, Mrs. Mason," Juanita said, "expecting him to come home with a bloody nose. And we particularly do not expect him to be bullied by the principal's very own daughter."

"Jenny is hardly a bully, Juanita, and I have warned Rodney and you about Rodney's behavior. Jenny is not the only child in this school who has complained about him, and it was only a matter of time before the whole situation blew up. I am sorry that it was my daughter, because that's not how we have raised her. But as I have watched your son push and push and push—with no sign of intervention from you, I might add—well, in all honesty, I must say I do understand why Jenny did what she did. I'm not condoning it, but I do understand it. Rodney has been the bully in this school, Juanita, not Jenny."

"Again, I must tell you, Mrs. Mason, that my husband and I do not take this kind of thing lightly. We do not send our children to school, even a school as scraggly as this one, to be violated."

Kate Mason felt her neck and left shoulder kink and knot up. For an instant, she thought she might lunge across her desk and grab Juanita Dimmer by the throat.

"VIOLATED?" she exploded. "You can ask the twelve-year-old girls in this school how they feel in the presence of Rodney if you want to start throwing around the term *violated*. And if you want to take this up with the school board, you may certainly do that. But rest assured I will be there, and I will bring with me every child in this school who cheered when they heard Jenny busted Rodney's nose."

Kate Mason took a deep breath and continued. "Now, Juanita," she said, "if I may ask you a question: Since you hold this school in such

low regard, why do you and Darryl send your children here? Why don't you send them to a private school if you are so unhappy with this one?"

Juanita Dimmer shifted in her seat, making a couple of swipes at lint stuck to her wool skirt. She decided to be nicer. Sort of. "My husband and I support the idea of education," she said.

"Good," Kate replied, "my husband and I do also."

"But we do not support the idea of having to pay for the education of our children twice, Mrs. Mason, which is essentially what we would be doing if we sent our boys to private school. Our property taxes pay for public education, swollen though the ranks may be with overpaid administrators." Juanita glanced slyly at Kate to make sure her jab hadn't been missed. It had not. "Therefore," she continued, "we will not pay for the private education of our sons until the United States government provides us with vouchers for doing so. It's that simple. Everybody else in the country gets to exercise their right to choose, and we should too."

"Well, Juanita," Kate said, "until that day comes, and while your sons are in this school, they will be expected to behave appropriately. I will not allow the students here to be bullied or badgered or harassed by one or two students who haven't learned how to get along."

"I hope you don't think you are describing *my* boys."

"Yes, Juanita, that's exactly who I mean and you know it. And one more thing. This school will no longer be held hostage by you and your First Amendment threat. If Rodney feels a need to espouse his beliefs, let him do it in your church. And if Jason needs to baptize some other children, let him do it in Sunday school. Your sons will no longer exhibit inappropriate behavior or they will forfeit the privilege of remaining in this school. Am I making myself clear?"

"Quite clear." Juanita's eyes had sharpened into daggers.

"Well, then," said Kate Mason, "I think this meeting is done. I am busy getting these children educated. Good day."

Juanita Dimmer rose so abruptly that even her dark hair shook. Since she kept it sprayed as stiff and round as an army helmet, any movement of it was as shocking as seeing the capital building dome sway in the wind, and just about as likely.

Like someone shot from a cannon, Juanita Dimmer blasted out of

Kate Mason's office. She never looked back, never paused to close the door, never even noticed papers swooshing off the table from the breeze of her departure, or the blonde twelve-year-old sitting outside the principal's office with her hand wrapped in ice.

Luckily, this was a Thursday. Sally Taylor, the school nurse, had been there to pack some gauze in Rodney's nose before sending him home, and to make sure Jenny's wallop hadn't broken any bones in her slender hand.

"Well, I gotta say this," Sally had told her, "—and if you tell your mother I said so I'll deny it—but Rodney Dimmer is a weenie and can't take a punch. But by golly, little miss, you can sure throw one." Sally squeezed Jenny's bicep a couple of times and made her blush. "Who taught you to hit like that?" she asked.

"My Grandma Knudsen," Jenny said. "She told me she cold-cocked a burglar with a punch one time. She told my dad he banged his head on the window, but that wasn't the truth. Grandma smacked him a good one. She thought my dad would worry too much if she said what really happened. What's *cold-cocked?*"

"It means she knocked him out cold." Then Sally Taylor added, "Your Grandma Knudsen taught you well." She gave Jenny the thumbs-up on the girl's way out of her office.

It was through the eyes of a warrior that Jenny Mason watched Juanita Dimmer's blistering presence shoot out of her mother's office. The young girl smiled the serene smile of someone who had fought the good fight. Oh, she was in trouble, she knew that much. Being the principal's daughter brought with it certain responsibilities Jenny knew her mom wouldn't back down on. Unwritten rules. Behaving yourself and not sassing were big ones. Not getting into fights was another. Busting somebody in the nose with your fist was an offense that was probably off the charts. Oh well, Jenny thought. It was, after all, a matter of honor.

Kate Mason stuck her head out the door and looked at her daughter. "Jenny," she said, "I need to talk to you now."

Jenny Mason left the bag of melting ice on the seat of her chair. She didn't want any extra sympathy for what she had done, and stuck her swollen hand in the pocket of her jeans. She'd probably at least be grounded for a month or more. Maybe even expelled or sent to a girls' refor-matory school. She didn't care. She held herself proudly and walked straight ahead, sure in her soul she'd done the right thing. No matter what happened to her, Jenny Mason knew in her heart that she'd do it again.

·29·

Kate Mason stood with her back to the door. She was staring out the window at Juanita Dimmer bustling down the walk toward the Dimmers' gray Oldsmobile, as if her girdle were ablaze. The plush car with its crushed velvet seats and whitewalls seemed completely out of place in this kind of country, almost as much as Darryl's Cadillac.

The principal could see Rodney in the front seat of the Olds, his head tilted back, holding a bloody handkerchief up against his nose. His face was red and puffy. Kate remained at the window, thinking, waiting until she heard her daughter settle herself into the chair across from the desk. She felt an odd admiration for her twelve-year old, and kept forcing the smile from her lips.

Even if she agreed with what Jenny had done, however, even if she completely understood the motivation behind it, Kate Mason knew she had drawn the line and that Jenny had crossed over it. The rules were the rules, no exceptions. Kate turned to look at her daughter.

"Jenny," she said calmly, "there are rules at this school, rules I have made as principal, that I expect each student to abide by."

"Yes, ma'am," said Jenny.

"Because you are my daughter, *especially* because you are my daughter, it is imperative that you obey the rules here. Do you understand why?"

"Yes, ma'am."

"Good. Now the rule about fighting is that there is not to be any. If there is, then whoever threw a punch is—and I don't care who started the fight—the person who threw a punch is to be suspended from school for three days. Today will be counted as one of those days. I will ask the nurse to give you a ride home. You will also miss Friday and Monday and will be allowed to be back in school on Tuesday. I want you to get your homework assignments from Mrs. Barstow, get your books, and get yourself to the nurse's office. Am I clear?"

"Yes, ma'am."

"Jenny, I need to ask you something else. Did Rodney Dimmer hit you or try to physically harm you in any way?"

"You mean other than making me sick to my stomach?"

"Jenny," Kate said, "this is not the time."

"No, ma'am," Jenny replied, "he didn't."

"Okay. Now, you know you are grounded for the weekend beginning today, and your dad will tell you whatever other punishment he feels necessary. For me, I want you to spend your weekend writing an essay. I want it to explain ways of handling conflict without fighting."

"Oh, Mom!" Jenny whined. Kate held up her hand.

"Listen to me," she said. "Haven't you told me how you wish all the people in the world could stop fighting and just get along?" Jenny nodded. "Well, then," Kate continued, "how do you think wars get started? It's when people are unable to sit down and work out their differences. They refuse to listen to one another and cease caring about what might be lost as a result of it."

Jenny slumped in her chair, exasperated and bored. Kate knew she needed to touch her daughter's heart and leaned forward on her elbows, straining her neck across the desk.

"Jen, listen," she said. "It is always good to take a stand against oppression and I know this is how you saw Rodney's behavior. And believe me, I'm not saying he didn't deserve what he got. All I'm saying is that there are many safe and reliable techniques for handling conflict that don't involve hitting. I want us to sit down together and learn what those are, then you can help me teach the other students how to handle situations like this that might come up, okay?"

"Okay." Jenny had tears in her eyes and the tip of her nose was beginning to turn red.

"At this moment, what I'm telling you does not feel fair, and it's a double-whammy being the daughter of the principal *and* the sheriff, I know," Kate said. Jenny nodded her head.

"More is expected of you, and I think it makes it tougher to be a kid. But, Jenny, we have always expected more of you, simply because your father and I have always known you have more to give. When we first brought you home from the hospital and looked into those beautiful eyes that were such a deep, deep blue, we knew we'd been blessed with the most special of children. We just knew, Jen, do you understand?"

Jenny's face softened toward her mother, as it always did toward either of her parents whenever they talked about her babyhood, and she smiled.

"Yes, Mom," she said, "I understand."

Kate was almost on the verge of tears and got herself together to return to the business of education.

"Well, then," she said, "you go pick up your things and I'll call Sally Taylor to give you a lift home. Make sure you get everything you need for your homework and reading assignments. I'll see you at home later and we'll talk about this with your dad."

Jenny walked out into the waiting area, pausing to grab the baggie of melted ice she'd left behind before heading to her locker.

"Jen," her mother called from her office.

"Yes, ma'am?"

"I am very proud of you." Jenny looked at her mother with a puzzled expression.

"Not for fighting," Kate continued, "but for being who you are. I'm proud to be the mother of a girl with such a good heart."

Jenny Mason blushed and waved to her mother before leaving, then took the stairs two at a time to her locker. She felt strong. She felt powerful. And, with the possible exception of being suspended from school and having to explain the whole thing to her father, she felt tremendously grateful to be her mother's daughter.

·30·

The snow came. On the very same afternoon Jenny Mason slugged Rodney Dimmer, big, luscious flakes swirled in the air, then drifted down onto the streets of Reliance like feathers from a down pillow. Even in a town as accustomed to winter weather as Reliance was, the first big snowfall always brought a ripple of excitement. Snow made people happy, friendlier. Snow even made people silly.

Tom Mason glanced up from his desk and out the window just as Dick Barstow emerged from his hardware store in his customary blue denim apron. Dick pretended to ice skate, sliding up and down the walk through the snow in front of his store, swinging his arms and sticking a leg straight out behind him. Then he vaulted into a really crummy single lutz and seemed to splatter onto the walk. Dick was the mayor of Reliance—a rotten skater, but a fun guy and very popular. His wife, Alice, was Jenny's teacher.

Wendell Metcalf was loaded down with a large bag and several buckets, snagging them in the doorway as he tried to exit the store and go around Dick. He looked surly, thought Tom, maybe even mad at Dick for having such a goofy, whoop-te-doo time. Well, Dick does look pretty silly, thought Tom, but Wendell usually looks mad. Too bad the rest of the world can't enjoy a spur-of-the-moment romp in the snow like Dick Barstow.

Tom turned back to the paperwork on his desk. Well, he thought, Wendell is not the only one in this town who's mad. The reports he held in his hands were recently filed complaints of vandalism. Mail boxes pushed over, cars spray-painted with racial slurs and antigay slogans. Even animals had been murdered, including a llama owned by the two men out on the Bend highway, Eric Holloway and Steve Dvorak. Wow, thought Tom, he'd had no idea llamas were so expensive. Actually, he'd had no idea Eric and Steve were gay, either. They told him so when they filed their complaint.

"We are not public people, Sheriff," Eric had said, "we just want to live our lives, raise our animals, and be happy."

"We are taxpayers, Sheriff," added Steve, as if indicating to Tom that his salary depended partly upon them. Eric scowled at his partner.

"That's not the point," Eric said. "The point is that over the past several months we have been the target of some vicious vandalism and terrible verbal assaults. We have chosen not to say anything because we are gay men. Apparently, we are not the only ones who know this."

"I kept telling him that the ORS people have radar," Steve said, wiggling his fingers up beside his head like antennae. "If a man expresses even the slightest interest in flatware or dishtowels, they'll nail him. That preacher, too, what's his name? Oh yes, Dimmer, at the Church of the One Big Ego. Have you heard the things he's been saying, Sheriff? Have you read this garbage the ORS is leaving in mailboxes?"

Tom nodded, wondering if these men knew he was a member of Darryl Dimmer's church. Hoping they did not.

"Not only is this stuff not true," Steve continued, "it's inflammatory, it's rabid, it's…it's…" Steve stumbled for the right words, "it's poorly written!"

Steve's last remark was really reaching—it made Eric snort and Tom wince. Flustered and embarrassed, Steve stalked off into the kitchen, grabbing a dishtowel and flapping it against the counter. Soon they heard the clanging of pots and pans.

"Forgive him," Eric said. "He taught English at Oregon State for many years. What he does now when he's upset is cook, so if you're up for chicken divan in a couple of hours, Sheriff, I'm sure we'll have plenty."

Eric smiled at Tom, who smiled back and shook his head no. "This whole thing has been terribly agitating for us both," Eric continued, "and, like I said, we are private people. We are both aware of the ramifications for gay people in speaking out. About almost anything, really. But we could not keep quiet after Camille was murdered.

"She was a llama, Sheriff, but Camille was like our child. I know how silly that must sound, but we got her when she was very young. Our purpose was to breed her. When she got old enough, though, every time we brought in some studly male to do the deed, she would look at us with those soulful eyes and those long, long eyelashes like we had betrayed her. If she had just spit at us, we could have handled that, but she didn't. She stared at us both and then looked away, like we'd shot her right through the heart.

"After three times of bringing in a male, feeling like the father of the bride at a shotgun wedding, Steve throwing a fit about 'some brute having his way with her,' and having to drag some horny, worked-up boy llama back out of the corral, we finally figured out that breeding our little girl was just not anything any of us wanted to do. Except the boy llama, of course. And his vote didn't count."

Eric's eyes misted up; his chin began to quiver. He stared out the window for a few seconds before continuing. "We can't sit by and let ourselves be bulldozed by these hatemongers," he said. "Not anymore. Not after this. That's why we called you. We know it may seem like not much of a big deal to you, but it's a very big deal to us. Today they kill our animals, tomorrow they kill us. That's how it feels, Sheriff."

Tom was writing furiously in his report book and finally looked up so that he could see Eric eye to eye. "Anytime the law is broken, it's a big deal," he said. "How much did you pay for Camille, do you remember?"

"We got her for four thousand dollars. Three years ago."

"Have you buried her body yet?" Tom asked.

"Yes," Eric said, "this morning, just before I called. I thought about waiting until after you had seen her, but Steve couldn't bear it. We were worried about coyotes coming down from the hills and having a snack. Her throat was cut, Sheriff, and it was pretty horrible." He covered his face with his hands.

"How could anyone get close enough to do that?" Tom asked.

"Listen. This llama would have sat in your lap if you'd let her. Camille was very loving, very trusting. It would never have occurred to her that someone would want to harm her. It never occurred to us, for that matter. Oh, dear God—" Eric brought his hands up to the side of his head and rocked with the pain of it. "We had no idea hatred ran this deep."

"You didn't see or hear anyone?" Tom asked gently.

"No. Nothing. These ORS pamphlets were beneath Camille's head. We've seen them before, left in our mailbox."

"I don't mean to insult you by asking this," Tom said, "but was Camille insured?"

"I figured it was part of your job to ask, so, no, I'm not insulted. The answer is no, she was not insured. We insured her when we first bought her, because we intended to breed her, to make her part of our business. Well, when that didn't work, when we fell in love with her and she became our very expensive pet, we let the insurance lapse. We could never replace that sweet creature with insurance money. We've both lost a lot more money than that on things we liked a lot less. That's the truth, Sheriff. I have documentation if you need to see it."

"No, that's okay. You have other llamas, right?"

"Yes, we do," said Eric.

"Were any of them injured?"

"No, they were in the back pasture. The barbarians, that's what Steve calls them. Camille liked the front pasture best. The grass is thicker, and she enjoyed watching the cars on the highway. At least, we made it up that she did. If it got too cold, she had direct access to the barn and her own special stall. It was heated, our little extravagance for her. The others huddled together for warmth out in the back, but Camille, well, she was our princess."

Tom finished his report and handed it to Eric to verify and sign. "I'll need to take a look at her before I go," he said.

"I understand that you do," said Eric. "She's buried behind the barn and her head is facing east—easier access to heaven, according to Steve. There's a shovel by the door. You won't have to dig much—there's only the one wound. Do you need me to come with you?"

"No," said Tom, "I'll do this alone. Let me know if anything else happens around your property. I'll be in touch if I come up with any leads. Don't be afraid to call, okay? Really. I mean it."

"Okay," said Eric, "thanks very much, Sheriff. We appreciate your help."

It took less than an hour for Tom Mason to uncover and inspect the llama's body. He was surprised at how small she was. Her eyelids were half open, the dried and frozen blood around her throat a dark crimson band. Tom thought Camille had the look of someone who'd staggered home from a Christmas party, passed out, and frozen to death. He searched the pasture where her body had been found. There was no clue as to who might have killed her, only a boot print in the mud he dug up with his pocketknife. Fresh snowfall had covered whatever other tracks there might have been. Tom drove back to his office and compared this case to the others in his ever-expanding folder marked Vandalism-Unsolved.

In the six years he'd been sheriff in Reliance, Tom Mason had never seen so many reports like this. Not even at Halloween or during spring break or the rodeo weekend over at Sisters had he ever investigated this much damage of property for no apparent reason. And the killing and wounding of animals, well, that just made him sick.

Tom punched in the numbers to forward the office phone to his home before locking up. He found himself wishing he had fought harder with the county over money to hire a deputy. *What does a sleepy little burg like Reliance need with two lawmen?* Everybody had practically laughed at him. *Why, the two of you would probably get all excited if something happened and shoot each other trying to run out of the jail.* That's what all the county and state bigwigs thought—it would be Mayberry all over again. Har-har-har!

They can say what they want, thought Tom, but when the lid blows on this vandalism and people start taking potshots at each other, maybe folks will sit up and take notice. He was only one man, after all, sworn to uphold the law. He could only do the best he could do, and he for sure couldn't be in every place at once.

Tom climbed into his patrol car, a metallic blue Jeep Cherokee, and slid the big file folder across the seat. Kate had called and asked him to come home early, something about a family meeting being in order.

Family meetings upset his stomach, actually. Family meetings usually meant Jenny was in trouble for something and he had to rack his brain thinking of an appropriate punishment for this beautiful blonde-headed kid he adored. This was the hard part.

The good part was that Jenny was always such a great sport about it. She did whatever he told her needed doing in record time and did it much better than he could have done it himself. Then Kate made brownies and the three of them read or watched television together. Maybe family meetings weren't so awful after all—except the part where he felt like the bad guy. But that usually didn't last long. No, not very long at all.

·31·

Well," Ted Schroeder said, and with a little too much finality for anybody's comfort, "I'm going to get me a goddamned gun, that's what I'm going to do." She folded her arms across her chest and leaned back against the couch so hard it made the rest of them sitting there pop forward like a line of marionettes.

They all knew that antigay harassment and vandalism were on the rise. The first two meetings of this crowd, trying to figure out what to do about it, had been more of a social gathering than anything else. So far they'd only thought of a name: Central Oregon Bigot Busters, or COBB. By this third get-together, however, almost everyone in the room had been affected by the hate. They were afraid, and ready to act.

Betty Ahern, Ted's partner of eight years, rolled her eyes toward the rest of the group and touched her lover's arm. "Oh shush, now, T," she said, "that's not going to solve the problem. Besides, you already have a gun, remember? It's that old deer rifle in the cedar chest." Betty looked around apologetically. "We never use it to hunt," she said. "Not anymore. Ted and Mitchell got an elk with it once, then Mitchell shot a snake with it, then we put it away and forgot about it. I use it to keep the lid of the cedar chest from dropping on my head when I have to drag out extra blankets." She smiled a weak smile. "I'm sorry," she added. "We don't even have shells for it anymore."

"Oh, for heaven's sake, Betty, don't apologize for being a hunter," Steve Dvorak said, "not in central Oregon. You only have to apologize for hunting if you live in Portland." The whole crowd gave a nervous laugh, not exactly sure what Steve meant by that, assuming that most Portlanders looked down on hunters and just bought their meat already packaged. After all, you didn't have to look the animal in the eye that way.

"Well, then," said Ted, still stuck, "I'm going to buy me some god-damned bullets, that's what I'm going to do. If they want a fight, then, by damn, they'll get one. I'll shoot the sonofabitches if they try to hurt me or my family or my animals."

A couple of people clapped their hands and whooped, but the whole conversation, this whole meeting, was making Cory nervous as a cat. She squirmed in her chair before popping up like a jack-in-the-box and heading toward the kitchen.

"Where are you going?" Leigh shouted at her from across the room. Cory turned and looked at her.

"To the kitchen," she said, "to get some coffee."

"Can't it wait, Cory? This is really important."

"I'll be right back."

"No," Leigh said, her gaze steady at Cory, "you won't."

Leigh was right, of course, and Cory knew it. Worse, Cory knew that everybody else knew it, too. She hated conflict and anger and con-frontation just about as much as any living human could. She felt her-self slinking into the kitchen, just like the chickenshit sloth she knew in her heart she was.

Pouring a cup of coffee, stirring in some milk and sugar, Cory stared out the kitchen window wishing it would all just go away. She wished she'd kept on driving the day she roared into Reliance. She wished she'd kept her big trap shut the night she offered to give Leigh O'Brien a ride home from the potluck over in Sisters—what was it now? Six years ago. Didn't seem that long at all.

She hadn't meant to fall in love with Leigh. She was fascinated by all those freckles, though. Initially, anyway, that was it. Freckles, freck-les, and more freckles, man alive! Cory had never seen anyone with that many freckles be that beautiful. It was sort of like looking at an aerial map of something that would all of a sudden smile at you. A brilliant white slash of perfect teeth erupting from a ground cover of reddish-brown, freckled terrain.

It hadn't taken more than a few dazzling smiles, a few heart-to-heart talks, and a couple of potluck dinners before Cory Miller's heart had sunk like a big rock in a deep lake and—*da-boosh!*—the woman was in love.

Now here she stood, hiding out in her own kitchen, wishing she'd never had to learn words like *discrimination* and *homophobia*, phrases like *equal protection under the law*, things people in her living room seemed obsessed with.

Truth was, if Cory Miller had her way, she and Leigh would just blow out of this place. That's how she felt about it right now, anyway. She couldn't have done it financially a few years ago. When she first got here, in fact, she was broke. Well, maybe not completely broke, but pretty badly bent. Alcohol had robbed her of money, focus, and ambition, but being in love with Leigh O'Brien had turned that around right quick and all of it was now a thing of the past. The far past.

By selling off their Pecos Fire salsa business and having the good sense to let Big Al's financial advisor invest the money for them, mostly in Microsoft and Nike, Cory and Leigh had as much money as they would ever need, even if their kid had to have braces and new sneakers every week.

Overseeing the Pioneer Foundation they'd started to help families and children with emotional problems was how Cory now filled up her days. It brought her and Leigh much joy to be able to do this. After all, just how much money could two people spend on themselves? It seemed foolish not to use it to help out somehow.

"Hooooooeee, gal!" her daddy had shouted to her on the phone. "You two sure landed with your butts in the butter on this one!"

Butts in the butter, indeed, thought Cory. We have all the money we need to go anywhere in the world we want, and the woman I love would rather just dig in, lock and load, and fight it out.

Cory drained her coffee, rinsed out the cup, and decided to wait in the kitchen until she'd heard everyone leave. Soon after, they all did. Ted sounded like she'd calmed down and everyone seemed to be in a good mood by the time Leigh said good-bye to the last ones and closed the door. Cory sat at the kitchen table until she felt Leigh's presence in the doorway before looking up.

"Mad at me?" she asked.

"Worse," Leigh said. "Disappointed."

"You know how I hate meetings."

"That's pretty lame, Cory. I know how you hate confrontation." Leigh began determinedly wiping the kitchen counter with a sponge.

"So what if I do?" asked Cory. "Is that a crime?"

"Only if you value your own freedom," Leigh said. "Or mine. Or your friends'. If you don't value that freedom, then don't let it bother you that you're..." Leigh's voice trailed off and she squinted her eyes, thinking.

"Chicken?" Cory asked.

"Worse."

"A coward?"

"Closer."

"Spineless?"

"Exactly."

Cory opened the refrigerator and stood staring at the contents, hoping something with whipped cream and lots of calories would suddenly leap out into her arms to occupy her. It didn't, so she turned to face Leigh.

"I keep getting the feeling," she said, "something bad is going to happen. Somebody's gonna get hurt."

"Something bad is already happening, Cory, don't you see that? The ORS wants to define our lives. They want to be able to tell the world who they think we are. If we allow them to do that, we'll lose whatever freedom we have. I can't believe you don't see that, that you can't feel it in your heart the way I do."

Leigh stopped cleaning nonexistent crumbs and stood staring at her partner until Cory looked her right in the eye. "They want to lump us in with pedophiles," Leigh continued, "and they want to put it in the Oregon constitution. I will lose my job, Cory. That's right, me. I will lose my job after having taught school for twenty years in this state, most of it in this town."

"Well," said Cory, "you don't really need your job, you know."

"And you don't really need a skull if you don't have any brains in there, you dipshit," Leigh said. "Whether or not I need my job is not the point. The point is that I will not lie about my life or who I am."

"I guess I don't see why we even have to bring it up. Seems like we all got along just fine when nobody knew about it."

"Nobody talked about it, Cory, and that's very different from not knowing. But let me tell you something, when we decided to have a family together, everything changed. Our commitment to each other was no longer something I could hang behind the door like a coat. Our commitment to each other, the tangible proof of that, was all of a sudden sticking out in front of me like a grocery cart. It's with me everywhere I go. And in a month, we'll bring a baby into the world who will be with us everywhere we go. What kind of a world do you want our child to grow up in? One where we have to lie about who we are so we don't lose our jobs? One where they kill our animals, or maybe even us? Well, not me, and if all you can think of to do is just go along to get along, then I'm not sure you're the person I thought you were."

Cory felt her cheeks flush as anger sparked across her eyes. Leigh had hit a nerve, and they both knew it. Once said, they didn't know what to say to undo it. Leigh placed both hands on her belly. She looked very tired. Overloaded.

"Do what you need to do, Cory," she said. "The baby and I are going to lie down and take a nap."

Leigh reached out to touch Cory's arm and Cory, still angry, jerked away, grabbing her jacket off the hook. She watched Leigh waddle off down the hall, doing the walk of a heavily pregnant woman.

·32·

ory scooped up her cap and gloves, feeling like the biggest jackass of all time, and slammed out the back door. She headed down the road toward Jimmy Heron's trailer.

When Cory Miller walked up Jimmy's driveway, she was surprised to see him outside on a ladder with a broom. He was trying to push snow off the top of the tacky little turquoise metal shack he called home. The wind was blowing and swirling snow up around his head. His ladder appeared to be sliding away from his feet. She sprinted over to grab him before he fell.

"I bet this isn't your usual line of work," she yelled to him, and Jimmy turned to see who it was just as she caught the ladder and moved it up under his feet again. By pure luck, he had put his Beltones in and was able to hear her.

"No," Jimmy said, "we never had much of a problem with snow on the roof where I come from. Of course, we didn't live in a trailer, either. And if we had, I don't think we would have chosen a turquoise one." Cory helped him climb down. "Thanks a lot," he said. "I worry that too much snow on the top will cave the roof in. And I have too much stuff, too many thoughts caving in on my head already."

Even though they smiled at each other, Cory could see the sadness in his eyes. She knew why they hadn't seen him in a while. He had been hibernating, nursing a wound so deep it would take years to heal. Perhaps it never would. She picked up a coil of frozen rope by the steps and threw one end over the trailer.

"Here," she said, "let's turn this into an easier job. You take this end, and I'll go around and we'll scrape it off. Shouldn't take long."

The pair worked slowly and silently, making three or four passes across the top of Jimmy's trailer with the rope until most of the snow was scraped away. He coiled the rope and pitched it under the steps, then motioned for her to join him inside.

"That was a pretty neat trick," Jimmy said.

"My daddy said if he couldn't raise me to be smart, at least he could raise me to be clever. I learned that little technique from him. That's how we scraped the mud off a car I sank in a stock tank once. It's the only rope trick I know," Cory added, "which is a source of great embarrassment for a Texas girl."

"Your dad is quite a character. Does he get up here to see you often?"

"No, my daddy is a bit of a roustabout. Has been ever since my mother died, maybe even before, but especially after she died his heart just hurt too bad. It's difficult for him to stay put for too long. He gets a case of the wanderlust and has to take off. You'll never catch Big Al with a boot nailed to the floor for very long, no sir."

"Was that hard on you growin' up?" Jimmy asked.

"Not too bad," Cory replied. "Could have been worse, I suppose. We had a lady who stayed with us and looked after things. And me. Her name was Polly. Polly Pickles was what I called her because she pickled everything from cucumbers to sweet corn. When she couldn't be there, I stayed with my Aunt Daisy and Uncle Shorty who lived close by. When I was fifteen and acting out, being a snot, I drove their tractor in a ditch and nearly flattened myself. Uncle Shorty phoned my dad. He was up on some oil rig in Oklahoma. Told him to get home quick before they rolled me up like a blueprint and shipped me to him in a tube. Daddy stuck around for longer periods of time after that, at least until I went off to college. It wasn't so bad. Like I say, it could've been a lot worse, I'm sure."

"Where did you go to college?" Jimmy asked.

"Southwest conference."

"All of 'em? That's a bunch of schools."

"Well, not all of them, I guess, but a lot. I went to four different schools in two years."

"What was your major?"

"Margaritas and Willie Nelson music."

"Oh. Want some coffee to thaw out?" Jimmy asked.

"You bet," Cory said, as they headed up the steps.

The inside of his trailer was warm and tidy. Certainly it smelled better than when Millie Jensen lived there.

Cory noticed Jimmy's stacks of mail sorted near the telephone and a picture box on the kitchen table. Several old photographs were lying about next to his coffee mug, a pen and pad of paper, a book of stamps and some envelopes. He had been writing letters.

Cory picked up one of the photographs. It was of a small boy, about age six, and two young women, probably in their early twenties. The boy was sitting in the saddle on a paint horse, grinning a snaggle-toothed smile, a too-big cowboy hat covering up his eyes. Both women sported tall cowboy hats, riding pants, and silky white blouses with dark neckerchiefs and shiny, knee-high boots like cowgirls wore in the 1920s. The young woman who looked quite a bit like Jimmy had a coiled rope slung over one shoulder and leather gloves gripped in her right hand. Cory stared at the picture.

"Is this you and your mom?" she asked.

"My sister," Jimmy said, putting down a mug of coffee for Cory and setting out sugar, a clean spoon, and a tiny can of Carnation milk. "This one right here, that's Della. She's quite a bit older than me, if you can imagine. And this is Bonnie, her…uh, her kindred spirit of many years." Jimmy's voice got shaky. "Bonnie just died," he said. "Last week. I got a letter from Della yesterday. Here, you can read it."

He handed Cory the cream-colored envelope and Cory held it in her hand, trying to make out the ancient scrawl. She sniffed it and noticed it smelled musty, like an old quilt, or the inside of a cedar chest. Then she turned it over and stared in astonishment at the wax seal with the JH in it before shaking out the letter to read:

December 2nd

Dearest Jim,

I appreciated getting the card from you with your new address so I don't have to spend a lot of time tracking you down. However, I am sad that I must share some difficult news with you which is that Bonnie passed away yesterday. She'd had another series of small strokes and so we knew it was just a matter of time and she died in her sleep. I feel very blessed that it was not a long ordeal, as I had dreaded her being any more incapacitated than she was. I did not mind caring for her, but she hated being taken care of quite a bit. I'm sure you remember how independent she was. Stubborn, too. We spent quite a bit of our lives trying to out-stubborn each other. It may be that I have won.

Do not worry about me, as I am being looked after to the point of nuisance by the young women from the co-op and other friends. Since we have both outlived most of our cohorts and relatives, there will be no service. I have told everyone who has called that flowers would be silly. I can look at Bonnie's Christmas cactus in the front hall and remember her anytime I want. It is in full bloom now, as I expect my Bonnie is as well.

There are decisions we both made while we were in good health and I want to tell you about them. At my passing, which I am not anticipating but know will come, even though Bonnie often told me I was too mean to die, our house and any monies left will go to the Women's Studies Dept. at the University. Over time, we have both come to feel this is important. I have designated to our young friends, Dana and Kim, which family items are to be shipped to you. It is not much, but there are some things you might treasure. My papers and books will go to the Women's Studies Library. Bonnie's artwork will be auctioned to raise money for them. All of the paperwork has been handled, so there will be no burden for you. I will keep Bonnie's ashes with me. After I die and am cremated, I have asked our young friends to bury us together at a secret spot and to place a couple of horseshoes in our grave for good luck. We may need it, who knows?

If I do not see you again in this life, Jim, do not be troubled by that, as I know we will be together—all of us—as a family, in the hereafter. It eases my mind to know this.

I understand more fully now your pain in losing Lou and my heart goes out to you. I feel very empty, already bored with my own company, and so I have been busy answering the phone calls and reading quite a bit. If I had Dandy, I would saddle up and go riding—all the way to the top of the bluff. And then I'd squint my eyes and hold my head just right and try to see clear up to heaven. Or maybe just Oklahoma. Remember that?

I love you,
Sis

Cory was crying by the time she finished reading Della's letter, and Jimmy handed her the Kleenex box. She gave her nose a good honk, then grabbed another tissue to wipe her eyes. "Wow," she said, "so Della and Bonnie were a team? Lovers? For how long?"

"I'm not sure," said Jimmy. "They met in college. It must have been around sixty-five years. Long time."

"Long time, I guess," said Cory. "And your whole family knew?"

"Well," Jimmy replied, "everybody knew without ever being told. In those days it was just not something people talked about. But my mother and father loved Bonnie and accepted her into our family just like their very own daughter, the way they welcomed my wife when we married. I only once heard Mother refer to Della and Bonnie's relationship as anything out of the ordinary, and then she called it 'nature's variation on a theme,' or something like that. Not anything bad."

"That's amazing!" exclaimed Cory. "It's hard to imagine—way back in the 1920s! And I thought *we* were being so progressive."

"What you folks are doing now," Jimmy said, "is being honest about it. That's not how people have been, not really. And don't think all that shuffling around didn't take its toll. I remember when my mother was dying. Della and Bonnie were both torn up. Everybody was. Right after they left Mother one day, Lou and I went in to see her. She took our hands and said, 'What do you think it is, Jimmy? Lou? What do you think it is about me?' We couldn't imagine what she was talking about, so we said, 'What do you mean, Mother?' And she said, I'll never forget this, she said, 'I love Della and Bonnie so much. I love both those fine young women so much and I am so proud of them. What is it about me that made them afraid to tell me about their life?' The truth may hurt, but it doesn't hurt as bad as holding back, especially with the people you love.

"I wish the times had been different, is all. I wish Della and Bonnie could've lived the life you and Leigh are living. Not that their life was a bad one, I don't think it was. And I'm sure they were much more open in Cambridge than they ever could have been in Texas. I just wish the times had been different and things had been easier for them."

Cory turned to the old man who had come from another life and was now her friend. Gently, she took his hand. "Jimmy," she said, "I think your family sounds wonderful. If only all of them could be right here, right now, having a cup of coffee with us and telling me all the family stories. This must be very sad for you, and if I could bundle up the sorrow and bury it in a deep pit, you know I would surely do that." Jimmy blushed and ducked his head, feeling a little embarrassed, but he did not pull his hand away.

"What I want you to know," Cory continued, "is that we truly are your friends, and if you need us in any way, we'll be here for you." Cory reached out and grabbed Jimmy by the back of the neck, pulling his big head down so she could hug him. "You're a good guy, Jimmy," she said. "I know it with my whole heart."

They said good-bye and waved as Cory banged her way out of the trailer and down the steps. She headed up Jimmy's gravel drive toward the road before the gray velvet of dusk enveloped her. As she walked up the road she could see Ned galloping toward her in his slew-footed run, his ears flapping wildly. He wore the big, goofy grin he always got on his face when he saw her. Leigh must have let him out to go look for her. The thought of it made Cory feel warm inside.

Ned skidded to a stop on the gravel at Cory's feet. He circled round and round her, dripping little happy drops and snorting as she rubbed his ears and smoothed his yellow coat. Then, with no more notice than a cocked brow and a challenging look in the eyes between them, they raced through the gathering darkness back up the road to their log house. "I can beat you," Cory yelled as she took off running. "Why, you're just a dawg!"

Jimmy Heron watched his new friends sprinting up the road, warmed by the joy he witnessed between them. He wished Della and Bonnie could have met these wonderful young people, been involved in their lives, and he hoped that Cory and Leigh would always be as brave as he saw them now. He wished that *he* had their courage. Most of all, though, he wished Lou, the shining light in his heart, was here to share it all with him.

In the lamplight and warmth from the woodstove, Leigh O'Brien sat in the rocker grading papers, a "double wedding ring" quilt draped over her stomach and legs. The burst of wind and energy when Cory and Ned thundered in the back door sent some of Leigh's papers flying. She could hear Ned's toenails scritching across the kitchen floor before he whammed into the bottom of the refrigerator, sending magnets clattering to the floor, and then the unmistakable sound of their big dog trying to drink all the water in his bowl in two huge gulps.

Jerry Garcia, asleep on the couch, awoke briefly at the sound of anything having to do with the refrigerator. Realizing no food was forthcoming, he rolled over onto his back to finish his nap. His fat, gray paws were curled up to his chest, and his hind legs stuck almost straight up in the air. He snored.

Leigh could feel the baby move as she rocked back, then forward, then back, then forward again. Finally, she managed to build enough momentum to vault herself out of the chair and push herself up to gather her papers. As long as she was up, since getting up was no longer an incidental thing to do, she decided to adjust the light on the aquarium and give the fish some food. Perry, the ever-hungry yellow perch, swam lazily to the top of the tank and opened wide, as he always did. Leigh could see the two little catfish, Hoover and Kirby—territorial creatures that they were—each carefully guarding a corner of the tank, waiting for some morsel to filter down their way. "Chow time, guys," she said, sprinkling in food.

Cory walked into the spacious living room, her cheeks and ears still red and cold. She inhaled deeply, breathing in the smell of pine from the logs and the cinnamon they kept in a kettle on the woodstove. It was a wonderful aroma, one that made her happy every time she came in the door. Leigh looked at her, not exactly sure what to say. "You were gone quite a while. Did you lose something?" Leigh finally asked.

"Yes," replied Cory, "I did."

"Did you find it?"

"Yes, I believe I did."

"What was it?"

Cory took a deep breath and smiled into Leigh's hazel eyes. "Pieces of my vertebrae," she said.

Transformation can take place in an instant, faster than the flicker of a thought. Courage can come out from its hiding place when least expected, when it is needed most. As gently as a whisper in the trees or a shadow across the canyon wall, courage pushes its way through, upward past fear. Then it settles itself across the shoulders like a comfortable old sweater. Things change, shift, making room for the beating of a brave heart. And once courage has found its place, there is no going back. Not ever.

·33·

t was a blustery Saturday afternoon. The rusty metal hook on the rope clanged loudly against the flagpole; the sky was flat and gray, the color of dolphins. Kate Mason, Jenny, Alice Barstow, and a gaggle of children of all ages stood shivering in the cold wind on the front walk of their school. Each of them was grinning up at the bright red ribbon they'd just succeeded in wrapping around the entire building, with some very much appreciated help from the mayor and Lloyd Russell, the school's maintenance man.

The ribbon, made from old sheets the kids had dyed red in art class and cut into long strips, swagged at various places around the building, then draped at perfect peaks right above the stone carving at the front entrance. RELIANCE PIONEER SCHOOL, it read. COURAGE, RELIANCE, TRUTH.

Painted in bright green on the red ribbon were the words, This School Is A Hate-Free Zone.

"Ith beyoooootifull," gushed Erin-Anne Turner, a second-grader caught up in the feeling of camaraderie and team effort. "It lookth like a great big Chrithmuth prethent." Her strawberry-blonde curls peeked out and fluttered in the wind from under the orange-and-black Oregon State hockey cap she wore. The freckles across the bridge of her nose looked drawn on. She beamed her snaggle-toothed smile at the group. "Merry Chrithmuth to our thcool from uth!" she shouted, and the whole group cheered.

Jenny Mason's essay, "Building A Better Community: Why It's Too Late For Hate," was the genesis of the banner. Her essay was based, in part, on a speech she had read by Dr. Martin Luther King, Jr., and one of his statements that had impressed her the most: "If we are oppressed every day...we must use the weapons of love, compassion and understanding for those who hate us…."

Spending most of the weekend after she had successfully deviated Rodney Dimmer's septum working on the essay, Jenny had also helped her dad clean out the attic and straighten up the garage as part of her punishment. True to form, Jenny and her dad had managed to have such a great time handling these chores together that Tom forgot he was supposed to be mad at his daughter. Besides, going through Jenny's boxed-up baby books had once again turned Tom Mason into the sentimental mushball the women in his life knew he was.

Back at school the next week, Alice Barstow had been so impressed by the elements of purity and logic in her student's paper that she had asked Kate for permission to let Jenny read it over the loudspeaker to the whole school. Then Dick Barstow took a copy of it with him to a mayors' meeting in Portland. In a matter of days, Jenny's essay had appeared not only in the *Oregonian* and the *Eugene Register-Guard,* but in a half dozen major papers thoughout the West. Nobody could have been more surprised about it than Jenny, and nobody could have been prouder than her parents.

The week before her daughter's essay went public, Kate Mason was adjusting a framed copy she'd just hung on the office wall when three fifth-graders from Leigh O'Brien's class appeared in her doorway. Sarah Bybee, Derrick Goldberg, and Lindy McAdoo stood there nervously. It was lunchtime.

"Mrs. Mason?" asked Lindy, "can we talk to you for a minute?"

Kate looked up and motioned for them to come in. "Sure," she said. "What's up?"

"We, uh, that is, all of us, not just the three of us, but all the kids in the school, well, most of the kids in the school, want to let you know how proud we are of Jenny," Lindy said.

"Oh," Kate said, "thank you. Thank you very much. Her father and I are proud of her, too."

"We also told Jenny," Derrick said.

"And Mrs. Barstow, too," added Lindy.

"We wanted to tell you what we were thinking about and see if this is an okay idea to you," said Sarah.

"And what's your idea?" asked Kate.

"A hate-free zone," said Derrick.

"A what?" asked Kate.

"A hate-free zone," Derrick repeated. "We want to make our school a totally hate-free zone. No hate allowed."

"Well," said Kate, "it sounds like a noble idea. Just how do you propose to go about doing that?"

Lindy McAdoo stepped forward and looked Kate Mason right in the eye. "Declare it," she said.

"*Declare it,*" Kate Mason repeated, figuring this was going to be a longer conversation than she'd first thought. She walked over and sat down in the chair behind her desk, motioning for them to drag over a couple of extra chairs and sit down.

"We told Miss O'Brien," Sarah explained, "that we wanted a school where everybody gets along. She asked us what we thought was the hardest part about going to school with so much conflict."

"And?" Kate asked.

"And," Sarah continued, "we decided that it just takes up too much of our time. That's it. Miss O'Brien says it 'splits our energy.' Somebody is always getting hurt or upset or mad. Besides, it doesn't feel good to any of us to be bullied. You just want to hate them back and that doesn't get us anywhere."

Kate stared at these sweet, thoughtful faces, astonished that their little heads were full of such high ideals, but not surprised in the least that these three students were in Leigh O'Brien's class.

"Do you realize that anytime there are human beings involved there will always be conflict of some sort?" she asked.

"Yes, ma'am, we do," said Derrick. "That's what Miss O'Brien said, too. But she also said that conflict doesn't have to involve hate. So, we decided to make our school a hate-free zone."

"Miss O'Brien said the first step in creating what you want is to declare it," said Lindy, smiling at the principal with a dazzling mouthful of braces, the rubber bands on them a startling shade of periwinkle. "So, that's what we're doing," she added, "and asking permission from you, of course, since you're the boss." She smiled at Kate again, and Kate could not help but smile back.

"And what happens beyond your declaration of what you want?"

Kate asked. "I certainly can't give you permission to paint it on the front of the school, I'm sure you know that."

Sarah Bybee was grinning so big Kate could tell the next part of this equation was her idea. "No, ma'am," Sarah said, "we knew we wouldn't be able to do that." She leaned forward, putting her elbows on Kate's desk. "But we can get close to that by wrapping a big banner around the school and we already figured out how. Show Mrs. Mason, Derrick."

Derrick Goldberg pushed his glasses up further on his nose, then unfolded the paper he took from the pocket of his plaid flannel shirt. In his careful, deliberate hand was an almost perfect drawing of the Reliance Pioneer School draped in a red ribbon with bright green letters announcing: This School Is A Hate-Free Zone. Kate smiled at the creativity and commitment of the children who sat with glistening faces before her. She looked at them.

"This is a good idea," she said. "How are we going to get the banner wrapped around the school? Have you thought of that?" Somehow, she knew they had. Sarah spoke up.

"Mr. Russell said he would do it," she said, "so none of the kids would fall off the top of the school. That's what he said, anyway."

"Good for Mr. Russell," Kate said.

"And Mayor Barstow said he would help," added Lindy, "and he'll give us any tools and nails we need—free of charge!" She felt the *free of charge* part was important to add.

"So the mayor has seen this plan?" asked Kate, and all three of the children nodded.

"Can we do it, Mrs. Mason?" Sarah asked.

"We'll do the work," said Lindy, "and hang it on the weekend. Mr. Russell said he would donate his time."

"And we'll pay for the stuff we need," added Derrick.

Kate reached down, pulling her wallet out of her purse. "Will you accept donations to your cause?" she asked, sliding twenty dollars out and handing it to Derrick.

"Wow," he said, "this is the biggest donation so far!"

"It's really only the third one," said Sarah. "Mrs. Barstow gave us five bucks. Miss O'Brien gave us ten." She looked at Kate. "We'll give you a refund if we don't need it all."

"That's okay," said Kate. "Take yourselves out to lunch. And, speaking of lunch, aren't the three of you missing yours right now?" She looked at her watch.

"It's fine," Sarah said, "we decided to skip lunch today to talk to you."

"This was more important," said Lindy.

"And it worked," added Derrick, stuffing the twenty dollars into his pants pocket.

Kate Mason ushered the three children out of her office, thanking them, making sure books and backpacks were matched up with the right kid. She reminded them to be sure and get their schoolwork done first before taking on any other projects. All three promised that they would.

She watched them walk together down the hall, punching each other's arms and giggling the proud feelings of a job well done. Then she turned and read Jenny's essay again, framed in rosewood, hanging in a perfect place of honor on her wall, and Kate Mason was sure she'd never felt fuller in her life.

Building A Better Community:
Why It's Too Late For Hate

The other day I punched a classmate in the nose because he was being a bully. I thought it would make me feel better, and it did, but only for a little while. When I realized that what I did would only make him hate me more, I felt very sad inside. I don't want to hate anyone, not really, only sometimes it is very hard not to. I don't want anyone to hate me, either, but I won't let myself be pushed around. I was feeling very confused about the whole thing.

My mom said to study history to see what works and what doesn't when it comes to dealing with hate. My dad said to pray about it. I did both. I read about Ghandi and how the Indian people followed the path of nonviolence in finally breaking the rule of the British Empire over them. Then I read about

Dr. Martin Luther King, Jr. and his ideas about using nonviolence as a way to secure civil rights for black people in America. When I prayed, God told me to love thy neighbor as thyself.

For all of history, winning wars has never meant winning hearts, and so the people who lose the war only feel hatred for the people who won. To me, that just feels like another war waiting to happen. I am in the seventh grade and am old enough to know that not everyone will always agree on everything. But I am also mature enough to know that hatred only creates more hatred.

My ancestors helped settle the town where I live, Reliance, Oregon. They came all the way across the country in a covered wagon on the Oregon Trail. All of the people who came with them were from different walks of life. Even though they didn't always agree, and maybe didn't even like each other, they knew they had to rely on one another or they would die. They learned to set aside their anger, even their hatred, and to work out their differences and get along in spite of everything. They had to. There was just no other way. If they didn't rely on each other, they would perish. That is how my town got its name, Reliance, and it makes me very proud to know that.

I cannot change the entire world but I know I can change my own world. To do this I must start with myself. I will not back down from what I believe to be right, but I will not close my heart to the rights of others to say what is true for them. I want to live in a happy, safe, loving world. To accomplish this, I know it must begin with me.

Jenny Mason
Reliance, Oregon

·34·

died of a heart attack, that's what I heard 'em say, and I guess I should've given up my smokes back when everybody else did. Actually, Jimmy was the only one who really went through quitting, since Lou was never hooked and I never made an effort to get unhooked. He said it wasn't all that tough, though. Lou, well, what Lou had to do was just stop firin' 'em up, 'cause she hardly did much more than light one and wave it around. She said the only reason she quit was because she got tired of burning holes in her tablecloths and dresses.

Jimmy just picked up his pack of Luckies one morning and said, "Nope, by God, I'm bigger than you are." He flushed those coffin nails down the toilet and never looked back. Me? Well, I inhaled all the way down to my toes. Camels, no filters. I bet if you looked hard enough, you could see smoke coming out of my socks.

Dying's not so hard, I gotta say that. Sort of like going through a revolving door, a quick and easy transition. At least, that's the way it was for me. Other people have lots of other stories.

Knowin' what I know now, and lookin' back on things, it seems silly the way humans have been killin' each other off since the beginning of time, like that's some big payback or something, like that's the true meaning of justice. 'Cause you know what? Dyin' ain't really the price you pay for whatever bad deeds you've done in your life, no matter how much we'd all like to think so. After all, everybody's going to kick the bucket sooner or later. It just feels like justice when you're lookin' at it from the other side.

Nope, the biggest price you pay for havin' been a jerk comes after your life is over and you get to take a look back. Not only do you see the pain you caused other folks, you also get to feel it. The Big Boss says if you miss the point of life while you're livin', the only way you can take in the *importance of love and understandin' is if you're able to feel the pain you inflicted. Then you can appreciate where you fell short of the mark. It's a simple process, really. Simple enough, even, for a red-headed country boy like me.*

·35·

endell Metcalf leaned back in his chair and studied the posters he'd made: NO SPECIAL RIGHTS FOR HOMOSEXUALS! They were red, white, and blue, as were the buckets Suzette had painted for him in which to collect donations. Good, he thought. After all, we're the real Americans, not those limp-wristed, East coast, screaming liberal faggots.

What we ought to do, he thought, is load them all up on a great big boat, send it out into the middle of the Atlantic Ocean, and sink it. Then we could see how many of their liberal pals would try to swim out and save them. He could just picture chubby, red-faced Teddy Kennedy getting yanked under the surf by schools of dykes and cross-dressers, all of them trying to save themselves by drowning each other. The thought of it made Wendell Metcalf almost laugh out loud, something he hadn't done very often in his life.

He dragged out one more piece of poster board, flattened it out with his palms, then slid the T-square from his desk drawer and proceeded to draw a perfect octagon. This would be one of his best, the universal sign people notice most often. They would do it instinctively, and he'd have their attention hooked before they knew what hit them. It would be red with a white border and in the center it would say STOP! Below it he would write: THE MILITANT HOMOSEXUAL AGENDA—VOTE YES ON MEASURE 19.

The venom oozing from Wendell Metcalf's pores as he finished up this last poster made the room smell sour, but he didn't notice. Nor did he notice that his shirt was soaked through and stuck to his back. All he knew was that with each task he completed in his efforts to get Measure 19 passed, he was one step closer to driving the stake through the heart of the monster who lived inside him. He could not rest. He would not stop.

·36·

The amber eye looked back at him, flat and unseeing, almost as dead as his own had been for most of his life. Donnie Zoeller picked up the severed head of the chicken with the tip of the big bowie knife he'd just used on it. He stood in front of the mirror watching himself hold the knife and the dripping, bloody head high in the air.

He was shirtless but felt no chill. He had just lifted weights for an hour or more and his muscles were pumped. The veins on his arms stood out like blue surgical tubing running just under his Aryan skin. He felt a rush almost like orgasm as the chicken's blood began to stream down his arm, mixing with the wet hair in his armpit and creating a raw, rank odor. This is how the victorious must feel, he thought, to be able to hold the bloody heads of the conquered high in the air for everyone to see.

The smell of his own body mixed with the bird's blood almost hypnotized him. He could not stop staring at his reflection, even as a crinkle deep in his brain registered the fact that someone else had entered the room. It was Mo, back from a stolen car run to Medford, who stood staring at the bizarre scene across the room.

"What the fuck are you doin', man?" he shouted, as Donnie turned slowly to face him.

Donnie Zoeller's face had taken on an angular look, almost pointed and ferret-like. His eyes were slitted and dull, the same color and flat look of damp clay. There was no soul behind them.

"Practicing," he said, turning back to look at himself in the mirror.

Mo felt himself shiver inside and something gripped tightly and then loosened just as quickly in his bowels. He was afraid he might shit himself.

"Practicing for what?" Mo asked.

"For when we take over," Donnie said.

"Take over what?" Mo asked. "This stupid town? Who needs it? They can have it, for all I care." He pitched a sack of junk food and snacks onto the rickety green table, hoping to act as natural as he could so Donnie wouldn't weird out. This bastard was nuts. Now Mo knew that for sure.

"No," Donnie Zoeller said, "this town is only the start. The world would be nice, but America will do." He finally lowered his arm, placed the knife with the chicken's head still on it in an empty Slurpee cup and set it by his homemade altar. With a deliberate, spooky slowness, he lit a candle, then turned back to face Mo. The odor in the room was putrid, worse than a butcher's shop on a hot day, what with the smelly kerosene heater fouling the air and the chicken's blood and God knows what else rotting away in this dump. Mo felt queasy, tried to hold his breath, didn't know what to do.

"So," Donnie asked, "what do you think?"

"About what?" Mo asked, trying to act casual.

"Don't be stupid," Donnie said, stroking his bloody arm. "This," he said, suddenly snatching the Slurpee cup off the altar and jamming it under Mo's chin.

Mo backed away, trying to push Donnie's hand from him, trying to keep from heaving right there on both of them. "Are you with me?" Donnie screamed, "or are you afraid? Do you think I'm brilliant? Do you think I'm crazy?"

Donnie followed him around the room as Mo scrambled like a crab. He was trying to hurry without running, to get away without being killed. His build was sloppy and unkempt, no match for Donnie's muscular physique. Donnie could kick his ass up to the top of Mt. Bachelor and back down without even having to take a deep breath. Mo knew that much in his heart.

In the shuffle backwards, Mo's feet got tangled in a discarded pizza box and he fell over. He lay flat on his back and totally vulnerable, before bolting upright as if spring-loaded. This is what he also knew: Donnie Zoeller could cut off his head just as easily as he had cut off the chicken's and never think twice about it. He tried to stay as calm as he could.

"Look, Z," Mo said, "this is getting too far out for me. I just wanted to have some fun and hang out, maybe make a little money now and then, you know?"

Donnie glared at Mo, inching slowly at him again with the Slurpee cup.

"I didn't sign on for killing and blood and guts and taking over the whole goddamned world," Mo said. There. It was out in the open. He waited for something to happen—the soundless slice of Donnie's big blade across his throat, the swift, sudden blast of Donnie's knee in his groin—something, but nothing happened. The smell in the room was awful.

Mo watched Donnie's face change as it took on an almost fatherly look. Was that compassion in his eyes? Concern? No, it couldn't be that, Mo was almost certain. Donnie brought his face within inches of Mo's and looked directly into his eyes. What Donnie was about to say was the very thing the Zoeller men had said to their children for generations, a tradition as true as the passing down of a pocketwatch. It is what every young boy in the family had heard from his father and grew up to say to his offspring, the very thing that had kept this family on its course of self-destruction.

"You," Donnie hissed at Mo, "are worthless."

By the time Mo had gathered his junk and slammed out of the dungeon-like room, Donnie Zoeller was in a trance, watching himself in the mirror as he sat surrounded by candles and pictures of Adolph Hitler, his hero, his idol.

Donnie glanced at his tattoos and noticed they seemed to be pulsating. The chicken's blood had dried to a crusty, reddish-brown webbing on his right arm which, at this moment, filled him with a thrilling anticipation. He felt alive, possibly for the first time since he had killed the llama. It did not occur to him that this feeling of exhilaration, this paradoxical aliveness, had come to him through the death of something else. He only knew that he would have to have this feeling again. Bigger. More. Soon.

·37·

The Reverend Darryl Dimmer was doing what he loved doing most in the world, counting the Lord's tax-free American money. He, being one of the Lord's chosen disciples, felt himself the perfect steward for the staggering amount of cash now flowing into the offices of the Mt. Goshen Church of the Righteous. After all, he was just as deserving as the next of his slice of this particular spiritual and financial pie.

Juanita's idea to take out ads for their antihomosexual videotape and audio cassette series in several national fundamentalist publications had been a stellar one, he had to admit. As a matter of fact, his wife's ability to keep a scorching eye on the bottom line continued to be a source of pleasure to him.

"You can't count on money from the people in Reliance, Darryl," she had said, "they're too fickle. I can feel it in my bones. Another mill just shut down and more people are out of work. It's unrealistic to think they won't run out of money to give. And besides, in case you haven't noticed, attendance has been down for the past three weeks. If this is a trend, then it's not a good sign. I think we should go national with it and I know just how to do it." She then waved an armload of magazines and newspapers in his face.

Darryl Dimmer had sat there rather dumbfounded. No, in fact, he hadn't noticed attendance being down, hadn't noticed that at all. He was glad his sweet wife was on top of things, just as she always managed to be, God bless her.

He smiled as he remembered how they had huddled together in his office that afternoon just last summer and put together a series of print ads. Juanita Dimmer instantly faxed them out to at least a dozen publications. Within days their phone was ringing off the hook with orders. Their mailbox was jammed with checks and money orders, even cash, along with requests for more information on ways to stop the militant homosexual agenda in America.

Darryl and Juanita Dimmer realized at once that they'd tapped into a motherlode. They had hit a vein of income so deep and wide all they had to do was prime the pump and hold the bucket as it came gushing out toward them.

If church attendance had dropped off, well, he could fix that one, Darryl Dimmer felt sure of it. It was just a matter of focus, and nobody could focus on getting what he wanted from a congregation better than the Reverend Darryl Dimmer. Why, Christmas was just around the corner and he always managed to pack the pews with his Christmas sermons: Joseph and Mary, poor but never on welfare; baby Jesus, sent to earth by God for the specific purpose of saving the United States of America from communism, the homosexuals, and the liberal elite; the virgin birth of our savior in a stable, proving that the slutty little tramps giving birth these days to a trainload of illegitimate bastards was God's answer to a nation gone bad. Why, there wasn't one of them in the lot worthy of touching the hem on the robe of the blessed virgin, not a single one of the despicable little jezebels pure enough to lick the dust off the sandals of Lord Jesus who, Reverend Dimmer was pretty certain about this, probably hated the wretched little harlots even more than he did. Fat chance any of them would have of ever experiencing a miracle in their lives.

Just as surely as he knew he was called to do the work of the Lord, Darryl Dimmer was certain nobody in the world could mix up a Fear of God cocktail like he could. Yessir, take your basic guilt, mix in a little fear, a little anger, a big dash of loathing, shake it all up and pretty soon you've got a congregation breathing fire and ready for more.

Darryl Dimmer had this number down. He'd done it one thousand times. No, he'd done it ten thousand times and, by God, he'd do it ten thousand more. He'd preach against the liberals and the communists and the homosexuals and the ecologists and all the New Age gurus until his vocal cords disintegrated if that's what it took to get his message across, if that's what it took to win.

He let out a big sigh and leaned back in the leather chair, staring

lovingly at the boxes and boxes of video and audio cassettes. His words—
his words, sent directly to him by God above—were about to set the
world on fire, a fire that would fume and smolder and burn until it
finally matched the one in his belly. It was a good feeling.

Darryl Dimmer stacked the checks together, wrapped a rubber band
around the currency, and dropped the change into the petty cash box.
Placing the checks and money in a leather bag, he slid it into his jacket
pocket, inside, next to his heart. He liked the feel of it next to him,
liked knowing this was only the beginning, just as he reveled in the
thought of doing God's work, saving America from evil, and expand-
ing his ever-growing portfolio. No reason why a person can't do well
while doing good, thought the Reverend Darryl Dimmer. No, praise
God, there was absolutely no reason for that at all.

·38·

Jimmy Heron was dreaming, and in this dream he was scuba diving through crystal turquoise waters with Lou and Curly Red. Brilliantly colored fish of every description swam around them. Bubbles surrounded their faces when they smiled at each other.

A banging at the door of his trailer made him stir. He struggled to get back into his dream, wanting to stay with the two people he loved most in the world. He knew that in the dream he must swim to the surface, but they both held onto his hands as if begging him not to go. When he attempted to swim upward with them, the weight was like trying to pull a bale of wet hay with each hand. Eventually, he had to release them.

Another knock, louder than the first, made him turn over in his bed facing the wall. Finally, three knocks—BOOM-BOOM-BOOM!— brought Jimmy Heron to consciousness and he sat straight up in bed, his eyes wide open. He looked at his watch and mashed in his Beltones. It was early afternoon. He got up to answer the door.

At the bottom of the steps stood Leigh O'Brien, pregnant and glowing. The sight of her almost took his breath away. Her dark red hair and purple-and-gray poncho stood out against the eye-frying whiteness of the snow. Jimmy Heron felt sure she was the most beautiful woman he'd ever seen. Then he felt instantly guilty for having a thought like that, as if he'd just cheated on Lou, even though he'd never really thought of his wife as beautiful. No, cute is mostly how he saw her, with such a spirit, such an aliveness, that from the time he first laid eyes on her, he knew he was a goner.

He smiled at Leigh and she smiled back up at him, shielding her eyes from the glare.

"You lose your way?" he asked, holding the door open with one hand, offering her the other. She lumbered up the steps, a Mama Bear kind of waddle, the coat he'd lent her slung over one shoulder.

"Nope," she said. "I needed to return this coat to you and to invite you up for sandwiches and festivities. And, I'll have you know, I'm under strict orders not to come back without you, so get yourself together and let's go."

"What's the occasion?"

"You'll see when we get there."

"I look a mess," Jimmy said. "Perhaps I should shave." He rubbed the stubble on his chin.

"When was the last time you shaved, Jimmy?" Leigh asked.

"This morning."

"Close enough. We've all seen whiskers before. Let's go."

Leigh's manner was determined, her voice no-nonsense. Jimmy began tucking in his shirttail, looking around for his glasses.

"What grade did you say you teach?" he asked.

"Fifth," she said.

"That explains why I feel like I'm ten years old," he replied.

Leigh O'Brien blushed, her freckles blending together just for the moment, as she realized what a schoolmarm she was being.

"I'm sorry, Jimmy," she said. "I'm so used to rounding up all the kids, and you know how ten-year olds dawdle and lag and make excuses and piddle, and, well, school's out now for Christmas vacation, but I guess I'm not out of school yet. Forgive me." She smiled at him again.

"Forgiven," he said, and grinned back at her.

Jimmy slid his big feet into some new waterproof boots, the ones with the rubber soles, and laced the skinny waxed laces up tight. Even brand new, they fit perfectly, like he'd had them for years and years. He was delighted about that since he'd learned the hard way how easy it was to bust your butt on ice and snow in the leather-soled cowboy boots he usually wore.

He grabbed a jacket and his hat, retrieved his leather gloves from the pocket, then went out the door and down the steps, helping Leigh after him. She held onto his arm tightly, as much to support him as herself, and they crept slowly up the driveway and onto the road, their bodies leaning into each other.

"You smell like my dad," Leigh said, nudging Jimmy's shoulder with her own.

"Your dad wears Old Spice?"

"If they make it in heaven, he's got it on," Leigh said.

"Oh," said Jimmy, "I'm sorry. I forgot he had died. How long ago?"

"Ten years. Next month."

"And how did he die? Do you mind my asking?"

"No," said Leigh, "I don't mind at all. He had renal cancer—kidney cancer—and lived for a couple of years after they found the tumor and removed it. Mother didn't last very long once he was gone, about four years before she passed away, too."

"Of cancer?" Jimmy asked.

"Heart attack," Leigh said. "She died in her sleep one night. I don't think it was a hard death; at least, I hope not. I'm just sorry I didn't have a chance to say good-bye like I did with Dad."

"Oh," Jimmy said, "I'm very sorry. What about brothers and sisters? Do you have any?"

"I have one brother. He's a rancher in eastern Oregon."

"Are you close?" asked Jimmy.

"We were as kids, but not anymore," Leigh said. "He and his wife don't approve of my—they say *lifestyle,* I say *life.* Since I'm not willing to be anybody other than who I am, well, it's just easier not to be around each other."

"Do you miss them?" Jimmy asked.

"Very much," Leigh replied. "And I miss my nephews, Drew and Nicholas. They were just little guys the last time I saw them, in first grade and kindergarten. Both of them called me Antly, like Aunt Leigh was all one word. They even used to write my name like that in the goofy letters I'd get from them every so often." Leigh fell silent and when Jimmy looked at her, tears were beginning a slow roll down both her cheeks.

"We can change the subject," he said.

"Oh, it's not a problem, Jimmy, just one of those disappointments I shove way to the back in there that pops out to take a swing at me from time to time." She squeezed his arm. "Thanks for listening," she said.

Arriving at the bottom of Cory and Leigh's driveway, Jimmy Heron stared up the hill toward the log home. He had no idea how he, a man nearing seventy years of age, and a totally pregnant woman nearing the moment of birth, were going to scale this icy mountain before them. Reading his thoughts, Leigh took him by the arm.

"Come on," she said. "This is easier than it looks. I followed Ned through here." She took off up the side of the drive, pulling herself upward on the low-slung branches of a giant juniper tree with one hand, cradling her belly with the other, nudging at rocks and roots for a toehold.

Jimmy kept up, staying right behind her, even resting one hand on the small of her back, as a gentleman would. "The trick is," she said, "to never, never stop. You just keep pulling and tugging and grabbing and sweating and climbing, until-you-get-all-the-way-to-the-top!"

They burst through the hedge at the crest of the hill beside the porch, pausing to catch their breath and whap each other's backs in wordless congratulations. When they could speak once again, Jimmy stared at Leigh in disbelief.

"My goodness," he said, "you are really strong! I always think of pregnant women as being so fragile."

"Fragile? Me? No way. I'm tough as a boot heel. Besides, I need the exercise. Of course, I've never had a baby before and I may change my tune once labor starts. Come on, let's go in the back. If we're lucky, Cory and Jonah will already have the hard part handled."

Leigh and Jimmy slipped in the back door, tiptoeing through the kitchen and dining room. They stood in the doorway, watching Cory and Jonah stretch out strand after strand of Christmas lights across the living room floor, checking to see if any were fizzled out. None were. The tree, a lush Noble fir, stood in the corner and was already ablaze with brilliant lights of every color.

"The problem, see," Cory was saying to Jonah, "is that we never seem to remember that we've already got enough lights to stretch from here to El Paso. One or both of us always buys another box or two and, well, as you can see, it's gotten away from us. We are out of control. I wonder if there's a 12-step program for Irresponsible Christmas Tree Light Consumers."

She reached for an empty box and handed it to Jonah. "Here," she said, coiling up the overflow strands of lights, "let's pack these up and I'll take them to the shelter in Bend. I think those folks could certainly use a little extra sparkle in their lives right now."

Jonah dropped the lights in the box. Cory was heading toward the dining room with them when she spotted Jimmy and Leigh in the doorway. She let out a yell, somewhere between a whoop and a hog call.

"Hooooooeee!" she shouted, "we've got Texas all over the place! I knew she'd talk you into coming along!" She ran over to Jimmy and gave him a big hug. Jonah bounded across the room to shake Jimmy's hand and pound his shoulder. Ned bolted awake from his nap and trotted over to nudge Jimmy's hand up with his big head and leave a happy drop or two on the toe of Jimmy's new Timberland boot.

"Glad you're here, Jimmy," Jonah said. "Really glad."

"And I appreciate the invitation," Jimmy replied. "I came to help, so what do you want me to do?" He glanced around at the boxes of ornaments.

"Ornaments," Cory said. "Grab 'em and go. The hard part, the lights, have already been handled by my friend Mr. Sullivan here, and yours truly. Now we're just down to the fun part."

She handed a box of homemade ornaments to Jimmy. He looked inside and saw little wooden reindeer, Santa Claus in a sleigh, a tiny cowboy boot, a wooden cardinal, a red Pegasus made of papier-mâché, and a carved wooden wreath with the words *Happy Yule, Y'all* across the front. In the bottom of the box he spotted a metal ornament painted like the Texas state flag. He picked it up and held it gingerly by the string.

"This may be my favorite one," he said, twirling the little flag in the air, glancing at Cory, who knew exactly what he meant.

"Mine, too," she said, giving Jimmy the Hook 'em Horns sign like some sort of secret handshake.

Within an hour, the group had beautifully adorned the tree, completing it with a tasteful strand of tiny, almost iridescent silver beads.

Checking to see that they had not overlooked anything, Jimmy fished an ornament out of the corner of the box. It had almost been forgotten—a small pink triangle on a string with *Peace* written on it. "What's this?" he asked.

"Oh, that one," Leigh laughed. "That's our Militant Homosexual Agenda. We asked every gay person we know if they had one and nobody did. We didn't, either, so we made our own. Last year or the year before, I think."

"Yeah," Cory said, "we got tired of the *Right* being the only ones who know what the homosexual agenda is. Every day Leigh would ask me, 'Honey, did you remember to pick up our agenda?' and I'd have to say, 'No, I didn't. Gosh, we must have left it at the motel and packed the towels instead.' So, now we don't have to worry about it. We have our very own."

"Cory," Leigh said, "there's a small box on the dining room table. Can you dash in there and get it?"

"I'm from west Texas," Cory replied indignantly. "I don't dash, I saunter." Then she strolled into the dining room while Leigh and Jonah looked at each other, rolling their eyes. "There," she said, bringing the box back and setting it down. Leigh opened it right away and carefully extracted the packing.

"This," Leigh said, lifting the angel gently out of the box, "is the most special ornament of all. Some of my kids made it for me when I taught second grade years ago. They named him Gabriel, and I promised to put him on top of every Christmas tree I ever decorated from then on. I'm not sure how they decided Gabriel had red hair, but he's cute, huh?" Jimmy nodded. "Look," Leigh said, "he's even got his own trumpet. I think he's playing 'Hello, Dolly.'"

"Oh, and look what I found in Bend," Cory said, pulling two long strands of what looked like cranberries out of a large bag. They were fake cranberries, small wooden balls painted dark red and strung together. "I thought this was just one of the most brilliant things I'd ever seen. They don't shrivel up or rot and fall off on the floor. They don't leak and stain your clothes or get stuck down in the cushions of the couch. And, best of all, we don't have to string them."

Cory and Leigh each grabbed an end and began draping the strands around the tree. Jonah placed the angel carefully on the tree's top branch, making sure the trumpet was in full view from the living room.

"We eliminated the popcorn a couple of years ago," Leigh said. "Our sociopathic dog"—she pointed to Ned with her head as he lay snoozing by the woodstove—"kept dragging long strings of it off the tree. He even toppled it once."

The four of them stepped back toward the dining room to admire their handiwork which, they all agreed, was awesome. Spectacular, actually, almost with a life of its own. The angel Gabriel, perched atop the tree, seemed to be smiling at them, as if at any moment he might put the trumpet up to his lips and blow like Harry James. They could not stop staring at it.

"This may be our most beautiful tree ever," Cory gushed.

"You say that every year, sweetheart," Leigh said, looping an arm through Cory's.

"And I mean it every year," Cory said.

Jimmy Heron suddenly felt himself so overwhelmed with emotion he thought he might burst.

"I thought I would never be doing this again," he said, "not without Lou, not without my wife." He sat down in one of the dining room chairs and leaned his elbows on the table, resting his head in his hands.

Cory and Leigh stayed with him as Jonah made his way to the kitchen and returned with plates of tuna sandwiches and fruit, glasses of water, and cups of spiced cider.

"I feel guilty that I'm actually having a good time," Jimmy said. "It seems like it all happened only yesterday, as if she were just here, right beside me, and then all of a sudden she's gone." He began to cry silently, his stomach bellowing in and out. Although neither of them knew what to say to comfort him, both women stayed close to him, touching his shoulder, or rubbing his neck or back now and then, while they let him grieve.

"We made pies for our friends for Christmas, did I tell you that? Just pies. I made the crust, Lou made the filling. We knew the favorite kind of almost every person in Montague County. Our neighbor, fella named Web Hardy, always said our pies were so good he just couldn't make up his mind. So Lou made him two, sometimes three. Pumpkin, blueberry, pecan, they were all good. And coconut. Coconut meringue. That was our favorite. We planned to open our own pie shop someday—it was a dream of ours. We talked about it all the time.

"We'd stopped off at Judd's Cafeteria in Killeen for coconut pie the day she got killed. Who would have thought that a simple decision like that could change your whole life? For a piece of pie. It doesn't make sense. It just doesn't make sense." He took a deep breath and let out a long sigh. Leigh took his hand.

"No, Jimmy," she said, "it doesn't make sense. So much of what happens in the world these days doesn't make sense. But the one thing I know that *does* make sense is to count on the people who love you to help you get through. We can be there for you, Jimmy, the part of the equation you can count on." She squeezed his hand.

"We're like rat terriers, Jimmy," Cory said. "We won't stop and we won't let go." She patted his shoulder. Jimmy shook his head, squeezing Leigh's hand and reaching to touch Cory's on his shoulder. "And I promise you something else," Cory said. "You will never again see a piece of pie in this house."

"Oh, no, now," he said, "I don't want you to give up something you like because of me."

"It's not a problem," Cory said. "I need to lose ten pounds anyway." She looked at the three of them as they stared back at her. "Okay, twenty... five. Besides," she added, "I make the best darned brownies in the whole Pacific Northwest."

·39·

By the time their meal was done and the kitchen cleaned up, the sun had just ducked behind the mountains and lent a pinkish hue to the gathering darkness. Jimmy Heron hugged both women as he said his good-byes, holding onto them both a little longer than he could ever have imagined holding onto, say, Winnie Bridwell, or any of the country women from back home to whom he could never fully explain the kind of pain he was feeling.

It seemed to him that he had been expected to buck up, knuckle down and get on with his life, when all he really wanted to do most of the time was peel his heart out of his chest and drop-kick it clear to the Gulf of Mexico in order to stop the pain.

Cory and Leigh understood this. Somehow, they just knew. He took comfort in the fact that he wasn't expected to be anything other than the way he was when he was with them. For this, he was thankful.

As Jimmy made his way toward the door, Jonah grabbed a jacket off the hook. "Hold on a second, Jimmy. I'll walk you home," he said, and took the older man's arm to help him down the steps and the hill beside the slippery drive.

On the road, the two walked along slowly, hands stuffed deep into their pockets, their breath coming out like smoke drifting away in the dusky air.

"Do you dream about your wife, Jimmy?" Jonah asked. "Have you seen her in your dreams yet?"

"Oh, yes," Jimmy replied. "I dreamed about her almost right away. I don't know if that's good or bad. I mean, I'm always glad to be able to see her, but then it's upsetting to me to realize it was only a dream." Jimmy sighed and hung his head for a moment, stabbing at the snow-covered gravel with the toe of his boot. "But I'd sure rather see her than not see her, so I guess that's my answer." He took a deep breath and leaned back, looking up into the tops of the trees. Or to heaven. The pines made a *swish-swish-swishing* sound in the wind.

Jonah thought for a moment before replying. "It's important to remember that a dream is more than a movie running in your head, Jimmy, don't you think? Your spirit, your soul—some would call it your deep psyche—is busy at work when you dream, teaching you, dropping hints that you can learn from. And if your dream happens to include people you love who have already left this earth, well, that's all the better. There is a Lakota word for that," he said. "It's *unma'ciya'tan,* which means 'from the other side, from the other world.' It is an honor, truly an honor, to be able to communicate with the other side, an honor usually reserved for the elders who are medicine men and women. My Uncle Jerome did it all the time and told me about it. That's how I grew up never fearing death.

"Repeated fasts and vision quests—*hanblecheya,* those are called—make it easier to speak with the Spirit World. Uncle Jerome taught me how, but I'm not as good at it as he was. Got too much white man in me, I guess."

"And explain to me just what a vision quest is," said Jimmy. "I hate to admit how ignorant I am about all of this. My wife and I would've thought a vision quest was when we went to Bowie to get our glasses checked." Jonah nodded and laughed a low, polite rumble.

"A vision quest is what it says," he said, "a seeking of clearer sight, a way to quiet your mind so you can hear the important voices when they come to you. For me, it works best to go off by myself in the woods for several days. The animals look out for me, Mother Earth nurtures me, and I understand more about why I'm here, what the plan is for all of us. Other people may have different ways, but this works best for me."

"How long does it take to be able to do that?" Jimmy asked.

"It takes as long as it takes. That's all, just as long as it takes. You see, Jimmy, in the Lakota language, there is no word for time, and that's often a frustrating thing for most people to understand, especially Anglos. 'They're an impatient species,' Uncle Jerome used to say, and he always added, 'No wonder they understand so little.'" Jonah looked at

Jimmy and smiled. "No offense," he said.

"None taken," replied Jimmy. "Do you see your uncle in your dreams?"

"Oh, yes," replied Jonah. "I see him quite often. He's always wearing a purple football jersey with a big number four on the front. That's how I know it's really him."

"And how's that?"

"Well, first, it's his big, ugly face with his two bottom teeth missing and the mole on the left side of his nose. Purple is a spiritual color and four is a sacred number for the Lakota people. And every single time he says to me, *Ma Lakota,* which means I am Lakota, the very first words he taught me. It's my Uncle Jerome, all right. Even my deep psyche couldn't make that one up."

The men walked along for another fifty yards in silence. As they climbed up the slick little slope, not much more than a big bump, really, to Jimmy's gravel driveway, Jonah caught hold of Jimmy's arm. "I have something to share with you, my friend," he said, "and you may do whatever you need to with this information." Jonah paused for a moment to gather his thoughts, to form his words clearly before he continued.

"In Native American culture," he said, "there is a name for deep loss. It is called a *giveaway* instead of *loss.* It is something of great importance to you which your spirit has already agreed to give up in order for something else to take its place. This is all part of your growth. It is one of the most difficult gifts we get, but we need to learn to look at it that way. The elders have told me this, and it has been my challenge, too, in this life.

"When you are able to again speak your truth, Jimmy, the sadness lifts and you can begin to take your power back. It is then that whatever is waiting to come into your life can enter. I wonder if this is the meaning behind such a tragic loss for you. Perhaps something or someone is on the verge of filling up that space. There is no way to know, of course, and it doesn't make your loss any less real, but it might make it hurt less if you can look at it that way."

Jimmy stared at Jonah for several seconds as the concept sank in. "Well," he said, finally, "it's something to think about."

"There is one other thing, my friend," Jonah said, looking even more solemn. "I have told this to no one and I want it to stay only between us." Jimmy nodded.

"I think I will be leaving this world soon, Jimmy," Jonah said. "I have seen it in my dreams, more and more recently. It is not frightening, but thrilling, actually, like looking forward to a wonderful trip. If it happens, I want you to know that we are friends, brothers in the truest sense of the word, and I will get through to you from the other side. I will tell your wife of your love for her, you can believe me on this." He squeezed Jimmy's arm in his strong hand.

"But why?" Jimmy asked. "How?"

"Those things are not important to know," Jonah said, "and, anyway, I could be wrong. I have been before. Many times. I just needed to tell you and let you know I am looking forward to it, that I am not afraid."

"Well," said Jimmy, feeling his eyes moisten, "I don't know if I get to vote on this one, but I cast my vote on the side that wants you to stick around. I am in need of a brother right now. I haven't had one in a long time."

"Since your friend Curly Red, right? I remember you told me about him. I know you miss him, but remember this: the shepherd always brings his flock back. Always. Some just get back to the barn sooner than others, that's all. Eventually, the barn will hold us all. Together. Don't you worry."

Jonah quickly gave Jimmy a hug. "I must go," he said. "*Toksa*—that's Lakota for 'we'll see you.' It's what you say when you see someone off." He turned and sprinted back up the driveway in that smooth, silent gait he had, so light on his feet he barely left a track in the snow. Looking back once, Jonah waved to Jimmy as he disappeared into the velvety darkness.

The cold night wind blew, shooting an icy gust off the top of Three-Fingered Jack as relentless and piercing as an arrow, chilling Jimmy Heron's back all the way through to the inside of his ribcage. He shivered against the wind, jamming his hands even further into his pockets.

"*Toksa,*" Jimmy Heron heard himself whisper, as the Spirit World sucked his voice right out of his mouth and straight up into the sky.

·40·

y Sunday, December 22nd, three days before Christmas, the town of Reliance, bathed in snow and Christmas cheer, looked like a painting or postcard of the perfect western town. Snow clung in poofy cotton balls to the branches and needles of the pines and junipers. It draped the craggy tops of monolithic volcanic boulders—such a dark red they almost looked purple—in the town square next to the bronze sculpture of the Oregon Trail Pioneers. Someone had encircled the bronze heads of the pioneer children with gold garlands, making them look like angels. HAPPY HOLLY-DAZE the sign said on the front door of the Wigwam Grill & Tavern. Over on the other side of the square, Dick Barstow had painted giant screws and bolts with stripes like candy canes onto the windows of his hardware store.

The town looked Sunday-morning sleepy with not much activity, only the occasional clickety rattle, like fingernails drumming on a countertop, of studded snow tires or chains across the powdery covering, as people began making their way to church or out for breakfast. Maybe at Hobo Hank's on the highway to Bend. Hank Thomason's steadfast refusal to close on Sunday despite pressure from the Mt. Goshen Church of the Righteous had given Darryl and Juanita Dimmer the excuse they needed to call his restaurant Heathen Hank's.

Every so often, a car would pass through the town square loaded to the top with kids and dogs and Christmas presents, a jumbled mass of yuletide cheer and wrapping paper, slushing its way to Grandma's for the holidays or a warmer climate somewhere.

In the shadow of Mt. Bachelor, at the Mt. Goshen Church of the Righteous, red poinsettias lined the stage and all the way up the aisle, one at the end of each pew. OUR SAVIOR IS BORN! shouted the banner hanging from the front of the stage, right below the chair where the

184

Reverend Darryl Dimmer parked his portly self to sweat and pant and recover at the end of each sermon.

Tom Mason, feeling antsy and out of place, sat toward the back of the sanctuary. Looking around, he noticed how many vacant pews there were. Probably a lot of folks are away for Christmas, he thought, although Darryl's Christmas sermons usually packed the house. At least that's the way he remembered it.

Although it pained him immensely, Tom was without his family, as well, on this Sunday morning, just as he had been at each church service since his daughter slugged the preacher's son in the nose. Jenny and Kate Mason were at services right now at the Methodist church on the road toward Redmond, after having put their collective foot down. They refused to ever again listen to the hateful rantings of Darryl Dimmer or watch the pious nodding of Juanita Dimmer's head in the front pew as she set the example for the congregation by nodding or applauding at appropriate places in the sermon.

For Tom Mason, it was like seeing everything and everyone here in an entirely different light.

She's a shill, thought Tom, as he watched Juanita, probably better dressed than most in her brown wool suit, but a shill nonetheless. Just as surely as a carnival barker sets up somebody to win a big prize and then parade around the fairgrounds with it, making sure everyone knows where it came from. Like the old men who were paid to yell "Bravo!" at the end of a concert to get the crowd started, Juanita Dimmer's job was to keep the enthusiasm for her husband's message revved up and furious, milking the congregation for all it was worth. The thought of it, and how obvious it was to him right at this moment, made Tom Mason feel sick to his stomach. Why was he only now seeing it? He felt ashamed that he'd not listened more closely to his daughter.

Tom looked at his watch, trying to figure out how much time was left. Maybe he could sneak out without creating a stink. What had he come here for? Was it to hear Darryl Dimmer rant on? Tom had already counted five times Darryl had said *militant homosexual agenda* this morning. Was it to hear his preacher thunder about the sorry state of the public school system? The liberal teachers and the lazy administrators? The Congress? The feminists? The environmentalists? The rest of society? Was it to watch Darryl Dimmer hold forth about the greed and sin and worthlessness of mankind? No. No, by God, Tom decided, that's not what he came to church for. It was supposed to be about teaching people how to love each other. How did all this other stuff get mixed up in it and still get called religion?

Tom Mason's mind was swirling when Darryl Dimmer's voice boomed out. "Ladies and gentlemen, I want you to know that my family has been the target of religious persecution, and I want you to know that we are not fearful, because Jesus has said that if you follow him, if you remain true to the task of following God, you will be persecuted. Say it with me—*I will be persecuted.*

"My oldest son's nose was almost broken a few weeks ago for no other reason than stating his religious beliefs."

There was an audible gasp from some people in the congregation, although Tom was pretty sure the first gasp came from Juanita, leading the way. She snatched Rodney Dimmer up by the collar and made him stand and face the rest of the congregation, showing them his swollen nose and the purplish-yellow puffiness still around his eyes. Rodney hung his head, trying for an instant to wrench himself free from his mother's grasp, as humiliated about being seen with his face all puffed up as for being slugged by a girl.

Tom felt his ears begin to get hot and knew the tips of them were turning red. He knew what Darryl Dimmer was saying to be a lie.

"My son's First Amendment rights, the right of free speech, were violated and his physical safety severely jeopardized," Reverend Dimmer continued, "and there is no doubt in my mind that it is all part of a larger conspiracy in this great nation to stifle free speech. It is a conspiracy of the left-wing liberals and their pansy, elitist friends to silence the real messengers of truth in America, the only ones who see the United States draped in the chains of Satan, the ones who are willing to stand up and say the truth about that.

"Well, I have news for Mr. Satan. I have a message for the Prince of Darkness. And I have news for the liberals in America. It is time for the Christians of this nation, the real Americans, to rise up and slay the dragon, to bring him to his slimy knees, to cut off his head and the heads of all who follow him into his lair of degradation and filth.

There won't be a closet big enough or deep enough for all of them to hide in. We will pursue. We will seek and destroy. We will smoke them out and burn them to ashes with the torches of truth placed firmly in the hands of God's true believers, and we will bask in the glory of righteousness as we march toward victory!"

The members of the congregation stood, cheering, with a fist or two shooting up and punching at the air. They had begun to sing as the organist boomed out "Onward Christian Soldiers," when they heard a man shouting wildly. Everyone turned to see their sheriff, Tom Mason, who had jumped out into the aisle and was yelling at the preacher, using his Bible as a pointer.

The organist, the last one to notice the commotion, finally stopped playing and the room fell silent. Somebody coughed a cough of embarrassment and awkwardness. The room felt too thick.

"You're not telling the truth, Darryl," shouted Tom. "Why do you insist on teaching people to hate each other? Where in the Bible does it say we should all hate everyone different from us? Tell me, Darryl, just where do you read that? I would really like to know!"

Tom waved his Bible at the stage and began walking toward the preacher, who was so startled at this outburst that he wiped his forehead harder than normal, knocking his hairpiece askew. Reverend Dimmer appeared to have a golf cap resting on the back of his head.

Juanita whirled in her seat to face Tom, her large brown eyes glaring at him like a startled beast of some sort. He about halfway expected her to snort and breathe fire, maybe paw at the plush, royal blue carpet with a big cloven hoof.

"Satan!" she hissed at Tom.

"Sinner!" somebody else shouted from across the room.

"Sinner, probably," said Tom. "Satan? I don't think so. And I don't think you believe that, either. But hating is a sin. And bearing false witness against your neighbor is a sin. Inciting people to acts of violence, however, is against the law. My job is to uphold it," Tom said, "and I won't sit idly by and watch the law get broken."

He looked around the room at the people in the sanctuary. Some of them looked frightened, others thoughtful or puzzled. And then others, like Juanita Dimmer and Wendell Metcalf, had looks of pure hatred on their faces. Suzette Metcalf, Tom noticed, wore that same distracted, disconnected look she always had, as if the whole idea of confrontation was just too icky to think about. She pulled a nail file from her purse and began a furious concentration on her cuticles, furrowing her brow at the thought of anything unpleasant.

Darryl Dimmer rose, straightening his hairpiece, sliding it forward and patting it into place. He began walking slowly, deliberately, toward the front of the stage. He was smiling in a condescending manner, as he might at a small, stupid boy.

"Tom, Tom, Tom," Darryl Dimmer said, "I see Satan has you wrapped securely in his claws today." He began to chuckle, and the sound of it made the blond hair on the back of Tom Mason's neck stand straight up.

The preacher reached out to touch him, and Tom jumped as if he'd been shocked by electricity. He stared back at Reverend Dimmer.

"Satan's not part of this equation today, Darryl. This is you. And me. And the truth," Tom said.

"Jesus, our dear, sweet Lamb of God, had his detractors, Tom," Darryl said. "Why even Peter, one of his very own disciples, Jesus said, would deny him three times before the cock crowed. And he did."

Tom turned and began walking up the aisle toward the main exit before he turned back to face the preacher one last time. He was breathing so hard he thought the back of his suit jacket would split open. He loosened his collar and tie with one quick jerk of his finger—so hard the top button of his shirt popped off and bounced under one of the pews—and swept back the perspiration now glistening across his forehead. A bead of sweat trickled down in front of his left ear. His knuckles were white against the redness of his skin and the worn black Bible he carried. He locked eyes with the minister's, as if they were in a duel to the death.

"The cock has crowed, Darryl," he said, pointing his finger, "and you're not Jesus, don't forget that part. Hatred wasn't part of his agenda, and that's all I ever hear you talk about anymore. No sir, in spite of what you might like to think, you're not Jesus Christ. You're not even close."

·41·

By Christmas Eve, most families in Reliance had turned inward, setting aside the gossip and hatred bubbling just below the surface of serenity, all of them still shocked at their sheriff's outburst at church. People had plenty to do and kept themselves busy getting the last of the presents bought, finalizing plans for Christmas dinner. Last-minute shoppers raced around gathering gifts, or dragging the remaining scraggly Christmas trees off the lots and home to decorate.

Jimmy Heron, when asked, had gently turned down Cory and Leigh's offer of having him spend the evening with them, since he was in a melancholy mood and felt no desire to change that. Something was pulling at him, drawing him in deeper, almost as if he should enter into the pain he was feeling, make it hurt even more, as much as he could stand and then some, in order to burst through it and out the other side. He was pushing the envelope of his own feelings without knowing why, without even knowing where it all would take him or what kind of shape he would be in when he was done. He felt like a naked man about to dive into a fire.

He reread and restacked the pile of Christmas cards on his kitchen table, surprised but pleased that so many people had chosen to remember him. Web Hardy and Buster Dan, Mona and Ted Lanier, and his sister Della. They had written to tell him how much he was missed and loved, and how they were all faring in their lives. Web Hardy had enclosed a snapshot of Buster Dan on his horse and had written *Don't forget us* at the side of the picture. Even ancient Winnie Bridwell had scratched across the bottom of a get well card, *Merry Christmas, Mrs. Ezekiel Bridwell.* A get well card? She must have gotten confused, Jimmy thought, but then again, maybe not.

He had not received this much mail since he'd taken up residence at 408 Wild Horse Road, and the feeling was both warm and wretched. If he hadn't lost his wife, his most precious gift, his giveaway, he'd be back in Texas at this very minute, putting the final touches on the pies he and Lou would be making for everyone. He'd be sparring with her about how to make the perfect crust, the juiciest turkey, and whether or not to put marshmallows on top of the yams this year.

His heart felt heavy and raw, almost as if the blood was dripping out of a big bullet hole right in the bottom of it. That was another thing: Why in the world hadn't that hateful, hollow-eyed bastard who put a bullet in his wife's brain had the simple courtesy to turn and blow a hole right through him at the same time, he thought. At least he and Lou could've gone together and he wouldn't be left behind to miss her with this unbearable ache, wondering what to do with the rest of his life.

Jimmy felt that familiar pinch behind his nose he always felt when he was about to cry, but he managed to push it down, hold it off for a bit longer. It seemed to him that once he started crying it was becoming harder and harder for him to stop. He knew he was setting himself up for a heartache, maybe a gut-buster of a bawling jag. But with the same morbid fascination of a bird to a snake, Jimmy Heron lifted the lid off the box of photographs sitting on the table before him and began, once again, to remember his life, the life he had treasured, with Lou.

Up the road, on Lavender Hill, the Central Oregon Bigot Busters meeting and Christmas gathering was winding down for the evening. Betty and Ted had taken Mitchell to his grandparents' house in Pendleton, and Eric and Steve were home with a sick llama, but the rest of the small crowd was enthusiastic. They pitched in to help Cory bring out snacks and the goofy gifts she had bought for everyone. Leigh, now heavily pregnant, with alternating bouts of levity and misery, hardly moved from the rocking chair the whole evening. Her belly had shifted sometime during the night, dropping, they assumed and Sally confirmed, as the baby turned, preparing for the grand entry—or exit, depending on how you looked at it.

Leigh was suddenly aware of walking differently, sort of low-slung, almost bowlegged, and had been that way ever since her struggle to get out of bed that morning. "I feel like I'm lugging a studded tire around in my pelvis," she said, "and I pee all the time. Is this normal?"

"Sure it is," said Willis. "My old man was just like that. Of course, his was prostate trouble, not pregnancy. Said his prostate was swollen up to the size of a canteen. Said it felt like he was sittin' on a horseshoe. With the nails still in it." Michelle, Willis's sweetheart, gave him a jab in the ribs with her elbow.

"Don't listen to him, Leigh," she said. "He runs off at the mouth. You shouldn't fret. If Sally says you're fine, then you're fine. Right, Sally?"

"Leigh-O," Sally said, "look at me. You are fine. The baby is fine. You are about to give birth, that's all. Now, I have written my home phone and my beeper number in bright red Magic Marker on at least two pieces of paper in every room in this house, plus the barn and out in Jonah's hideaway. You or Cory or Jonah are to call me the very instant things start happening. Don't worry so much—you don't want to make the baby all jittery. We'll have to name him Felipe."

Sally picked up the nervous little dog in his sock and snuggled him close to her neck. Felipe, momentarily soothed by Sally's warmth, stopped shaking for a millisecond and sighed, letting out a little pop of a dog-burp as he exhaled. The laughter of everyone in the room, however, revved him right back up and he shook, awaiting Armageddon.

Sally looked at her watch. "Glenn?" she called. "Honey? 'Bout ready to go?"

Cory and Glenn walked back into the living room as Glenn wiped powdered sugar from the last of the brownies off his beard. "So," Cory said to Glenn, "we've got a deal then? You know you're the one I trust most in the world to build it. I'd try it myself, but it needs to be done in the twentieth century. Besides, I'm still limping from my last encounter with a power tool." She pointed down to her foot. Glenn nodded at Cory and they shook hands. Cory glanced over at Michelle and Willis and gave them the okay sign.

"What's this?" asked Leigh. "What's going on?"

"Is this some big secret?" asked Sally.

"No," Cory said. "I just didn't want to bring it up until everything was settled." She glanced at Leigh. "We're starting a new restaurant."

"We are??" Leigh rolled her eyes and leaned back so quickly in the rocker she almost tipped over. Sally caught the arm of the chair and held it.

"Cory," Leigh said, exasperated, "I don't believe you and how you decide these things without—"

"Now, wait a minute," Cory interrupted, "the truth is we are helping Michelle and Willis start their own restaurant." She looked at Michelle. "Can I tell this?" she asked, and Michelle nodded. "Seems our friend, the Prince of Darkness, Mr. Wendell Metcalf, put one of his ORS donation buckets and a bunch of antigay literature right out on the bar at the Wigwam. Michelle protested to Lars, and when Lars refused to remove it, she called him a bigot, draped her apron right across his big bald head, slapped her tray in his gut, and walked out."

"Wow, Michelle," Sally said, "that was really a brave thing to do." Michelle blushed and held up her hand, then curled her arm like a body builder and made a little pimple of a muscle with her skinny bicep.

"Soooo," Cory continued, "I bought the building adjacent to the BP and Glenn's gonna remodel it for us. We'll call it The Filling Station, and Leigh and I will be silent partners."

"The two of you—silent?" Willis guffawed. "This is getting to be more miraculous by the minute."

"Quiet, man," Cory said, "or I'll be there tomorrow with my very own tools and then you'll be sorry."

"Oh," Willis said, helping Michelle with her coat. "Please. Forgive me. Please, not that." They made their way toward the door, hugging Cory and waving to Leigh and the others on the way out.

"Merry Christmas, y'all, and don't forget to wear those buttons proudly!" Cory shouted to the group as they headed out the door with their NO ON 19 bumper stickers flapping, campaign buttons pinned to their chests. "If you don't, you'll have to answer to Michelle!" Michelle turned and flashed a big smile at Cory, and Willis honked his horn and waved before they headed the truck down the drive.

At the bottom of the hill, Sally and Glenn's rattletrap VW bus spasmed itself into an asthmatic-sounding start, wheezing and groaning as Glenn ground it into gear.

"If you can't find 'em, grind 'em!" Cory yelled to Glenn, who shook a big fist at her out the window as he drove off.

Cory shut the door and turned to face Leigh, who was smiling at her from the rocker. The underwater glow from the aquarium lights made her face look angelic, almost translucent.

"You've got a big heart, my love," Leigh said.

"And, luckily," Cory said, "a big bank account to help things along." She took hold of Leigh's hand. "I think we all get stuck, trapped into thinking there's only one way to work it out. That's just not true. All I did was present Michelle and Willis with another option, a bigger opportunity. Sometimes bravery warrants its own special reward. You know—jumping off the edge you've been afraid of, then realizing you can fly after all."

She sat on the floor beside the rocker and placed a hand gently on Leigh's belly.

"How's the baby?" she asked.

"Sleeping right now, I think. Maybe mapping out an escape route. Filling out college application forms. Something that requires concentration and silence, for which I am grateful. This is one frisky little cowpoke we've got in here."

"So, whaddya think?" asked Cory. "Boy or girl? Alien life-form?"

"I haven't a clue," said Leigh. "Sally says to stay loose about it since we'll get what we get. I'm inclined to take her advice."

"Good plan," said Cory. "I'm with you. When will Jonah be back?"

"In a couple of days, he said. Maybe longer. He also said not to worry, so I'm trying my best."

"And where did he go?"

"To the woods was all he told me. I don't think he ever really maps anything out before he goes off. He just goes."

"Did he take some food with him?"

"Carrots and beets," Leigh said, "'to stay grounded.' He dropped off Christmas presents before he left. They're in the kitchen. Did you get a gift for him from us?"

"Yes, I did," Cory said. "A pot of geraniums."

"No!" Leigh replied. "You didn't. He hates those. Did we ever figure out why?"

"He can't remember. All he knows is that when he looks at them, it makes his teeth hurt. Anyway, I was kidding. I didn't get him geraniums. I got him a compass. Perhaps it was a poor choice."

"Not as bad as geraniums would have been. Don't worry, honey," Leigh said, "I gave him a big batch of dried sage I had in the barn and he was thrilled. We can get him a new sweater when he gets back. That is, if he doesn't freeze to death before then."

"Did you remind him this is winter?" Cory asked.

"I did."

"And he said?"

"He said, 'I know. Pretty, isn't it?'"

Both women sat in silence for the next few minutes, staring at the aquarium, where the fish swam slowly, lazily, with tiny gills puffing in and out. Leigh lightly stroked the hair on the back of Cory's head, letting it drop through her fingers.

"When I met you," she said, "your hair was mostly dark brown. Now it's mostly gray. Am I making you old?"

"No," Cory replied, "you are making me brave. Courage takes a lot of energy, at least it does for me. Worrying about my hair turning gray makes me old." Both women fell silent again.

"Are you happy, Cory?" Leigh asked, finally.

"About what?"

"You. Me. You and me. This baby of ours."

"Most of the time."

"And the other times?" Leigh asked.

"I'm ecstatic."

Across town, Wendell Metcalf watched Darryl Dimmer's metallic blue Cadillac speed off into the night. Rodney and Jason punched each other's arms amidst the Christmas packages in the back seat. *Brats,* thought Wendell, glad that he and Suzette shared the same view about children.

In his hands, placed there only moments before by the good reverend, was a check made out to the Oregon Reformation Society from Harley Dixon of the Americana Foundation in Virginia for fifty thousand dollars. Darryl Dimmer had received one for twice that amount from Mr. Dixon, a multimillionaire who had held the only U.S. government contract for the manufacturing of military clothing for the past forty years. Oh, there had been other bidders, even other manufacturers who had won bids. But thanks to some high-level friends and influence pedaling in Congress, nobody ever bothered to notice that each manufacturing operation was owned by Harley Dixon or his Americana Unlimited Corporation.

Harley Dixon had seen Wendell Metcalf on CNN and on the NBC *Nightly News* representing the fight against gay rights in Oregon. He had also become an avid listener to the fiery sermons of the Reverend Darryl Dimmer via audio and video cassette. Having lost his favorite grandson to AIDS only two years before, Harley Dixon had chosen to blame the gay community for the downfall of the America he had loved, honored, and gotten rich off of all his life. Besides, it was the queers who had corrupted his beloved Michael. Harley Dixon was sure of it.

Wendell's hand was shaking as he showed the check to his wife. "Ooooh, Daddy," Suzette purred, "this is our biggest one-time donation so far." She snatched the check from his hand to endorse it with their bank stamp and to jot down the name and address of the donor for future reference. Anyone with this much money to give to people he'd never even met would have much more to share once the battle really heated up, Suzette was certain.

She stuck the check into the zippered bag along with the others, making a note to herself to hotfoot it to the bank as soon as it reopened after Christmas. Money that could be earning interest should never be left sitting around idle.

Wendell looked over at their shiny silver Christmas tree with the bright blue lights and ornaments. Twenty ornaments, to be exact, since both he and Suzette felt any more than that would be cluttered and unnecessary. Blue lights, blue Christmas balls, silver wrapping paper for the four gifts under the tree—two for him and two for her. Everything was neat and clean and uniform.

There was something about having everything condensed and tidy, and the very same year after year, that appealed to both of them. For Suzette it was the simple fact that she liked things neatly packaged. It made her feel clean, orderly, and efficient. For Wendell it was somewhat more complicated. Just as crazy people often button their shirts all the way to the top for fear of flying apart, Wendell's complete control of his world helped keep at bay the monster he knew lived inside him. If Wendell didn't keep it completely chained, this monster, the wild one, would throw back its head and scream at the night.

In his dungeon-like room lit only by the candles at his altar, Donnie Zoeller stared into the mirror at his pecs and biceps as they bulged each time he lifted the barbell into a simple curl. Emotionally he was pumped, as pumped as the veins running the length of his arms just under the white skin. He had killed again. At least he was pretty sure he had, this time by poisoning one of the faggots' stupid llamas. Just some arsenic mixed with oats and molasses, that's all he'd used.

It had been easy enough, even though he'd had to hop the fence and run off down the hill right after he'd done it. He'd just barely had time to spray a black swastika on the back of the barn before the llama started belching and farting and puking and then screaming—Jeezus, what a sound! Like someone had slammed a car door on its nuts or something.

Donnie remembered seeing lights come on at the back of the queers' house and took off, but the memory of it all made him smile. He could do it again, oh yes. Real easy. No problem. And he wondered if a faggot would make that same screeching, high-pitched wail when death was near.

In their white house with the green shutters out on the road to Redmond, Tom Mason and his family were spending Christmas Eve as they always did: with Kate's mother, Edith Knudsen, and her gentleman companion, Silly Carl, a retired postal worker. The large living room was fragrant with the smell of the Christmas tree, butter cookies sprinkled with nutmeg, and the applesauce gingerbread Edith Knudsen was famous for. Presents spilled out from under the tree almost to the middle of the room. Most of them were for Jenny, the apple of everyone's eye. After their traditional nontraditional Christmas Eve dinner of vegetable soup, grapefruit salad, and homemade bread, the family played Monopoly until Jenny Mason had cleaned everyone's clock. She employed brilliant and strategic financial moves well beyond her twelve years. The game ended, finally, only after Silly Carl threatened to kidnap Trapper, the miniature schnauzer asleep in his lap, and never return him. Maybe he would even ship him off to Russia where, Silly Carl had heard, schnauzers were a delicacy the Russians ate with borscht, whatever that was. Some sort of Commie food, he supposed.

At 408 Wildhorse Road, Jimmy Heron had fallen into a fitful sleep in the turquoise trailer. His bed, always too small and cramped for his big frame, was rumpled. Covers were strewn around and spilling onto the floor as he tossed and sweated, flailing his arms and crying out for the people he loved.

Earlier, he had looked at as many family photographs and reread as many love letters as he could stand. Then Jimmy Heron had sobbed for what had seemed like hours before finally dragging himself from the table and into his pajamas to go to bed. He felt spent, like his bones were dry and his skin sagging on him, as if there was no blood or oxygen left in his body that wasn't used up and ready to be discarded. If someone, some force, could pick him up at this moment and break his body across its knee like a dead tree branch, Jimmy Heron was sure his blood and bones would crumble out of him like coffee grounds.

What was it that young woman had said to him? The waitress in—where was it? Montana? Wyoming? Sharon, that was her name, the one with the kind eyes. "I know it doesn't feel like it right now, mister, but it will get better. You will heal from this." That's what she had said, Jimmy remembered, as Sharon's words floated up to catch him in the air and hold him while he drifted off to sleep.

Will call. Wilco. Will Shakespeare. Will work for food. Last will and testament. Will you marry me? Will heal from this. These were the words Jimmy Heron saw, all of them in bright yellow letters, painted onto the side of a dark green army duffel bag. The bag belonged to Curly Red. Jimmy could see him just as plain as day in the dream. He was packing things into the bag, filling it up fast and furious with as much stuff as he could cram in there. Boots. A cowboy hat. A Texas flag. Tools.

197

Overalls. Bowls. Army mess kits. A big container of salsa. An extra ear.

Next to the duffel bag was a large wooden box shaped like a boomerang. It was full of red candy hearts. What was that? A big box of red candy hearts? On each heart was the word *Love*. Curly Red picked the biggest one out of the boomerang box and held it up. It seemed to be pulsating, beating, as if it were alive. The polished oak wood of the box gave off a steady golden glow.

"See, Bimmy?" he said, "all the love you've ever given is coming right back to you again." And as Curly Red held the heart up higher for Jimmy to see, the word *Love* transformed into the face of Lou Heron, smiling her cute little dimpled smile at him.

"I love you, Jimbo," she said. "Don't forget. Don't worry. I'm never far away." Then she winked and doodled her fingers at him like she had done almost every day from the kitchen window.

Jimmy reached for her in his sleep, stretching up to touch her face, to brush the back of his hand across her cheek as he'd always done. Instead, he caught his fingertips on the reading lamp clamped to the headboard and it woke him. He let out a sigh and stared for a minute into the darkness while his vision cleared. The hardest part about waking up was the sameness of everything. Nothing had changed. Lou was still dead. He was still here without her, and the stretch of what looked to be the rest of his life was endless. His giveaway. Shit.

The kitchen faucet dripped into a saucer left in the sink, sounding like a lead pipe dropping onto a garage floor. Pulling himself out of bed and trudging into the kitchen, he gave the faucet a hard twist, then peeked out through the blinds at the moonlight hitting the top of Three-Fingered Jack. How long before he could see them, the people he loved, again? How long would it take? How long would he last?

Jimmy shuffled back toward his bed through the cramped trailer, suddenly overwhelmed by the fact that this was his first Christmas in almost fifty years without the woman he loved. It wasn't only that he missed her, although that was certainly right up there at the top of the list. It was more than that. It was as if he no longer had any place to put the love he felt. Like he had a gift to offer that nobody would take. There was no need for him. Even the love and friendship from the new people in his life, Leigh and Cory and Jonah, was not enough to fill the void.

Jimmy Heron sat down on the edge of his creaky bed and held his head in his hands. This was his dark night of the soul, the night he would begin to call his spirit back. Surrender was near on Christmas Eve. He let out a mournful wail, a cry from the bones of him, boiled up from the marrow, ragged and painful. Then, in the darkness, deep in the loneliness and despair of a man whose life had been forever changed by senseless hatred and tragedy, James Jefferson Heron sank to his knees beside his bed, clasped his hands tightly together, and prayed. For courage. For healing. For deliverance. For something about which to be grateful.

·42·

So, I'm thinkin' by now you must've figured out this whole story and I don't have to yammer on about it all anymore. But just in case you're not as bright as I thought, I'll give you some clues. First of all, it ain't hard. What pains the Big Guy the most is how difficult humans have made the task of loving each other. Seems they'd all rather beat each other over the head with dogma and point out each other's shortcomings instead of really seeing into each other's hearts.

Well, they'd better watch out is all I gotta say, 'cause their karma's fixin' to run over their dogma. And all I mean by that is this. As humans, we live in a world of reap and sow. You put out love and you'll get it back by the trainload, but you put out hatred and it'll bite your butt like a big dog. Karma's a good word, one I didn't learn until I "graduated." No, I never heard it once, not one single time growin' up in Montague County, but I saw it in action a lot.

The second thing you need to know is that whatever your life is now, well, you chose it. Yep, you heard me, you already picked it out ahead of time. You mapped out the big blueprint with the power hitters up here, to learn whatever lessons you needed to back on old schoolhouse earth.

Now, I gotta tell ya, that was a tough one for me to get a handle on, seein' as how I lost my family at such a young age and all. I remember what ran through my mind when I found out this is how it's set up: Why would I pick that? What was I thinking? But you know what? The more I pondered it the more I came to realize that if I hadn't lost my family, I wouldn't have found Jimmy, or Mr. and Mrs. Heron, or Lou, and they were as much of a family to me as a fella'd ever want. Lookin' back at it, I'd say I was a pretty lucky guy. And, knowin' what I know now about already havin' picked it out and all, I have to admit I wasn't the poor dumb hayseed I always assumed I was.

snow angels on the side of Lavender Hill.

She felt that familiar pressure in her lower abdomen, a heavy, imminent feeling, letting her know her bladder needed emptying. Leigh stared at Ned, who hadn't moved an inch, his droopy eye and droopy ear making him look all that much more concerned and loyal. His grin got bigger.

"Ned," she said, making his droopy parts perk right up, "you are my rescue team today, my trusty steed. Now, sit." The big dog instantly sat down with a loud *whump,* his obedience surprising them both. Leigh caught hold of his collar. "Stay," she said, holding on with both hands and sliding her feet off the edge of the bed. "Now," she said, "I need you to understand me as you never have before." She looked him straight in the eye and he stared back at her, dedicated to his mission, whatever it was. "Stand up, Ned," she said gently, and he did it, with Leigh still clinging to his collar. She was red in the face and panting. Her bladder felt like it was about to explode and send her flying around the room, sputtering the death knell of a birthday balloon. "Now, back up, Ned," she said, and the dog just stood there, as if wondering what to do next.

Leigh dropped her head and thought for a few seconds before shouting at him in a voice normally reserved for saving a child from impending doom on the school playground. "REVERSE!" she screamed, her face fully of fury. The look in her eye and the sheer volume of [her] voice spooked the dog so that he almost ran backwards, pull[ing] right out of bed, onto her feet and halfway down the h[all]... ded to a stop two feet from the bathroom door. "... she said, rubbing his big head and smoothi[ng]... around. "Now if we can just do somethi[ng]... we can enter you in a contest of some sort. ... or something like that. We'll paint flames con... chromeplate your toenails. Trust me, you'll be...

Leigh went into the bathroom, closing the d... time Cory came back in from the barn she could he... ning. She put on a pot of coffee, then dragged some... of the freezer and slid them into the oven. She was sit... peeling oranges onto the counter, when Leigh wadd...

See what's happenin' is that we are all evolvin', all of us, on sort of one big spiritual evolutionary trail. I had trouble with that one too, especially since I figured I was about as spiritual as a bucket of axle grease. I'd just wanted to go back as one of Jimmy and Lou's horses. I'd just carnation I wanted to eat oats and alfalfa all day and get a bath with warm water once a week. He said then that all I'd ever learn would be how to be a better horse, and I realized he had a point there. I'll keep you stuck in the spin cycle using the name of God ... hang out and eat oats ... well, let's just say you'll have a long, long time. Now I gotta get my stuff Oh, and you want to know what? Hatred, pure and simple. Now I'm gettin' to make through eternity? with the skinny on every- to make a quick buck caught in the auger over that one for a long, long time. caught in the auger over that one I'm much obliged to be able to bend your ear with thing, to fill you in on how this all plays out. Yep, looks like I got me a lesson or packed and my paperwork filled out 'cause you see, I'm gettin' a lesson two more to learn and maybe, just maybe, I'll help somebody else learn a trip back to old schoolhouse earth a lesson or two while I'm there. Once I'm there they say I won't remember much of this afterlife stuff at all, seein' as how that'd take away the whole point of goin'. Sort of like havin' a cheat sheet, I guess. It's just too bad, I say, that we all have to die in order to remember as much as I can 'cause it's the sweetest, purest, grandest I'll remember there is. So, are you wonderin' if my next trip will be as a Texan? Doe... like it. Nope, not other than in an indirect, once-removed k... really give you a lot of information until you're already Maybe a cousin, or something like that. To tell you the tr... fixin' to buck, but I think I've signed on to home of minded Oregonians. Damned straight, though, that my soul will is branded on me—lone star fl... cowboy b...

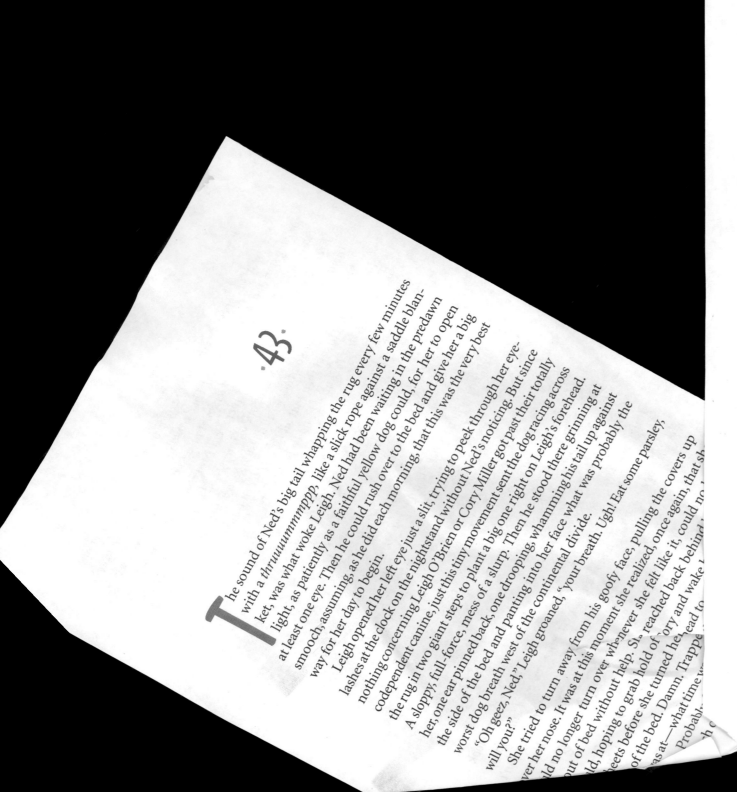

43

The sound of Ned's big tail whapping the rug every few minutes with a *thruuuummmppp*, like a slick rope against a saddle blanket, was what woke Leigh. Ned had been waiting in the predawn light, as patiently as a faithful yellow dog could, for her to open at least one eye. Then he could rush over to the bed and give her a big smooch, assuming, as he did each morning, that this was the very best way for her day to begin.

Leigh opened her left eye just a slit, trying to peek through her eyelashes at the clock on the nightstand without Ned's noticing. But since nothing concerning Leigh O'Brien or Cory Miller got past their totally codependent canine, just this tiny movement sent the dog racing across the rug in two giant steps to plant a big one right on Leigh's forehead. A sloppy, full-force, mess of a slurp. Then he stood there grinning at her, one ear pinned back, one drooping, whamming his tail up against the side of the bed and panting into her face what was probably the worst dog breath west of the continental divide.

"Oh geez, Ned," Leigh groaned, "your breath. Ugh! Eat some parsley, will you?"

She tried to turn away from his goofy face, pulling the covers up over her nose. It was at this moment she realized, once again, that she could no longer turn over wh never she felt like it, could no[...] out of bed without help. S[...] reached back behind [...] [...]ld, hoping to grab hold of Cory and wake [...] [...]eets before she turned he[...]ead to [...] [...] of the bed. Damn. Trappe[...] [...]as at—what time w[...] Probabl[...]

kitchen.

Leigh was so scrubbed and shiny, even her freckles sparkled. Her wet, auburn hair hung in dark ringlets around her face and onto the shoulders of her green robe. She was beautiful. Cory felt her own heart skip a beat when she looked at Leigh, astonished that it could hold as much love as she felt in this moment. She got up off the stool, staring at Leigh with the same awe and intensity she might have if gazing upon a beautiful gemstone or a dazzling sunset.

"Where were you?" Leigh asked. "I had to talk Ned into pulling me out of bed." Ned, sprawled out by his food bowl, lifted his head and thwacked his tail on the kitchen floor at the mention of his name.

"I was out in the barn, uh, manger, making sure everyone was fed. Jerry Garcia got himself wrapped up in a feed sack in the hay and, I swear, he looked just like Baby Jesus. Oh, and remind me to talk to Glenn about replacing that big support beam, maybe in the spring. It's so old and brittle and it groans so loudly when the wind blows I always think it's about to snap in two. Sounds like the ghost of Sir Loin bellowing to Meems. Probably breaks her heart."

"Jerry followed you out to the barn? What's gotten into him?" Leigh asked.

"It's Christmas," Cory said. "He forgot himself. Maybe he thinks being Baby Jesus is his job for the day. Don't worry, he followed me back in. If I know him, he's asleep by the woodstove as we speak."

She glanced at Leigh, then looked at her ponderously, cocking her head and squinting. "You look," Cory said, struggling for the right word, "um, well, shorter."

"I am bowed out," Leigh said. "What I've lost in height is now in front of me. I feel like half a set of parentheses." She rubbed both hands against the small of her back.

"Yeah," Cory said, "I guess maybe that's it. Wow. I feel like we should be doing a countdown of some sort, like your belly is that big ball in Times Square and it's about to drop."

"I think that's an apt description," Leigh said.

"Oh, I didn't mean it in a negative way—"

"And I didn't take it that way," Leigh said. "I agree with you. Really. I just hope I'm ready for this."

See, what's happenin' is that we are all evolvin', all of us, on sort of one big spiritual evolutionary trail. I had trouble with that one, too, especially since I figured I was about as spiritual as a bucket of axle grease. I remember tellin' a fella that if there really was such a thing as reincarnation I wanted to go back as one of Jimmy and Lou's horses. I'd just hang out and eat oats and alfalfa all day and get a bath with warm water once a week. He said then that all I'd ever learn would be how to be a better horse, and I realized he had a point there.

Oh, and you want to know what'll keep you stuck in the spin cycle through eternity? Hatred, pure and simple. And using the name of God to make a quick buck—well, let's just say you'll have your cojones caught in the auger over that one for a long, long time.

I'm much obliged to be able to bend your ear with the skinny on everything, to fill you in on how this all plays out. Now I gotta get my stuff packed and my paperwork filled out 'cause, you see, I'm gettin' to make a trip back to old schoolhouse earth. Yep, looks like I got me a lesson or two more to learn and maybe, just maybe, I'll help somebody else learn a lesson or two while I'm there.

Once I'm there they say I won't remember much of this afterlife stuff at all, seein' as how that'd take away the whole point of goin'. Sort of like havin' a cheat sheet, I guess. It's just too bad, I say, that we all have to die in order to remember where we came from. I can tell you this, though— I'll remember as much as I can 'cause it's the sweetest, purest, grandest thing there is.

So, are you wonderin' if my next trip will be as a Texan? Doesn't look like it. Nope, not other than in an indirect, once-removed kind of way. Maybe a cousin, or something like that. To tell you the truth, they don't really give you a lot of information until you're already in the chute and fixin' to buck, but I think I've signed on to be one of those independent-minded Oregonians.

Damned straight, though, that my soul will always be a Texan. Texas is branded on me—lone star flag, cowboy hat, boots and all.

·43·

The sound of Ned's big tail whapping the rug every few minutes with a *thruuuummmppp*, like a slick rope against a saddle blanket, was what woke Leigh. Ned had been waiting in the predawn light, as patiently as a faithful yellow dog could, for her to open at least one eye. Then he could rush over to the bed and give her a big smooch, assuming, as he did each morning, that this was the very best way for her day to begin.

Leigh opened her left eye just a slit, trying to peek through her eyelashes at the clock on the nightstand without Ned's noticing. But since nothing concerning Leigh O'Brien or Cory Miller got past their totally codependent canine, just this tiny movement sent the dog racing across the rug in two giant steps to plant a big one right on Leigh's forehead. A sloppy, full-force, mess of a slurp. Then he stood there grinning at her, one ear pinned back, one drooping, whamming his tail up against the side of the bed and panting into her face what was probably the worst dog breath west of the continental divide.

"Oh geez, Ned," Leigh groaned, "your breath. Ugh! Eat some parsley, will you?"

She tried to turn away from his goofy face, pulling the covers up over her nose. It was at this moment she realized, once again, that she could no longer turn over whenever she felt like it, could no longer pop out of bed without help. She reached back behind her as far as she could, hoping to grab hold of Cory and wake her. Her hand patted the sheets before she turned her head to see the empty space on Cory's side of the bed. Damn. Trapped, that's how she felt. No telling where Cory was at—what time was it? Six-fifteen on Christmas morning, she thought. Probably feeding the animals in the barn or, Leigh imagined with a touch of jealousy, she could just as easily be making snow angels on the side of Lavender Hill.

She felt that familiar pressure in her lower abdomen, a heavy, imminent feeling, letting her know her bladder needed emptying. Leigh stared at Ned, who hadn't moved an inch, his droopy eye and droopy ear making him look all that much more concerned and loyal. His grin got bigger.

"Ned," she said, making his droopy parts perk right up, "you are my rescue team today, my trusty steed. Now, sit." The big dog instantly sat down with a loud *whump*, his obedience surprising them both. Leigh caught hold of his collar. "Stay," she said, holding on with both hands and sliding her feet off the edge of the bed. "Now," she said, "I need you to understand me as you never have before." She looked him straight in the eye and he stared back at her, dedicated to his mission, whatever it was. "Stand up, Ned," she said gently, and he did it, with Leigh still clinging to his collar. She was red in the face and panting. Her bladder felt like it was about to explode and send her flying around the room, sputtering the death knell of a birthday balloon. "Now, back up, Ned," she said, and the dog just stood there, as if wondering what to do next.

Leigh dropped her head and thought for a few seconds before shouting at him in a voice normally reserved for saving a child from impending doom on the school playground. "REVERSE!" she screamed, her face fully of fury. The look in her eye and the sheer volume of her voice spooked the dog so that he almost ran backwards, pulling her right out of bed, onto her feet and halfway down the hall. They skidded to a stop two feet from the bathroom door. "Way to go, buddy!" she said, rubbing his big head and smoothing his coat as he pranced around. "Now if we can just do something about your breath maybe we can enter you in a contest of some sort. Monster Dog Tractor Pull, or something like that. We'll paint flames coming out of your ribs and chromeplate your toenails. Trust me, you'll be a hit."

Leigh went into the bathroom, closing the door after her. By the time Cory came back in from the barn she could hear the shower running. She put on a pot of coffee, then dragged some breakfast rolls out of the freezer and slid them into the oven. She was sitting on a stool, peeling oranges onto the counter, when Leigh waddled into the kitchen.

Leigh was so scrubbed and shiny, even her freckles sparkled. Her wet, auburn hair hung in dark ringlets around her face and onto the shoulders of her green robe. She was beautiful. Cory felt her own heart skip a beat when she looked at Leigh, astonished that it could hold as much love as she felt in this moment. She got up off the stool, staring at Leigh with the same awe and intensity she might have if gazing upon a beautiful gemstone or a dazzling sunset.

"Where were you?" Leigh asked. "I had to talk Ned into pulling me out of bed." Ned, sprawled out by his food bowl, lifted his head and thwacked his tail on the kitchen floor at the mention of his name.

"I was out in the barn, uh, manger, making sure everyone was fed. Jerry Garcia got himself wrapped up in a feed sack in the hay and, I swear, he looked just like Baby Jesus. Oh, and remind me to talk to Glenn about replacing that big support beam, maybe in the spring. It's so old and brittle and it groans so loudly when the wind blows I always think it's about to snap in two. Sounds like the ghost of Sir Loin bellowing to Meems. Probably breaks her heart."

"Jerry followed you out to the barn? What's gotten into him?" Leigh asked.

"It's Christmas," Cory said. "He forgot himself. Maybe he thinks being Baby Jesus is his job for the day. Don't worry, he followed me back in. If I know him, he's asleep by the woodstove as we speak."

She glanced at Leigh, then looked at her ponderously, cocking her head and squinting. "You look," Cory said, struggling for the right word, "um, well, shorter."

"I am bowed out," Leigh said. "What I've lost in height is now in front of me. I feel like half a set of parentheses." She rubbed both hands against the small of her back.

"Yeah," Cory said, "I guess maybe that's it. Wow. I feel like we should be doing a countdown of some sort, like your belly is that big ball in Times Square and it's about to drop."

"I think that's an apt description," Leigh said.

"Oh, I didn't mean it in a negative way—"

"And I didn't take it that way," Leigh said. "I agree with you. Really. I just hope I'm ready for this."

"For what?" Cory asked. "Motherhood?"

"Birth," said Leigh. "I've been ready to be a mom forever."

The smell of cinnamon began to fill the kitchen. Both women bustled around, grabbing plates and napkins, filling coffee cups and loading up a tray to take into the living room.

Cory filled the thermos with the remaining coffee, turned down the oven, and slipped a couple of buns back in to stay warm. Then she scooped a handful of orange wedges into a plastic bag. "We'll take these to Jimmy when we go, okay?"

"Good idea. Do you have any thoughts about Christmas dinner?" Leigh asked. "I've been so preoccupied, I—"

"Not a problem," Cory said. "I've got it all figured out, the perfect Christmas dinner. Perfect. Guess."

"Don't tell me—reindeer stew and cranberry Jell-O."

"Nope."

"Fudge and Divinity sandwiches."

"Nuh-uh. Give up?"

"I give."

"Shepherd's pie."

"Perfect!" said Leigh. "Now, where did I put my frankincense and myrrh?" Then they slapped high fives across the kitchen counter and made their way into the living room, where the bejeweled tree, in all its splendor and glory, stood with arms outstretched to embrace them.

For the next two hours, Cory and Leigh opened their gifts—some for Leigh, some for Cory, some for the animals, and a whole bunch for the new baby. Then Cory showered while Leigh packed up the brunch for Jimmy and his gifts from the two of them and from Jonah.

Ned, sporting a new purple collar, got a quick brushing from Leigh. Cory grabbed a Magic Marker and some stick-on name tags from the kitchen junk drawer, scribbled something on three of them, and slapped them onto Leigh, Ned, and herself before they headed out the door.

Leigh's Subaru wagon erupted into an unenthusiastic, cold start and shimmied for a bit until it warmed up.

"We could have walked, you know," said Leigh. "I'm only pregnant, not an invalid."

"This is safer," Cory said, pumping the brakes to ease the car down the icy hill. The studded tires crunched on the frozen gravel, like rocks rattling in a pan. "Besides, what if the baby decides to show up today? Do you want to give birth on the side of an icy road, in the snow? I don't think so."

"It just seems overly cautious to me," Leigh said.

"Belt and suspenders," Cory replied, "that's what Big Al would tell us, belt and suspenders." She jabbed at the air with her forefinger the way her dad always did when he was making a point.

"That reminds me," said Leigh, "have you talked to him?"

"Yesterday," Cory responded. "He called while you were napping to say Merry Christmas. He's in Bermuda, as planned."

"He's having fun?" Leigh asked.

"Sounded like it. He's met a 'lady friend,' he said. She's there on vacation with two other women. They call themselves the Bermuda Triangle—is that a hoot? He wouldn't tell me anything about her, other than the fact that she has all her own teeth, she hasn't dyed her hair, and they're learning to line dance."

"In Bermuda?" Leigh asked.

"Go figure," said Cory.

In less than two minutes, Cory crept to a stop in front of Jimmy Heron's crimped and dingy turquoise trailer. Rust and dirt streamed down like tears from the corners of the old metal screens. It made the whole place look morose. The thin ribbon of smoke curling up from the chimney let them know he was up.

"Poor Jimmy," Leigh said. "I don't know how he can stand to live in this place. It just doesn't seem to fit him. I mean, it worked for Millie, but then, Millie's a renegade, probably only a step or two up from a bag lady. It sure doesn't look like it works very well for him. Bless his heart." She and Cory both stared out the window at the sagging, sad-looking trailer. Ned whined and yelped from the back, ready to get out.

"Yep," said Cory, "for a man who's used to sandstone, oak, and leather, I'd say this is definitely a step down. Come on, let's see if we can brighten his day."

Like a soldier on new terrain, Ned vaulted from the back of the station wagon when Cory lifted the hatch, then circled around sniffing and hiked his leg on the closest tree.

Leigh struggled a little, but managed to extricate herself from the Subaru without help, feeling somewhat empowered despite the enormous bulk she was lugging around. She gathered the food and presents from the back seat while Cory, coffee thermos in hand, knocked on the door of the trailer.

Lying on his bed, thinking about his dream the night before, it took Jimmy a while to realize he had company, to jam in his Beltones and pull on his robe. He often could not recognize voices without his hearing aids, but a dog's bark was something he could pick up and Ned's was especially burly and loud. When Jimmy finally opened the door, he saw three eager faces grinning up at him. There was food, coffee, presents, and a hand-lettered name tag stuck on each of them—Cory, Leigh and Ned—declaring in big red letters: I'M THE GIFT!

The sight of them warmed Jimmy's heart, sending a shot of love right straight up his spine, so intense it almost felt like joy, and he could not help but smile at them. He ran a big hand over his face, still salty and crusty with dried tears and sweat from the night before. He wished he had shaved in the past couple of days, wished he had cleaned the place up a little and not left everything strewn about, wished Lou was here to meet his new friends, wished he could think of something more gracious to say to them on this Christmas morning than "Come in," but he couldn't. He held the door open with one hand and motioned them in with the other. "Please," was all he could say.

The energy of extra people and a big dog inside the tiny trailer made the small space feel even more cramped. Jimmy found himself hurrying about picking up clothes and boots and other debris of everyday living. "This place is a mess," he said, "and so am I." He felt embarrassed to be seen as such a slob since he had always been rather fastidious about keeping himself and his space clean and in order. When he headed for the kitchen to attack dirty dishes in the sink, Cory held up her hand.

"Stop, Jimmy!" she yelled. "For goodness sakes, do you think we've never seen a messy house before? Here, you go get yourself washed up. We'll handle this and get you something to eat." She placed a hand on his back, nudging him toward the bathroom. "Go on, now. Git." She shoved him in there and shut the door behind him.

While Jimmy showered, shaved and got himself dressed, the two women tidied up his place and did the dishes in the sink. The aroma of cinnamon and coffee filled the trailer, stifling the dog-smell of Ned, who had fallen asleep by the woodstove. Rolls and orange sections were on plates and the thermos of coffee was set on the table with cups and spoons, a bowl of sugar, and a tiny can of Carnation evaporated milk Jimmy always kept in the refrigerator.

"What is it about old dudes and this milk?" Cory asked, holding up the can toward the kitchen light as if she expected to be able to see through it or, even more miraculously, decipher the label on the side of the can without her reading glasses. "My dad always has this milk for his coffee. My Grandpa Homer did. So did my Uncle Shorty, and Silly Carl. Willis's Dad, Pap—now, there's a name for you. He should be grateful his last name isn't Smear. Or Test. Anyway, why do you suppose all of these guys use it? Is there some giant warehouse where you can go and get it for free if you're over sixty-five and male?"

"I suppose," Leigh said, distractedly, thumbing through an ancient issue of *Reader's Digest*.

"Do you think they think it's good?" Cory asked after a bit, holding up the can again.

"What?" asked Leigh, exasperated, looking up.

"This stuff," Cory replied. "This milk. I mean, it isn't exactly fresh. No telling when they canned it. Maybe they should call it Reincarnation evaporated milk. "

"Cory," Leigh said, "has it occurred to you that maybe they just like it?"

Jimmy emerged from the back room wearing a green plaid flannel shirt and a pair of dark gray Dickies. His clothes were a little wrinkled but clean, and he smelled of Dial soap, shaving cream, and Old Spice. Long wisps of wet gray hair lay slicked across his head. The pink scalp beneath it was shiny. As he sat down at the table, Leigh leaned across to wipe a splotch of lather off his face by his ear.

"Merry Christmas, Jimmy," she said. "You look handsome."

"Oh, now," he said, "thank you, but *handsome* isn't a word I've applied to myself in a long time. I look, well, let's just say I look presentable. And the truth is, if the two of you and Ned hadn't shown up today, I'd probably still be in my skivvies, looking like a bum. So, I owe you a debt of gratitude. Again."

"How 'bout some breakfast, Jimmy?" Cory asked. "Our treat."

Cory and Leigh sipped their coffee while Jimmy ate some of the breakfast rolls and orange sections. Their conversation was gentle and easy. Neither of the women pressed him for information, preferring to let him share whatever he felt he needed to. When he was finished with the food, Cory slid three small packages across the table toward Jimmy. "Beware of geeks bearing gifts," she said. "I think that's the saying, isn't it? Here, this one's from Ned."

Jimmy tore off the green-striped wrapping paper and opened the box to find a pair of handsewn leather slippers. He held them up to admire the workmanship. They were deerskin, the leather a buttery shade of gold, the smell of them like the inside of a saddle shop. Jimmy held the slippers to his nose and sniffed.

"Oh," he said, "these are beautiful. Very nice. Thank you, Ned. You are always so busy, I can't imagine when you'd find the time to shop." The big dog whapped his tail on the floor without opening an eye.

"Here," Cory said, pointing to a small red package for Jimmy to open next, "this one is from Leigh and me." When Jimmy got the wrapping paper off, he found a Swiss army knife complete with three blades, tweezers, a fish scaler, and a bottle opener. He spent a few minutes opening and closing the knife, admiring its precision.

"I don't suppose you knew I needed a new knife, did you?" he asked. "I always thought I'd buy myself one of these sometime. The one I have was my dad's; that's the only reason I keep it." He slipped his old one out of his pants pocket and set it on the table. Leigh picked it up and began trying to pry the rusty blades out of it. Only one stunted blade emerged easily. The rest stayed stuck.

"Nope," Cory said. "Lucky guess. Everybody likes a Swiss army knife."

"This is a wonderful present," Jimmy said. "Thank you very much. I appreciate your thoughtfulness."

The final gift, the one from Jonah, was flat, something wrapped in a plush piece of purple corduroy. Leigh slid it toward Jimmy. "This is from Jonah," she said. "He told me you would understand."

Jimmy carefully unwrapped the material to reveal a long, bluish-gray feather. The pearl-colored quill was thick and round, the consistency of a toenail. The hue of the feather went from dusty beige to dark brownish-gray to almost a steel blue and then black as it tapered toward the end. It was perfect, as exquisite as the connection had been the day Jimmy saved the bird's life. It was a few seconds before Jimmy realized that all three of them were holding their breath.

He opened the note Jonah had enclosed with the feather, his hand shaking. It was as if he had discovered some treasure, some ancient writing that would decipher the meaning of life. It said, simply: *Jimmy, your teacher left you a gift by the river, Heron to Heron. I saved it for you. Merry Christmas, my brother. Toksa, Jonah.*

Jimmy felt himself overwhelmed for an instant at the kindness just laid at his feet. But worse, he felt guilty. He had been so wrapped up in his own despair he had not thought to get gifts for his new friends.

He had rarely met people so spontaneously loving as these young people who lived up the hill from him. Oh, his friends in Texas loved him, he knew that, but actively participating in his healing was not part of their plan as it was with Cory, Leigh, and Jonah. His new friends seemed to want to hold him up until he got well, to help him endure while the wound closed.

"I feel ashamed," he said, finally, his voice breaking.

"But why?" Cory and Leigh said simultaneously.

"I…I've been so sad, so self-absorbed, that I didn't think to get Christmas presents for you. I have nothing to give…"

His voice broke and he leaned his face into his hands, sliding his fingertips up under the edge of his glasses to cover his eyes. Leigh placed a hand on his arm. Cory shot up from her chair and jumped across the room toward Ned.

"Keep your eyes shut, Jimmy," she shouted. "I'm about to prove you wrong." In quick succession, Jimmy heard a sound—*sschtuck, sschtuck, sschtuck*—like Velcro, or cockleburs being pulled off wool socks, then felt *fwap-fwap-fwap* onto his stomach, his chest, and the middle of his forehead.

"Open your eyes now, Jimmy," Cory said. He did and, looking at his shirt and then peeling one away from his eyebrows, he saw three stick-on tags. I'M THE GIFT! I'M THE GIFT! I'M THE GIFT! the tags shouted to the world, making Jimmy Heron laugh in spite of himself.

"For us?" Cory said in mock surprise. "You shouldn't have!" She grabbed Jimmy around the neck and kissed his cheek. Leigh leaned across the table and touched the side of his head. She looked into his eyes.

"Knowing you is our biggest gift, Jimmy," she said. "We are so grateful to have you in our life."

Jimmy was overcome with emotion; he didn't know what to say. His face screwed up like a Cabbage Patch doll and all he could do was shake his head yes. Finally, when the spasm in his diaphragm subsided, the words leaked out of him, like warm air escaping from a secret place in the soul.

"Lou and I had no children," he said, "but we just accepted that as the way things went. We weren't bitter about it, although right at first we did feel a little shortchanged. We did accept it, though, and just decided to play out the hand we were dealt, that's all. But if we had," he stopped for a moment to get his breath, "if we had had children, I, that is, we, uh…yes, we would have wanted them to be like you."

In a few minutes the women rose to say good-bye, hugging Jimmy Heron. He had decided to go for a walk in the snow and was wrestling himself into his jacket and gloves. Leigh placed his hat on his head at a jaunty angle and turned his collar up close around his neck.

"Sure you don't want some company?" Cory asked. "I don't mind walking with you. Or we could send Ned."

"No," Jimmy replied. "I'll be fine alone right now. I'd prefer it, actually, just for a bit."

"Join us for dinner, then?" asked Leigh. "We'll eat around five. Be careful, Jimmy. The ice and snow get very slick on these rocks."

Cory bundled Ned into the back of the wagon and Leigh wedged into the passenger's seat. Then Cory ran back around to wrap Jimmy in a bear hug before hopping into the car and starting it up. She and Leigh looked back once as they headed up the gravel drive toward the road. They saw him climbing through the fence, heading toward the river. Cory beeped the horn and Jimmy turned to them to wave.

"Merry Christmas, Jimmy!" she yelled, adding, "We love you!" as the car turned left and headed up the hill.

Jimmy Heron stood alone in the snowy field with his left hand held up high in the air, his palm outstretched toward the women. In his right, with the gentlest pressure of his fingertips, he held the perfect feather of the Great Blue Heron. "I love you, too," he said, almost in a whisper. He looked up toward the sky. "All of you. I love you, too."

·44·

he Deschutes River ran slow and cold this time of year, the deepest color of blue. It was like some massive sleeping serpent hibernating, awaiting the snowmelt and spring runoff as a signal to shake itself from slumber and slither across the land, to roar and hiss if it needed to, demanding its due respect.

The river waited silently, dozing with eyes barely closed, breathing in, breathing out, for the aliveness of a new spring to warm its belly and set it free.

Jimmy Heron waited as well. He sat on a volcanic boulder, the very same one he'd seen Jonah perched atop watching him set the heron free. Jimmy chose a bare patch of rock and watched the Deschutes pool and swirl, as if it were dreaming, and then fall into an indigo silence.

He felt surprisingly unburdened, at least for the moment, of that awful feeling, the one he'd had every day since Lou's death—that something was missing, something vital and irreplaceable.

He smiled at his memories of her, thankful for them, not resentful that there would be no more memories of Lou to be made. The feeling of serenity and contentment startled him. Maybe this was what this whole business of life was about, he thought. Gratitude. Being grateful for what you've got and doing the best you can with it.

Lou had been right when she said that life was too short, especially if it's a life you've loved. Looking back, though, he couldn't imagine much he'd have done differently. Now his life had changed dramatically—there was definitely a void with Lou gone. But Jimmy felt certain he'd have people he could love with his new friends. Lou would have loved them, too; Jimmy knew it in his soul.

He gently felt in his shirt pocket for the heron's feather, resting by his heart, and gave it a soft stroke. Slipping the Swiss army knife from his pants pocket, he rolled the smooth red enamel around in his palm. It was heavy and warm from the heat of his own body, the stainless steel blades glistening in the snow's bright light. He pulled out the shortest blade, ran his thumb lightly along the edge of it, then scratched into a blotch of ice on the boulder next to where he sat. He carved slowly and carefully so as not to damage the blade of his new and treasured gift:

JIMMY LOVES LOU

LOVES JIMMY

LOVES LIFE

CHRISTMAS DAY & FOREVER

·45·

Tom Mason slowly sipped his coffee out of a deep turquoise mug. The thick edge of the mug was slick and rounded, almost mesmerizing to him as he rubbed it against his lower lip. The coffee was creamy and smooth with foamy milk floating on the top, an entirely different brew from the Hills Brothers he scooped out of a large can and heaped into the old corroded coffeemaker at his office every day. Drinking this stuff almost made him happy.

"What's this on the top?" he asked. "Cinnamon?"

"From Madagascar," replied Steve Dvorak, smiling smugly, pleased the sheriff had noticed. "And nutmeg."

"From Foodway," added Eric, narrowing his eyes at Steve.

"So, what does the vet say about your llama?" asked Tom. "Will he recover? Do you know what the medical costs will be?"

"Our doc says we're lucky we got to Stewart in time," Eric responded. He screams just like a girl when he's upset, like twenty third-grade girls at recess, actually. When we heard that awful noise we both dashed outside. Whoever poisoned him tagged the back of our barn with a big swastika and ran off. We didn't see anyone or hear a car or anything. It was creepy." Eric leaned back on the sofa, shaking his head.

"Yes," Tom said, "I saw the swastika, and I managed to follow some tracks to the highway before I lost them in the slush. Tire tracks ran all over everything after that."

"And?" Steve asked.

"And the footprints I saw seemed to match the mud print I dug up from beside your barn when your first llama was killed," said Tom. "Looks like there's only one person doing this, so that's good news."

"But...," Steve added, becoming peevish.

"But," Tom replied, "unless I go around town examining everyone's

215

feet, or catch someone in the act, this print's not going to do us a whole lot of good." Tom was becoming frustrated; the last thing he needed right now was to be reminded that his job was not getting done. He was irked at Steve and was just about ready to say something he'd regret later when Eric changed the direction of their conversation, bringing it back around to the subject of their sick llama.

"Our vet doesn't know what the final cost will be, Sheriff. He's got to keep Stewart on various medications and under observation for some time. It might wind up costing us more than we paid for him. We don't know yet."

"I don't suppose I have to tell you how terrifying this is to us, Sheriff. And something else—" Steve stood behind the sofa, his arms rigid against the back of it as he talked—"I have a gun. Two guns, actually, a pistol and a rifle, and I'm not afraid to use either one to protect our lives and our property."

Tom felt himself wince at the thought of everybody in the county being worked up enough to start blasting away at each other. Tomorrow was New Year's Eve, and no telling who or what would raise a ruckus, or worse. He rose to make his way back out to his Jeep, his shoulders aching from the weight of his worry. "I don't blame either of you for wanting to protect yourselves," he said. "Really, I don't. I just want to caution you to be careful. What we don't need around here is a shootout."

"We're awfully tired of being the target of this, Sheriff," Eric said. "I'm sure you can understand how terrible this feels." He eased himself and Tom out the front door before Steve blew a fuse. Eric could feel it coming.

"Not unless he was gay, he couldn't understand it, Eric, not in a million years could he ever understand it!" Steve shouted from the living room as Eric rushed Tom out onto the porch, closing the door behind them.

"Forgive him, Sheriff," Eric said. "This has all been too much. We've both just about had it."

"I'm sure," Tom said, "and he's probably right. Maybe I couldn't ever really understand. Even though I've been the target of hatred over something I did, it was never over who I was. But I can tell you this: I would not sit still and see my family terrorized and my property destroyed, and I won't stand for it happening to the families I've sworn to protect. That's my promise."

"Thanks, Tom," said Eric. "Thanks a lot. We appreciate it."

Eric was standing in his shirtsleeves, shivering, with his fingers tucked into each armpit. He quickly whipped one hand out and offered it to Tom, who gave it a good, strong shake.

Within seconds the sheriff was heading up the long drive toward the highway, glancing back once in the rearview mirror to see the coziness of lamplight in the sprawling house on the D-H Ranch. It surprised him that he liked these two gay men as much as he did, just as it surprised him when he remembered that he'd referred to them as a family. Despite Steve's propensity for fit-throwing and dramatic flair, Tom felt them both to be pretty fine fellows.

Maybe Kate was right, he thought, maybe this is just the way some people are. Maybe one of the reasons he'd thought homosexuality was such an aberration was because he didn't know any homosexuals. Oh sure, he knew Cory and Leigh, but he never thought about their being gay until Jenny had mentioned it, and he'd always liked them both. Maybe he knew a lot more homosexual people than he thought. Maybe they just never got to say so, out of fear, probably, of losing jobs or friends. Or maybe they were afraid of exactly what was happening in Reliance right now, this hatred so vicious and divisive it was about to blow the whole town apart. And what was it they were doing that was so wrong? Loving each other? It seemed awfully hard to work up a lot of hatred over that.

Jenny and Kate had nailed it, Tom thought. Darryl Dimmer swings his Bible around like a torch, trying to sear and scorch anyone who doesn't believe or behave or act or think like he does, spewing hatred in the name of God. Tom Mason shivered as a trickle of cold sweat ran down his neck. Recalling his own position on the matter just a couple of months before, he felt ashamed of his close-mindedness.

The problem, he realized, was not so much what Darryl Dimmer preached, but that ordinary people, like him, had never bothered to stand up and say no, never bothered to do anything. He made a mental note to speak to Dick Barstow tomorrow about the possibility of a town meeting. Folks needed to talk to each other before things got out of hand. Maybe the good people of Reliance could still be counted on to work things out before hatred chewed them up and swallowed them, burping up sour memories.

·46·

I t was a little after 8:00 P.M. when the phone rang. Leigh, her head and upper body stuck almost completely in the back of the bottom cabinet, pots and pans strewn about, yelled, "Somebody get that, okay?" Cory looked up at Jonah, who had his hand in an institutional-sized jar of pickled jalapeños, the juice running to his elbow when he held it up in the air. He shook his head no. The phone rang again. Cory dropped the chunk of Tillamook cheddar onto the cutting board and grabbed a dishtowel to wipe the cheese glops off her hands before she snared the phone off the wall. It was Sally.

"Happy New Year!" Cory said. "What are we doing? If you must know, it's New Year's Eve and we've just started our annual pick-up basketball game. Leigh's playing point guard—you should see her! She's never blocked like this before in her life.... Of course, I'm kidding, whaddya think, silly? You mean what are we doing *really?* Well, at this moment, we're out to break the world record for the number of batches of nachos eaten by three humans. Jonah and I plan to write a book about it. Yep. We're gonna call it: *The Hundredth Jalapeño: Approaching Critical Mass In The World Of Nachos.*

"Leigh, however, is not competing in this event. No, she's out to see how many drawers and cabinets she can rearrange in one day's time. It took me an hour to find the cheese grater. I may never again see my socks or underwear. We are at her mercy, I'm afraid...What?...Oh yes, we heard...No, Steve and Eric are staying home with a sick llama. The party's been moved to Ted and Betty's...No, no, we'll be fine, Sally...No, really...Leigh feels great. Honest, she does. She hasn't been this energetic in ages. You'd think she was on speed or something. Maybe we'll call her Ampheta-Mom. I bought her a case of Diet Dr. Pepper and a whole container of those red licorice strips and she's happy as a clam.

She uses them like straws to suck the Dr. Pepper through…Well, she just chews the ends off and sucks it through…How should I know why she does that? You're the midwife. Yes, I agree it's too weird for words, but that's what she wants. That and nachos. She wants nachos. Nachos with extra jalapeños. So, we're doing our best to accommodate. If anybody burps close to the firewood, there could be trouble…no, now don't be a pest about this. You and Glenn go on and have a good time. Give everybody our love. We're just gonna stick close to home tonight and play it safe. We'll be here apologizing to our colons…okay …don't worry, Sally. Now, go on…yes, I have all your phone numbers …yes, yes, yes, I will call you…now, hang up the phone, okay? I'm gonna hang up on you, Sally, if you don't hush now, and it would be a really bad memory for us both…yes, we love you, too. 'Bye."

She slipped the phone back in its cradle and leaned up against the wall. "That was Sally," she said, "who worries entirely too much for a medical professional if you ask me. So, what are your plans for the evening?" Cory asked Jonah as she slid the last batch of nachos under the broiler. "Hot date? Party? Spinning straw into gold?"

"Nothing quite so spectacular," Jonah replied. "I'm meditating, then going to bed."

"I swear, Jonah, you meditate so much sometimes we think you're going to disappear, just poof away like some vapor. I always about halfway expect to look out and see you hovering above the barn." She wiggled her fingers in the air indicating spookiness.

"If you do see me hovering above the barn," Jonah said, "I hope I have a hammer and nails with me. There's a big hole in the roof on the south side. Have you seen it?"

Cory rolled her eyes and let her shoulders droop. "Don't remind me," she said. "I was giving it a big dose of benign neglect. The roof and the cracked support beam. If the wind doesn't blow it over before then, I'll get Glenn to fix it up in the spring. We'll build a new barn, too, down the hill, for the critters. With a heater in it even. I'm kind of scared to put them in the old one, but it gets so cold I hate to leave them out. Mimi would come in the house if we'd let her, but the horses are happy anywhere they can get extra oats. So the barn is it, at least for now. It's such a wonderful old thing, I hate to knock it over and get rid of it."

"Knock what wonderful old thing over and get rid of it?" Leigh asked, waddling back into the kitchen. "Me?" Her cleaning and rearranging rampage had taken her all the way out to the laundry room and back and she stood there with a bucket full of cleaning supplies. Her face was sweaty and glistening, almost glowing. A waft of Pine Sol followed her into the room, making her smell antiseptic and tidy.

"Never!" Jonah and Cory said simultaneously.

"Actually," Cory said, "we were thinking of selling you at auction. Being the most pregnant lesbian in central Oregon ought to be worth something, don't you think?"

"Cute," Leigh said, "but bear in mind that I am now the only one in this household who really and truly knows where everything is. Your socks are being held hostage, perhaps even for a ransom." She gave Cory a smug smile, patting her cheek as she passed by.

"Oh, gee, I forgot about that," Cory said. "I guess that makes you too valuable to unload." She reached out and gave Leigh's arm a squeeze.

"Exactly my point," said Leigh, "so don't mess with me."

"Say, did you see this?" Cory asked. "We got a Christmas card from Millie Jensen. Jeepers, it smells like the inside of her truck. Ugh!"

"What does it say?" asked Leigh. Leigh gazed over Cory's shoulder trying to make out the scratching on the inside of the card.

"Here's what I think it says. She sure can't spell: *'I hate this guddam town. My son-in-law is a tird and my dog is mizerbell here. That Jimmy-fella that baugt my place ain't died yet has he? I'd bye it back quik. Your frend, Millie J.'*"

The smell of smoke and scorching tortilla chips was suddenly in the room. "Nachos are ready!" shouted Jonah, grabbing a mitt and sliding them out of the oven. Cheese was still bubbling and crackling and running onto the cookie sheet. The sharp vinegary smell of roasted, pickled jalapeños made Jonah's eyes water. He held the tray at arm's length before setting it on the butcher block in the center of the kitchen. The three of them pulled up stools before digging in. It took Leigh a couple of tries, in a semi-vaulting movement, before she managed to get her body completely up on hers, hooking her toes underneath one of the bars at the bottom for safety. Each simple task seemed a major accomplishment these days.

"Dibs on the burnt ones," said Cory.

"Dibs on the extra jalapeños," said Leigh.

"Dibs on the perfect ones," said Jonah.

By 9:00 P.M. the last batch of nachos had been consumed. By 9:30 P.M., the three friends were well into homemade gingerbread, Red Zinger tea, and a hot game of canasta. At 11:00 P.M., Jonah finally added the scores and flopped the pencil and his cards onto the table. "I can't win against two women who know how to go out with a concealed hand," he said, "and are shameless about it."

"Better a concealed hand than a concealed weapon," said Leigh.

"I went out with a concealed hickey once," Cory said. Jonah and Leigh both stared at her. This was going to be a good one, they could tell. "It was in high school," Cory continued. "I was a junior, I think. Thank God it was winter time. I wore a turtleneck sweater for days— weeks, even. My dad would have yanked me sideways if he'd ever seen it, and he'd have thrown Keith Maroney off a cliff. I'd probably still be grounded, picking corn in some big field out in Plainview, Texas— hunkered over from the back-breaking work, my skin like the end of an old moccasin, a big gap where my front teeth used to be, tired, but loyal, a hard worker, everyone would say—"

"Why would your teeth be missing?" Jonah interrupted.

"Because I would have passed out in the blistering sun—"

"Please!" said Leigh. "Stop!"

"And fallen straight down on my face—"

"There's no end to this, is there?" Jonah asked.

"Not yet," Leigh said. "I'm afraid you just primed the pump."

"After having given up my meager water rations to those less fortunate than myself," Cory added. "That's just how I am, you know. Selfless goodness through and through, that's me."

"But the big question," said Leigh, "is this: would you still have Keith Maroney's hickey on your neck?"

"Of course," said Cory. "It was a serious hickey. Only, by this time it would look like a very old tattoo. Maybe a birthmark. Or a thrombosis of some sort. In the shape of Florida. Or Italy."

"Ladies," said Jonah, "I must go." He pushed away from the table, swirling himself into his jacket in one quick motion. "Happy New Year. I love you." He hugged them both to his chest at once. "Send Ned out to get me if you need to, even though I have to tell you I don't know nuthin' 'bout birthin' babies."

"Neither do we," said Leigh, "but we won't have to tonight. Really. I feel fine. In the immortal words of James Brown," Leigh added, skittering up a head of steam and then sliding across the tiles in her house slippers toward the refrigerator, "Whoa! I feel good, na-nuh, na-nuh, na-nuh-na-nuh…" She wiggled her butt and began bopping with the dishtowel draped through the handle on the fridge. Jonah and Cory stared at her in disbelief, then looked at each other.

Cory shook her head and took a deep breath before she continued. "We've got Sally's beeper number," she said. "And Sally's home phone number. And Sally's work number. And Sally's social security number, for heaven's sake. Don't worry. See you tomorrow."

With that, Jonah was out the door and down the back steps, whooshing out into the darkness toward his cabin without a sound. Even the patches of snow and ice, crusted over by the surprisingly warm evening wind, became velvet under his feet, leaving no tracks.

By 11:30 P.M., the current year seemed to be dragging its heels, unwilling to give up its space to the fledgling New Year. Cory and Leigh, having decided to stay awake long enough for a New Year kiss, were now both asleep. Ned was on his back by the woodstove and appeared to be in a coma. His tongue lolled out of the side of his mouth like some skinny piece of purplish rubber as he lay snoring like an old man.

Leigh was in the rocker, her feet propped on the edge of the coffee table, her favorite quilt draped across her abdomen and legs. Her fingers were laced together protectively over the mound of her pregnant belly. *What's In A Name?* rested on the floor beside her chair. Cory was on the couch, her legs splayed out, with Jerry Garcia snoozing in the crook of her knee. *Don't Call Him Bubba And Don't Call Her Sissy, Either,* a book about naming babies written by a woman from Austin, rested on Cory's chest. A yellow legal pad was on the floor with a list of several potential names: Dylan, Jordan, and Brett showed up in both the column marked BOY and the one marked GIRL.

Leigh felt the movement in her lower abdomen at about the same time she heard the gurgling rumble of Ned's growl. Then a piercing pain shot straight through to her back almost taking her breath away. She lurched forward in the rocker, bent in the middle, feeling as if she'd been tossed onto a spear, not able to stand or lean back. "Cory," she whispered, gasping. "Cory," was all she could say as the pain came again.

Surfacing from her slumber, Cory rolled over. She mumbled something to Leigh that sounded like, "Warned you about too many jalapeños," then pinned Jerry Garcia's fat head between her knees. The cat yowled with everything in him just as Ned jumped to his feet, barking in his guard-dog voice, the fur on his neck standing straight up. Cory fell off the couch and Ned bolted, lunging through the living room and dining room, and was halfway into the kitchen when Jonah burst through the back door. The whole scene had a Keystone Cops feel to it.

"Cory!" he screamed, grabbing the fire extinguisher from the laundry room, "Come quick! The barn's on fire! CORY!" His voice was urgent, electric, almost shrill, a surprising sound coming from him.

Not realizing Leigh was in pain, Cory scrambled up from the floor at the sound of Jonah's voice. She charged through the house, pulling on her boots as she hopped down the back steps and ran toward the barn. The amber glow of flames silhouetted the barn against the night sky and Cory could hear Mimi's plaintive bellowing and the *bam!bam!bam!* of the tenacious bovine trying to cow-kick her way out of the barn.

Ned barked and yelped, leaping up against the creaky old building, as if the force of his voice could somehow extinguish the flames or cut a hole in the side of the barn, freeing the animals trapped inside. The terrified horses screamed out into the night, against the heat, against the flames. Piercing, awful sounds.

Jonah foamed the door while Cory dragged the hose around, praying it wasn't frozen up, praying it would reach far enough. She said, "Thank You, God," when she realized it wasn't and it would and with plenty of hose to spare. "Get the side before it gets to the hay!" she yelled and pitched the nozzle to Jonah, who nodded and took off running around the side of the barn with the hose. It was then that Cory noticed he was barefoot, his feet flying across the patches of snow and ice, flashing against the darkness.

The door to the barn was the color of charcoal and still hot to the touch, as hot as the top of their woodstove, when Cory managed to get it open by wrapping the handle in the bottom of her shirt. The black, acrid smoke whooshed out of the barn, roiling into a sooty tidal wave. Cory covered her face with her arm. It was sweltering inside, and the old barn groaned from the heat and trauma. Underneath the choking bite of smoke was the unmistakable smell of gasoline.

Mesa, the buckskin, bolted past Cory, wild-eyed. Froth, gray from the smoke, dripped from her nose and mouth. Lakota, the paint, reared and bucked until Cory was able to slip a feed sack over his eyes and her belt around his neck to lead him out. Snaring his head in a halter and rope left on the fence post, she tied him up next to the tool shed fifty yards away. She talked to the skittish horse to soothe him as he danced around and snorted. She hugged his neck and rubbed the singed black mane, which smelled of smoke and terror and burned hair.

Running back to retrieve her cow, Cory saw Mimi emerge from the smoldering barn. The cow limped along, crunching a mouthful of cow-cakes in that slow, side-to-side grinding of her big, square teeth. She sauntered past Cory with no more than a nudge, a belligerent kind of push with her flank as if to say, *What kept you?* The cow had a funny look on her face, not exactly angry, more like put out, inconvenienced, bored with this particular drama. After all, she walked around with a reminder of hatred—bullet fragments imbedded deep in her shoulder—every day.

Cory heard Jonah's voice, gentle once again, behind her. "It's out," he said. His face was streaked with smoke as he worked to coil the hose over his arm. They looked at each other and their eyes registered their fear. War had been declared on them. Nothing about it felt like a fair fight.

"Who would do this to us?" Cory asked. Her voice almost broke and she looked away quickly to keep from crying.

"Evil spirits," Jonah replied. "Or crazy ones."

"Mesa freaked and took off," Cory said. "I hope we don't find her dead in a ditch in the morning. She'll run forever."

"I'll go get her," Jonah said. "Don't worry. I'll speak to her in the Lakota language. She always comes when I do that."

"It works? For true?" Cory asked. Jonah nodded.

"Well," he said, "it helps if I have an armful of alfalfa."

"Thanks, Jonah," Cory said. "I'll get the others tucked in. I'll put them by the shed and close off the corral. Cowcakes and oats ought to calm everybody down and keep them happy. Oh, and Jonah," she glanced down at his feet, "put some shoes on, will you? It's still winter, in case you haven't noticed."

"Thank you for thinking of me," he said, smiling at her, "but I don't need them right now." He ripped a chunk of alfalfa from the end of a bale and took off down the hill, his gait smooth and untroubled. The tail of his shirt flapped at her like sea-going passengers waving bon voyage with white handkerchiefs. Cory watched the bottoms of his feet slapping at the night, churning like slats on a paddle wheel, until he was out of sight.

·47·

Nobody saw Jonah Sullivan die, nobody on the earth plane, anyway. He'd just brought Mesa back up from the pasture and turned her loose in the corral with Lakota. Having completed his mission, Jonah had walked back into the smoldering barn to check on everything, to make sure no fire was about to break out again, and to put away the halters.

At the precise moment the main support beam in the ancient barn finally gave way, groaning like an Orca before breaking in two and crashing down onto the young man's neck, Cory Miller lay unconscious not fifty yards away. The blood from a gash in her forehead stained the patch of crusty snow beneath her.

Jonah had not seen her, either. He had not seen fire blazing from the front and back porches of Cory and Leigh's home, had not seen Cory and Ned running up the hill. Nor had he seen the evil banshee scream out of the front hedge straight at them, wallop Cory aside the head with a red gas can, and almost break Ned's jaw with a sudden, vicious kick from thick-soled boots and another to the ribs for good measure.

The dog lay on his side, almost unconscious, barely wheezing breath in and out, his paw as close to Cory as he could get it. A patch of blood-soaked denim jean material hung from a bottom tooth.

The smell of smoke blowing down the hill brought Ned back to consciousness; his heart and his duty brought the wounded animal back to his feet. He stood, wobbly, and tried to bark, coughing up blood. He shook his head to clear it. His right eye was almost swollen shut. He barked again, and his voice sounded more like Ned. Then he looked up the hill toward the cabin, quickly licked Cory on the chin, and took off down the road, his breathing labored, toward Jimmy Heron's.

Who could ever know the dog's thought processes during all of this? He wasn't Lassie, after all, a dog who would probably have grabbed the nozzle of the hose, put out the fire, delivered the baby, and done a load of laundry. No, he was just Ned, doing his dog-job the best way he knew how. He was going for help.

Inside his trailer, Jimmy Heron had dozed off on his bed fully clothed with a *Field and Stream* magazine fanned out on his chest. His Beltones rested in a saucer on the nightstand beside him. He was not dreaming, but the rumble of Ned's bark outside made him think he was. As he awoke, the wall of the trailer vibrated behind his head with each burly bark. What is that sound? he thought. A dog barking? A cannon going off somewhere? He sat up and slipped his hearing aids in, then padded to the door in his sock feet to peek out the window.

At the bottom of the steps he saw Ned, barking with great effort, listing to the side in between barks. The dog looked hurt, beat up, like he'd been hit by a car. Jimmy eased the door open to let him in and realized Ned couldn't make it up the steps. Rushing down to gather the dog up, Jimmy noticed light coming through the bare trees, something unusual, an orange glow from up on Lavender Hill—fire! "Oh, Jesus-God," he said, as he scooped Ned up like a calf and rushed him into the trailer, placing him gently onto the rug by the woodstove. "You hold on, buddy," he said, "I'll be back real quick."

Jimmy slid his feet into his boots, not even bothering to lace them, grabbed his jacket and raced out the door and up the drive. He punched his arms into the sleeves as he ran along the road, his bootlaces flapping and clicking with each movement, his ring of locksmith keys banging against his hip in sync with his stride. He ran faster than he knew he could run, his toes barely touching the gravel, as if God had him by the hair.

Jimmy could see from the road that there was fire at both doors. Shit! Fat chance he'd have of picking either lock. When he made it to the top of the drive and burst through the hedge, he was right next to the row of living room windows. He looked inside and was sickened to see through the haze of smoke what he thought was Leigh. She was crumpled into a heap on the floor, a quilt pulled up over her face. She looked like a rag doll.

He could not see Cory or Jonah anywhere. "CORY! JONAH!" Jimmy shouted as he slipped off his jacket and wrapped it around his fist. He punched through the glass in three quick hits, then hoisted himself up and slid through the window, ripping the front of his shirt and grazing his skin on some jagged shards.

Jimmy kept as low as he could to escape the smoke and scrambled over to Leigh. She was still conscious, but barely so. "Leigh," he said, "it's me, Jimmy. Where are Cory and Jonah? I don't see them."

"Oh, Jimmy," Leigh said, opening her eyes for just a moment, "they're outside. Ned, too, I think. Something caught fire and—"

"Leigh," he interrupted, "listen to me. The house is on fire. Right now. We've got to get you out of here." He unraveled her from the quilt and gave the end of it a quick dunk in the aquarium. Wrapping it around her again, he brought the wet part up over her face. He scooped her up, surprised at how light she seemed, as both of them choked on the smoke. Water began leaking from her in a steady gush and splashed onto the floor.

"I was afraid of that," Leigh said. "Don't worry about finding a hose to fight the fire, Jimmy, just grab me by the arms and sling me around the room." She smiled up at him. He stared back at her, the way he had stared at Lou on the last day of her life, astonished she could think of something funny to say at a time like this. He started toward the kitchen where the smoke seemed less dense and spotted Jerry Garcia cowering in the corner of the dining room. Squatting down quickly, he grabbed the cat and plopped him right in the middle of Leigh.

"Sorry, Jerry," Jimmy said, "but I don't have time to coax you." The three of them raced through the dining room, the kitchen, the laundry room, picking up speed like a locomotive. At the last second, Jimmy Heron dropped his shoulder, turned slightly, and blasted through the smoking door with his back, sending splintered boards and glass flying. He and Leigh and Jerry seemed to be in slow motion, suspended for a few seconds in midair before sprawling out onto the backyard.

Jerry Garcia hit the ground like a sack of oats and scampered off into the bushes to hide. Jimmy crawled over to Leigh on his hands and knees, lifting up her head and resting it on his leg. "Leigh," he whispered, "are you okay?"

"Jimmy," she said, pulling her knees up, "the baby's on the way. Please help me. Please."

Not knowing what else to do, Jimmy positioned himself between her knees and, unsure exactly why, he began to pull the laces out of one of his boots. Leigh was puffing and panting when she suddenly let out a scream. Jimmy caught hold of her hand and gingerly lifted the quilt and her nightgown to see what was happening. "Forgive me," he said.

"Forgiven," Leigh replied, panting and puffing once again.

"I see the head," Jimmy said, pulling the edge of the quilt up under Leigh's bottom. "Can you push once more?"

"AAAAAARRRRGGGH!" replied Leigh, pushing with all her might. Her face looked almost purple and the veins stuck out on the side of her face. The infant suddenly shot out of her, surprising them both. Jimmy managed to catch the baby, a wiggly, gooey life form, before it skidded across the ground. He ran a finger quickly around the inside of the baby's mouth to check for mucus, and squeezed the nostrils downward, just like he would do with a newborn colt. He wiped its face and head off with the quilt and then fished around in his pants for his new knife. Tying the umbilical cord off with the lace from his boot, he severed it quickly and the baby let out a bleating wail, sounding quite a bit like a baby goat.

Jimmy gathered the infant up and talked to it softly before placing it on Leigh's chest. Somehow, he knew this child, had felt the spirit of this new being entwined with his own from the instant he caught the infant in his arms. "Hey-bub, hey-bub, hey-bub," he cooed until the tiny boy, wrapped up in the edge of the quilt like a little burrito, settled down. Jimmy glanced at his watch and noticed it was now one minute into the New Year. "The two of you have a son," he said to Leigh. "Happy New Year," he added, and began to cry. It was not a weeping of sadness, nor of joy, really. It was recognition, connection, a reunion of souls.

The *ka-POW!* of Sally and Glenn's VW bus backfiring as it puttered up the hill made Jimmy and Leigh both flinch. It sounded like gunfire. The bus rattled itself to a wheezy halt, then Sally and Glenn hit the ground moving. Sally headed toward the back with her bag in hand, the one in which she carried everything she would ever need to do anything ever asked of her. Glenn took off toward the front. When Jimmy saw Sally racing toward them, he couldn't remember feeling quite so relieved in all his life. He gave her a quick wave and dashed off to help Glenn, who was lumbering around the corner of the house with a hose. Glenn looked like a bear on the run.

Sally instantly set to work checking the baby and delivering the placenta, which zipped out of Leigh as quickly as a forward pass. Sally plopped the jellied mass into a plastic bag to save as Jonah had asked her to. It was to be buried, in the Native American custom, in a sacred manner.

"We called twice," she said, "and when nobody called us back we got worried. Where's Cory? And Jonah?"

"They both ran outside to put the fire out, I think. Are they okay? Are the animals all right?"

Sally smiled at Leigh. "I'm sure they are, sweetie," she said, "don't worry. So, here we are in the new "natural setting" delivery room. You're not cold are you?" Leigh shook her head no. "Looks like you've done just fine on your own," Sally said. "This certainly didn't take as long as first births usually do. How long were you in labor?"

"Not long," said Leigh. "Actually, I wouldn't even really call it labor, not even very hard work. I've had PTA meetings tougher than this."

Sally checked the baby from stem to stern, listening to his heart, moving his arms and legs back and forth, running her thumbnail along the outside of his foot to test for certain reflexes. Then she wrapped him tightly in a receiving blanket she pulled out of her bag and handed him back to Leigh. Sally pulled a knit cap onto the baby's head. "He's perfect, Leigh-O," Sally said, "just perfect." Sally hugged her friend's neck.

Glenn and Jimmy put the house fire out. It had not ruined as much as they had feared. The front porch would have to be replaced and the back door, of course, where Jimmy and Leigh crashed through it. Plus a log or two just to be safe. Neither of them had even noticed the scorched barn, so concerned had they been with Leigh, the baby, and the house.

"So, where are Cory and Jonah?" Leigh asked. "Should we go look for them? This is making me nervous."

"I'll go. Don't worry," Jimmy said, and started to get up.

The three of them—Jimmy, Sally, and Glenn—were huddled around Leigh and the baby when Glenn suddenly arched his back and looked up, as if sniffing the air for danger. Jimmy felt every muscle in his body tense, and he crouched back down, ready for a fight, as they watched someone moving toward them from the direction of the barn, someone staggering through the darkness. It was Cory. They all recognized her at the same time she saw them.

"So, what is this—a picnic scene in the middle of the night? And on New Year's Eve, too. Where is Dick Clark when we need him?" Cory said, holding her hand over the cut above her eye. "Am I the only one who knows it's still winter? The wind is so warm, though…why is that? Man, do I have a headache."

Sally ran over to her, placed an arm around her shoulders, and helped her sit down on the ground next to the group. "Let me take a look," she said, easing Cory's fingers away from the wound. Blood was dried and caked around the cut which had already begun to close, and the goose egg had turned an ugly shade of jade. Sally daubed at it with some antiseptic from her bag as Cory flinched, yanking her head away. "Who did this to you?" Sally asked.

"Don't know," Cory said. "We heard some guy running at us—he was screaming like a maniac—and then he hit me in the head with a gas can. At least, I think it was a gas can. Must have been high octane. The last thing I saw was red. Where's Ned? He was with me—"

"Ned's at my place," Jimmy spoke up. "Looks like he got kicked, but I think he'll be all right. Don't you worry."

"I hope he bit the sonofabitch," Cory said.

"Cory, where's Jonah?" asked Leigh.

"He's gone after Mesa. She ran off right after we got the barn fire out. He'll be back soon."

"They set your barn on fire, too?" Sally was incredulous. Glenn and Jimmy instantly jumped up and took off toward the barn.

"Sally, call the sheriff," Jimmy yelled, as he and Glenn raced away. Sally started to get up when Leigh stopped her.

"No, Sally," Leigh said, "we can handle that later. Right now I want to have everyone I love around me. I don't care who did this. Really, I don't. I just want everyone safe. Please. Tom can catch somebody later. Please. Sit. I don't want everyone all scattered out." Sally knelt back down beside her friend.

"I need a drink of water," said Cory.

"I have water," said Sally, reaching for the bottle in her bag and handing it to Cory, who took two big swigs.

"I could sure use an aspirin," Cory said as she scooted on her butt up next to Leigh.

"I have aspirin," Sally said, rummaging deep into her bag, a seemingly bottomless container of medical essentials. She handed a couple over.

"Interested in sharing that quilt?" Cory asked Leigh. "Am I the only one getting chilled?" She rubbed her arms with her hands.

"I'm fine," said Sally.

"Me, too," said Leigh, "not cold a bit. But I can't share my quilt with you."

"Why not?" Cory asked. Leigh eased the quilt away from her breast, exposing the tiny, sleeping face resting there. The infant's face was red and scrinched, his tiny fingers gathered up under his chin. His eyelids fluttered for just a second and then settled back down.

"This is why," Leigh said, showing Cory the baby. "Our package arrived while you were out. Special delivery, thanks to our friend Jimmy."

Cory's mouth dropped open. She stared at the baby, reaching over to touch his silken cheek. "We have a boy, Cory," Leigh said, "a son." All three reached out to touch one another's shoulders, forming a protective circle, a womb, around the newborn life.

Although nobody on the earth plane ever noticed, wind blew a cloud up from the valley. It hovered above the old barn and rested there for a few seconds before another breeze, a stronger one, pushed the cloud into its own constellation, a different shape. The cloud wrestled with the wind briefly, then disappeared as silently as a vapor, as quickly as a dream.

·48·

Three weeks later, on the windy hill by Cerebrum Rock, Cory, Leigh, and their newly christened son, Jefferson Miller O'Brien, gathered. The minister of the Methodist church, Chuck Kimberling, and other friends—Jimmy Heron, members of the COBB group, Tom, Kate, and Jenny Mason, Dick and Alice Barstow, plus several children from the Reliance Pioneer School—were also in attendance. They were there to say good-bye to the spirit of Jonah Sullivan, whose ashes rested in a small covered wooden bowl on top of the volcanic boulder.

Reverend Kimberling, an ex-Marine turned hippie turned logger turned fishing guide turned minister, led the ceremony. He was a wiry man whose ruddy cheeks and pale blue eyes had faced many sunrises on the river. His hair and almost-too-big mustache had grayed early in his life, on a hillside in Vietnam.

A great-great-grandmother from a Cherokee tribe in Tennessee was somewhere up his family totem pole. Respect for his own Cherokee heritage and for Native American people led Chuck Kimberling to weave Native wisdom into his sermons. His theology was simple: love each other, be grateful for the life you were given, harm no one and no thing. Oh, and have a good time, that was important, too. He had chosen the Methodists because they would let him drink beer and dance.

Lifting the lid off the bowl, Chuck Kimberling scooped up a handful of ashes. "Oh Lord, our God," he said, "we commend to you the spirit of our friend, Jonah Sullivan." Flinging his hand in the air, Reverend Kimberling watched the wind sweep Jonah's ashes up in the sky and down toward the valley, disappearing within seconds. "As your son Jesus was sent to the earth to teach us how to love each other, so was Jonah Sullivan, a truly gentle soul. We are all blessed to have had

Jonah with us for this time and we thank you for him."

Leigh began to weep softly, snuggling the baby up closer to her neck. Red fuzz peeked out from under the edge of the infant's blue knit cap and fluttered in the wind.

"Tunkashila," the reverend continued, holding his open palms toward the sky, "receive our brother with open arms. Great Spirit, welcome him home."

One by one, beginning with Leigh and Cory, each person took some ashes and did the same until two-thirds of the ashes in the bowl had been set free by the wind. The last person to release Jonah's ashes was little Erin-Anne Turner. When she held her open palm toward the sky, a gust of wind swirled the dusty remains up. It formed a mini-cyclone of spirit and matter right before her eyes, then flitted away like so much stardust. She giggled.

Reverend Kimberling put the lid back on the bowl. Kneeling beside the freshly dug hole just below Cerebrum Rock, he lowered the carved wooden container into the grave. The clean smell of the earth mixed in the air. Leigh passed the baby to Jimmy and stepped forward, going on her knees to slip the placenta out of its plastic bag and into the grave. Cory knelt across from her.

"In some Native American cultures," Leigh said, "particularly the Navajo, after a child is born, burial of the placenta, the sack in which the baby lives inside the mother, is of great importance." Ever the teacher, she glanced at the children to make sure they understood. "Some believe it will influence the spirit and life of the child born. We could not think of a better place for this than with our friend Jonah. We loved him very much, and we know his spirit will look after our son."

"His gentleness will be with us always," Cory added. "We are very grateful to have known him." Her chin began to quiver and she hung her head. Tears streamed down her cheeks. "We will miss him," she said, barely able to squeeze the words out. "We will miss him so much."

Again, one by one, each person at the funeral filed past the grave to drop in an item—a bundle of dried flowers, a pretty stone, a strand of beads, a note of good-bye. Erin-Anne Turner dropped in a tangerine she'd saved from her lunch and her greatly loved, almost bald Malibu Barbie. She smiled as she did so, pleased with herself, her gift, and her sacrifice. Evidence of the impending arrival of her big teeth flashed like tiny, white stalactites emerging from her gums. Alice Barstow and Kate Mason both began to weep.

Jimmy Heron carefully handed the baby to Sally and reached inside his jacket to his shirt pocket. Giving the feather a gentle stroke before he pulled it out, Jimmy walked over slowly toward the grave. Handing the heron's feather to Leigh, who gently placed it in the grave, Jimmy turned to face the rest of the group. "I didn't know Jonah very long," he said, "but he was my friend. I will miss him." Jimmy struggled for the right words. "He saw into my heart and tried to ease the pain. He was my brother." And then Jimmy Heron fell silent in order to keep from crying.

Walking back up the hill after the service with his arms draped protectively across Cory and Leigh's shoulders, Jimmy felt heavy with sadness, but also extraordinarily strong. It was as if some puzzling gift he'd unexpectedly received finally made sense. As if, after all that had happened in his life in the past few months, he knew in his core that everything was for a reason, that everything would be all right. Something had shifted in his bones, deep in the marrow of who he was.

·49·

The sound was like bees swarming around a hive, alive with excitement and anticipation, even though a certain anxiety was present in the air, like the feeling just before a big prizefight. Someone was bound to come away bloody.

The town hall in downtown Reliance, Oregon was already packed, and still people were filing in—people from Sisters and Bend and Redmond and even smaller towns in central Oregon, all of them anxious to hear what was to be said on this night.

Snow had fallen again the week before, thick and relentless, and had clogged routes in and out of town for several days. Even though it had warmed up considerably by the first week of March and the roads were mostly slushy, occasional bursts of icy wind off the top of Three-Fingered Jack kept everyone bundled up against the cold. People were far too warm once inside, and coats and hats and boots overflowed from the racks and began piling up in a corner as they got themselves more comfortable and settled in.

The room was divided into two distinct camps at first. Members of the Oregon Reformation Society and the Mt. Goshen Church of the Righteous sat on the right side, and members of the Central Oregon Bigot Busters and their friends sat on the left. As space became less available, however, many people found themselves shoulder to shoulder with people they considered the enemy, trying not to touch for fear of contamination. The room began to feel almost claustrophobic.

Leigh and Cory sat in a row toward the front with Jimmy, Sally and Glenn, and a few other members of COBB. Jimmy had his legs crossed with the new baby boy propped up in the crook of his knee. A fat little fist was wrapped securely around his index finger and a bootied foot, which had kicked its way out of the blanket, was now jabbing him in the groin. But Jimmy Heron didn't mind in the least.

Jefferson Miller O'Brien, now two months old, had been nursed and burped and had a diaper changed. He was now in that fuzzy place babies get to just before sleep, alternately grinning and cooing and then drifting off. Having learned at less than a month old the power of a big, gooey smile, the baby was reluctant to give it up for such a silly thing as sleep. His toothless grin seemed to bring the house down and leave all the people who adored him clamoring for more. He was a smart boy and not the least bit stingy with the joy he brought.

Darryl and Juanita Dimmer clearly led the delegation sitting on the right. Both of them leaned forward in their seats next to the aisle, poised and seemingly ready to pounce. Reverend Dimmer, his red leather Bible in hand, was sweating and tugging at his cotton-and-wool-blend sweater, a creamy lemon color. Juanita had talked him into wearing it so he would look more approachable, just in case any fence-sitters could be persuaded to their point of view.

Juanita Dimmer tried her best to act casual, although curiosity would occasionally get the best of her. This would cause her to swivel abruptly in her seat and cast a scowling eye toward people sitting on the left side of the room. Once a woman of great warmth and beauty, self-righteousness had hardened and stained her over the years so that her features had taken on an almost cartoonish appearance. She looked as if she might snort or bray at any moment. Light bounced off the back of her hair and her husband's toupee. Both, true to form, were sprayed as stiff as Tupperware bowls.

Wendell Metcalf sat far to the right, brooding and sullen, with his arms clamped firmly across his chest, as if holding all the hatred in the world stuffed deep inside him. Antigay literature and YES ON 19 stickers bulged from the pocket of his corduroy jacket, and he itched for the chance to stand on his chair and fling them at all the assholes in this room like so much confetti. *Fuckin' fag-lovers.*

Suzette Metcalf sat next to Wendell, laboriously filing her nails— buffing, sweeping off her tweed skirt, holding her hands up to the light to admire her work. Suzette could not understand what all the fuss was about, or why there even had to be a meeting about such an unseemly issue. Any fool could see that gay people were just not supposed to be here.

It wasn't that she made a moral judgment about it; it was simply that "those people" didn't square up with Suzette Metcalf and her idea of normal, of orderliness. If they all had to be eliminated, well, then so much the better. Just call her when it was over. The turmoil seemed unnecessary when the solution was so simple: get rid of them.

Suzette worked on her nails and glanced over toward the left side of the room. Yes, she thought, that would be the perfect solution. Everybody knew it, and it might as well start in Reliance as anyplace else. It would be messy at first, but everything could be cleaned up. Cleaned up and tidy again. In the world of Suzette Metcalf, that was the most important thing.

Tom Mason and Dick Barstow sat at a table at the front of the room to act as mediators of this showdown. As mayor of Reliance and an all-around amiable guy, Dick knew the names of almost everyone in the room. He could not keep himself from waving and glad-handing whenever possible, just to let folks know he was thinking of them.

Tom Mason, whose big idea this meeting was in the first place, looked strained and unsettled, as if waiting for a bomb to explode, or for pistols to be drawn. He fidgeted in his chair and tapped the end of his pencil on the table until the lead broke off, secretly miffed at Dick for acting as though this were some big political rally.

Jenny Mason, sitting just a couple of rows back with her mom, would occasionally catch her dad's eye and grin at him, making a silly face to try and get him to lighten up. It didn't work. As much as he loved her, as easy as it had always been for him to turn into mush at the slightest smile from her, on this night Tom Mason's mind was on other things. He was wondering how to create a safer more loving Reliance in which his precious daughter could grow up.

Glancing at his watch, Tom noticed it was 7:40, already ten minutes past the time they'd agreed to begin. He cleared his throat. "We need to start this meeting now," he said, running his gaze around the crowded room. "I'll try to make this as brief as possible and let everyone have a time to speak. As you are aware, a ballot measure has been approved to appear before the public in the election coming up this fall. It is Ballot Measure #19, and if you haven't heard about it by now, you've been living in a cave somewhere.

"The purpose of this ballot measure is to change the wording of the Oregon Constitution so that it will declare homosexuality, and I'm quoting here, '…abnormal, wrong, unnatural and perverse…,' and—"

"That's exactly what it is!" shouted Wendell Metcalf from across the room. "Ballot Measure 19 is to save Oregon and the rest of America from—"

"Oh, tie a knot in it, Wendell!" yelled Steve Dvorak from the other side, as Eric pulled him back down in his chair.

"Wait!" shouted Tom, who took a long, slow breath. "This is exactly what we don't need—people shouting at each other. Now, just hold off until you get your turn to speak. I'm not here to tell you how to vote on this measure. That's not my job. My job is to uphold the law and protect the citizens of this town, and right now this town feels like it's about to explode. We have had rampant vandalism—animals slaughtered, property defaced, death threats left in mailboxes. Two of our citizens even had their house and barn set on fire." Tom paused to look at the faces in the audience before he continued. "These two people were home at the time, asleep. It is clear that the fire was intended to kill them both. One of our citizens, Jonah Sullivan, actually did die as a direct result of that fire. He was only twenty-five years old." There was a gasp from somewhere in the back of the room, maybe even from the group on the right.

"I hope you're not accusing me or my congregation of murder or attempted murder, Sheriff," Darryl Dimmer spoke up. He had an almost wicked grin on his face, as if he were challenging the sheriff to do just that very thing.

"We'll sue you for slander," Juanita chimed in.

"I'm not accusing anyone here of anything, Darryl. Keep your shirt on," said Tom, the irritation rising in his voice. "All I'm saying is that this has gotten out of hand, this hatred, this intolerance. It has got to stop before we all wind up hating each other, before someone else gets killed. And I have to tell you, Darryl, that your sermons are not helping. If enough hateful and divisive rhetoric is spewed out week after week, there will always be someone willing, some sociopath willing to act on those words. Don't fool yourself into thinking it won't happen. It already has, and not just in our town, but across the country. I'm just trying to keep any more of it from happening here in Reliance."

Darryl Dimmer's face and neck seemed to expand, to puff out, and a bruising purplish color began creeping up the sides of his head and around his ears. He stood and pointed his Bible at Tom. "You'll burn in hell before you tell me how to preach a sermon in my own church, Tom Mason. You can count on that, you and your whole lobotomized, liberal leftist, Communistic crowd." A foamy coating of spit had gathered at the corners of the reverend's mouth. Juanita tugged at his sweater, pulling him back down onto his chair before he had a stroke.

Leigh O'Brien stood on the other side of the room. "I have something to say," she said, and turned to face the crowd. "Most of you know me since I have taught your children at some time or other over the past twenty years. You probably also know that a lot of the conflict here in Reliance revolves around the fact that my partner, Cory, and I decided to have a family together. Before that, everybody knew without having to be told about our lives. My regret comes from the fact that we were accomplices in this. We didn't lie about it, but we didn't stand up and say the truth, either. I have realized in the past year just what a shameful thing that was." Leigh took a deep breath and looked around the room. "I am an American and an Oregonian. I deserve exactly the same rights as everyone else is entitled to."

"But you do have the same rights, you stupid dyke!" shouted Wendell Metcalf. "You just don't get to have special rights." Leigh whirled and glared at him.

"Equal rights are not special rights. As long as your marriage is legal and mine is not, Wendell, don't talk to me about special rights," Leigh said. "As long as you cannot be fired from a job for being who you are and you want to be able to vote on whether or not I can, don't waste your breath."

"How dare you even mention a marriage sanctioned by God in the same breath with that reprehensible pile of perversion you're in that you call a relationship." Juanita Dimmer spat the words out staccato-like, as if she were expelling watermelon seeds.

"Now hold on a second, sister," Cory said. She stood, feeling a little shaky, but gathering steam as she continued. "I find it really offensive that you think the love I feel for Leigh is somehow 'less than' whatever you think real, true love, or relationship, or marriage is. I've kept my mouth shut and I've gone along to get along, but enough is enough, and I'm here to tell you that this love is no less real, no less passionate, and no less blessed than any other love.

"If the only way the two of you can make yourselves feel better is by trying to make everyone else feel bad, then you're just pissin' up a rope, as far as I'm concerned. I am no longer going to sit around and be nice while you define to the rest of the world who or what you think I am, who Leigh is, or what our family and friends mean to us.

"If you want a fight, then, by God, let's draw a line in the dirt, because you'll be sorry for the day you ever turned over my rock. I will be like a gila monster on the fat part of your thigh for the rest of your days. I won't give up and I won't let go. You can cut off my head and I won't ease up. I'll be clamped down hard, grinning right in your face until your final breath."

Cory was standing with her index finger jabbing at the air to make a point. She surprised herself, realizing she had stopped speaking and was still pointing with her finger at the silence.

She looked at the audience and blushed, her ears turning a dark crimson. Then she sat down slowly. Never having been so bold or outspoken or confrontational in her entire life, she felt shell-shocked. She was stunned at the words and emotion that had flown out of her, as if she had been channeling for some being that actually had a spine. She grinned a slow grin. Well, that wasn't nearly the traumatic episode she'd always imagined. No body parts fell to the floor. Her head didn't explode. She actually felt stronger, taller, held up by something powerful and true.

Leigh and Sally both stared at Cory, their jaws dropped open and hanging loose like nutcrackers. The entire room sat in stunned silence for several seconds.

Suddenly, the left side of the audience exploded into applause so loud and rapid-fire it sounded like potatoes being lowered into a deep fryer. Whoops and hollers peppered the outburst. Ted and Betty both jumped to their feet and punched their fists in the air. Even a few people who'd had the misfortune to arrive at the meeting late and had been forced to sit on the right side of the room burst into applause. Juanita pivoted in her seat and glared at them. Pestilence would have been easier to bear than the hateful gaze of Juanita Dimmer. *You'll go to hell!* She mouthed the words at them, just to remind them of the clout she was sure she carried with the Lord.

Tom Mason stood and placed his hands on his hips, looking more like a basketball coach than a sheriff. "This meeting wasn't designed to be a pep rally," he admonished, "or a shouting match. I want us all to have the decency and respect to let each other speak and to finish what we have to say without being interrupted or insulted. Is that too much to ask?"

A young man stood on the left side of the room. He was no more than sixteen or seventeen, handsome, with clear blue eyes, cleft chin, and a short, muscular build. His dark brown hair was parted on the right and combed straight across. It was Mitchell, Betty and Ted's son. "I have something to say," he said, clearing his throat. "My mom realized she was gay when I was nine years old and she never lied to me about that. She said she wanted me to grow up to be a truthful man and she couldn't expect that if she wasn't a truthful mother. She and my father had been divorced for almost a year.

"When she fell in love with Ted, uh, Theodora, I tried my best to hate them both because I didn't want to be different. I didn't want my family to be different from any other families. But you know what? I couldn't do it, I just couldn't do it. And it wasn't because I was a nicer kid, or more sensitive, or more forgiving. I was just as big a jerk as you'd ever want to meet. It was simply that, well, I love my mom, and who could not love Ted? She has helped raise me just as if I was her very own son. She taught me to fly fish and to hunt for elk. She showed me how to whitewater raft and she helped me figure out how to do calculus problems so I wouldn't flunk math. She also showed me how to iron my own shirts, and I bet not many teenage boys know how to do that." He tugged at his freshly pressed shirt and smiled. "I ironed this one," he said, proud of his handiwork.

"I guess one of the most important parts, though," he continued, "was that she and my mom never interfered in my relationship with my dad. They never tried to push their life or their point of view on me or anybody. They love each other and they love me, and I don't see anything wrong with that at all. I just figured it was time I stood up in front of everybody to say how much I love them, both of them, and that all the ballot measures in the world will never change that."

In the midst of steady applause, Mitchell sat down next to his mother, who was wiping her eyes and snuffling and blowing her nose into a pink Kleenex. No parents ever felt more proud of a child than did these two women in this moment. Betty patted Mitchell's leg with her free hand. Ted reached over and squeezed the back of his neck with a callused paw, oddly adorned with an elaborate gold ring cradling a ruby the size of a prune pit. The brilliant crimson hue of the stone perfectly matched the red in Ted's flannel shirt, and was probably her idea of dressing up.

Darryl Dimmer rose and pulled his sweater back down over the dome of his belly where it had rolled up. Then he adjusted it in the back across his buttocks. He remembered how exposed he felt wearing anything other than a suit jacket or sports coat. He flipped open his Bible, as if he were searching for the appropriate scripture, as if he hadn't had his finger stuck right there on that particular page the entire evening. He raised his eyebrows toward Tom Mason. "I assume," he said, "that this still being America, the members of the Christian community still have the right of free speech." Tom nodded, bored with Darryl's theatrics. "Well, then," the reverend continued, "I am here, along with my gracious and lovely wife and other upstanding citizens, to tell you why we are in support of Ballot Measure 19." He adjusted his glasses on his nose.

"According to my Bible," he said, "the inspired word of God, in the book of Leviticus, chapter 18, verse 22, the Lord states very explicitly, and I quote, 'Do not lie with mankind as with womankind. It is an abomination.'" Darryl Dimmer snapped his Bible shut with a flourish and looked at the crowd, as if that would end the argument right then and there. "It is my duty as a Christian and as a minister of the faith," he said, "to stamp out those things that are an abomination to the Lord."

Sally Taylor shot up from her seat on the other side of the room.

"But Leigh and Cory don't lie with mankind as with womankind," she said. "They don't lie with mankind at all!" She turned to look at her friends. "Hey, guys," she said, "you're home free. Thanks a lot for pointing that out, Darryl. You twerp."

Peels of laughter from the crowd died down after a few seconds, but not before Darryl Dimmer's hand flashed in the air, an obscene gesture about to spring forth. It did not. Thank God, thought Juanita Dimmer, who looked as if she might faint. She tugged at her husband's sleeve and whispered something terse into his ear. He nodded his head, admonished.

From the back of the room a sandy-haired woman spoke. "My name is Jane McAdoo," she said, "and this is my husband Terry." She motioned to the tall, slender man standing beside her. "We have four daughters. Our oldest one, Lindy, is a student in Leigh O'Brien's class, and we know Lindy thinks the world of her. The children in her class are not interested in her sexual orientation. Even if they knew what it meant, it's no more important to them than her eye color. What they are interested in is that she is a terrific teacher who loves them and challenges them to be their best. As the parents of one of her students, I can tell you that that is what we are interested in, as well.

"We are not what you'd call religious people," Jane McAdoo continued. "I mean, we believe in God; we just don't happen to think churches are the best way to practice our beliefs, so we're not here to fight that battle one way or another. But we are here to fight for fairness, and we both believe this ballot measure is completely unfair. Not only is it unfair to the gay and lesbian people of this community and this state, it is unfair to all the rest of us who are now boxed into the position of having to vote for or against the rights of an entire group of people. Can you imagine how it would feel if you were in the group being voted on? It almost makes me nauseous to think about it. I'd rather not have to vote on this issue at all, but since we do, we are both here to voice our opposition to Ballot Measure 19 and to the behavior of the zealots who have forced us into this divisiveness. It's not what we want for our community, and it's certainly not the way we intend to raise our girls."

Jane and Terry McAdoo both smiled at Leigh O'Brien, who raised her hand to them in acknowledgment and appreciation as the crowd applauded.

Lloyd Russell and his wife, Emma, stood on the left side of the room. He was an older black man, deep in color, with salty hair. His eyebrows peaked, making him look bemused. His wife was younger, about fifty, small, with amber eyes. Her skin was the color of creamy coffee. "We moved here from the South," he said. "We thought there would be less of this kind of thing goin' on the further north we got. But we were wrong."

Each time Mr. Russell ended a phrase or paused for a breath, his wife muttered, "It's true, it's true."

"Don't misunderstand me, now," he continued, "most folks here are good. But there's a big difference between feelin' accepted and feelin' like people are just puttin' up with you. We know both feelings, and they're not the same.

"I helped those kids hang the banner on the school," he said, "and I realized they were takin' a stand. Then I understood how I wasn't bein' nearly as brave as they were. All I did was bang in some nails and stretch some rope. Well, tonight my wife and I are here to take a stand against this ballot measure. 'Injustice anywhere is a threat to justice everywhere,' that's what Dr. King said."

"It's true, it's true," Emma Russell averred.

Buoyed by the bravery of the Russells, another black woman, Marlene Burke, a first-grade teacher, rose to speak. She was a lovely woman in her thirties. Gentle, soft-spoken, and motherly, she was every parent's dream of a first-grade teacher.

"I am a Christian," she said. "I believe what I read in my Bible. I believe the lessons in there that I am supposed to learn. I believe the rules I should abide by. But I believe I am supposed to apply those rules only to me, not everyone else. And you know what? It takes up all of my time. All of my time. I don't have the energy or even the interest to run around trying to police everybody else's behavior. I don't think that's what God intended us to do." She sat back down to sustained applause.

Darryl Dimmer spoke from his seat. "When a group of sinful people want to push their ways down the throats of the American people, they must be stopped! Homosexuals have sex out in the open, they ride through town with no clothes on, they—"

The doors on the far side of the meeting room suddenly burst open. Like the entrance a gunslinger makes into a saloon looking for a showdown, Millie Jensen, back from Fargo and anticipating a ruckus, swaggered in, all five feet one inch of her. Her appearance and odor were as weathered and ragged as ever, somewhere between a fishing boat and a dog's blanket.

Jimmy Heron could not help but smile when he realized she was in the very same clothes he had seen her in when he bought her trailer several months before. The only change he could discern was that her gimme cap was cleaner, possibly even a new one, and her polyester stretch pants appeared to be on backward—way too tight across the belly and sagging like an empty laundry sack in the seat.

Millie walked slowly down the aisle until she was standing directly beside Darryl and Juanita Dimmer. They were both leaning so far to the right, trying to get away from Millie without running, they looked like ancient headstones in an old country cemetery about to fall over.

Millie definitely had swaggering down to an art form. "Still usin' the Good Book to beat people over the head, Dimmer?" she said. "Why, I've even seen your ugly face on books and tapes floatin' around all the way out in Fargo. Makin' a lot of money, are ya, spoutin' your own special brand of fire and brimstone bullshit? Gettin' people to hate each other and make you a rich man, are ya?" She poked him on the shoulder with a bony finger. Darryl grimaced and pulled away.

"Get away from me, you old reprobate," he muttered.

"Naw," Millie said, "I thought you and me could swap scriptures for a while, preacher. I'm sure you know more than just that one in Leviticus you keep sayin' over and over. Does the sound of a cash register go off in your big old head every time you say it, is that how it works? Or don't you ever read any other part of your Bible? Maybe you're just into 'selective scripturizin', maybe that's the problem. Just pick and choose the one that suits your purpose, is that how it works? How 'bout Leviticus 19, verse 17, that says—now you correct me if I get it wrong—it says, 'Thou shalt not hate thy brother in thine heart.' Ever hear of that one? Naw, something tells me you skipped right over it. Then, let's try Leviticus 19, verse 11: 'Ye shall not steal, neither deal falsely, nor lie to one another.'"

"How dare you call me a liar or a thief, you filthy pile of vermin!" Darryl shouted at her. "Sheriff, must my wife and I be subjected to this? You said this was to be a civilized discussion." Reverend Dimmer was almost whining.

"You're the only one who's shouting, Darryl," Tom said, chuckling at Millie's surprising knowledge of scripture.

"I was here when you and Miz Juanita floated into this town, Dimmer," Millie said. "You were poor and skinny, both of you, and I even washed up a few times and went to your Bible meetings. I have to say, they were almost enjoyable a time or two, even though, I gotta tell you, any twelve-year old can quote scripture better than you, Dimmer. *Quote* is the key word here, not makin' it up as you go along like you do, Reverend. I kept forgivin' you for it because I thought maybe your heart was in the right place. Boy, was I ever wrong about that one! Don't fool yourself by thinkin' I'm the only one who noticed that your sermons changed; they got big and swollen and nasty. And so did your looks, your waistline, and your bank account I'd bet my last can of Bag Balm on that one. When you started using hatred to make yourself a rich man, well, let's just say I know a viper when I see one, especially a great big fat viper with a rat stuck in its belly!"

"You'll go to hell for threatening a man of the cloth," Juanita Dimmer hissed at Millie.

"Oh, pipe down, you self-righteous sack of wet brownies," Millie shot back. "You'll go to the cardiac unit at St. Vincent's in Portland if you and Darryl don't ease up on the spareribs!" she croaked, cracking herself up and slapping her leg.

She threw back her head, as if she were about to yodel, and shouted into the air, "Leviticus 3, verse 17: 'It shall be a perpetual statute for your generations throughout all your dwellings that ye eat neither fat nor blood.' I don't know about the blood part, although it may apply to you since your hate sermons have been suckin' the life blood out of this town for a long time, but I do know fat when I see it, and the both of you are carryin' around more than your share. You're so hot on the book of Leviticus, why haven't you read the whole thing? How 'bout Leviticus 11, verse 7? 'Eat not the swine, though he divide the hoof and be clovenfooted, yet he cheweth not the cud, he is unclean to you.' Or were those some kind of special vegetarian-soybean fake pork chops you were chowing down on at the Wigwam before Wednesday night prayer meetings? Lars oughta be grateful the hand of God ain't struck all of you down before now."

Darryl Dimmer was struggling to keep himself composed, figuring he had forfeited far too much ground in almost shooting the bird at Sally Taylor. "Eating pork chops can hardly be classified as the same kind of sinful behavior as homosexual acts."

"Sez who?" dared Millie. "You? Juanita? The two of you sanctimonious know-it-alls get to pick and choose your sins? Well, now, that's sure a relief to all the rest of us run-of-the-mill sinners, especially since we was countin' on you to help us get our worthless feet inside the edge of heaven's door. Why, homosexuality ain't even made it to the top ten. You remember the top ten, don't you—the Ten Commandments? Like, 'Thou shalt not bear false witness against thy neighbor.' Stuff like that."

"But since you're partial to the book of Leviticus, let's see what else we can milk out of it. Seems to me if you believed everything in Leviticus, you'd have a beard, uncut, hangin' all the way down your big old gut by now, and, oh, I know, how 'bout this one: Leviticus 19, verse 19 says, 'Neither shall a garment of mingled fabric touch thy skin.' Millie reached over and stretched out the back of Darryl's sweater, peeking in over the tops of her glasses. "Oops, Dimmer," she said, "you're caught again." Millie faked a look of compassion toward the minister. "This just ain't your night, is it, Reverend?" she asked, clucking her tongue. "Says here you're wearing cotton and wool, with just a touch of rayon for that elegant look, no doubt." She wrinkled up her nose and made a face. "Eeeewwwwwwww," she said, "all mixed together, too." She flicked the ends of her fingers in the air, as if trying to rid herself of something nasty.

Darryl Dimmer's face had turned purple with rage and his head began to shake ever so slightly, as if a palsy had dropped upon him. "Do not put your hands on me again, you witch," he said slowly through clenched teeth. Millie whirled and looked Darryl Dimmer square in the eye.

"Oh, just one last time, please, I can't stop myself," she said, suddenly leaping at him like Troll lunging for a Milkbone, snatching the toupee from the preacher's head.

The sound of the tape strips ripping made everyone in the room cringe. Millie flounced to the front of the room with it, waving it in the air like an enemy scalp. "Say, everybody," she said, glancing at the underside of it, "why, there's not a natural fiber in this thing at all. One hundred percent acrylic, that's what it says, and it's from Topper's in San Francisco, too. Tell us all the truth, Dimmer, do you venture down to that—what did you call it?—that city of Sodom, very often? Your pecker's gonna fall off, don't you know that? That's exactly what you tell everyone in those vile tapes of yours, isn't it?"

Millie pitched the toupee back onto Darryl Dimmer's lap, as he sat stunned, almost on the verge of tears. The two long strips of raw skin on his bald spot looked like a bad sunburn, or a football helmet for the Michigan Wolverines. Juanita Dimmer rummaged wildly through her purse, looking for the .22-caliber handgun she almost always carried.

"Enough!" shouted Tom Mason from the front of the room. "That's enough, Millie. You've had your say. Now sit down. Please."

"My dog's in the truck," Millie said, jutting her whiskered chin up in the air. "I'll wait outside with him." And she marched herself back up the aisle and out the door to scattered applause from most of the people in the room. Whether or not they agreed with her position, folks admired her performance. Millie did have a flair for the dramatic in spite of her tendency to go overboard. Nobody had ever heard Darryl Dimmer challenged on scripture, or any other thing, with such verve.

Darryl wrestled his hair back onto his head and stood up. He took a deep breath, trying his best to look composed and in command of the situation. "Satan arrives among the faithful in many forms," he said, "even as a filthy, foul-talking woman in need of a bath. But I am steady in the Lord and I won't be deterred. I will keep on, do you hear me? And I will rid this great nation of ours—our white, Christian nation—of every homosexual, every mixed-race person, every nonbeliever. I will drive them all into a pit of fire for all the world to see."

"Just kill them," said the tiny voice of Suzette Metcalf. She never stood, never even looked up from the finishing work she was doing on her nails. "I don't see what's so wrong with that."

There was an astonished silence. Darryl Dimmer's words were still sinking in, and now this.

"What? Are you saying you think it's okay to kill people because they're gay?" Tom asked. He could not believe what he was hearing. Everyone in the room stared at her, faces marked by incredulity. Wendell Metcalf slid so far down in his seat that the lapels on his corduroy jacket almost covered his face. Even though he partially agreed with his wife, he'd rather nobody knew about it.

"Sure," Suzette said.

"Do you realize that's murder?" Tom said.

"Well, not really, it's not," replied Suzette. "Homosexuals aren't really people, so they don't count. It's not really murder, it's more like animal control." She looked up, her face as emotionless and blank as chalk and stared back at the people who were staring at her. "Why don't you see that?" she asked them. "Everything they do just makes a great big mess. AIDS, for example. Everybody knows it's all their fault and God is getting back at them by making them all sick. If we kill the rest of them, we're just helping God out as far as I can see. Homosexuals just want to have sex with children and they are all infected with AIDS. Everybody knows that. Don't you know that? It's been proven."

"Bullshit!" Leigh O'Brien shouted, jumping to her feet. The baby, sound asleep on Jimmy Heron's leg, was startled at the sound and jerked both tiny fists in the air. Jimmy picked him up, snuggling the infant up close to his neck, patting the baby's bottom with a big hand.

"You'd better get your facts straight, Suzette, before you shoot your mouth off. Ninety-seven percent of the convicted pedophiles in this country are white heterosexual males. In the last school year there were ten instances of sexual misconduct of a teacher toward a student in the state of Oregon. Nine were of a heterosexual nature and one was of a homosexual nature. That makes it 90 percent to 10 percent, with the heterosexuals ahead by a wide margin. Those are the facts, Suzette, the facts."

Leigh O'Brien stopped to take a breath, grateful to have had a chance to use the information she'd gotten from the Oregon Departments of Education and Corrections. Her freckles were vivid, almost alive on her face, and her hair had frizzed out around her head. She looked electric. She continued to stand—it was clear she wasn't through. "Does that mean," Leigh went on, "we should worry about protecting our children from all heterosexual people? Or from all homosexual people? No. It means we should worry about protecting our children from pedophiles, Suzette. A pedophile is a pedophile and I'm really sick of hearing the lies and reading the garbage the ORS and the religious Right keep pumping out about who I am and what you think it is I do with my life.

"You keep saying I have some homosexual agenda, and I'm here to tell you that no gay person I know has ever heard of it other than from you. You are the authors of this so-called homosexual agenda, not us. And before you go around advocating the murder of every gay person in America, you'd better check real close on the limbs of your family tree. Chances are there are more gay people than you know about, certainly more than would tell the truth to you about their lives. One in ten, Suzette, those are the odds."

"Those numbers are incorrect," Suzette shot back. "Everybody knows gay people lie about how many of them there are so they can get special rights."

"Those numbers are more correct than any the ORS makes up," Leigh said, returning fire, "and nobody is asking for special rights of any kind—only equal rights. Besides, what difference do the numbers make? Is even one murder okay? Just how many cousins are you willing to snuff for being gay, Suzette? Two? Four? You and Wendell will certainly be a hit at your next family reunion."

"Sister Metcalf is just voicing her own opinion. She certainly has every right to do that, am I right, Sheriff?" Darryl Dimmer smiled a sickly smile at Tom. "I'm sure the gracious lady was speaking metaphorically."

"No I wasn't," said Suzette, not exactly sure what *metaphorically* meant, although she was afraid they thought she was kidding and she most certainly was not.

"Nobody has the right to incite people to violence, Darryl," Tom said, "particularly murder. You and I have talked about this before."

"And in my sermons at the Mt. Goshen Church of the Righteous our message is to love the sinner, hate the sin." The preacher was trying desperately to back-pedal. "The U.S. Constitution allows us that right."

"Pardon me, Darryl, but I've been to your church and that's not what you teach at all." Tom felt his neck getting hot.

"Are you calling me a liar, Sheriff?"

"If the shoe fits, Reverend."

"Read I John, chapter 2, verse 9." It was the slow, steady, strong voice of Chuck Kimberling from the back of the room. Everyone turned to see who was speaking. "This particular scripture is one of the most powerful. 'He who says he is in the light and hates his brother is in the darkness still.' That's what it says. I think maybe you should concentrate on that scripture, Darryl, rather than wearing out the book of Leviticus."

Chuck Kimberling walked slowly to the front of the room and stood next to Tom Mason. In his faded Levi's and work shirt, Reverend Kimberling could just as easily have been a farmer in from the fields. Darryl Dimmer rose and pointed his Bible at them both.

"I don't need some environmental-wacko hippie-preacher telling me what to read when it comes to the inspired word of God, Mr. Methodist Pervert-Lover. Go hug a tree and leave the salvation of America to me."

"Okay, Darryl," said Chuck, "but remember, 'Hurt not the earth, neither the sea, nor the trees.' That's in the Bible, too, only you can't make money off of it, can you? No, hatred has become big business in this country, the primary business in some churches, I'm ashamed to say. I think you've made all the money you're going to make off the citizens of central Oregon because I'm really tired of seeing this whole town, this whole community, torn apart due to your rantings. There's only one thing I want to know, Darryl. Just what part of "...love thy neighbor as thyself" is so hard for you and your pals to understand?"

"Jesus Christ never commanded me to love a bunch of queers, Kimberling. That's all part of the homosexual agenda, too, you idiot. They want every pantywaist preacher in the country to feel sorry for them, to forgive them, to love them no matter what wicked, evil, perverted things they do—"

"Hey, I'm a Buddhist," said Eric Holloway from across the room. "What makes you think I'm obligated to pay any attention to what you or your religion says anyway? America is still a free country, Mr. Preacher, and that includes the freedom to choose how I believe."

"This is a Christian nation," the reverend said, "founded on Christian principles, and those principles do not include people who cannot keep their Satanic impulses under control—"

"My oldest brother died of AIDS four years ago." From the front of the room, people heard the soft, gentle voice of Glenn Taylor, who was breaking his usual silence to stand and speak his truth. For many in the audience this was the first time they'd ever heard his voice. He stared at the whole group for a few seconds. "He was the kindest man, my big brother was," Glenn continued, breathing in slowly to cover the shakiness in his voice. "He drove each day to deliver meals to AIDS and hospice patients in Chicago, where he lived. When he was too weak to drive or walk, he went to a nearby park in his wheelchair to share lunch with an old man he'd befriended. And when he became too weak to leave his apartment, he wrote letters of encouragement and sent cards to others he thought might be in need of a kind word. He was neither wicked, nor evil, nor perverted. He was only a good man who got sick.

"My family and I didn't know David was ill, or even that he was gay. We are a clan of loggers, mostly, and I guess he was afraid to tell us. I'm ashamed we let our macho image get in the way of everything that was really important. We found out that David had died when I got a letter from Mr. Madison, Mr. Daniel Madison, his friend from the park. I read it over again so many times I almost memorized every word. Mr. Madison told me many things about my brother in his letter, but what I remember most is this: '*You can be proud of your brother David. He had an angel's heart, so it is not surprising to me that he was not here on the earth for very long.*'"

Glenn Taylor stared directly at Darryl Dimmer. "I will always regret not saying good-bye to my brother, or telling him how much I loved him. Don't think for a minute I won't defend his good name from the likes of you."

Glenn sat back down just as abruptly as he had stood, looking frail and fragile for a big man—crumpled, almost deflated, as if the pressure and guilt of a thousand missed chances had suddenly been released from him. Sally Taylor leaned in close and swung an arm around her husband, kissing him quickly on the shoulder. Her blonde hair draped across her arm and down her back like a shiny yellow ribbon. Tonight was the first time Glenn had spoken about David's death; the first time he had shared the piercing pain in his heart with anyone other than his wife.

"I have something to say to everyone," said Ray Clooney, the florist, the only one in town. He was a slightly built man with thinning grayish hair, and a nervous, almost panicked look about him. Like he might dash off or pass out at any second.

"I've never told anyone this," Ray continued, "but I figured now is the time. I always felt I would lose business, or that maybe someone would try to kill me…someone did try to kill me once, in Toronto." Ray's eyes clouded over at the memory and his hands began to shake, so he stuffed them deep into his pockets. He looked like a man badly in need of a cigarette.

"I was only twenty-two years old," he went on, "just a kid. These boys jumped me as I was coming out of a bar. They were about my age, maybe younger, maybe even in high school. They dragged me across a street and into a parking lot, where they tried to kick me to death. They broke two of my ribs and my left collarbone, then one of them hit me with a chain and put my eye out." He pulled the lower lid of his right eye down. "This eye is a fake one. See? See the red stitches on the bottom? See how real they make the eye look? It was the surgeon's idea and I thought he did a superb job."

Caught up in the moment and remembering how conscientious and meticulous the Canadian surgeon had been, Ray sounded more like he'd just had a fender repaired than an eyeball replaced. "So," he continued, "after that exciting little experience, it seemed safer to me to keep quiet and lay low, and that's what I've done. For thirty years that's what I've done. But I am fifty-two years old now and I don't want to be afraid the rest of my life. So I'm standing up tonight to announce to you that I am a gay man."

He waited, almost cringing, for something to happen. Leigh O'Brien noticed how much Ray reminded her of Felipe, Sally and Glenn's neurotic little dog. Ray looked around the room at all the faces and they looked right back at him, expecting him to add something more. Finally, Cory broke the silence.

"Oh, please, Ray," she said, "tell us something we don't already know. That's like telling us the sky is blue. Don't you imagine people have figured it out by now?"

"Don't you get on my case, Cory Miller. There is a big difference between assuming that people know and knowing that they know. And people don't really know until they hear it from my lips." For an instant, Ray looked as if he might cry.

"You're right," Cory said, instantly regretting her flippant remark. "I was wrong. I didn't mean to hurt your feelings. What you just did was very brave."

"Thank you," Ray said, feeling vindicated as he sat back down. "Thank you," he said once more, looking rather smug.

Lars Stenvold stood on the right side of the room. He was short and round and bald, with beefy, hairy arms protruding from rolled-up sleeves. He looked around the room before speaking. "I am a Christian man," he said, "and I believe what the Bible says, most of it, anyway. But I have to admit that my opinion of homosexual people was formed mostly from the literature I've read in the past year." He glanced at Wendell Metcalf as he said this. "It just never occurred to me that I actually knew so many gay people in person. I mean, I never thought about it. My friends were just my friends, not people I would have to think about voting against. Since this ballot measure business started, it seems to be the only thing any of us in this town think about anymore. I wish it had never come up, that's what I wish."

"Me, too," said Dick Barstow from the front of the room, almost under his breath.

Lars picked up a red, white, and blue ORS donation bucket from the floor and held it out toward Wendell Metcalf. "Having this stinking thing around was a big mistake," he said, "so you take it back. Just take it back. Get it away from me. I've lost business over this, and employees, and friends. And I feel like we're all about to lose our town. I won't do it. I feel like we've all lost way too much over this already."

Darryl Dimmer jumped to his feet, whirling to confront Lars, whom he now saw as his own personal Judas. "And you *will* lose your town and your state and your country, you moron, if you don't take a stand this minute for righteousness!" he shouted. "These slimy perverts want to take everything over, can't you understand that? We must hate them. We must—"

"Hatred killed my wife," said Jimmy Heron, who had just passed his adopted grandson over to Cory and stood to face the crowd. The clarity of his statement caused people to hold their breath, as if the world might crack open from the exquisite pain of its truth. "The policemen told me and then I read in the newspaper that the man who pulled the trigger hated just about everybody—women, gay people, black people, Jewish people. The guy even hated his own mother.

"None of that mattered to me at the time because my pain was too big and I was still too raw. My wife was everything to me—my heart, my strength, my life. I only knew that she was gone and I could never get her back." Jimmy paused for a few seconds to gather himself as the painful memories of Killeen flooded inside him. "This is so much bigger than politics. Or religion. So much bigger. I want everyone to think about what this kind of hateful thought and hateful talk can do. It is poison. Lou, my wife, said that very thing on the day she died, and she was right. It's poison for all of us. Like anthrax through a herd, is what it is. Hateful talk is dangerous, no matter which side it comes from. It can get people killed.

"My wife was not the only one who died that day. Twenty-four people died and twenty-seven others were wounded, all because one crazy and hate-filled man felt it was okay for him to act on it. Can you imagine how many lives were affected just like mine because of that? He didn't even know us, didn't have any idea who we were. It didn't matter to him who he killed.

"Is that really what you want for your town? I can't believe it is. I hope with all my heart it isn't. I don't want anyone else to have to go through this kind of grief. It is too hard, believe me, too awful—" Jimmy's voice broke and he sat down abruptly and put his face in his hands, sobbing into them silently, his body shuddering from the wound.

Leigh O'Brien placed a hand on his back and gently patted. Chuck Kimberling walked quickly to the aisle where Jimmy Heron sat, kneeling down to place a strong hand on Jimmy's shoulder.

Darryl Dimmer sank back down to his chair, knowing better than to confront this kind of emotion with an outpouring of rage. Dick Barstow looked completely uncomfortable and nervously tapped his toes under the table where he sat. He wished he could make a run for it, to somewhere else where life was easier and conflicts such as this one were unheard of. Jenny Mason had turned in her chair and was glaring at Darryl Dimmer with slitty eyes, hoping he could feel just how creepy and evil she thought he was.

Without warning, Wendell Metcalf vaulted out of his seat, grabbing Suzette by the arm. Her bottle of pearlized Mauve Interlude nail polish bounced off her lap and clattered to the floor, rolling toward the front of the room as Wendell dragged her to her feet. She assumed, correctly, that they must be leaving.

Slinging a fistful of ORS literature at the crowd, Wendell shouted at the top of his lungs, "This whole meeting is horseshit! Do you hear me? It is horseshit!"

He stormed up the aisle, dragging Suzette by the arm, kicking the door to the front hall open. Her high heels made a scrabbling noise, like a poodle's toenails on concrete, and the people inside could hear Suzette's whiny voice plaintively wailing. "But, Daddy," she cried, "my coat! Wait! I've got to find my coat...it's over in the corner...wait—"

"Fuck the coat. Let's go," said Wendell, before the outside door slammed shut, and in just a few seconds there was the sound of tires squealing across pavement and gravel and leftover icy slush, past the town hall.

Darryl Dimmer rose slowly and closed his red leather Bible with a flourish. "It is clear to me," he said, "that Satan has this entire town by the throat. Wickedness and evil and perversion might prevail in this den of Sodom, but I shall have no more to do with it. My hands are washed of this place."

With that, he gripped Juanita's elbow, forcing her to her feet in spite of her reluctance to leave. She would rather have stayed a little longer to duke it out. They began making their way up the aisle, their last-minute stab at self-righteous indignation hampered by the fact that Darryl's toupee was slightly askew, listing toward the left side of his head like a satellite dish.

Steve Dvorak, trying to keep from laughing, stifled a snort which sounded a lot worse than it actually was. Cory Miller fought off a terrific urge to yell, "Don't let the door hit you in the butt on the way out." She could not help but clap and let out a whoop, however, when she heard the front door finally close behind the Dimmers.

Others in the room followed suit. Steve and Eric slapped a manly high five; Betty and Ted hugged Mitchell; Kate Mason hugged Jenny. Lars Stenvold walked across the room to shake Ray Clooney's hand.

Finally, Tom Mason spoke up to end the meeting, even though some of the people toward the back of the room had already wandered out into the front hall and were scrambling through the pile of coats. Dick Barstow looked practically exhilarated with gratitude and relief that the whole thing was done and that he hadn't had to speak. He quickly bolted up the aisle to grab Alice by the hand and make his way out before any more trouble started brewing.

"If nobody has anything else to add," Tom said, "this meeting is now adjourned." He walked over to put his arms around his wife and daughter. Jenny Mason smiled up at the face of her daddy and placed her blonde head against his chest. He cradled the back of his daughter's head with his hand and looked at his wife. "Let's go home," was all he could think of to say.

Outside, in the cold breeze, Leigh kissed Sally and Glenn good-bye and bundled the baby up even tighter. Cory spotted Millie's olive-drab truck parked over by the Oregon Trail sculpture and tugged on Jimmy's sleeve.

"Let's see what Millie's up to," she said. "I hope she's not planning on spending the night in her truck. She'll freeze to death…hey, I know! Why don't you bunk with us, Jimmy, and offer to let her use the trailer? Is that okay with you? You can have the guest room. Or, better yet, you can sleep in the bunkhouse. How 'bout that? That'd give you some privacy. Besides, you know how cranky we all get when we don't see you everyday, especially you-know-who." She wiggled her eyebrows at him, cocking her head toward the baby.

"Oh, yes," he said, grateful almost to the point of euphoria not just to be out of that cramped trailer but to be anywhere closer to the baby.

Even though Jimmy only lived up the road, even though he had finally quit making excuses as to why he showed up at Leigh and Cory's house two and three times a day since the baby's arrival, the idea of being that much closer was thrilling to him. The tiny, red-headed boy's goofy grin was, by now, so firmly embedded in Jimmy Heron's heart that not seeing it was almost torture for the old man.

Neither of them could have known at the time how a simple, friendly gesture could change their lives, yet again, forever, just as no one who came to the meeting could have known that courageous hearts standing and speaking their truth would change the course of a community about to implode on itself.

Within a week, Jimmy Heron was firmly ensconced in his new place in the bunkhouse at Cory and Leigh's. So thrilled, so delighted was he to be out of the dented turquoise trailer that he chose not to sell it back to Millie, even though she offered to buy it and pay top dollar. He simply gave it to her.

For her part, Millie Jensen said she had fit in at her daughter's house in the suburbs like "tits on a boar hog," and that's why she'd made her way back to central Oregon from Fargo. That, and the fact that Troll had growled and barked so much at her son-in-law—even peed on the guy's shoes once—they'd made the poor ugly dog stay out in the garage.

By pure luck, Millie Jensen had roared and backfired her way into town on the same evening as the big meeting; a poster on the wall at Hobo Hank's had told her the time and place. She had been waiting for the chance of a showdown with Darryl Dimmer for years.

Jimmy loved the bunkhouse and the spacious feel of it, the smell of the pine logs, and the memory of Jonah, which was steady and comforting all around him. He had a refrigerator, a tiny stove, and a big bed in which to stretch out his long frame. The shelves, filled with Jonah's books and Jimmy's pictures of Lou and Curly Red, his parents, Della and Bonnie, and Web and Buster Dan, held plenty for him to read and lots to think about and remember.

It made him feel good to be in this place. Content, not sad, almost anxious to see what each day held for him from here on out. Most of all, though, Jimmy Heron loved the feeling of being part of a family, which Leigh and Cory and little Jeff all considered him to be. Although the main people in his life were no longer blood relations, sometimes good hearts holding fast to each other create the most important family of all. It was a blessing for him, a gift. Serendipity.

·50·

Wendell Metcalf smoothed strapping tape across the last of the boxes in his office and pushed them up against the far wall, closer to the door. All the easier to get them out of here when the movers came.

Glad to have that done, he sat at his desk, leaned back in the chair, and looked around the place one last time. He wouldn't miss it. No, not at all. Wouldn't miss anything about this backward town, this stupid state, or the brainless homos who lived here. They could take this whole goddamned wretched place and shove it as far as he was concerned.

The day after the town meeting, Wendell was up early, before dawn, hammering away in the basement. By 6:00 A.M., a FOR SALE sign stood, rigid and defiant, in the Metcalfs' front yard. By 8:00 A.M., following a series of phone calls, Wendell had decided what he and Suzette would do. There was a place for them, he knew, a place and a cause that could use his tenacity and fury and Suzette's startling ability with money and numbers. There was a place where they would be appreciated, even acknowledged and loved, for what they were trying to do.

It would be the same mission, of course, just in a different location, with a group of people as dedicated as he was. And there was still plenty of time before the November elections to make an impact, to let them know he was somebody to be reckoned with.

Wendell had placed the receiver back in the cradle on the desk after the last phone call that morning, feeling almost giddy with excitement. He smacked a fist into his other hand with the determination of a man who could see no way of turning back. Then, on a lined yellow legal pad, he had drawn a long arrow and written with a determined hand: *Amendment 2—Ground Zero—Colorado Springs.*

On the outskirts of town, in the basement room of the abandoned building, Donnie Zoeller knelt in front of his altar for the final time and stared at his reflection in the mirror. Reaching down behind him, he ran his hand over the swollen and bruised calf muscle finally starting to heal from the bite. *Stupid motherfucking dog.*

It was time to make a move and Donnie knew it, time to say good-bye to this zit of a town and head for a friendlier climate. Things were getting too hot. All of his stuff was almost packed and ready to go. He would leave tonight, he decided, by walking out to the highway, faking a stupid, nonthreatening grin on his face, then hitchiking his way northeast to someplace else.

Donnie had heard of a skinhead group that had taken over places in Utah at Mt. Zion National Park, but the thought of spending time that close to Mormons gave him the creeps. Reaching across the table next to his altar he picked up the bootlegged copy of *Romper Stomper,* a skinhead movie filmed at the Aryan Nation compound near Hayden Lake just the year before. He'd stolen it off a guy from Phoenix who'd been passing through Medford last summer after they had watched it together.

Donnie thought for a moment about the thrill of seeing those men repeating their motto together: "I am proud of my white heritage, proud of my Aryan blood," and he remembered the thrill shooting up his spine, that feeling of belonging, of being important for the first time in his life. He rolled the video cartridge around and around in his hand and slid it quickly under his arm, almost as if to put his scent on it.

The candle flickering in the mirror brought Donnie Zoeller's mind back into focus on his purpose. Breathing deeply, he closed his eyes for a moment. When he opened them and saw his close-cropped blond hair, the flattened bridge of his nose, and the need in his eyes, he knew where he should be. He would go to Hayden Lake. In Idaho. Where there were more of him.

Before he left, though, there was one last thing he had to do, one last way to make a mark on this place, just in case he ever decided to come back and reclaim his turf. Donnie Zoeller stood up and in one swift motion tore his T-shirt up and off over his head so he could see

263

the muscles on his chest and arms bulge. Bending forward slightly from the waist, he tightened his abdomen, smiling to himself as the hardened muscles popped to the surface of his smooth white skin and rippled, ever so slightly. He felt himself start to breathe faster, shallow breaths, and beads of sweat formed on his upper lip. He unzipped his pants and pulled his flaccid penis out, working the fat and sleepy shaft back and forth in his palm, like a father slowly awakening a napping child. Then Donnie Zoeller walked around the filthy, foul-smelling room with his head thrown back, pissing on the walls and laughing out loud until his balls ached.

Out on the highway, behind a majestic stand of ponderosa pines, the hook on the rope outside Darryl Dimmer's office at the Mt. Goshen Church of the Righteous clanged against the metal pole insistently, sounding like church bells. Darryl Dimmer took this as a sign, an omen, and rubbed his sweaty palms on his pants. Since the day after the town meeting, he had been recording sermon after sermon, sending them out to be dubbed and mass-produced for sale. He would not be slowed down by the humiliation he suffered at the hands of the town of Reliance. He would show those morally stunted heathens. Oh, yes, he would.

His latest book about the militant homosexual agenda, *America: Godless Nation Uncovered,* subsidized for printing and distribution by Harley Dixon of the Americana Foundation, was on its way to Christian bookstores across the United States right now. It was also being offered, of course, by mail order. This book would make Reverend Darryl Dimmer a nationally recognized name, one honored and respected among the Christian Right, one feared by the liberal left. It would also make him a multi-millionaire, he was sure of it.

The U.S. map spread out on his desk was new, folding out easily like an accordion shade. Darryl Dimmer smoothed down the edges and focused his gaze to the right of Oregon. He and Juanita and the boys would be moving, most likely within the next two weeks, just as soon as they could get packed. They had yanked their kids out of that socialist school the very next day after the town meeting. Juanita had insisted on doing this task herself as the final insult to Kate Mason, even though Kate was more than delighted to be rid of the two Dimmer boys. Juanita had decided to home school their children, she had told Kate, since the public schools could not be trusted to instill the proper Christian values in its students.

Indeed, Juanita had made a half-hearted try at home schooling over the next couple of days by flipping through some home schooling information and texts, but she found them tedious. The thought, moreover, of having to spend the entire day with her two sons was almost more than she could bear. She took to her bed with a migraine, preferring to let Maxine, their maid, handle them. Thus far, Maxine had not been able to pry the boys away from rotations between the television, the refrigerator, and the Nintendo game and that, in truth, was just as fine with Juanita as it was with them.

Rodney and Jason Dimmer's home-schooling was the last thing on their father's mind at this moment, however. In fact, when they got to their new home, Darryl Dimmer planned to start his very own Christian school, an institution of learning so spectacular, so immersed in biblical teachings, it would put any public school in America to total shame. Total, absolute shame. His boys would be leaders there, young men all the other children would look up to and want to emulate. The tuition would be steep, he knew that much; it had to be, of course, but it could be built with tax-free money. School vouchers from the government would help pay for the rest of it, just as soon as he and other founders of Christian schools could pull enough strings to get school-choice measures passed in Congress. His new friend and benefactor, Harley Dixon, would help with money donations and arm-twisting, Darryl felt sure. Harley was old and ugly and mean, but he had grit, by God, and a bank account big enough to get anything he really wanted. This new Christian school would be a moneymaker, no doubt about it, and it would be the wave of the future.

Darryl Dimmer leaned back in his chair and momentarily considered Chuck Kimberling's comments and what Millie Jensen, that grizzled old witch, had said to him at the town meeting. He could vaguely remember a time when his sermons had been gentle ramblings about loving each other, following the teachings of Jesus and all that. He sputtered his lips in disgust at the memory. Pablum, that's what it was. Certainly not sermons worth writing home about, nothing with any teeth in it. No bite or guts.

He had been a brand-new minister then, fresh out of seminary. It seemed like a million years ago. Most certainly, it was a million dollars ago. When Darryl Dimmer had discovered the secret that set his sermons ablaze, aiming at an enemy—whether it was the prochoice murderers, the government, the environmentalists, the feminists, or the homosexuals—well, all he had to do was look at the ledger, the numbers, and see which way of preaching was the better idea. His beloved wife had pointed that out to him right off, and he'd been grateful to her ever since. After all, if the Lord had not intended the Dimmer family to prosper by preaching the gospel, He would have silenced them.

Easing the drawer of his polished desk open, Darryl Dimmer unscrewed the cap of a felt-tip pen and carefully circled on the map what he felt sure would be their new home. It was clear to him that the town of Reliance, perhaps even the state of Oregon, would never be persuaded to deal as harshly as he would like with the wicked homosexual perverts.

He was tired of beating his head against the wall, tired of the humiliation. He needed to go where he could get a stronger foothold, where God-fearing people—the ones who hated the government and loved the Lord—would stand beside him and march toward victory in taking America back. He wanted to be where there were people unafraid to speak of an Aryan nation, an untarnished America.

Darryl Dimmer needed to be where he was sure there were more people just like him; where, in particular, Juanita had noticed an unusually large number of orders for Darryl's tapes and books originated: Sand Point, Idaho.

Thus, the fog soon lifted off the town of Reliance, Oregon, as the people remembered who they were and how their town got its name. Within days after the departure of the Dimmer family, the Metcalfs, and Donnie Zoeller, that cloud—the fearful, suspicious look of neighbor distrusting neighbor—shifted. The hatred began to fizzle out like a Roman candle.

People who had not spoken to each other in months would shake hands in the middle of the street, even hug, as friends do when they've been apart for too long. Reliance, Oregon was becoming a sweet place to live once again.

Sheriff Tom Mason hung onto the dried and caked-mud boot print, though. After packing it carefully in styrofoam, he wrote all the information on top of the box and wedged it into the bottom drawer of his filing cabinet. And, just in case, he kept the bullets in his gun. Hatred had left their small community for now, but hatred, Tom Mason knew, just like bad colds and bad habits, had a way of circling back. Never again would he be blindsided.

In Cambridge, Massachusetts one night, as the earth rolled over on its belly, Della Heron did the same and never woke up, passing from this life to the next as peacefully as a butterfly settling on a cactus flower. Just as she had known in her heart the way it would happen, her Bonnie was there to greet her, to take her hand and help her step across, to welcome her home.

The box of items arriving from Cambridge for Jimmy Heron contained scrapbooks, photographs, some letters, and a miniature pair of well-oiled and preserved red cowboy boots that the note attached said had belonged to him. Della had taken them with her when she and Bonnie moved away to remind them of her baby brother.

Leigh left her teaching job to be a full-time mom. The baby grew under the watchful and adoring eyes of his mother, Cory, his grandpa Jimmy, and everyone else whose heart he captured. The baby had sparkly brown eyes and a sweet smile, with a dimple in his left cheek deep enough to curl up and snooze in. Just a glance from this small boy could lasso any stranger within fifty yards, but it was his dark copper curls that made everybody in the county want to touch his head. And even though Leigh and Cory always made sure they told each person the child's name was Jeff, nobody who ever saw him could keep from calling him Curly Red.

The little guy was born in Oregon, but there was Texas somewhere deep in his soul. Jimmy and Cory and Leigh knew it from the time Jeff spoke his first word. It was *salsa*.

·51·

E ighteen months later, Jimmy Heron's business had just gotten off the ground, thanks to the large kitchen Cory had asked Glenn to build onto the bunkhouse. Jimmy's new stove with its commercial-sized oven sat on gleaming tiles. That, and a loose and easy contract with Gary Tollefson, a former hippie and good-hearted guy from Minnesota who now made a very nice living as owner/operator of Crusty's Gourmet Pies catalog business in Bend, were all Jimmy needed to transform an old dream into something now workable for him. His rapport with Gary, and the reliable overnight services of Federal Express and UPS, kept everything running smoothly—he had discovered both carriers willing to ship pies that stayed plenty cool if he packed them properly.

Though his oven could accommodate six pies at once, Jimmy felt he still had better control of things if he kept it to three. Four, max. Three meringue pies rested carefully on the top shelf of Jimmy's Kenmore. Pies cooled on windowsills, on counters, on top of the fridge, and pie boxes, all white and flat, just waiting to be folded into shape, were stacked and shiny on the table.

Earlier that morning, after their usual Saturday morning breakfast together, Jimmy had walked around his house holding his red-headed grandson on his arm. Little Curly Red would point to the pies, one by one, then look deeply into Jimmy's eyes as if the answer to each question would open the door to the meaning of life for everyone.

"Dat?" the baby asked.

"Apple," Jimmy replied.

"Dat?"

"Peach."

"Dat?"

"Rhubarb," Jimmy answered, and the baby frowned.

"Boo-rob?" he asked.

"Roo-barb," Jimmy repeated, "you've never had that before."

"Dood?" He was just about as earnest a support system as Jimmy Heron could have asked for.

"Oh, yes," Jimmy said, "they're all very good."

"Dood," the baby replied, shaking his head up and down, giving his approval like the inspector for quality control before Jimmy took the boy by the hand and walked him back home.

Jimmy Heron's dream of opening his own pie shop was a dream he had shared with Lou. Without her he knew it would feel hollow. Torturous, even. Being a pie supplier, however, particularly for someone as easy going as Gary, well, this was not only simple, most of the time it was downright fun. It helped Jimmy fill up his days, he made a little extra money, and he was good at it. *Piece of cake.* That's what Lou would have said about this set-up.

Later in the day, Jimmy sat quietly folding pie boxes into shape. Country music played gently from the kitchen radio. This would be his tenth shipment for Gary, his biggest one so far, including the meringue pies he'd only recently added to his list. It felt like a milestone, as if a threshold into a new life for him had just been crossed. And it was his birthday, his seventy-first.

Jimmy glanced across the table at the birthday cards he'd gotten from Web Hardy and Buster Dan, plus a photograph of the two of them with Web's new wife. *Can't wait to meet you, Jimmy!* she'd written on the back, and *With love, Nan Hardy.*

Winnie Bridwell, who must be a thousand years old by now, Jimmy thought, sent her usual get well card birthday wishes, which could add up to love if held in the right perspective. All she wrote was: *When are you coming back? Signed, Mrs. Ezekiel Bridwell.*

Jimmy missed them, sure, but the ache was different now, not so ragged or painful as before, and he actually found himself glad that today was his birthday, like he'd already gone through the fire and had burst out to the other side. Today was his day, but it did not feel scary, nor was it even lonely. It felt easy. What a surprise, Jimmy thought. Easy.

He heard Ned's bark outside just before the knock at his door. When he opened it, Jimmy Heron was shocked to see not only Cory, Leigh, and the baby, but Sally and Glenn, several members of the COBB group, Tom, Kate, and Jenny Mason, and even a few neighbors. Some people held balloons and flowers. Somebody held up a cake and waved it back and forth. "HAPPY BIRTHDAY, JIMMY!" the crowd shouted at once causing Jimmy Heron to blush and almost run back in the house before he decided to stay put and accept whatever good wishes were about to be cast upon him.

Millie Jensen and Troll sat on the hood of Millie's filthy truck, where Troll howled at nothing in particular. Ned zigzagged his way through the crowd, sniffing and snuffling his head up under a hand or two for some pets before finally settling down with his rump on Leigh's foot and his paw on Cory's so they couldn't get away. It was his job.

Leigh set the squirming Jefferson Miller O'Brien down and the baby boy took off at a dead run, hopping up the steps and smashing face first into Jimmy Heron's knees before he finally stopped, and Jimmy scooped the child up next to his shoulder. "Who loves you, Curly Red?" Jimmy asked, and the baby banged the old man square in the chest with a pudgy hand.

"Bimmy!" he said.

"Your present's on the railing there, Jimmy," Sally Taylor said. "Glenn just finished it today. That's what those hooks are for. I know Cory told you they were for hanging baskets, but that wasn't the truth." She pointed to the S-hooks hanging right above his head and he glanced up.

"Cory's always had a loose grip on the truth!" shouted Willis from the back of the crowd.

"Pipe down, man," Cory said, "or I'll tell all your secrets. I'll even make some up, then you'll be sorry." She faked a scowl toward the back of the group.

"Go ahead, Jimmy," Leigh urged, "take a look."

Reaching over to the railing, Jimmy picked up a wooden plaque and stared at it. He felt the tiniest gasp from deep within his chest as he took in its full meaning, and his eyes filled with tears. He blew feathery wisps of sawdust off the board and held it up toward his grandson for some help. The boy puffed out his little cheeks and blew while everyone in the crowd waited, not quite knowing what to say or do.

A single tear rolled down Jimmy's cheek. Deep within the salty matrix of that single tear was all the love, joy, sorrow, and loss of a million memories. It was a life story, a love story. It was life itself.

The S-hooks stretched, as if to help catch hold of their new treasure, and Jimmy Heron met them with the plaque where the summer wind blew against it. It rocked, ever so gently, back and forth, back and forth. Cory and Leigh began the applause, the tears and cheers for this old man and their love for him, for a dream come true, and for all it took to make it so.

The beautiful wooden plaque, hand-carved by Glenn Taylor for his friend Jimmy Heron, read simply:

JIMMY AND LOU'S PIE SHOP

COCONUT MERINGUE, OUR SPECIALTY

Firebrand Books is an award-winning feminist and lesbian publishing house. We are committed to producing quality work in a wide variety of genres by ethnically and racially diverse authors. Now in our fourteenth year, we have over ninety titles in print.

A free catalog is available on request from Firebrand Books, 141 The Commons, Ithaca, New York 14850, 607-272-0000.

Visit our website at www.firebrandbooks.com.